I0831642

M.P. DESMARAIS

Desiderata

First edition

ISBN: 979-8-9923235-2-8

This book was professionally typeset on Reedsy.
Find out more at reedsy.com

Prologue

"What did you come here looking for?" the time-tested titan asked aloud.

He knew the fallen fighter probably couldn't hear him anymore. It was just the usual question he asked.

A state of disappointment ensnared him then, as he looked down at that broken warrior. The large and once powerful man remained unresponsive, and he faded from consciousness on the floor.

"You had me so expectant, so hopeful…" the titan went on. "Pick up your sword, your blaster. Come at me with something, with *everything*!" he roared as his shouting escalated.

It was to no avail. The weakening man, of such vast notoriety and past promise, lay hopelessly bleeding out and nearly dead. The titan stared hatefully at the man, who now seemed little more than a blood-gurgling heap of shredded flesh and broken bones. He challenged him a final time through clenched teeth. "Show me that some embers still burn in your heart, from that great conflagration I know once set it aflame."

Still, nothing of consequence.

The duel between the two men had not satiated the battle lust that the victor of this fight continued to harbor, to his great and persisting frustration. That victor was a man known as Armando—a man who now breathed a great sigh of disappointment. His mind fell back over the years, scouring his memories for someone he had ever faced who had been of the caliber he now knew himself to be. It troubled him greatly that no one was occurring to him.

Then, his mind did land on one man in particular, though it was for reasons not immediately clear to him. He had been an older man, more than twice the age Armando was back then. That was around the time he had come to power in Ezmondia. That old fool had dared to defy him and stand against him. Of course, he had subsequently paid with his life for the transgression.

There had been a certain … uniqueness, a particular rarity about the way that man had carried himself, the way he spoke, the way he fought. A little unnerving at first, perhaps, but not so much that it mattered in the end, as far as was apparent to Armando at the time, anyway.

The man's son had been there, and he couldn't have been much older than Armando had been. This son had also taken up his sword against him, as his father had. He was more reckless with his wielding of it, though perhaps still fairly skilled. Armando hadn't really gotten much of a sense of that skill, though; he had bashed him over the head with the hilt of his sword after the emotional son overbalanced and missed him with one of his first strikes. He knocked him unconscious and probably rendered him foggy-brained, with a hazy memory of why he woke up later with a pounding headache and a dead father. Armando's face creased with a wicked smile at the memory. Perhaps some dormant talent in the man came alive after that encounter, but he doubted it.

Anyway, that son wasn't really crossing his mind for his or even his father's fighting prowess. Why was he thinking of this encounter, then? After considering it for a short while, he finally settled on why: it had been something the son had said to him. What was it? Something odd, something … dramatic.

Armando then thought of a conversation he'd just had earlier that day with his second-in-command, a woman named Mercedes. She was a little like that in conversation, too, he supposed. She did speak in an unusual manner sometimes—at least, as compared to the general citizenry living in his empire, Ezmondia. Not that the citizens of the country that made up the remainder of the continent of Gracyr—a country known as Makeva—spoke anything like her, either. It mostly annoyed him, really, and she had a way of beating around a point, hovering closely but never really getting to it. Armando was a man who generally favored concisely made points in conversations.

He thought of that word she had used earlier when speaking to him. That was why this long-ago encounter was coming to his mind now. That son had used the same word she'd used earlier—a word he figured in all likelihood hadn't been spoken to him in all these years since. That word from today, and from all those years ago ... was "desiderata."

How curious it was, the memories that came back to a person with the most random reminders. Armando didn't think further of the matter, though. It was unlikely that the man's son—whatever his name was—had gone on to make much of himself, and perhaps he didn't even survive long after that.

Armando left the massive indoor arena and headed upstairs toward one of the main hallways of the grandiose building known as the Castle. He walked past many expensive trinkets displayed in cases, the spoils of wars and battles past, and passed a myriad of fine paintings depicting battles even older and grander. Many were morbid scenes, favoring shades of red and themes grotesque and macabre. Such was commonly the preference of Armando, the emperor who reigned over the empire of Ezmondia, along with some minimal influence from others on what was dubbed the Elite Council.

Armando was a large man, standing at close to seven feet tall, and was a formidable enemy to anyone foolish enough to challenge him. His influence was strong, his grip over his inner circle—and in general, the public of Ezmondia—unsurpassed. Massive media campaigns were spread out over the ubiquitous vidscreens and other media throughout nearly all residences of Ezmondia. They conditioned the people. It had been going on for a long time: a campaign to bend and guide minds to Armando's designs, as the people, usually to a great though gradual extent, all became products of the information they consumed. Indeed, Armando, now some twenty years the emperor of Ezmondia, had unquestionably great if not absolute power and influence here.

And yet he had come to be such a slave—though he did not know it—to that very power he thought he could command.

1

Chapter One

The word had barely left the referee's lips, and they instantly crossed their weapons, almost as if some tangible force had been holding them back. It was as if there were an invisible barrier that held until that very moment, when that single word was spoken that finally permitted those weapons to come together—*"Begin!"*

The blade wielders went to work, sparring with a seeming—if unusual—degree of playfulness, almost as if they were toying with each other. The combatants had been battling other contestants in the tournament all week and had watched each other's tactics with increasing interest.

The city of Nethereel was holding its most highly anticipated and celebrated annual competition. Even so, the crowd swelled even larger than expected for the final fight of the tournament, with many attendees particularly interested to see this pair cross swords.

Gerrard was the older of the two fighters by perhaps half a decade. He had won the tournament for years now and was widely expected to continue his winning streak this year as well. He was popular in Nethereel and across much if not all of the country the city was located in. That country was known as Makeva, a land located northwest of the empire of Ezmondia, on the continent of Gracyr.

Gerrard normally favored his own larger sword, rather than the smaller ones provided by the tournament—but he was bound by the same rules as everyone else and didn't mind playing by them. What perhaps did trouble him at that moment though was how even when wielding the smaller weapon, and even with the betting odds continuing to favor him, he could still feel how his movements had slowed since last year and years past. They felt sluggish, and the competition—whether as a result of his advancing age and this creeping slowness, or the improved caliber of the other contestants—was becoming more challenging every year. He certainly couldn't say he had never broken a sweat in the tournament before, but it seemed to him at this particular moment that he never felt it before so much as he did now.

Still, the pair traded blows with a sort of lighthearted appreciation for each other's skill, and it lent a further surge of excitement to what was already a true spectacle for the audience to watch. His opponent was a somewhat ragged-looking female fighter, rough-edged and likely not coming at him from a place of wealth and success. And of course, a place of wealth and success was where most would say Gerrard hailed from in his more recent years.

Perhaps she didn't have his wealth or resources, but she had considerable speed, strength, and skill. And any perceived raggedness did little to detract from her natural beauty. She appeared to be middle-aged and more youthful than him, and she stood many inches shorter, though he was not a particularly tall man.

Though he rarely succumbed to such things during combat, Gerrard actually found himself admiring the woman's appearance. She was quick, with fast reflexes, and she had an athletic frame, and a lovely shade of auburn hair—and though it was tied too tightly back to be sure, he suspected she didn't have the gray streaks running through it that coursed through his own more mundane, simply toned brown hair.

Still, even Gerrard appeared otherwise far younger than his older age would suggest. He rapidly traded blows back and forth with the energetic, younger female fighter. And he managed to keep ever present in his mind that he could not afford to let looks detract from the task at hand—which was, of course, at least one more year of winning this thing.

Andromeda was the woman's name. She was a newcomer to the city and this competition. She was from a much more sparsely populated area, a small town farther north and close to the coast. She had trained with her father, who had bequeathed to her the weapon with which she usually fought: a bejeweled saber.

Her father was a man who, unlike Gerrard, was not so widely known. The man had lived and died in that little town she was from, a town called Elazora. She couldn't do that. She knew she was talented—though she questioned whether sword fighting in arena games was really her true calling, or if it really embodied whatever it was that she was best at doing. Her father, though, had been a careful and dedicated teacher, and she had learned much from him before he died years ago. He had wanted her to be better than him. That was what would be needed, he had told her, to be able to make it in the world she had been born into—which hadn't exactly struck her as uplifting at the time. Eventually, though, as the years rolled on, she came to appreciate the difficulty of navigating the modern world, and she came to understand the wisdom of his advice.

Despite the heavy thoughts weighing on her as she found herself involuntarily reflecting on these things, she grinned now as she fought this "living legend," as Gerrard was sometimes referred to. If this was the best Makeva could offer, she didn't seem so far behind. Surely, she could be of great use to someone of some means in the city, if she could hold her own in the final round of the tournament with such a living legend of the blade. Could she beat him, even? She pondered the possibility. She was doubtful, but she didn't dwell on those doubts. Even if she could, she questioned that she wanted to. She certainly didn't want to gravely harm or slay him; he seemed to possess too much potential for her to waste it like that. But of course, it was not uncommon for people to be injured, even with the dulled blades the tournament provided.

This man might present an opportunity, she considered, for a rather effective partnership. Not necessarily in a romantic sort of way, though she didn't rule out that possibility, either. He was a little older, but seemed solid and strong. He had a hardened sort of personality about him, and an inviting sort of handsomeness that she could appreciate. Andromeda understood and often considered the benefits of teaming up with all sorts of people for all manner of various adventures. She often strived to mentally uncover and dissect the talents and skills of others, and to consider what they could accomplish with her help—or what she could accomplish with theirs.

She didn't end up having to make any big decisions about whether she truly wanted to take down the reigning champion in the tournament or not. After one particularly heated exchange of deflecting and returning strikes against each other, Gerrard's sword came slashing across and found a momentary lapse in her defenses. The blade halted an inch or two from her face, and she froze, thankful that he had ceased the weapon's momentum.

"Well fought," Gerrard complimented her, smiling slightly.

Andromeda thought to quickly fall back and come in at him with heightened assertiveness and ferocity, to capitalize on his foolishness for stopping short. He had not truly won—not without striking that winning blow. She considered her precarious situation for a few moments, but ultimately yielded all the same in what was honestly, to her, a clear defeat. She smiled more widely than him and echoed his words back at him with a personal touch. "Well fought … Gerrard."

* * *

Second place in the competition fetched plenty of coin for Andromeda to get well ahead for the time being. She was smiling to herself, thinking about it all as she ambled along through Nethereel, caught up in the post-tournament excitement that was like electricity in the air. Many gamblers celebrated their winnings, while those gamblers who fell short drowned their disappointment in potent libations and deeper debt. Many carts and booths lined the city streets, with merchants and salespeople trying to catch tournament attendees for a final impulse buy—which was often one of the spicy burritos popular in the city, or some small souvenir by which they could fondly remember their attendance.

Andromeda glanced into the windows of shops she passed. She was tempted several times, but not to the point of actually venturing inside. At least, for a while she wasn't, anyway. When she came upon one particular shop, she did find herself traversing through its doorway. The shop sold weapons that were of increasing rarity in the world. They were blaster weapons that ran on magic largely lost in the modern age. Their production had ceased long ago—though a rare few did still possess the knowledge and skill to create their ammunition. She asked the shopkeeper to show her one of the blasters that had caught her eye in the shop's window, and the man happily obliged.

"One of the last ones ever made, we believe, so one of the newest you'll find, and perhaps one of the most advanced," said the man convincingly, with clear designs of selling her on it quickly. He led her to the shooting range in the back of the place, indicating to his assistant to watch the front of the store.

"Hard to pass up an opportunity to show this off, especially to a finalist in the tournament this year!" he exclaimed. He loaded a couple rounds into the cartridge and inserted it up into the handle of the weapon. The first bullet entered the blaster's empty chamber. "Just class D rounds for our demonstration, if you don't mind, miss," he said, referring to the lowest class of available ammunition.

The blaster bullets, Andromeda knew from her father, who had once carried a blaster like this, were categorized in classes A through D. There were further subcategories of A bullets, though those were all exceedingly rare, and particularly so with the Quadri-As, of which there might not even be any left in existence. Magic was an increasingly rare phenomenon in the reality they lived in, and the magics that commanded such power as those high-level rounds did, in all likelihood, were already gone from the world.

"That'll be just fine," responded Andromeda sincerely, with her typical sweetness and understanding. She happily accepted the low-class ammo for the demonstration.

The shopkeeper fired the first blast, handling the powerful recoil masterfully. The shot tore through the target bullseye in an explosion of fireworks, which were then readily contained by the magical forcefield that surrounded the target. Then he set the weapon down on the small table in front of them. The target was immediately refreshed by the magic of the place, and it appeared again as new.

"Take a shot. Let me know what you think," the salesman invited.

Andromeda lifted the blaster, and not devoid of familiarity with such a weapon, leveled the barrel, aimed at her target down the range, and squeezed the trigger. She was, of course, not so accustomed to it as her father had been, or even as she once was, and the recoil did surprise her slightly. She was prepared enough, though, and still managed to easily hit the target—though not with the precision and practiced ease the salesman had demonstrated.

"It feels good," she stated plainly, not wanting to sound too enthusiastic and potentially drive up the price on herself. "What does this blaster go for, pricewise?" she inquired.

The man's answer drew an involuntary and reflexive frown from her. Andromeda could barely afford it and couldn't justify the purchase, however enamored she might have been with the thing.

Andromeda thought about it another moment. She locked eyes with the shopkeeper, if only for the sake of her very typical tendency to try to connect with new people. "An earlier model at a lower price would suit my needs just fine, I think," she concluded with her characteristically clear tone.

The shopkeeper nodded understandingly. He guided her back to the front of the store, and he walked her over to a case of lower-cost blasters. "The first test run was on me. You'll have to pay a rental fee to test out another. You'll have to purchase the ammo for it, too," he informed her.

She nodded in acknowledgment. As she looked over the case, one did stand out to her in particular. She pointed to it, trying to seem fairly indifferent to the salesman. "What's the story with this one?" she asked conversationally.

“Came in just yesterday,” he replied. “I don’t see many of this venerable age still in such fine working order, actually. Single-shot blaster, but if you can get by with that, it may be just right for you. It looks old, I know, but I do promise you that it still shoots straight. Aside from that, though, I’m afraid I can’t tell you much about it.”

The blaster had engravings on its handle, but they were far too faded to be legible. That wasn’t so unusual, though it did frustrate Andromeda slightly. She was curious about the history of the thing. She agreed to the rental fee, purchased a bullet, and went out back again to test-fire it.

The blaster lit up the prettiest shade of violet when she squeezed the trigger. Other than that, it didn’t seem too remarkable. It did seem to function all right, despite its age, though. The price was low, too—so low that even if she didn’t get a whole lot of use out of it, it would probably be worth the coin.

She purchased the blaster, a holster, and a few low-level rounds for the weapon. She strapped the holster to her side and couldn’t help but take a few moments to marvel at how nicely the weapon seemed to complement her saber at her other hip.

She exited the shop and continued on her way. The better part of an hour later, Andromeda reached an establishment along the lines of what she had been searching for: a local tavern. She followed the din of a rather rowdy-sounding band of musicians coming from inside.

2

Chapter Two

The sign in front of the rickety, older-looking building was broken, the final word apparently missing from the sign stating the name of the establishment. Liberty's Last ... *something*, the place was called.

Inside, the place was busy and full of people chattering and clamoring about the fights of the tournament that week. No one seemed to take much notice of Andromeda as she entered and made her way over to the bartender, who was also the owner of the tavern.

Gerrard did see Andromeda enter from his seat at a table toward the back of the place. He wasn't dedicated, though, to any fleeting ideas he may have had of engaging with her again. He was largely just here to enjoy the company of a couple of old friends.

"So, what'd you think of the tournament this year, Gerry?" asked one of them, a man named Cid. "Caught what I could of it after my arrival from my trip—shame I missed so much of the excitement and festivities this year."

Gerrard regarded his friend Cid, who was just back from another fishing trip. The man had done well for himself over the years, really wasn't even in great need to continue working—not with the wealth he had already managed to amass over his life. He had been careful to save and careful with his expenses. It did help that fishing was a lucrative business—and he owned his. Still, it wasn't the most predictable means of employment; Gerrard had to grant him that much. He nodded at the man, in apparent forgiveness for missing most of the tournament—or at least, acceptance of the circumstances and a willingness to move past them.

Not that Gerrard was so worried about his friends making it; the tournament was basically the same as it had been for many years preceding the current one.

Well, perhaps not, he considered briefly, thinking of the second-place fighter he had just watched enter Liberty's Last, one of his favorite restaurants in Nethereel. She had given him a fair measure more trouble—and thrill—than he had been accustomed to in recent years.

"What can I say?" Gerrard responded in his usual worn, stoic voice. "I do feel myself getting older, maybe slower."

"You looked plenty fast to me! Even against all those twenty- and thirty-somethings!" chimed in Gerrard's other friend, a local businessman named Carmine. "Imagine the glory one of them could capture should they manage to lay low the living legend that is Gerrard!" he continued, swigging another mouthful of his favorite ale and seeming to have already tasted a fair share of it.

Gerrard smiled a little at his remarks. His father had been the swordsman, really, but a couple decades back, Gerrard had come to take it more seriously. He had still never wanted to make a career out of it, and indeed had pursued a career elsewhere, but it seemed that the tournament, the arena, had always called to him—and it had long been a calling he couldn't completely deny.

He still didn't get the fulfillment that he longed for from his sword fighting, though; he sought to make a difference elsewhere in the world with more important work. Yet his fights and the blood that he spilled were what was bringing him the wealth and earning him all the fame and reverence from the people of Makeva. To him, it was all a terribly upside-down state of affairs.

"I appreciate it, Carmine," responded Gerrard in a reassuring tone, granting another fairly rare smile to one of his oldest and most trusted friends.

"So, are you headed back to Akastair soon, to continue your work there?" Cid prodded.

"I'll be relaxing here in town for the start of the weekend, at least through tomorrow. I'll catch the train back there early on Sunday, I think," replied Gerrard casually.

Gerrard thought then about what he regarded as his more meaningful work. Some old maps recently discovered by the company he worked for, Old Guard Mining, had tipped them off to the location of rare deposits of several valuable elements out on the outskirts of Akastair. The company was drilling for samples to analyze, running various tests, laying some groundwork, and developing preliminary plans for a new mine there. Things did seem to be going promisingly so far, though he and many others had initially been skeptical of a mine with so much potential so nearby to where the company had already been stationed for some time.

There had been a new spark of interest in the city of Akastair of late, as a result of his company's rejuvenated interests over there. Carmine was even considering expanding his business operations to Akastair, though he hadn't yet considered the matter in great depth. He did already seem unendingly busy with his current business pursuits. It felt good to Carmine, though, to get out with Cid and Gerrard for a change. It had been far too long a time.

"A toast," Carmine began as he raised his flagon and clinked it against his friends', "to one of the greatest sword fighters in Makeva—our friend Gerrard!"

The trio then drank deeply of their frothy beverages, in mutual appreciation of the too-rare moment they were sharing.

Meanwhile, on the other side of the restaurant and over at the bar, another conversation was starting up.

"What'll you have?" asked Lydia, the dark-haired owner and operator of Liberty's Last. The woman approaching her was someone she didn't immediately recognize. Not that this surprised her, though; there were plenty of customers from adjoining and even faraway communities currently in Nethereel.

Andromeda began to speak, but was cut short by Lydia, who suddenly recognized her after dwelling on the matter for a moment.

"You were second in the tournament! Nicely done!" Lydia cut in. "I'm Lydia. It's a pleasure!" she excitedly said, and she extended her hand warmly. Lydia had known there was something vaguely familiar about the woman, and she was glad she had realized who she was—a tournament finalist and an impressive fighter, one only bested by her old friend Gerrard.

"Oh, thank you," responded Andromeda appreciatively. "My first time. I had fun, though, for sure, and what a great learning experience, too."

Andromeda paused a few moments, wondering if she would be cut off again by another excited outburst. Then, judging it to be safe, she continued, "I'll have something among the sweeter and lighter of the libations you have available, I think," she said, a little indecisively.

Lydia regarded her with more interest than she usually gave her customers, especially around the time of the tournament. After all, many were out-of-towners that she might well never see again. And those types didn't tend to be the greatest tippers, regardless of how much of her attention she gave them. Lydia was quite impressed, though, with the swordplay she had witnessed from Andromeda and the way patrons of her tavern had been excitedly recounting her final fight with Gerrard.

As she let her eyes linger on Andromeda, she happened to notice the archaic-looking blaster at her hip. "Where did you come by such a relic?" asked Lydia, indicating the blaster. She slid a fruity and colorful drink over to Andromeda.

Andromeda took a sip before answering the pleasant younger woman, immediately feeling more interested in engaging with her. "Here in the city, actually. Some small blaster shop I happened by on my way here."

"You made sure the thing still fires first before you sealed the deal, I hope?" Lydia said teasingly, before flashing a disarming smile.

"Yes, of course," replied Andromeda, smiling and chuckling a little before taking another sip of the sweet beverage.

"Not sure I've seen one so ancient in working order before. Do you know much about it?" Lydia asked. She moved her hand in a circling motion, indicating for Andromeda to turn her body and let her take a better look.

Andromeda turned slightly, and the view afforded Lydia a better view of the weapon—and the athletic frame it was strapped to.

"There must be a story worth knowing there," Lydia observed. "Where are you headed?"

Lydia didn't normally drink while working, but she made a rare exception, given the unusual circumstances. She mixed up one of her favorite and most potent concoctions and sipped it while listening to Andromeda's response.

"The seller wasn't able to tell me much about it, really. He had just come by it himself. I was glad to be able to acquire it quite inexpensively though—at least compared to some of the other blasters he was showcasing, anyway," Andromeda remarked. Then her mind caught up to Lydia's question. "As far as where I'm headed, I'm sort of trying to figure that out, actually," she admitted honestly. "I'm new around here. You seem perceptive, though," Andromeda said as she narrowed her eyes playfully. "You probably didn't need me to tell you that." She flashed another smile before draining more of her glass.

"Well, you may want to inquire with the blaster shop owner over in Akastair; he might possibly know something about it. And anyway, Akastair is a lovely place to visit, even if it may be a little costly to linger long around," Lydia suggested. Andromeda noted that her eyes continued to dwell on her a little longer than necessary.

Andromeda smiled warmly, noting Lydia's persisting interest. "Maybe I shall," she responded cryptically.

Lydia was intrigued by her. And it was certainly true the owner of the blaster shop might know or be able to find something out about the blaster. He had a fair degree of notoriety for his historical knowledge of many old relics. More than that, though, Lydia was intrigued with the prospect of sending Andromeda in the direction Gerrard was also headed. She could tell by his occasional glances over at Andromeda he had some kind of lingering interest in her. They seemed like they'd make a powerful team, though what might come of it all, she couldn't be sure.

Lydia motioned to an employee to take over the bar, then she drained what was left of her glass and poured another pair of beverages for herself and Andromeda. She moved to the other side of the bar to play the customer role for a while. She would ... further investigate the compatibility of the two of them—just herself and Andromeda, if not Andromeda and Gerrard as well.

***

Some hours later, Andromeda awoke to the sound of pounding rain coming down on the roof. Her head was pounding a bit, too. Those fruity drinks, she lamented, had such a tendency of intoxicating her more than she realized. In any case, the side effects were relatively mild. She likely only felt them at all because the rain had happened to wake her. *A couple more hours of rest,* she thought. *A couple more hours, and I'll feel perfectly normal.*

Normal... she reflected momentarily as she chuckled lightly to herself. Even in her most normal state, she didn't really fit into that category well at all.

3

Chapter Three

In a different section of the city, another woman, who was younger by perhaps a decade, was pondering her own inability to fit society's various cookie-cutter molds.

Regina was reeling through some inner turmoil, the mental aftermath of what had been a crushing blow to her recent dream of winning the tournament in Nethereel. She was considering that perhaps her life was a rather large lie, and she was challenging her foundations and several long-standing perspectives she had harbored. Such was often the way with the fiery but contemplative Regina.

These sleepless contemplations weren't typical for her on a Saturday morning; she would certainly rather have still been in bed like Andromeda. Not that she knew Andromeda, though she did now know *of* her, having watched the exciting and conclusive final match of the tournament between her and Gerrard.

I could have beat him, she thought. Regina had developed a plan to defeat Gerrard, had banked on him being in the final matchup of the tournament. Perhaps she could have proven successful with that plan, too. But alas, she had been eliminated in one of the first fights, and she was stripped of the opportunity. She had felt like it was her turn to win this event. She had fought in a few events over the last few years and had studied the man and his technique, his stance, and his skills, in depth and with great care. She hadn't managed to secure the victory against Gerrard, though. For that matter, she hadn't succeeded in making it through the tournament far enough to end up matching with him. Still, she knew she could have defeated him, if only she had managed to get that far. At this point, after coming up short again, she was reconsidering the path she had been taking for years now.

This wasn't so uncommon a thing for her, though. She, with some degree of regularity, often remade herself from the ashes of what she had been before. She was constantly challenging herself, making herself question what she believed, and was always striving to improve herself. She had also come to romanticize and thoroughly fall in love with this idea of being champion of the tournament in Nethereel. She had romanticized all kinds of things over the years like that—a side effect, she supposed, of being so painfully introspective.

Her ideas about how she could be the one to defeat Gerrard, essentially the living legend, had been fueled greatly by her grandfather, from whom she had learned much. The man had actually known Gerrard's father, one of the primary people who had trained Gerrard in the fighting style with which he now fought. There were weaknesses she perceived that she felt she could have exploited, had she only gotten closer.

How she had fantasized about being victorious, about being champion, just a week before! She had even entertained the notion that it might be something like her destiny to accomplish that feat. *What a fool I am to always get so carried away like that,* she reflected. She felt she might have staked too much on it to now be able sustain herself in the face of this unfortunate outcome. Still, on some level, she didn't have much along the lines of regret. It was all experience, an opportunity to find and open other doors. She simply needed to reappraise herself and her views, take an objective look at her situation, and formulate a new path forward. None of that was to say she was unemotional about her current situation though; her thoughts at that moment were quite emotional.

That was why she lashed out more intensely than intended when a young man recklessly bolting down the road in the opposite direction practically rammed right into her. She shifted her weight right before the impact and turned her body sideways to avoid the brunt of it. The slight collision was still enough to bring them both crashing to the ground in a misshapen heap.

"Run much?" she snarled at him, not really hurt, but not happy about the situation, either.

"Very sorry, miss, please forgive—" the rushing man began as he sprang back to his feet, but he was off running again before finishing his apology.

Regina had managed a few observations about the hurried man: dark eyes, and dark hair, too, which was not that long, but certainly not as short as was the usual style for males in the area. He was perhaps a full decade younger than her, maybe roughly a quarter century old. He was also quite muscular, and he had an impressive-looking shield strapped on his back, which bore a rather intricate design. There was a snake on it, set against a background of a full moon and a starry night sky.

A few moments later, she found the presence of mind to check her pockets. She hoped she hadn't been mugged by this person. She quickly determined everything to be copacetic, then simply shrugged and continued on her way to the train station—though she hadn't quite unraveled the mystery of where she was going next.

* * *

Gerrard awoke in the late hours of the morning, in his room on the upper level of Liberty's Last. He got up from his bed and began a morning routine of stretches and a brief workout. Then he organized his belongings, to try and make packing most of it up later as quick and easy as possible. He wanted to get an early start the next morning.

He went through a mental list of things he wanted to get to before his departure. After the workout, up next was breakfast downstairs in the restaurant. He also had an old friend, Duncan, to meet at his shop downtown. He wanted to also take his favorite post-tournament hike out to a waterfall outside Nethereel. It had become something of a tradition for him to make the trip annually after the tournament, and he found the experience calming, even therapeutic. He had the thought to check out a local armorer or weaponsmith, too, if he returned to Nethereel early enough. Then, of course, there should be dinner, probably just back at the tavern. Then, hopefully, early to bed and early to rise the next morning to head to the train station.

The stairs creaked noticeably as he made his way down to the ground-level restaurant and bar a few moments later. He gave a friendly wave to a familiar employee and another woman, a friend of his named Lydia, over at the bar. He sat himself at an open table in the lively and crowded restaurant. It was busier than the norm; surely many people were still around from the tournament that had bolstered the usual number of patrons.

"Good morning," he greeted the waitress who approached with a relaxed tone. "I'll have eggs scrambled with cheese, and toast, please."

"Anything at all for you," she responded warmly, recognizing him immediately. "It's supposed to be a scorcher of a day—anything to drink?" the waitress asked.

"Just a glass of water, thank you," Gerrard replied, more impassively.

"Sure, darlin'," the woman responded simply but warmly again, then headed off.

Gerrard thought over the forecast the waitress had mentioned, momentarily reconsidering his planned hike. It was summertime in Makeva, and temperatures were certainly picking up, though they still usually stayed milder where they were—relatively far to the north on the continent of Gracyr. He reflected, but ultimately determined he would not stray from his usual tradition. Besides, he had just picked up an extra canteen this week, and he had plenty in his travel bag to keep him going for the duration of what was really, for him, an easy hike.

"Maybe I'll just take my shortcut this time around," he said to himself aloud, not intending for anyone to hear or respond.

"What's that, sweetheart?" inquired another waitress passing by, who happened to hear him say something.

"Oh, apologies. Nothing, miss," he replied courteously.

"Okay, well, you let me know if there's anything else," she said, and she smiled and moved on to a group of new customers that had just sat down.

Soon, Gerrard was finishing the last few bites of his meal, and he tried to take a few extra seconds to enjoy the moment, as he felt others around him rushing. People so often seemed that way to him—in a hurry from one pressing matter to the next, and so often they seemed to possess no real depth of understanding of why they rushed through so much of their lives. *These seemingly inconsequential moments have such a subtle way of linking together to define our days, weeks, months, and years,* he remembered as he swallowed his last bite of food.

Gerrard counted out a few coppers for the meal and left them on the table, along with an additional tip for the pleasant waitress. He headed back up to his room briefly to grab his large, two-handed claymore and his travel bag. Then he went back down to the ground level and out of Liberty's Last. He strode out onto the streets of Nethereel, following those he knew would take him out of the city and eventually to the remote and forested trails beyond—those he knew would get him to the waterfall.

Outside, the city was bustling. Vendors lined the streets, capitalizing on every impulse to buy something that they could find or create before everyone headed home. It was doubtful that any of them were very disappointed with their profits so far—it seemed to have been another record turnout for tournament attendance this year—but Gerrard could still appreciate the sellers' final push to maximize profits. Economic times were far from at their peak in Makeva, and the woes of the world increasingly weighed on its residents. It was easy to forget all that, though, in the current surroundings. All those around him seemed caught up in the excitement of the moment.

It also helped, Gerrard figured, that it didn't seem like the surely strained hydropower energy systems in the city were faltering yet. Such energy systems failing was becoming common in recent years across Gracyr. It was a consequence of relying on power plants that were dependent on water for generating electricity, in what was an increasingly dry environment across the continent.

He continued on that train of thought for much of the time he strolled through the city and out past its limits. *So curious*, he thought, how the problems of the world seemed to increase every year. And there seemed to be more and more of an emphasis on—and more advertising for—this annual tournament he participated in, but not for so many more critical things.

In his view, there were matters more consequential to the world than pushing throwaway products and sensationalizing fleeting championships. Yet the marketing by all the largest companies of Gracyr seemed to fall primarily on such lesser things, and it was all done to the exclusion of far more important matters—at least, if one cared to think in terms of the continuance and advancement of humanity, anyway.

He could see what an opportunity it was for these companies to get their names in front of the public again and again, to get themselves to be ever more present in their minds, to generate more profit and secure more influence and power. But what a misguided joke it all was, and it was all laid so bare in front of him at this point in his life—so much so that it was almost comical. And yet it persisted and worsened year after year, to what he knew was the detriment of the human race. Even the company he worked for—Old Guard Mining, which accomplished many great things for humans and their advancement—was not innocent. They always wanted Gerrard to be in the tournament, to exclusively sponsor him, for that alluring stream of credits and coin that invariably flowed to them after each successive victory.

It was fine by him, though; he'd wear the company logo and colors. They sponsored the event itself, too. You could find the company name, mission statement, and logo around the city and the arena during the tournament every year. Larger companies with deeper pockets advertised even more. Even in the mining sector, there were many with more capital and resources, financial and otherwise. And there was no shortage of things in and around the tournament to pour money into, so as to build up one's organization in the minds of the attendees.

Even so, Old Guard Mining always set coin aside for what they saw as irresistible investments, even in the face of so many advertising options. Gerrard, given the exponential growth of his popularity with the people—and particularly with this Nethereelan tournament crowd over the years—was someone clearly seen to be an investment of that caliber.

Gerrard sighed a bit, considering it all, as he started up the hilly slopes and woodsy path. Maybe he felt they were buying him, that he was selling himself out to them. He appreciated some of the work the company did, and surely, they were not the worst. But still, he hardly stood for everything that the company seemed to. That was maybe the greater problem here: how people were associating him now with all manner of things about the company he did not agree with.

He had been with Old Guard Mining for decades. That was a relatively unusual feat in the times he was living in. People more commonly bounced around between numerous employers, always seeking the bigger, better deal. Gerrard suspected he might care more than the average person about whatever the company that was paying him stood for. But for him, it was more important to be doing work he believed in, or at least to work for a company he believed in, than however much it was they were paying him.

Fortunately, Gerrard didn't need the pay so much. He had amassed enough wealth for a lifetime, so long as he wasn't wasting it too ridiculously and recklessly. And he was actually so much in the public eye now that he could, to a limited extent, even sway some of the public's opinions. He had even protested some actions by his company in the past, and the pressure he generated from the public actually swayed the behemoth business—an achievement that struck him as a fairly profound feat.

Not that he cared much to be invoking that sort of power, unless he found it critically necessary. And anyway, in terms of the state of what was going on in modern-day Gracyr, the company was doing comparatively little harm, considering all the countless others doing far worse. Anyway, looking past the negative aspects of the company that he worked for, it was still a means to do a lot of good in the world, even if Gerrard didn't wholeheartedly agree with everything being done.

The city of Nethereel was gradually shrinking into the distance. When he looked back now, the trees largely concealed his view of its many buildings. And as he continued to distance himself from it, he found himself thinking of his daughter, of walking with her in woods not so unlike these when she was younger. He had spent great amounts of time away from his daughter while she was growing up. He had gone on many long trips after getting into the mining work with Old Guard. He'd been away for weeks at a time, which didn't always work well with having a young child. He was able to make great coin while away on those trips, though, and it got them by, sometimes even comfortably so—he and his daughter, and her mother.

He thought of their small potato farm and the time he had been able to spend back at home with the two of them. His home time was largely just defined by more work planting or harvesting potatoes, but those were simpler times, upon which he thought back on fondly.

His daughter's mother and he, they had come to be distanced from each other over time though. But their daughter was grown now, so it didn't matter so much. That young girl had gone on to admirably stay on to help the family potato business, which had grown to be bigger than back then. Even so, Gerrard understood it had still been struggling in recent years.

Gerrard followed the trail as it wound around some large boulders, and he made his way over to the shortcut path. It would take him to the scenic and remote waterfall, and by means of that path, it wasn't far away now.

He was not aware that since his last visit to the place, some rather unseemly ruffians had carved out the area for their nefarious affairs.

4

Chapter Four

Regina strode into the central area of the train station in Nethereel. Her short, slender frame was swallowed up by the intimidating immensity of the place. It was a central hub for many trains from numerous different companies and lines coming together. The trains ran on the combustion of hydrogen fuel, and many had been outfitted with the latest in comfort, style, and luxury for the relatively upscale city of Nethereel. The trains levitated almost magically over the rails by means of powerful magnets, which saved them from significant wear and tear and energy loss from friction. Even if Regina had held far higher expectations, the grandeur of the place would not have disappointed her. Perhaps it was still outmatched by Akastair—the city where she had spent much more of her life—but not by much.

She sighed then, thinking about her current predicament. Perhaps she should just return home to Akastair for a while and contemplate what her next moves should be. She could see the upsides and downsides of pursuing all kinds of directions, on all sorts of paths, but thinking over it then, none of it was doing much to placate her growing anxiety. She'd had her plan of training for the tournament, entering, defeating Gerrard, and becoming champion, and then taking off on a new career course from there. Multiple losses over multiple years had now led her to feel the need to cut those losses and take an entirely different direction. But despite all her best-laid plans for success, the last course had still not worked out. Where could she possibly turn now?

She spent a few unsuccessful moments trying to cast things in a positive and optimistic light, to make all her efforts in Nethereel seem like they weren't an utter waste of time. She couldn't shake the nagging feeling that more time in Nethereel was just leading to more wasted potential.

But that train of pessimistic thought was thrown entirely into question a few moments later. Regina saw a familiar figure rushing through the crowds at the station, and her mind was immediately at work reconfiguring the circumstances that led her to such pessimism. *Maybe still being here isn't such a negative thing, after all,* she thought as she considered that seeing this young man again might not be a coincidence. She was, after all, weary of believing in such things. She knew there was a destiny carved in the stars for her—so long as she had it in her to find it.

Doesn't he ever get tired? she wondered, watching him. She glanced again at the intricate image on the shield on his back. She couldn't feel any magic on or about the thing—and she was quite sensitive to such things. *Maybe it's something about the design itself?* she thought as she pored through her memory for any vague recollection of the design. *Is the shield magical? Is it energizing him? Why are thoughts of the item gnawing at me now?*

There was something there—something in her memory she couldn't quite reach. Were her thoughts being scrambled, magically hindered by something? Was she just more forgetful than she used to be? Maybe the memory was just too dated to come back easily.

Regina could usually sense magic around her. She had always held a certain level of attunement to such things in the world. And she carried a magic shield herself, which was capable of greatly enhancing that ability. She could sense her shield activating then, perhaps in some reflexive defensive maneuver. Then she saw what no one else could in the huge room, save for the dark-eyed, dark-haired man rushing through the crowds that she'd recognized from earlier.

Regina's eyes glowed with a faint golden tinge while her shield granted her sight of the forces at work before her. She recognized the seal now, a symbol associated with a malicious group that was unknown to the general public. They were said to be criminals, murderers, thieves, scoundrels, all manner of wretched things, though they did—if you believed the stories, anyway—adhere to some sort of inner code and principles. They were called the Order of Oranlak, and now, in seeing what she had been straining to see, Regina questioned whether she really wanted to see it at all.

The shield the man held still seemed otherwise ordinary. The same could not be said of the marvelous longsword this running man had at his side. It was clearly of potent and ancient magic, perhaps even more so than Regina's magic shield. Thoroughly intrigued, she needed to know more about the sword. Her shield was perhaps the strongest magic she had ever witnessed, and to see something like this now was an incredible rarity, indeed.

Has something about this man's sword actually been clouding my thoughts as well? Remarkable! she thought, with just a tinge of horror creeping in at the possible implications. Still, she found herself driven to unveil more of this mounting mystery.

She could see now what the man was running away from. His pursuers had not been observable at first, but as her eyes dwelled on the man, she came to see them. *They were literally jumping in and out of shadows!*

Regina gathered that if you didn't deal in such dark magic yourself, or didn't otherwise have something like the attunement or magic means that she had, this was not an enemy you could likely defend yourself very effectively against.

Perhaps the runner is an initiate of Oranlak gone rogue or something. Or maybe, a petty thief trying to escape with his ill-gotten gains? Regina surmised. *Maybe he's just taking a shot at an evil empire that could do with being knocked down a bit, for the good of all Gracyr,* she thought, and appreciated the sort of person this man might be if something along those lines were actually true. *Maybe he's just looking for new and exciting ways to get into trouble, like I seem to be,* she thought, and laughed a little to herself.

She weighed her options and played out in her mind the consequences of the different actions she could take. Just then, the man dodged a sudden strike from one of his pursuers, while in an amazing synchronicity, the other adversary also lunged and managed a glancing blow to the man's side. He didn't launch a counterattack though; he seemed to favor using whatever time he had to focus on running away. He dodged into a train car with a lit sign that said, UNDERGOING MAINTENANCE.

Figuring he meant to just take his chances with however far he could get with it anyway, she quickly moved to board the train car, too. Perhaps she could help him dispatch the pursuers, or perhaps the train would actually still take off, and she could continue following this strange but interesting mystery.

The slightly wounded man hadn't bothered to attempt finding any of the door locks, probably figuring the shadow-jumping pair that pursued him wouldn't be significantly hindered even if he found and activated them.

As Regina made her way to the doors of the train car, she considered that, though. These two pursuers had probably been expending a significant portion of their magic on all the shadow jumping; it might've been worth the man's effort to get them to expend a little more. The faster they ran out, the quicker they would become more easily beatable adversaries. Of course, she could also appreciate that the chased didn't exactly have an overwhelming abundance of time to be considering every action in great depth.

She quickened her pace as she saw the train come back online, and she made it through the door to the train car just as it started to move forward. The train was on its way.

With the train now rolling along, Regina made her way up through several connected train cars, and then she came upon the trio she'd been following.

The man being pursued by the Oranlak gang members was up against the far wall of the train car. Perhaps the door at his back that led to the next car was not unlocked, as the others had been that she had just passed through. He was brandishing his glowing red longsword. He managed a few strained words between gasping breaths.

"I didn't want it to have to come to this," he warned the pair, who had backed him up against that wall. He slashed at the shadow magic user closest to him, an attack that was easily dodged. But then something unexpected followed the strike.

Regina blinked in disbelief as she saw what appeared to be a giant scorpion materializing in the air between the man and the Oranlak gang members. She actually looked on with a measure of admiration, as these dealers in darkness, these shadow-commanding sorcerers, did not even flinch. Then when the scorpion turned and viciously stung one of them—without either even moving to dodge or defend—she realized the truth of the matter. *Apparently, these two can't even see the potent magic that has just been conjured to strike one of them down. Fascinating... and terrifying,* she thought.

The vicious and perhaps venomous tail of the thing pierced one of the men's throats, and he collapsed lifelessly to the floor. Then the magical specter of the scorpion vanished. The other gang member seemed to be caught off guard by the sudden collapse of his comrade, and he quickly fell victim to a slash from the summoner's mighty sword.

Alarms were going off on the train and all over the station, though the latter was fast fading in the distance behind them now. The train sputtered and rattled ominously, but it seemed to at least be holding together as it barreled along down the length of tracks out of the city and toward the tree line beyond.

Regina didn't immediately settle on her next actions, other than to drop down behind some seating and look up ahead to the end of the car. She found herself harboring some doubts about the wisdom of hitching a ride on that train.

How could I have let myself be the victim of such an impulse? Why did I dive into this disaster that's going to leave me cleaved in half by that vicious red blade, or drowning in my own blood from a magical scorpion's sting? The commonsense questions mounted in Regina's mind as she looked on at the man and the scene up ahead of her.

* * *

As he ventured up the trails to the waterfall, and as the temperature was similarly climbing, Gerrard was considering that perhaps he should have met his friend before heading out. Hopefully, the earlier start would position him to be able to return to Nethereel before the day was out. He reached into his travel bag for a drink, and he swallowed a few gulps of water from one of his canteens.

Shortly after, Gerrard finally came upon the waterfall. It was the usual beautiful sight to behold. He watched the water pouring and tumbling down a great distance below the height that the trail had taken him up to, and even still, he had to look up high to see where the falls descended from.

He sat down and considered the simple splendor of the scene for some time. His thoughts gave way to memories of visiting the place many years before. He could recall bringing his daughter and her mother there years ago. Even before that, he remembered being there with his own father and mother on some long-ago trip. He basked for a while in the moment.

Gerrard pondered the comicality of it all, the ridiculousness and absurdity of the games he seemed to enjoy playing with himself and the world. He saw with refreshed clarity what a shallow game it all was, compared to the depths of emotion and thought the waterfall stirred in him now. But he acknowledged to himself that to try to convey that it all was merely a "game" would be misleading to many. That would imply he didn't take any of it seriously. And that wasn't so at all. If it was a game, it was one he took very seriously.

He was drawn from his contemplations by a loud voice, quickly shushed by other, more whispering ones. Gerrard was immediately on his guard and slunk away as quickly and stealthily as he could to some nearby shrubs. He couldn't make out the voices due to their distance and the roaring of the waterfall, but he gathered that the group seemed not to have noticed him. He laughed a little at himself, thinking he was overreacting by running and hiding. Then he noticed the group for what they were, seeing a seal that contained a snake against a moon on the plate armor of one of them. These were members of the Order of Oranlak, a nefarious band of criminals with tendrils that reached out all across Gracyr.

The group approached a mossy patch of rock to the side of the waterfall. One tapped in what seemed to be a specific and complicated pattern on the rock. Gerrard edged a bit closer, knowing any rustling he made was likely to be drowned out by the waterfall. The moss glowed a vibrant and powerful shade of green in what suddenly took the form of a large rectangle. *The outline of a doorway*, Gerrard thought. The large rectangle of glowing rock collapsed into the stone and slid out of the way, out of sight into the chamber beyond. The chamber seemed to instantly come alight inside, and Gerrard found himself moving toward the entryway himself.

It surely crossed his mind then to turn around and head back. But he felt as if some force was driving him forward. It was a force he couldn't deny, despite the obvious logic he could see in just getting out of there. He managed to close the distance to where the Oranlak group had been standing, and to slide inside into the strange chamber, just before the stone wall magically glided back into place and sealed the doorway.

5

Chapter Five

Andromeda awoke then, almost in perfect timing with the sealing of that chamber all those miles away.

She had slept many hours past what she had intended; she could immediately tell by the level of sunlight in the room. It was also becoming quite hot in her room there on the upper floor of Liberty's Last. She recalled Lydia mentioning, between swigs of a sweet alcohol that turned her stomach to remember, that today was going to feature some rather hot temperatures.

She went through a few morning stretches. Then she strapped on her holster and blaster, and she sheathed her saber at her opposite hip. Her saber was a vicious and deadly curved blade that had been wielded by her father eons ago. She reflected on how it felt like it had been too long since even she'd had the opportunity to put the weapon to use—particularly since the tournament rules had not allowed her to use it in the arena.

Such an opportunity, however, was to be presented to Andromeda sooner than she was anticipating.

She grabbed her backpack with her gear and supplies and headed downstairs to the restaurant and bar area. She caught a glimpse of her new friend, Lydia, over at the bar, and gave her a friendly wave as she moved to sit at one of the few remaining open tables—one that appeared to have just been cleared by the waitstaff.

A waitress stopped by her table and inquired what she would like, and as the timing was suitable more so for lunch than breakfast, Andromeda asked for her lunch recommendation.

"What's popular here? What do people usually rave about?" Andromeda asked, looking to catch the woman's eyes. The waitress's focus was somewhere else, though, or perhaps her heart wasn't in customer service, as she barely looked at Andromeda.

"I'd go with the soup du jour, and the steak sandwiches are my personal favorite, as well as a typical favorite here. They're saucy and meaty and well worth the coin, I'd say," answered the waitress, a little more pleasantly as her mind seemed to linger on the appetizing menu option.

Andromeda nodded approvingly, and she added a glass of juice to the order.

She was just finishing up her food and counting out some copper coins for the bill when her new friend briefly paused by her table.

"Sleep well, Miss Andromeda?" asked Lydia, with a touch of concern in her voice, perhaps feeling she had led her new friend to imbibe more alcohol last night than she had wanted to.

"A little longer than I meant to, but well, all the same," Andromeda said, and she smiled reassuringly. In truth, she'd had more of those fruity, frothy things last night than she had planned to—more of them than she had in years. But it was more important to Andromeda to just have a positive interaction with the alluring and friendly Lydia than to get into any of that.

"I ... just wanted to remark that you look very much like the adventuring sort. Are you going out on a new one today?" Lydia asked.

"Oh, well, I'm in sort of a limbo at the moment, actually. Maybe looking for a new one, though, a new direction to take—maybe," Andromeda replied.

"Well, there are a lot of scenic spots around that'd be ideal for finding one," Lydia began, but then paused to ponder something for a moment. "Why don't you check this place out, see if you might find some adventure there?" She pulled out a brochure from her front apron pocket and opened it to show Andromeda a map. Lydia circled an area of the map, then went on to elaborate. "I've heard some gossip from a lot of our customers about some interesting things apparently happening over in this area," she explained, pointing. "Local authorities haven't turned up much in their investigations—but maybe you have eyes for things they don't. If, say, some unscrupulous operations are, in fact, being conducted over there ... there are several rewards and bounties for information and people of interest... Do be careful, though, miss," Lydia said, smiling as she departed, but not lingering to hear or gauge Andromeda's response.

That made sense to Andromeda, though, looking around at the buzzing bar and restaurant. Lydia certainly appeared to have no shortage of work to get to.

As she walked away, Lydia considered how she sincerely wanted whatever was going on out by that waterfall to die down. Perhaps more importantly, though, it was an opportunity to bring together a pair of people she thought would make an incredible team.

Had Lydia waited around a few more moments to hear her response, Andromeda would have simply expressed that she would give it some consideration. She wasn't keen on making any immediate, spur-of-the-moment commitments, but she was intrigued.

Andromeda headed outside and in the direction of the base of operations for the local authorities in Nethereel, a place she had walked past several times over the course of the tournament.

It wasn't far, and she came upon it a short while later. She went inside the large building and entered the lobby area. She asked the officer at the front desk about recent calls to the public for assistance with any pending investigations in the area or in the woods out by the waterfall. She inquired about information related to any concerns people had, what was going on out there, and what bounties were available, if any.

She hadn't given much thought to any serious ideas about pursuing the title of bounty hunter for herself, but she also wasn't firmly opposed. After all, she did need something new, by her own admission, and certainly needed to keep an open mind. And it did seem apparent that she had some skills that could be useful in that line of work.

The largest bounties were on some particularly dangerous-sounding criminals, naturally. Some were even speculated to have connections to large criminal enterprises. It struck Andromeda as concerning that such organized criminal groups could be looking to take a serious stake in the area or were even possibly already operating there.

I wonder what brought them here, she thought. She had never encountered the groups detailed in the paperwork the officer provided for her reference, though she had certainly heard of some. They made her think of the stories she had heard of a particularly evil group known as Oranlak. They were a mysterious group, not even widely accepted to truly exist. But there was no mention of that particular group in the paperwork.

Could such a degree of darkness have designs for this pleasant city and the surrounding area? More importantly, is it something I want to involve myself with? she thought.

She thought of the shadow magic Oranlak gang members were said to command—at least in the stories. Andromeda had long suspected much of it to be true, though she hadn't encountered anything she considered to be concrete evidence of any of it. Gracyr seemed an often-dark place, though, and she had little difficulty in accepting that such darkness could possibly exist.

Still, Andromeda often felt doubtful that such an allegedly large organization could exist and not be widely known to be real. And if they could wield such powerful magic—the sort that largely was lost to the modern world—could such a thing really be kept under wraps? That magic, in the stories she had heard in her youth, was the stuff of nightmares. Supposedly, those using it too much or too long even risked becoming less human, and more like some monster of the shadow realm.

She shuddered slightly. That didn't seem like a worthwhile trade-off at all to her. Such an unnatural, abnormal transition, for what she knew was a shallow power that would never satisfy one's soul. Although, she could certainly acknowledge to herself, it was astounding what could come to seem like a good idea to a person exposed to the wrong environment for long enough.

Drawing herself back to the moment, she skimmed through the paperwork the officer provided her. The information being called for from the public was any that would lead to uncovering an alleged base of operations for one of a number of criminal bands theorized to have interests in the area. Information about why they were here to begin with, or any other information one might consider "potentially relevant" was also of interest. The monetary rewards were certainly noteworthy, and Andromeda determined she would seek out this location Lydia had circled on the map she'd provided.

She started out of the building and on her way at once. She couldn't help but notice how excited she was. She had a new mission and purpose to work toward—one she hoped would take her closer to solving the larger predicament that had necessitated her journey out of Elazora. And she also now had a mysterious case to crack, something she was finding she also treasured.

* * *

The trio that Gerrard had followed into the magically lit chamber had already moved on down a tunnel ahead, one of several breaking off from the main chamber he stood in. He wasn't looking for it at that moment—but if he had been, he might have uncovered a valuable clue as to why the Order of Oranlak was operating in the place.

There were a few streaks of red-colored rock barely perceptible to a casual onlooker, but still visible to one familiar with and scrutinizing for it. It was a substance called crimson fluorite, embedded in the rock on the far side of the chamber from where Gerrard stood. The substance was a rich and beautifully deep shade of red. It was prized for its use in making a particular metal alloy, and it was sometimes sought for use in extravagant jewelry as well. More importantly, it often contained another substance of even greater value—at least to someone who knew its potential and how to extract it. Lutetium was a silvery-white substance that could be drawn from the crimson fluorite, and it was a key to unlocking great magical power.

There was a decreasing reliance on magic in Gracyr; it was generally falling out of favor. It was increasingly costly and rare, and also inaccessible, and more and more frequently, it was capable of being replaced by advancements of the modern age. Some didn't feel the full reasons that magic was fading in the world were *entirely* clear, though. Gerrard's opinion was that, beyond these other factors, people with great power in Gracyr simply saw it as a threat to the order of things.

Lutetium was needed to create the ammunition for Gerrard's blaster and all blasters remaining in Gracyr. And only an ever-dwindling few knew how to work with it and create the ammunition.

Gerrard held some of the rare and sought-after A-level rounds, and even a few in the more advanced subcategories of them that existed. Bullets of such great power had become wondrously rare over his lifetime; it felt like a long time since he'd fired anything so powerful. Not that a person generally needed something more destructive than the basic A-level blaster rounds anyway.

Gerrard, though, at that moment, was not so far removed from a future time when he might—not that he was at all aware of it at that fateful moment.

Gerrard selected one of the tunnels to head down—the one he believed the trio had taken. He wasn't entirely sure it was the tunnel he should take, regardless—but alas, as with many times in his life, he was being presented with a choice between many options, which had among them many possible upsides and downsides. And once again, none of them seemed indisputably better than any of the others. He made a decisive and reasonable choice when one simply had to be made. Gerrard began down the largest, the central tunnel.

6

Chapter Six

The train ride that took Regina from the Nethereel station was a tumultuous one. As they moved farther from the city, the train intermittently slipped and grinded on the tracks, and awful sounds emanated from the engine. The ride became so turbulent at one point that Regina felt like the train cars were going to detach, or like the one she was in would simply explode.

After what was just a few minutes, though they felt to her like hours, the train did quiet, and those feelings thankfully passed.

"You can come out now. It's … sort of safe. I've bought us … some time," came a deep and low voice, speaking slowly. It was the man with the red, scorpion-summoning sword.

Regina paused, frozen where she knelt for a few more moments, hoping the man was addressing some other stowaway. She remained unmoving and in silence for what felt like a long time. She then heard the man's footsteps moving through the train car toward her, past the rows of empty seats and closing in.

She stood to the full height of her approximately five-and-a-half-foot frame when she knew he was just a few rows ahead. She held her shield defensively out in front of her, her longsword in her other arm at the ready. She tried not to come across in any overly threatening manner. "Impressive display," she managed through her unease, in what was almost her normal voice—one much higher and louder than the one that had just addressed her.

The man remained stone-faced and silent as he looked her over.

"What was all that about?" she asked, attempting again to move along the conversation.

"I took something from them. You were witnessing their attempt to get it back," the man finally answered, cryptically. And that voice of his, like smoke, only added to the mystery of the peculiar circumstances Regina found herself in.

She stared back at him for a few moments and decided his response was likely truthful. It did only seem to lead to further questions, though.

"What was so important that they lost their lives trying to get it back?" Regina asked, her silvery voice trying to pierce the stubborn veil that shrouded her situation.

Still the man visibly hesitated—perhaps because he was not much of a liar, but didn't want to yield much information to her, either.

She changed the subject. "What's your name?" she asked.

"Hector."

"Well, Hector ... what now?" asked Regina, shrugging her shoulders in an exaggerated motion, smiling slightly.

She wasn't sure, but it almost looked like Hector nearly cracked a smile himself.

In truth, Hector was considering how he might begin to attempt to explain it all—the preposterous situation he was digging himself into, especially to someone he barely knew, especially when he questioned how long he even wanted her around.

"What is your name?" he asked, tonelessly, but borrowing the woman's tactic a little.

"My name is Regina," she replied formally. Then she didn't let up, but graciously reworded her question. "So, Hector, what should we be doing about this runaway train we're on?"

"Well, those two—they were from ... an organization that is ... up to something outside the city. Near the waterfall in the forest," he began, answering her question a little more broadly. "Hopefully, this train can get me closer to that place. And preferably ... quickly."

"Okay, and what interest do ya have in all that, though?" she delved, genuinely curious. But she could see the younger man was disinclined to talk much—secretive, perhaps, maybe the sort to keep things to himself, or perhaps he was just the sort to think too much about simple questions. She didn't want to fault him for that, though. She couldn't—not considering her own idealistic tendency to romanticize and waste time on all kinds of unnecessary things.

"Well," he said, speaking up, but noticeably restricting his response a bit, "I suppose I was thinking my life needed to be made a little more interesting, and felt this whole thing seemed a grand opportunity."

Regina expected sarcasm, but there was none. The man's voice was matter-of-fact. So, she just chuckled slightly, a little artificially, but she did manage a sincere smile. "So, this train is taking us there? To this waterfall?" she asked.

Hector looked at the screen behind him, hanging down from the ceiling of the train car. There was a map displayed there. He judged they were indeed headed in the right direction. This occurred to him at that instant as somewhat miraculous, because his priorities had been much more focused on escaping those shadow-jumping assassins than on where exactly he was sending himself.

"It does look like this train will be getting us close to where we need to be going. So long as we jump off at the right time," he remarked.

"Ya sound a little surprised about that," Regina observed. "And ... jump off?" she asked, sounding a touch alarmed.

Hector nodded. "That's correct."

But her countenance suggested he needed to elaborate a bit.

"The brakes were under maintenance, among other things ... but it appears we can still slow the train. We won't be fully stopping it, though, whether we want to or not," he said flatly, without any degree of the horror that was creeping onto Regina's face.

"Any way we can be getting off a little less dangerously?" she asked, as calmly as she was able to at that moment.

Hector shook his head. "Even if we could stop this thing, it'd only give the authorities more time to catch up to us, and they won't be far behind as it is. Better the train keeps on and continues giving them something to chase, distracting them from us and where we're headed."

Regina considered again the logic of her own recent decisions. But she didn't question Hector's reasoning just then. She surely didn't want to get tied up with the authorities over the theft of some hydromagnetic train barreling out of Nethereel—particularly one that was likely now headed toward its inevitable destruction.

7

Chapter Seven

In Imadazan—which was widely known as the grandest city of Ezmondia, and as one of the most populous—Mercedes sat mulling over the most pressing problem of her day. She sat comfortably, sinking into the large, plush chair in her capital city office. She leaned forward in a moment of frustration, though, and she tapped her hand against her cheek as she contemplated. Then her eyes happened to fall on an object on the wall on the other side of the large room. It was her favorite weapon: an ornate, and mostly symbolic, mace. Its metal shaft was decorated with rare gemstones that made it seem excessively fancy, but its head was a knobbed, blunt, spiked affair, capable of deadly damage. It was the weapon customarily carried by the second-in-command to the emperor, and it had been bestowed upon her by the very same: their leader, Armando.

Mercedes stood to the full height of her voluptuous, five-and-three-quarter-foot frame, which was tall for most females of the region. She had taken on a softer and rounder appearance in more recent years, having sunk deeper into the luxuries and relative ease of life in the capitol building, the place generally referred to as the Castle.

She didn't regard that change with much concern, though. Even if she had been far less attractive, she would still have no shortage of would-be suitors vying for her attention, especially given the powerful position Armando had appointed her to.

She was midway through her thirties now, and she had known Armando since she was very young. The case could be made, even, that she knew the man better than anyone. Somehow, though, that didn't seem to be making her current predicament any easier to work through.

She had been tasked by Armando with solving an elephantine problem plaguing the empire. And of course, annoyingly, it now fell on her to find a solution to what was an age-old issue. It was a problem that had persisted from long before she was ever in power—or alive, for that matter. The present issue, simply stated, was that the people of Ezmondia were having too few children. Fertility rates were down, and it was not serving the longevity of Armando's empire well.

It wasn't the biggest problem he could have conceivably charged her with—and Ezmondia certainly had no shortage of problems—but such considerations as these didn't do much to alleviate Mercedes's current frustration. *What does he expect me to do about this?* she agonized repeatedly to herself.

She thought about what had changed over the course of her life that had so exacerbated this problem, to the point that it had become the crisis it now was. She thought of her younger years, of how she remembered feeling. There was a stability back then, and a feeling of being more protected, safer, that even her current surroundings couldn't match, and she had been of far more modest means back then. Ezmondia—all of Gracyr, really—was far from the place it had been back then in those simpler times ... or was it?

She wondered, *Is it truly the objective reality that things have so changed since then? Or is this belief just stemming from a shift in my own perspective over time, leading to a differing perception of what is, in fact, the same?*

Her increasing age and deeper analysis of things certainly played a role in forming her current perceptions. She reached through her thoughts for examples of more material, more palpable changes. She thought of traditions, commonplace in her youth, that few now bothered to carry on with. *That's a rather objective observation*, she thought. *Is there a connection?*

Life in Ezmondia—or really anywhere in Gracyr, for that matter—had certainly never been perfect. That fact held true throughout all of her living memory, and beyond.

Through her ongoing deliberations, she came to determine it was necessary to continue moving forward, but that they still needed a return to some aspects, some *traditions*, perhaps, of the past. Agonize over it as she did, she still couldn't convince herself anything in particular was the absolute cause or the incontrovertible solution. She ultimately resolved to accept they needed to try some things she could conceivably see leading to a solution, and just see how it played out.

Ideally, those things should be succinctly and easily explainable to Armando. He wouldn't want technicalities and pages of empty rhetoric to digest. He needed the sort of clear-cut and concrete solution he was always comfortable with. And if the proposed solution could not be something he would be immediately comfortable with, then it at least needed to be of the sort he could stomach with minimal persuasion from his second-in-command.

That was the way with Armando: he wanted quick and easy answers to vastly complicated problems. And he wanted a solution in line with how he viewed the world—an effortlessly digestible solution, and preferably one that wasn't going to take long to materialize, either.

Armando's end goal for this current task was pretty much rooted in what all his short-term goals were rooted in: a desire to concentrate and centralize more power more closely around himself. He wanted more control over military forces, which he also wanted made stronger. For that, he needed a steadier and reinforced pipeline of new recruits, and that was a significant connection to the more direct issue of low fertility rates that she had been given to address now.

The problem of too few children was not serving the empire well for a number of reasons though. It was just perhaps most concerning to Armando that his long-term militaristic aspirations were jeopardized as a result. And he did recognize that new soldiers from any new programs they might implement might not be substantially coming into play until a distant future when they would reach adulthood, but the importance of the matter was largely just the public perception. He wanted the people to see the infrastructure, the groundwork of what was coming tomorrow—and that alone would be building the strength of his empire in their minds, and he knew it could be as effectively built up there as anywhere.

As word would spread from there, before they ever even physically advanced on their enemies, those enemies would grow weaker, and Armando's power would grow stronger. And it wouldn't even matter whether those enemies lay within some rebel band inside the Ezmondian Empire, or beyond its borders. They would all inevitably be defanged, and he would concentrate ever more strength for himself. And of course, Mercedes reflected, Armando's ambitions would never be quelled simply by better controlling what he already had. He desired more.

That being said, Armando's call for a more rigid, more "effective" framework for the education of the public was still another top priority. This was education for essentially everyone, surely, but more critically, the youth—including those now being born, and those soon to be.

The lights flickered in Mercedes's office just then, disrupting her thoughts with a gentle reminder of an even more gargantuan problem than the fertility crisis.

The worsening droughts, and the consequently failing hydroelectric dams, were necessitating the temporary cutting of electricity to whole sections of the empire, sometimes for hours at a time. And it was not something that had been improving or seemed at all poised to improve in the future. Conditions might improve or worsen over a span of any given few months, mostly with the changing rainy or dry seasons, but observed over years, things were clearly taking a drastic turn for the worse. It was a dire problem, because the vast majority of the electricity in their empire came from their hydroelectric dam operations.

Mercedes wasn't certain that the top priority problem she had been assigned was the one she should be focused on addressing first, but it really wasn't her place to waste time questioning the orders of her superior.

Refocusing after a few moments, Mercedes's thoughts finally settled back on their current education system in Ezmondia. Many small changes had been instituted in the years since Armando had come to reign. He wasn't one to favor such minor alterations and had openly criticized the benefits of many of these changes as being infinitesimal. The Elite Council, she knew, was holding back his too far-reaching, too ground-shaking ideas.

The subtlety, the gradualness was important, she understood. As it was, she could still see how all these changes since he had come to power could be construed in the minds of the masses as conditioning—or worse, brainwashing, if one wanted to be extreme about it. She knew most residents wouldn't think too deeply about it all, though. Anyway, even if they were upset, they had adequate distractions draining their motivation to keep them from doing anything about it.

Still, she, Armando, and the Elite Council didn't need to be instituting too many changes that could be easily labeled extreme. For the sake of the longevity and stability of the empire—things she did care passionately about—they needed to avoid doing such things.

Beyond such incentives as those that she had for continuing her work, she also considered, as she let her mind slip back to old crushes from her youth, that she was also just a great and long-standing admirer of that fiery strength Armando had. And his sort of leadership suited her need for societal stability quite well. Sure, it needed to be lightly checked from time to time, but there wasn't much in the way of uprisings or rebellions; people fell in line with little fuss, trusting the circles of elites with so much of everything in their lives. The elites were protecting people, eliminating conflict and worry over countless things, something that one might call a *freer* society inevitably suffered from. And that was all to say nothing of how comfortable her lifestyle had become in recent times.

So, Mercedes was pleased to be advancing more or less whatever Armando deemed important—whether it was truly something of direct benefit to the empire, or even if it was just something for his own personal benefit.

She considered elements that some grand campaign could contain that might reinforce to the masses the importance of producing offspring. The "stability of the empire" might be too distanced a notion from their day-today lives to really be a strong selling point. *Something forging a more direct, deeper emotional connection, maybe?*

If a new media campaign, or some new education process was introduced to people at a young age, their minds would be much more easily molded to what Armando wanted. *What a slow progression it would be, though!* she thought. *It won't be enough, or it won't come to fruition fast enough, for Armando's liking.*

She thought over her own experiences throughout her life, considering to what extent they were generalizable to the current population of the empire. She also considered that she could set an example and have a child herself, and she wondered how effective a course that would be for solving this issue. It would, of course, detract from her work, for the sake of what Armando would just call a single child, which he would likely not find acceptable. She considered laying out a hard truth that they were going to have to just focus on doing better with the children who were now very young and born hereafter.

No, she thought. *We need to be building up the value of having more children now—in the minds of the potential parents we have among the population now, and with the resources and the systems we currently have in place. We can't wait to just do better tomorrow. It'll be too late for Armando, if not for Ezmondia. We need to be constantly talking about the importance of this to the public, and to be working on appropriate incentives today.*

* * *

It was as Mercedes was contemplating these things that, far and away up north and to the west, Andromeda was finally crossing into the forest that held the waterfall. She trekked to the area Lydia had circled on her map. Andromeda had crossed some train tracks a while back, but was now thoroughly surrounded by trees and nature, a setting she found far more peaceful than the bustle of the city.

She began up the first steep hill she encountered, onto a largely overgrown trail that seemed to be the correct path to get to the waterfall area. She strolled along another few minutes before she heard the rattling and barreling of what she suspected was a malfunctioning train traveling along the tracks she had just crossed before entering the woods.

That train sure sounds noisy, she thought. She turned her head and attempted to look back through the trees to see what was causing the ruckus. It was indeed a train, and as she regarded it, she was surprised to observe it slowing—basically in the middle of nowhere, so far from a station. She was then even more surprised to see a pair of people jumping off the slowing train.

She ran off the trail and hid behind some large boulders not far off. She curiously watched the scene unfolding.

The pair was a bit scuffed up, but they seemed to have endured the jump off of the hydromagnetic train just fine. The train picked up speed again as it noisily moved off into the distance, and shortly thereafter, it was gone from sight.

Andromeda had taken the hydromagnetic trains around Makeva many times throughout her life. She knew from experience that their nearly frictionless gliding over the tracks didn't produce any real noise at all, so it was clear there was something going very wrong with that particular one.

No wonder they were willing to risk their lives jumping off the thing, she thought.

She couldn't make out the few words they were exchanging as they walked along and into the forest. The man appeared to be in his mid-twenties, and she could plainly see he possessed a muscular build. He seemed shorter than the average male, but not by much. He was perhaps a few inches taller than the female he was with.

The female was the better part of a decade older than him, she guessed—something like a decade younger than herself. The woman was perhaps slightly taller than Andromeda, and maybe a little thinner and less athletic.

What are they doing out here like this? Andromeda wondered. The female had a remarkable-looking shield, but a much less impressive-looking sword.

The man's red sword seemed on par with the quality of that shield, though—it was a deadly-looking weapon. As they began to move up ahead and past where she hid, Andromeda saw he had a shield on his back as well.

Or is it truly a shield? she thought. She wasn't entirely certain. It had an emblem emblazoned on it—one she recognized after a few moments. It was the alleged symbol of the fabled Order of Oranlak. The realization immediately quickened her heartbeat and set her on her guard. She couldn't see anything else on or about the pair that really made her think they were of that criminal gang, though. They also weren't triggering any memory of the bounties she had reviewed back in Nethereel. Perhaps they didn't know what they carried and had just stolen it from one of the Oranlak—maybe they had taken it as a trophy.

What kind of person would openly antagonize the Oranlak? she pondered with a degree of excitement. Perhaps they'd be helpful allies. Perhaps she could be of use to them, as well.

She'd gone so far as to have the thought, but she wasn't looking to immediately put any such theory to the test. Right then, though, she suspected she was going to have to, as the man suddenly halted and looked cautiously over in her direction.

His right hand gripped the hilt of that marvelous sword he had at his left hip.

* * *

Gerrard made his way carefully and silently down the central tunnel, and he continued on for some time. While he did so, he considered, a multitude of times, what madness had driven him to run into the place, and whether it was all going to cost him something like his freedom or even his life. Perhaps only for his own peace of mind, he reached a hand back more than once to grasp the familiar hilt of the massive sword strapped across his back. The powerful claymore was his favored weapon, and one he could harness to devastating effect. Of course, he knew the tactics this particular band might employ against him might put him at a considerable disadvantage, particularly in the increasingly claustrophobic place he was delving deeper into.

He touched the blaster at his hip for further reassurance. He thought perhaps he might favor the six-chambered firearm over his sword on this particular venture.

He walked past some boreholes in the rock walls and observed crates of typical mining supplies, including explosive powder. And he thought at once that he would need to be careful where he aimed his blaster.

They seemed fairly well outfitted. There were several nice-looking diamond-coated drills. As an employee of a mining company, he knew this environment relatively well. The holes he walked past appeared to be exploratory; those drilling them must have been checking for some resource the group suspected to be nearby. And he was naturally quite curious to know what that resource might be.

How many years had he been coming to this place, not knowing something valuable enough to draw the attention of this powerful criminal band was so close?

He heard voices then, so he halted his progress into the tunnel. They were coming from up ahead, where there was more light. He slowly resumed his previous pace. One of the voices elevated suddenly and sharply, apparently berating an underling for something.

What is it all about, the yelling, this whole mining operation I've managed to stumble into? he wondered. But he wondered these things only briefly, as a sudden loss of consciousness came over him, just an instant after a poisoned crossbow bolt penetrated the back of his shoulder.

* * *

"What's wrong?!" Regina yelled to the younger man, who had stopped for some reason and ended up well behind her on the trail.

Hector winced at Regina's louder-than-necessary inquiry. He glared silently at her, and as he did so, he moved his head slightly toward one of the boulders, just back and off the trail a bit. He hoped she would get the hint of what their situation potentially was.

He felt the vague presence of another human there, through the magic of his sword, Kazahvir. Not that he wanted to share that explicitly with Regina. It occurred to him how she might question how he could have known someone was there, though, and he didn't know how he would respond if she asked.

Let her think I've a keen ear for such things, he thought.

Hector advanced slowly toward the boulder that loomed ever larger before him. As he did so, Andromeda carefully but quickly weighed what course of action she should take. She knew she couldn't let indecisiveness get a hold of her now.

She could run, she considered. She could come out and prepare to fight the duo. Maybe she could talk or reason with them. *Maybe we could all be friends?* she thought, smiling slightly to herself, despite the possibly dire situation. Of course, if they were of the Order, they certainly weren't going to be her friends. And she also knew she wouldn't be persuading those fanatic zealots of much.

Still, she really had the sense that these two were something different. She stepped out from behind the boulder a moment later.

"Hello there. Greetings!" she called to the two fellow travelers. "I'm, um..." she started. "... not looking for any trouble or anything!"

Hector slowed, then stopped his advance. "That's what I would expect a person in your situation to say," he challenged coldly, not putting his sword away. He couldn't call upon the scorpion again today, but he still remained confident he could take this person down. He considered, though, with his typical caution and guardedness, that he might have some trouble if Regina and this new woman happened to be in league with each other, and they both decided to come at him.

He carefully regarded the woman who had stepped from behind the boulder. She was perhaps two decades older than he and a few inches shorter. She looked toned and athletic, but not so bulky and muscular as he was. She had a gorgeous-looking sword, with a vicious and threatening curve to its blade—a saber, he recognized. He judged that someone with so fine a weapon in all likelihood had a fair measure of skill, and he, of course, was aware of the tournament that had just ended in Nethereel. She wasn't taking a very threatening stance against him, though.

He regarded the blaster at her opposite hip. He sincerely questioned whether the archaic thing would even manage to fire if she succeeded in pulling the trigger.

"You're not with that wretched Oranlak, are you?" Andromeda said, breaking the brief silence between them.

"I don't care to be associated with that group at all," Hector responded flatly.

"You probably shouldn't march around with one of their emblems so prominently displayed on your back like that, then, you know," Andromeda teased lightly, and flashed him her usual disarming smile.

Despite himself, and his typical don't-wear-your-heart-on-your-sleeve stance on things, his face did crease into a slight smile.

"Fair enough," he replied. He felt his guard almost automatically lowering a bit, though it was a feeling that worried him. *Is there something more about this one, too?* he thought with a degree of concern. Were her words tinged with some sort of magic he couldn't detect? Perhaps soaked in some spell of enchantment?

Hector felt his general distrust for others begin to take hold, and he was careful to keep his countenance firm and not betraying much.

"What are you after?" he inquired of the older female, still not lowering his weapon. Regina remained where she was, more or less where she had been the whole time—still just looking on, he supposed, trying to gauge the situation.

"Well, I'm on something of an adventure—hopefully one that ends with a significant payout, actually. That's … not something you'd fault me for, is it?" Andromeda asked, gambling on what course of conversation would appeal to the untrusting swordsman. She paused briefly, then continued. "Happy to join with you. You could use the help, if you know what you're headed into," she added, in what she hoped was a convincing bluff. After all, she didn't even know what they were headed into.

Hector did lower his weapon slightly then. There seemed to be some sincerity there. And he sensed a certain level of skill in this newcomer that intrigued him. It seemed she was just charismatic, not that she was casting any literal spell. No real magic seemed to be about her—insofar as he could judge with Kazahvir, anyway. And the fact that he could think of no instance before where his sword had been wrong in such a matter did reassure him.

Yes, the partnership could be beneficial, he thought—or rather, *they* thought, since the thoughts of the magical sentience of his sword merged with his own. He still didn't favor the idea of having another new person so close to him whom he wasn't entirely sure he could trust. Of course, for Hector, that category included essentially every human in existence.

"What is your name?" he asked the woman.

"Andromeda," she answered, locking eyes and flashing a hopeful smile.

"Nice name," he responded, though with too much plainness and lack of emotion for Andromeda to gauge for sure if he really meant it. "Hector," he added.

Regina yelled from farther away, "That's a beautiful name! I'm Regina!"

Hector reflexively winced. It was a little louder than he was comfortable with, particularly given that members of Oranlak could well be within earshot of them.

To her credit, Regina did realize her mistake, though. And that was even before catching Hector's brief, targeted scowl, after which, she concluded immediately that she had to be more careful.

Then, with introductions (and pleasantries, more or less) completed, the trio continued onward together, moving up the mostly overgrown path and deeper into the forest.

8

Chapter Eight

He was younger suddenly, revisiting a past argument he'd had with his daughter, who was back in her late teenage years again. Even now, after so many years, the nightmarelike memory seemed as painful and potent as the real experience had been. And perhaps it was even more so than whatever vile poison had felled him.

He retained the strangest sort of awareness in this dream state the poison had plunged him into, but the blend of dreams and reality left Gerrard confused about which of the two he was really trapped in at that moment.

He reflected that this was one of the only arguments he could remember having with his daughter. He had been a fairly passive parent, and his daughter, Shannon, hadn't been particularly badly behaved or troubled in her young life. Gerrard also valued control of himself and his emotions, so he didn't believe in getting angry really—at least, not unless it was intentional. In this memory, though, this anger had not been intentional; it had been the culmination of many things building up that had finally driven him beyond the limits of his usual impeccable level of self-control.

He had been tired and frustrated from some number of difficult months. His health had been faltering, and he had on this particular day lost his job. Nerve pains weighed on his mind even as they did on his physical body. These shooting, intermittent pains were the result of years of hard labor that had worn on his body. His lungs were damaged from too much dust from the mines, and he was often stricken with terrible bouts of coughing and wheezing.

In a sense, it had been a great thing for him that his employment had ended. It would, as time ultimately showed, lengthen his expected remaining lifespan, and he would ultimately go on to find better employment that wasn't so physically demanding.

Still, the job loss had put him in a precarious position and served to help push his mind to the brink of its resilience that day. He had been exhausting himself, putting incredible effort into the work he was doing leading up to his termination. He had been let go on grounds of not following an obscure safety protocol—or so the official paperwork stated. This happened to him, even though far more profound safety measures were almost openly neglected on a daily basis—at least if you were holding to a strict interpretation of what the rules and guidelines for their industry were.

Regardless, that craziness had still been far from what was needed to have pushed him to the point that Gerrard had been on that day. In this scene he lived through again now, he felt the pangs of responsibility and failure weighing on him. And those pins and needles in his shoulder and his legs. Furthermore, he hadn't eaten a proper meal for days. And then his daughter—whom he cared for more than anyone in the world, and who was so painfully oblivious to all of these things—was angrily accusing him of not caring about her.

He had not expressed support for her decision to throw her life away—not that he had put it in so concise and inflammatory a manner when he was speaking with her about it. He'd had some reservations about some of the life decisions she had been making. Still, the angry exchange hadn't been a long one.

Too many distractions vying for our time, dividing our attention, Gerrard thought as he considered the memory. That was one reality of the world that had only grown worse with the passage of all the years he had lived through.

He remembered thinking some good had probably come of the conversation, that there was a point or two he made that he could be reasonably confident had sunk in with her. Still, she had gone on to run off with that young man, despite her father's protests.

Fortunately, she had come back home not long after. Apparently, the young man hadn't thought through some critical elements of the plan he had pitched to her, despite his older and presumably wiser age.

Gerrard remembered she had called him and her mother to come get her, after she had lost her credentials, her train boarding pass, and her coin card. Coin cards were an alternative monetary means that allowed someone to expend units for goods and services, rather than the copper, silver, and gold coins more common throughout much of Makeva.

At least she hadn't left again after that. A few years later, though, Gerrard remembered, their family had reached a point where their situation was no longer financially sustainable. Something had to change. It was also that failing financial situation that led to the deterioration of his relationship with Shannon's mother.

He ended up taking extra work, taking jobs out on fishing vessels, sometimes on months-long trips, which was where he also ended up meeting his longtime friend, Cid. The funds had somewhat stabilized the situation they were in, and Gerrard stuck by his family to see Shannon through to adulthood.

After that, it hadn't made much sense for him to stay around, and he departed from their farm. He had taken up sword fighting again, something he had largely forsaken in years prior, as changing financial needs had demanded more time spent working and less time spent playing. Oh, how he marveled at how readily so much of it came back to him, though, when he had the time to practice it again and think back through those old memories. It hadn't paid so well at first, but he didn't need to make the same kind of coin as he had when he had a family depending on him—and in not so long a time, it came to pay far better than anything else he could have done.

He hadn't been back to their farm for many years, but understood his daughter was still likely there with her mother, helping to keep the place running. He wondered about the kind of person she had gone on to be through adulthood. He thought of the things he had tried to convey to her, and the advice he had given, and wondered now how much of it persisted through the years.

He thought of another exchange he'd had with her, and something he had said.

"In life you'll find," he recalled telling her those many years ago, *"that maybe everything can be reinterpreted, reconfigured in your mind to produce an entirely different conclusion. Apply a different viewpoint, a different angle, or put the details in a different level of context, and you can extract a rather contrary meaning."* He recognized now that he was saying this to a probably-too-young-to-understand version of his daughter.

He went on in his memory.

"Imagine, for example, that you are in your class at the academy. You are reading a book at your desk, surrounded by other students at their desks, all before the teacher, who is at her desk. You read this book, turning page by page through it as you do so. You start from the front, moving through it as you read toward the end of the book," he began to explain. He paused and asked whether she understood, and Shannon readily nodded.

"Now," he continued, "the teacher at her desk tells you to put your book down and to come to the front of the room. Then you, acting as the obedient student that you are..." Gerrard paused again and smiled at his daughter. "... stand up from your desk and proceed by walking forward *to the front of the classroom. You walk forward to get to the front—that's common logic, yes?" he said, then paused to see her nod in agreement before proceeding again.*

"Yes, only, we've just established that sometimes you go backward—as in, to the end of the book—to actually go forward," he said as he smiled again at the pondering child. "If you started flipping to the front of that book, you'd be going backward. And so, to go to the front is not always to go forward," he explained.

Shannon's face gradually seemed to go from a countenance of confusion to one of understanding.

Then Gerrard took a step back, figuratively speaking, and tried to paint the bigger picture of his point.

"You'll find in life, Shannon, that you can argue this way or that way on anything. It is all just a matter of the spin you want to put on it, whatever the perspective is you want to apply to it. Play around with the interpretation of phrases and ideas, look at them through the lenses that are the experience of another. Focus on or emphasize particular details, or do not, and you can shift the perceptions of others and yourself." He paused to reflect on his own words.

He looked off into the distance. The sun was nearly down, and darkness was overtaking the final fading light of the day that had passed. He considered the great openness and peacefulness of that place, their potato farm, for just a few fleeting moments before he picked up his explanation again.

"You are, in a very real sense, in control of the world you live in. Think about how one day, the world is a beautiful place, and how pleased you are with it. But then sometimes, perhaps the very next day, something awful happens that you didn't want, at school or something—nothing even in the larger world—and then suddenly, the world is a terrible place, and you feel thoroughly displeased with it. You're focusing on different aspects of the world to draw different conclusions about it. The world is essentially the very same place it was that preceding day, and yet it seems so different to you, even separated by just that single day. And this cycle will repeat, this shifting will persist through your life," he informed her.

Gerrard could see that his daughter was probably reaching her mental limit on how much her mind was going to absorb from him that day, but he continued on a little longer anyway. Perhaps some would still get through, he thought, or maybe he just wanted to do it for his own benefit, to work through his own thoughts—to see how well he could articulate what seemed so simple in his mind, but somehow became complex in the process of putting into words.

"My dear daughter," he continued, "it seems to me that it is often not the reality of what a situation actually is that's important, but rather the perception of what that situation is ... and perhaps how many people have a similar perception," he said.

His explanation turned toward a warning then. "Be wary of those who will abuse this truth, who will weaponize vast amounts of information and pound it into the minds of the common people, by means of whatever mediums dominate communication in the present day. They will create the perception they desire to, irrespective of whatever the reality is, for their own self-serving and often destructive pursuits. And they will destroy themselves as fully, if not more so, than they destroy others—though they may never come to see themselves for the victims they truly are. Generations of people can be ... manipulated by such means, by the weaponization of information dominance, as the minds of the masses can repeatedly be exposed to the views of a select few with too much power for their own good. People so subjected will all inevitably become, to a greater extent, whatever those select few have designed—as we all become products of our environment, products of what we are consuming," he said, finishing his warning.

Shannon finally spoke up, her young mind grasping at least that her father was concerned, and that he was trying to warn her of something she needed to watch out for. "What can be done about this, Father?"

"Defend, arm ... guard yourself," Gerrard responded sternly. "Immerse yourself in truths as absolute and powerful as you can find. Let them be your foundation, and ground yourself well in that foundation," he continued, as he thought of how the words reminded him of his own father and the way he had lived his life.

"Hold fast to that all-important foundation. Choose well what you use to build it, and with great care," he advised. "You will be tempted to compromise those core beliefs countless times. Challenge them, yes, make them stronger, let them be tested, but take great care and time with changing them. You will be tempted to go beyond what you know in your heart to be right, and if you let yourself be so moved, half the battle is already lost for you," he said, then again considered the darkness settling over the farm. They needed to be heading inside shortly.

Still, he heard himself resuming again, in what perhaps he might have thought was some fateful moment at the time.

"Stay true to what you believe and have always believed. Hold your ground. The first step you take off that solid foundation—that step will take you a farther distance from your salvation than the thousand that will almost inevitably follow. Seek to educate others, to work with them and understand them, as well as to learn more about yourself. But do not compromise yourself, Shannon," he finished.

Then the two of them headed back inside their large farmhouse, darkness now fully enveloping their farm.

Other moments from across the years flashed through Gerrard's mind, but eventually, his mind settled on one memory in particular—another of him and his daughter, Shannon. The penultimate memory that occurred to him then was of when she had been following some trend or another that had been bothering him, something others her age were all caught up in. It was some movement they were all falling in line with, something he took to be wrong and dangerous.

"Don't let them put you in some neat little box like that, Shannon," he scolded. "Don't aspire to have these silly labels put on you," he continued. "Don't ... seek to be summed up by a generalization or stereotype—these things that poison the public discourse and harm our society. They serve primarily to just make us more tribal and distracted and to make society more divided. Be ... capable of fitting in, but make the deliberate decision not to," he finished.

He recalled, in considering this memory now, the many times he had advised her to be skeptical about things, to not just accept things as some indisputable truth.

"Let us say," he told her on one such occasion, "that I aspire to create a peaceful world—devoid of worries and conflict..." He paused to verbally reflect on the imagined world. "What a kind of life, huh? No conflict... Ever read a good story that didn't have a good conflict?"

Then he looked down and shook his head at the absurdity of it, and let the question hang for a few more moments.

Then he continued through the lesson he was attempting to teach. "Let's say you don't take this as being a very realistic goal, that you don't believe in the achievability of this 'world peace.' Now, in my mind, I am basically just trying to convey that I don't want people mercilessly slain by tyrants and evil people. And let's say that I'm not delving much further into that concept—that I'm mostly just trying to say essentially that much to you. But let us say that you take my viewpoint further, looking into the realities that would need to be forged to make such a thing real—the costs, the consequences, the possible avenues we'd have to follow, and all manner of things that could go wrong along the way—and you immediately feel compelled to argue with the man who is suggesting such horrible things be done in Gracyr.

"You perhaps might think I mean to take away the right of goodly folk to defend

themselves. Though I may just be dreaming superficial dreams and not thinking about the means and consequences, I may well still bring us to the point of an argument in sharing what is truly just a kindhearted and well-intentioned—though perhaps short-sighted and ill-advised—idea. We, in this scenario, have a different understanding of what is being talked about—which is going to lead to assumptions and unnecessary conflict if we do not also mutually harbor the understanding that greater depth and analysis, and maybe clearer definitions, are needed to further explore the views of the other. We may, in all likelihood in this scenario, be led to disagree with each other—when in time, we could find that we actually agree," he finished in the memory.

A final memory surged through his mind then. He was writing a message in a greeting card to her—perhaps it had been a birthday card.

You can do it, Shannon. Carve your dreams into that cold, unyielding rock we call reality. Forge them with the fires blazing in your heart, and will them into existence with the power of your mind—and with your belief and faith that it can be done.

He had drafted a longer letter, but in going to transpose it to the actual card, he had decided that just that shorter section was better as its own message.

But he saw then in his memory the rest of that letter.

I suspect I will fall short in my life of accomplishing what this world desperately needs someone to do. And I know the trials of your generation will be the worse for it. You are going to need to be better than I ever could have been, if you are even going to have a chance in the world of tomorrow. But I promise you, if ever I have promised you anything, that you, so much your father's daughter, but more—the daughter of two incredible parents—have every ounce of that profound potential in you.

The poison was doing its cruel work, encroaching on the borders of that letter's image in his mind. It slowly swallowed it up and plunged Gerrard into a deepening blackness, one he fully expected to be what finally overcame him. And he felt he was correct then in the prediction he'd made in the unused letter. His life was about to end, and he was going to fall desperately short of accomplishing all the work he still had ahead of him.

9

Chapter Nine

The unlikely trio continued their trek up toward the waterfall site. Along the way, the woods seemed typical to them, unremarkable. The trail they traveled along continued to be mostly overgrown, but there was still a vague path there they could follow. They were cautious—about their surroundings, but also about each other, and they kept a fair distance from one another.

Hector was particularly careful and guarded toward his new allies. He didn't have much evidence from them—not directly—to really doubt their sincerity or think they meant to harm him; he knew it just had more to do with the way his life had been for so long before then.

He also knew his lack of trust for others was amplified by the mental intrusions of the sentient weapon, Kazahvir, which poured feelings of skepticism into his mind incessantly. Regardless, Hector wasn't an overly trusting person anyway—not toward others, or toward Kazahvir, either, for that matter.

Perhaps, though, that was part of why he felt such a bond with the sword. They had a mutual distrust for the world they existed in. He wondered, not for the first time, how long Kazahvir had been in existence. His mind was wandering a bit, as the group's surroundings continued to seem unthreatening and mundane. Who had forged and enchanted the thing?

Who had the previous owners been? Had they lived through to old age?

The answer to that last question, Hector had to figure, was *probably not.* He doubted the sword's patience would last with anyone not constantly seeking some exciting, world-changing idea. He also knew from his time with the sword that someone very much older than Hector would probably not last long, either. And he sincerely questioned how long he could even keep pace with the expectations of the thing.

He also reconsidered then his use of the word *owners.* He actually had some doubt that anyone could rightly be called an owner of Kazahvir.

He knew himself to be of formidable mental will and physical strength, and of course, he had the natural energy and hunger of youth on his side, too—yet often, even he could barely contain the power that spilled forth from the sword. A less strong-willed, more clouded or divided mind would have no hope of restraining the might of the weapon. Such a person would be consumed and dominated, thoroughly and easily, by Kazahvir.

Why doesn't it just seek a wielder more like that—weaker-willed and more easily dominated? he pondered. It was a question he had returned to many times already, though. Perhaps such a person would seem to Kazahvir to be likely to be less effective at achieving its greater ambitions, though surely it could employ such a tactic if it simply wanted to transport itself across Gracyr.

Regina drew him from his contemplations then with her question to Andromeda, which also broke the trio's longstanding silence.

"You were in the tournament, weren't ya? I recognize ya now!" she said enthusiastically, letting up on her quiet streak a bit, but still taking care to keep her noise level minimized, despite her mounting excitement.

"Yes," Andromeda replied more reservedly, but with a smile. "Were you watching me compete?" she asked in a tone that almost struck Hector as teasing.

"I think everyone in Nethereel was watching ya in the last round!" she excitedly exclaimed. Then she slapped a hand over her mouth in an exaggerated motion, to signify to her companions that she realized she was getting a little loud.

Andromeda's eyes darted around the area, but still, nothing seemed ominous or unusual.

"It's okay; we don't seem to have company," Andromeda reassured Regina. "Even if we did encounter them, we could probably get away by saying we're just visiting some old stomping grounds or something. I'm sure other travelers happen by this place from time to time. They can't possibly make every person stumbling by vanish without a trace—not without drawing the scrutiny of greater powers of law enforcement. Surely, they don't want those eyes on whatever it is they're up to around here."

Hector spoke up to challenge that sentiment, though. "We would do well not to underestimate what they are capable of," he warned.

Andromeda nodded. She lowered her voice and more quietly continued the previous conversation Regina had struck up with her. "I'm glad you enjoyed the show," she said, rightly judging that she had, just from Regina's excited tone.

"I thought ya were going to bring down Gerrard this year for sure," Regina said, with the slightest tinge of jealousy creeping into her voice.

The perceptive Andromeda still recognized it, though. Hector may have, too, had he not been distracted by the revelation that Andromeda was of such formidable skill that she had nearly defeated the legendary Gerrard in Nethereel's tournament.

"In *what* round did you face him?" Hector looked over and asked, questioning what he thought he'd heard from Regina.

"Ya must not've been watching the end of the tournament," Regina cut in.

Hector was not one to outwardly express much emotion, but his eyes did widen at what he took as Regina's confirmation of what he thought he had heard.

Such strange and interesting times I'm living in, Hector thought as he regarded his situation anew. *To have stumbled upon so skilled a fighter, who was nearly the champion of Nethereel's sword fighting tournament this year, and in such unusual circumstances. I would do well,* he reflected, *to keep my guard up around her.*

Of course, that was something the ever-at-the-ready fighter he was generally did around everyone, anyway.

"Do you come to the tournament every year?" Andromeda inquired of her fast-forming friend.

"This was the third time for me," Regina answered "I've been in it each year. This was finally going to be *my year*, too," she lamented, thinking about those broken dreams. "It would have been fantastic to have been the champ, but I haven't even managed to get a shot at Gerrard yet," she said, sighing. "My grandfather knew Gerrard's father, forged weapons for 'im—or, at least, that's what he always claimed in his wild stories," she added, and a little nostalgically, Andromeda noticed.

"It's okay," Regina concluded. "I'll set myself to working on other dreams. This tournament's a dead end for me, I think. There must be something more fruitful I can put my mind to."

Andromeda, almost involuntarily, felt herself slip into analyzing the younger female. Regina usually spoke fast, at least when she seemed comfortable with the situation. She was a little loud and had a high-pitched voice, but not an unpleasant one. She was friendly and optimistic sounding, and she seemed to be a suitable friend to keep around.

Andromeda couldn't be sure, but Regina seemed to hail from a background of some wealth or other significant means. Not the type to have spent many nights starving for something to eat. The woman was impulsive, but she seemed too thoughtful to be uneducated. And she didn't appear to have the mind of someone who had been plagued by constant hardship, like perhaps her other travel companion did—just judging from his untrusting disposition.

"I certainly appreciate that enduring optimism you possess," Andromeda said, smiling warmly at Regina, and just picking one of many compliments she could have given her. "But do you have the focus to settle on one such goal in particular, do you think?" Andromeda playfully jabbed.

Regina figured the older female was just being jokingly critical of Regina's younger age, and the limited attention span her generation was known for. But she wasn't doing it in a mean way. And anyway, perhaps she had already exhibited some behavior or another that lent a degree of credibility to the lighthearted accusation. Regina resolved to take it as Andromeda just being friendly.

So, she just embraced it and laughed a little, in such a way as to suggest it was preposterous that she didn't have the needed focus. In actuality, though, she wasn't entirely confident she did. She knew her dreamy pursuits of ever-changing priorities could be a little chaotic, and a little unfocused, at least from time to time.

Andromeda seemed to harbor some skepticism about that confidence Regina was attempting to portray, though. The older woman looked upon her doubtfully.

"Well, suppose I don't always," Regina conceded. "But even if my focus is shaken after this recent venture, I don't doubt at all that I can get myself back together more focused than before," she declared more confidently.

She pulled away from her thoughts about herself, and she managed some questions in return for the inquisitive Andromeda. Regina was curious; she wanted to dig in a little deeper and understand her better. "Haven't seen ya before at the tournament or otherwise. You new this year? Where ya from?" Regina asked.

"I was new this year," Andromeda answered.

"Pretty admirable performance for a first-timer, wouldn't ya say, Hector?" Regina said, taking a shot at bringing Hector into the conversation.

Hector barely acknowledged the question, mostly just grunted and maintained his vigilance of the surrounding area and his focus on moving forward.

"I'm from a small town well north of here," Andromeda added. "I've never actually been so far from there before, so a lot of all this—being around so many people and all—is rather new to me."

Regina considered how interesting it was to have encountered Andromeda—this person who was new to the scene, who possessed the skill to measure up to the talents of those who had grown up with the Nethereel sword fighting tournament.

But that train of thought halted as she haphazardly stumbled into Hector, who had stopped suddenly.

"Ahh!" Regina said, steadying herself quickly after nearly falling over.

Hector seemed momentarily annoyed, but he didn't dwell on it. "Okay, you were getting me back for before when I ran into you in Nethereel. That's fine," he said, seeming to justify it more for his own mental sake than for hers.

"Y-yeah! That's right. I owed ya that!" she said, suddenly feeling justified. "Actually, I didn't knock *you* over. I'm not sure we can say we're even," she quipped, pretending to hold a grudge about something she truthfully wasn't worried about.

Hector might have smiled slightly; it was hard to tell with him. But he did at least remark, "Anyway ... we're finally here."

The waterfall they approached was breathtaking. The crystal-clear water tumbled from well above the trio's heads down onto rocks a great distance beneath their feet. They stood in awe for a few moments before Regina broke the group's silence.

"It's a wonder they haven't harnessed the waterfall here for power for the city yet... A bit unusual, I'd say," said Regina, drawing from her university studies on energy solutions.

Then, Hector wordlessly unstrapped the shield that was not a shield from his back and moved to press it against the stone wall at the side of the waterfall. When nothing happened, he stepped slightly to the side and tried again in a new spot. He pressed it repeatedly to overlapping spots on the stone.

"It's around here somewhere," he remarked to his curious companions, feeling the females' eyes on him.

Then, suddenly, the emblem and wall flashed orange, and the stone wall collapsed inward, revealing a doorway. The trio saw a large chamber and tunnels beyond as it seemed to magically come alight inside. They stepped in, pausing just inside the large chamber, and looked around for a few moments. Suddenly, the stone wall behind them restored itself, sealing them inside.

"We're ... trapped in here?" Regina asked, a touch of unease creeping into her voice. "And I guess it's a key you've been carrying all this time, huh?"

"Doesn't much matter," Hector said as he shrugged. "The only way out for us is onward. And yes … a key," he confirmed.

To more than you know, he thought excitedly, as he led the way deeper into the chamber.

10

Chapter Ten

The black-cloaked woman drummed her fingers anxiously on her oaken desk. She had been tasked with taking charge of the operation here at Waterfall Ridge, the name her criminal band commonly used to refer to the place. She was in charge since, apparently, her predecessor had overstepped, or perhaps he had fallen short of expectations; precise details of his departure hadn't been made abundantly clear.

In any case, this new assignment was a promotion. And she was quite thrilled with the opportunity, despite how she could easily construe the reassignment as a considerable risk, particularly given the suddenness and mysteriousness surrounding the open position.

The cloaked woman's name was Ursula. She sometimes came across—to those in their organization who didn't know her—as rather unthreatening in appearance. That mostly had to do with her diminutive size, at least as compared to many of the hulking members of the Order's ranks. But anyone who really knew Ursula saw beyond any seeming weakness in her physical form.

She had come to be one of the most adept among the Order of Oranlak with their signature abilities, those that they were known and feared for: their shadow abilities. She could walk between shadows, weave through them, even spend time in that other place, the shadow realm. She knew of the denizens that lurked in that otherworldly place and had spent significant time in their presence, watching and learning, before summoning some of the mightiest into the human world.

She had shown great skill even from a young age, when she first became involved with Oranlak. And that skill had only amplified through the decades. At this point in her middle-aged life, she had spent more time in the shadow realm than most others of their Order. It had won her countless fights and valuable respect. As a consequence, though, she had taken on some characteristics of that other realm, where it was said humans were not even meant to go.

She did not appear entirely human to anyone who spent just a little time considering her. The color of her eyes had changed from green to almost black, and her hair had taken on a silver tone. It was not the gray color of aging—it retained a pleasant sort of richness, and in fact, she appeared far younger than her actual age. Her skin color had changed, too, gradually taking on an unusual grayness.

The changes were not all physical, a fact particularly obvious to anyone who had known Ursula well in her younger years. She had become far less considerate of the lives of others, and her lust for power had escalated tremendously. Such qualities were typical among members of Oranlak, and even among some notable individuals presently in partnership with their criminal organization, in other sorts of powerful positions.

In any case, despite her intensifying lack of humanity, she was still at least partly human, and those frustrating human feelings of anxiety still affected her at times, as they did in this moment.

She now had the problem—which really had nothing to do with her own actions—of this outsider who had stumbled into Oranlak's operation at Waterfall Ridge. She'd had the impulse to kill him outright for being foolish enough to be here, and for possessing the forbidden knowledge that was the location of Oranlak's base.

She'd had reservations about the setup of their base here ever since she'd been briefed on the place. It had, many years in the past, been a natural setting popular with tourists visiting the area. It had mostly been abandoned and forgotten over the years, but their gang knew there were those who still remembered the place and might visit it. They had known from the start that they would have to take measures to stay hidden, and that the occasional disappearance of someone who happened to see something they shouldn't have might become necessary.

Still, the appeal of the place, which was theorized to contain rich veins of crimson fluorite, was too great to dismiss, even with notable risks involved.

Anyway, now it had happened: someone had actually discovered the entrance to their waterfall base, and he had seen the mine they were developing and actively working in.

She could not bring herself to immediately kill this one, as one of her "helpful" informants had let her know that this particular transgressor was popular and well known locally. He was, so she'd been told, a champion of the tournament in nearby Nethereel, whose disappearance would undoubtedly trigger a highly unwelcome degree of scrutiny of the area and her gang's operation at Waterfall Ridge.

So, now she puzzled over her dilemma. She considered first, of course, just proceeding to kill him anyway. But she also considered that the operation they had going here really wasn't going so smoothly or optimally. The yield of lutetium they were extracting from the crimson fluorite was relatively low and of frustratingly poor quality. There was also less of the crimson fluorite than had even been proposed in the projections. And those proposals had been leaned on heavily by the staunch advocates of the mine, who had convinced leadership to pursue the controversial project in the first place.

Someone is probably going to be executed over that blunder, she thought.

Her mind then wandered to other paths to power she found more promising, which she rather wished she was a part of. There were recent findings that not far from their current location at Waterfall Ridge, farther eastward and on the coast, there was vastly more potential. The location was near to Akastair, a great and well-known city in the country they were now in, Makeva.

The Order of Oranlak had exhumed fragments of an apparent spacecraft outside Akastair. They had been tracing its theoretical trajectory into the ocean, and they were actively researching and learning more about the ship every day. It was presumably proof of aliens' existence, something that had never been proven in the known history of Gracyr.

There was also a substance Oranlak had found, something they had dubbed "promethium." It was a substance previously unknown to humanity, so far as they could determine, and it seemed to possess some promising characteristics—of particular note, its capacity to produce electricity. In the opinion of the most highly positioned members of the Order, it held great promise for taking their gang to new heights of wealth and power.

She had been dreaming of being involved with those not-so-far-away efforts, but she had mostly put them to bed when she took her assignment at Waterfall Ridge. That was, at least, until the new team she was supervising uncovered a possible connection between the two projects.

The network of mines they were developing at the waterfall was actually a further development and expansion of an old, abandoned mine. They had little information on the old mine, and it was mostly collapsed and forgotten. Even the considerable reach of Oranlak could locate little surviving literature on the place at all. But in some deep chambers of the ancient mine, which they had partially broken through to with explosives, the group now under her command had found some old journals and maps. One of the maps her underlings had brought her seemed to show rich deposits of crimson fluorite near Akastair, near where Oranlak was already present and investigating some of the old wreckage from that alien ship. Interestingly, the alien ship and the mineral deposits were described throughout a number of the journals. Such deposits would likely contain more potent lutetium than what they were getting from the crimson fluorite they were mining at Waterfall Ridge—if the maps and associated writings were accurate. At the time, her mind had immediately gone to ideas of how she could best benefit from this potentially advantageous set of circumstances.

And now this situation with this trespasser was rekindling those previous dreams of hers about that other project. She again found herself thinking about how she could get out of the increasingly problematic and less fruitful circumstances at Waterfall Ridge. Could she get herself into Oranlak's more promising designs near Akastair?

She had a thought, and with great expediency, she developed it into a plan. Ursula began to contact her superior. She activated the screen on her clonra device, an electronic communicator she wore on her wrist and forearm. A hologram image of her supervisor materialized a short distance in front of her in the room, generated by the wearable device, in what was, for Ursula, just a few excited heartbeats.

Mercedes's voice emanated from the clonra device as the hologram turned, as if regarding her.

"This better be good, or you're going to be doing a lot of unpleasant tasks for the next week, Ursula," Mercedes threatened. "With all that apparent excess time you have over there," she continued, narrowing her eyes. It was her typical extremely-bossy-to-her-inferiors tone, Ursula observed. And of course, the group that composed her *inferiors* was pretty much everyone these days.

Ursula restrained herself. Mercedes had somehow managed to surpass her in station and in power, which was a frustrating reality. Mercedes wasn't even of the Oranlak, but she *was* practically in charge of the empire of Ezmondia. And as the elite upper circles of the empire were in extensive dealings with Ursula's gang of late, it had become Ursula's charge, by the supreme leadership of the Order of Oranlak, to answer to this woman.

Hence it was that Ursula had to demonstrate a measure of tact and respect—an increasingly unusual situation for the powerful shadow-walker, who had climbed most of the ranks through the Order of Oranlak.

"We have a situation over here—" Ursula began.

Mercedes cut her off. "Managed to break things over there already, huh?"

Before Ursula answered, she first paused to consider how satisfying it would be to slay her supposed *superior*, in what would probably just take a few seconds of close combat.

"There was a chain of events already unfolding, regardless of what actions I took in the brief time since I've arrived here," Ursula calmly and formally replied.

It wasn't so apparent a thing to Ursula, but her voice transmitted to Mercedes's ears with what almost seemed like an echo. Perhaps it had just been a slight glitch in the tech, Mercedes reasoned. Even so, she couldn't deny the effective way it compounded with that eerie tonelessness of Ursula's voice. The not-entirely-human creature sounded almost ghoulish or phantomlike.

Mercedes wasn't one to be intimidated easily, but she did listen attentively, her hologram image staring back silently at Ursula.

Ursula knew an image of herself was also being generated for Mercedes through her own clonra device. She couldn't let her face, posture, or tone show weakness or a lack of confidence; it would be too provocative and tempting a thing for Mercedes to pounce upon, and such things could easily be betrayed by the detail of the hologram image that the technology generated.

"A man of some renown locally, for his performance in the Nethereelan fighting tournament, has found and entered our base of operations here. He is in irons now, locked up in another chamber. He was apparently sightseeing at the waterfall, then saw and followed some of our Order inside. I'm told by my informants that the waterfall was known to him in his younger years, and that he was visiting the place because it holds sentimental value to him. A not insignificant number of people in Makeva, and particularly Nethereel, knew this Gerrard enjoys this place and would have come here after the tournament concluded," Ursula said, then paused briefly, having, she believed, provided succinct but sufficient context for the current predicament.

"His death is essentially now necessary, but it will rouse significant suspicion and trouble for our operations here for the foreseeable future. He will be consequentially sought, and his disappearance is likely to be investigated thoroughly," she went on.

She did not stop speaking for long. Ursula did not want Mercedes to come to harbor the impression she was waiting for her superior to figure out how to solve her problem. She knew Mercedes would expect her to deal with it effectively herself.

"I propose we kill this man, regardless. Our operation here has not been proceeding as hoped. We should abandon our efforts, which have yielded only a limited amount of the lutetium we came for, in favor of more lucrative exploits we have learned of from the journals, logbooks, and maps we have uncovered here. There is a far more promising mine that can be developed nearer to the city of Akastair, not far from our current project already underway in that vicinity, regarding the alien vessel," Ursula said.

She went on after a moment's pause. "The findings are being further reviewed, but my team assures me they are quite promising and highly likely to be accurate," she finished. Then she carefully watched for Mercedes's response.

Mercedes appeared to consider the proposal. "Send me what information you have to substantiate this confidence of yours. I do hope, for your sake, that I find it as compelling as you do. Also, do send along the outstanding report for this past week's progress. I will prioritize looking this information over and respond soon," she said, narrowing her eyes dangerously as she looked for Ursula's response.

Mercedes didn't like being troubled with more headaches from Waterfall Ridge, like Ursula's predecessor had unendingly bothered her with, but she couldn't immediately dismiss the promise of what Ursula described. The empire had been aware of the potential for veins of crimson fluorite to exist in that area for some time, and they were interested in finally making some progress on that front. She was right that Waterfall Ridge had been less than hoped for; it had actually been a colossal waste of funds and time, and Mercedes could entertain the notion it was time to cut their losses with the place.

The shadow-walker nodded in acceptance of the command and in agreement with the course of action. Then Mercedes terminated the communication.

Ursula immediately set to work compiling the information requested, to transmit it to Mercedes back at the Castle. Hopefully, this would lead to bigger and better things for both her and the rest of the Order of Oranlak.

As she moved to do this, her thoughts of the potential of this opportunity distracted her significantly.

There were vidscreens on the walls of her large office space. They showed video footage from myriad cameras mounted throughout the base's upper level and its entry chamber. So, it was fortunate for the three trespassers, who appeared on a few of those vidscreens, that Ursula had been so distracted in those critical moments.

Those three would have been hard-pressed to defeat the powerful shadow creature Ursula had become.

11

Chapter Eleven

The entry chamber, and the shallower tunnels branching off from it, did not contain any miners or members of the Order. They had already moved on into deeper tunnels. They only now moved through this upper area to enter the base and proceed deeper into the tunnels where the crimson fluorite was actively being mined.

Most of the humans at the base were indeed at too great a distance from Hector for him to detect them through his enchanted sword. He could feel one weak, static life force in one chamber down below them. The person perhaps was asleep, but was also likely injured, possibly even close to death. There was one other presence also, he noted after a few additional moments. It was farther from them, significantly deeper down. Hector was surprised he even sensed it. The distance seemed too great, judging by what he was usually capable of sensing.

As he considered that, he began to find it mildly alarming. The obvious conclusion was that this other entity, whether it was human or otherwise, was particularly powerful.

He did not let realizations about the nature of that other life force spill onto his emotionless face, though. He just looked to the pair he traveled with and signaled for them to follow as he started off down one of the tunnels leading out of that main chamber. But he did so with what struck the others as unusual surety. Andromeda, in particular, found herself curious about the seeming confidence he had about that specific tunnel being the right one to take.

"How do you know this is the way we should be going?" she asked quietly.

He turned and regarded her. "Just … a feeling," he answered, less than convincingly.

Andromeda opted not to pry, though she sensed there was more than Hector was unveiling. She looked over at Regina, who didn't seem like she was planning to question or challenge the situation. So, they started off and carried on. Andromeda took care to glance behind them periodically as they moved through the tunnel, trying to watch their backs.

It was unsettling how easily they seemed to be making their way through this apparent stronghold of the Oranlak. Still, they proceeded carefully, silently, through the remainder of that shallow tunnel. Hector was quiet, too, but he seemed shockingly sure that there wasn't anyone around any given bend or turn in the tunnel.

The trio came upon a chamber at the end of that tunnel—one far smaller than the one they had entered when they stepped into the base. They also saw that the current purpose of this one was to serve as a dungeon, as on the far wall was chained a familiar man, bloodied and battered.

* * *

Mercedes stood up from the desk in her office, which was in the grand capitol building known as the Castle. She reflected briefly on Ursula's words about this promising lead of hers. Then she shrugged, mostly undecided on the matter. She resolved to see what Ursula came up with and to give it her objective consideration. She suspected Ursula had personal interests that were mostly driving this proposal of hers, but she recognized, too, the potential for mutual benefit, and for a greater benefit to the interests of Ezmondia.

Maybe Ursula was just consumed by her need to take another human life; perhaps it had been too long since she'd had an opportunity. Maybe she treasured the thought of bringing down someone so skilled in the arena as this prisoner of hers apparently was.

If he's really such a talent, Armando would perhaps like a go at him, too, she thought. But she dismissed the idea. She had enough on her mind without trying to cater to the man's obsession with finding his next kill, which always needed to be someone stronger and worthier than whatever poor soul he'd last slain. That whole obsession, to Mercedes, was an unwelcome distraction from more important work, and one that didn't do much for her personal wishes for self-preservation to be prioritized over the next big thrill.

Even if Ursula's suggested course was largely wrought from self-interest, and even if it hadn't been clearly holding potential for their greater designs, Ursula was still too useful to punish too harshly, despite Mercedes's own tough stance toward the woman. She wouldn't have her executed like she'd had her predecessor executed, she decided, even if these alleged leads did end up being an utter waste of time. She also wasn't sure if perhaps the leaders of Oranlak might protest in her case, as Ursula did seem more powerful and might be more valuable to them.

She thought then, though, of how Ursula seemed as power-obsessed as Armando. *Dangerous to deal with, but also perhaps more useful because she is that way,* she thought.

She also couldn't help but contrast the shadow-walking monster with herself, if only to put her mind at ease with how different they were. She had been dealing with Ursula more often than her counterparts lately and had rarely spoken with anyone higher up their chain of command. Ursula must have been one of the more ambitious of those few of the Oranlak at her high level in their hierarchy, she thought.

Mercedes didn't mind ambition or those holding positions of power; she could surely relate. Yet the idea of this person—if indeed that was what she could still rightly even be called—disgusted her. Ursula seemed to have such an incredible disregard for the past, tradition, and custom. She certainly didn't care to be restricted by the laws of the world they lived in—not given her embrace of the shadow realm and those otherworldly powers.

Mercedes shuddered a bit at the thought. It was unnatural, inappropriate to combine oneself as a human with other beings and worlds so controversial. Ursula didn't care about preservation of the past, about not violating things that should be inviolable, about stability and their homeland of Ezmondia. In that way, she was far worse than Armando. Ursula was even more obsessed with raw power, and she didn't harbor other, more human weaknesses or desires, like Armando did. And Armando didn't forsake his own human world and betray it for the dark place beyond the void that thankfully separated their worlds.

Still, she lamented, it seemed Armando was not so different that he was beyond working with someone who would do such things as Ursula would, even if he would not personally take the steps she had taken. She admired him at that moment, though she often did, perhaps for the simple fact that he had accomplished so much of what he wanted without compromising so much of his humanity. And others like Ursula—they had given so much more to still not get nearly as far.

Yes, despite Ursula's apparent value to Armando, Mercedes still had no great affection for that creature. Mercedes even had a few grudges beyond the truths she was considering about her in those moments, but she could accept that they were relatively minor offenses. Not that she, as the second-in-command of the empire of Ezmondia, was going to be told about what was or wasn't a *minor* offense.

She continued to fight through her own arguments with herself, to further justify continuing to work with Ursula. Perhaps, she told herself—not for the first time—the power of the Order of Oranlak could bring a greater level of control over the people of their empire for her, Armando, and the Elite Council. With greater control, they could better protect the still-largely-uneducated masses from themselves.

How often, she thought as she looked down and shook her head in disgust, *do people fail to realize what is best for them? We'll remedy that.* Still, she couldn't help but linger on the thought that it was unfortunate they had to resort to dealing with some of the entities they did to save people from themselves.

She resolved to put away further thoughts on this matter for now. She'd surely be revisiting them again at some point. For now, she needed to make some progress on the pressing issue Armando had most recently charged her with.

She returned to her prior contemplations about military strength for the future and the fertility rates dilemma. The interruption from Ursula had, at least in part, been something of a welcome distraction from the mental roadblock she had been suffering from while trying to work through those other issues. Maybe coming back to them now would offer a fresh perspective.

Mercedes knew she had to play the board as it had been left for her to play. The existing infrastructure of society and the current perspectives of the masses needed to be put to use to solve the issue Armando wanted her to solve. They needed more children and a stronger military. It needed to be sufficiently gradual so as to gently guide the masses toward thinking it was their own idea, but the plan needed to be efficient enough to meet Armando's expectations as well. And there perhaps needed to be a rather direct emotional connection with the people to tie in with the results Armando needed of them.

She thought of traditions of the past she remembered—those still alive and well, and those well lost to time. She thought of her life. What had she personally been conditioned to believe that many others also had been? What was important to her generation and those even younger? What had transpired over the course of her lifetime that tied so many of them together?

She thought then of the previous emperor, Armando's predecessor. That man had been ancient when he died, had reigned for countless years over the empire. And he had sought to build up a particular framework in the minds of his people over most of that reign. It had been majorly self-serving, but of course, emperors throughout Ezmondia's history were hardly catalogued for their altruistic pursuits.

It was, generally speaking, the importance of the elders; that was something that had been ingrained in many of the minds of people currently living in the Ezmondian Empire. Countless campaigns by Armando's predecessor had seen to it. It had been built into them to respect and admire and strive to please and care for their elders. The malleable minds of the youth had been shaped since the cradle to hold that perspective. It was even likely a reason the situation with insufficient births had come to be so dire as it now was. Many had prioritized just seeing to and caring for the elders to the exclusion of all else. To have also had children would have gobbled up all the rest of the time the younger adults had. While attending academies of learning across Ezmondia throughout their youth, and into young adulthood, the amount of mandatory time spent as caretakers for elders was considerable. And it hadn't always left the young with much time to enjoy their youth. Mercedes herself could certainly relate.

The consensus among the vast majority of the youth had come to be that their elders had done so much, and deserved to be given much back. And now, she could capitalize on that. She could infuse a sense of urgency into the matter: they didn't have forever, their time was running short, and more people were rapidly growing into old age.

The elders would be so useful for this, she thought excitedly. The Ezmondian elites would just exploit their very existence. And in so doing, they would motivate those who were able to have and raise more offspring. Even if it were deceptive, it would be so much for their own sakes, and thus justified. Yes, they could portray to the public that the elders needed them to step up and do their part, and many would fall in line to do just that. And as long as the connection could be simply and constantly made, with an appropriate measure of subtlety, they could bring about potentially all sorts of new behaviors.

That's the framework already in place that I could repurpose, she thought. Wasn't it needed, after all, that they have more of the young to care for more of the old? After all, surely there was still a degree of self-preservation in them all. They would, in time, be direct beneficiaries of their own efforts, a nice add-in—though of course, that point itself was probably too far removed from most peoples' day-to-day to carry much weight on its own. In any case, that was a tie-in that hadn't been exploited, a connection that hadn't been made sufficiently clear to the public ... yet.

Elaborate media campaigns over vidscreens and radio waves would build in the people's minds the value, the greatness of having children. And it would be embellished, romanticized, and emotionally tied to what people have been conditioned to value all their lives: serving their elders. People doing this would be rewarded, revered, respected, and valued. They would have feelings of success and meaning and fulfillment. *Yes,* she thought, *such a campaign could be profoundly effective.*

Mercedes saw her vidscreen printer activate then; something was coming through. Her thoughts were driven back to the matter with Ursula. She started thinking about that other project going on near Akastair. And she inevitably thought of their empire's energy struggles. The issue, succinctly summarized, was that the climate of Gracyr was becoming far drier. And much of the power across Gracyr was generated by means of hydropower, generally by hydroelectric dams that generated electricity.

Some limited technological advancements had begun to provide alternatives, but they were not seen as comparable to or capable of replacing hydropower, particularly in Ezmondia. That was a problem, since hydropower was a failing system in these times of drying reservoirs and inadequate rainfall. The drier wet seasons, and the dry seasons that were even drier than they had been in the past were weighing more heavily on their society, year after year.

Therein lay the true promise, though, Mercedes believed, of this alien vessel. Aboard that ship—or at least within the fragments of it they'd uncovered on land—they had found the new substance called promethium. Their scientists had found that the stuff could be burned to produce electricity, and they, of course, were in desperate need of such new, alternate power sources.

The Elite Council—and of course she and Armando and the partners they were in league with—would all stand to profit immensely from solving so massive a problem as the energy crisis in Ezmondia. Makeva would be a likely and profitable market, too, though the crisis had not yet grown to the same level there yet.

They lacked the means to create more of the promethium, though, and once burned, the source of energy was expended; more of it would always be needed. They had only recovered a limited amount of the substance. Furthermore, there were some words of caution from the scientists studying it. Apparently, it had some rather toxic effects if not used carefully, and perhaps even if it was. There were also longer-term environmental considerations; apparently, over some great span of time, it might create larger problems for Gracyr.

Mercedes didn't follow the technicalities or particulars closely, but she understood the main points, as well as the stance of those who worked for her. It would solve the problems of today, though they didn't fully understand the process by which it was solving them, but it would possibly create different problems at some distant future time. Of course, the more immediate and enticing conclusion was that they would be buying time and becoming incredibly wealthy and powerful—more so than they already were—in the process of using the stuff.

There was vastly more of the promethium; it was just harder to get to. Their extensive resources, enhanced in partnership with the Order of Oranlak, had enabled them to find the remainder of the alien spaceship, sunken deep beneath the surface in the waters off Akastair.

The submerged vessel was colossal. It had flooded, perhaps eons ago when it crashed. Maybe at the time, none of the area had been underwater—or perhaps the crash ended with most of the ship in the water, then sinking deep. Either way, the current situation was that the ship was in a watery grave at a great depth in the Eastern Sea, and they needed to retrieve its cargo.

They had managed the task of getting down to the sunken ship. The operation to search for and survey the vessel had been expensive and time-consuming. It was also difficult, specialized work that required certain people with particular skills and abilities, of which a very finite supply existed.

But that was all a different matter than the task now at hand. The rapid succession of documents spewing from her vidscreen printer slowed and then ceased, and she could see that it was indeed the response from Ursula. She moved to quickly review and consider them to make a judgment, putting other concerns out of her mind for the time being.

12

Chapter Twelve

Andromeda was first to rush across the room to Gerrard's aid. Regina followed, while Hector hung back, his guard still up, eyes darting around with what might have seemed like slight paranoia to his fellow travelers, had they been paying attention to him at that moment.

Andromeda got to Gerrard's side and urgently but quietly asked him, "Gerrard, are you all right?" She put the palm of her warm hand to his deadly cold cheek.

His dark eyes shot open, and he pulled himself from the grasp of the poison with the help of Andromeda's warm caress. He had tears in his eyes. Unbeknownst to his rescuers, though, they were more the result of the contents of his dreams than the physical pain he was suffering.

His memory of this person touching his face came slowly back to him.

"Andromeda? Where are we? Why're ... you here?" he asked groggily. He attempted to move and found he couldn't. He was chained to the stone wall of the dark chamber they were in. His mind then shoved aside these lesser questions, though, as he asked a sudden and more urgent one. "Can you get me free?"

"Try the keys hanging over there," interjected Hector. "They seem very dated in their tactics," he observed, his voice just loud enough to be heard, his eyes continuing to scan their surroundings.

"Suppose they weren't expecting us. Clearly didn't go to great lengths to secure him if one of those keys actually works," remarked Regina. She ran over to retrieve the keys hanging on a hook lodged into another wall of the chamber. She trotted back and handed them to Andromeda.

Hector continued to ponder the situation as the others worked to free Gerrard. He thought it interesting that the Oranlak hadn't just killed him outright. *Perhaps they recognized him for who he is, and knew it would cause trouble to kill him, and are presently deliberating their next actions*, he considered silently.

Hector felt the hunger of his sword defeating its patience as it tugged on his attention. It didn't care for such trivial considerations; it wanted to move on to the greater prize of the place, something it and its wielder mutually agreed to be information—information that would lead them to a far greater adventure and level of excitement than this place could afford them.

One of the keys worked. With a satisfying *click*, the shackles opened, and Gerrard fell off the wall—and practically into Andromeda's arms. She did blush slightly at the way he fell into her, but it probably wasn't noticeable to Gerrard or her companions—or at least, so she quickly convinced herself.

Hector spoke again, looking on at the spectacle. "If you two are finished, we should be getting on to an efficient investigation of this place, and then hopefully, to a speedy departure." But he said the words with such a lack of emotion that he left Andromeda unsure whether he saw her blush or not.

More important things to worry about, she reminded herself.

Gerrard managed to get to his feet and compose himself. He then tried his strength and moved a few successful steps, and then more confidently closed the rest of the distance to a nearby table that had his confiscated claymore and blaster on it.

"You've such a peculiar way of speaking," Regina criticized Hector, though she maintained a friendly and almost admiring tone.

Hector decided not to bother responding to her comment, and seeing as Gerrard could stand and had Andromeda close by for support if needed, he continued down one of the two tunnels out of that chamber that seemed to lead deeper into the mines. He opted for the one not leading to the unnervingly strong force he felt. He questioned whether the four of them were capable of defeating whatever that was. And strangely, Kazahvir was silent as he passed up that opportunity to engage such an apparently worthy opponent. But he admitted to himself, and so simultaneously to Kazahvir as well, that he was okay with that.

In defiance of the aching pains coursing through his body from the poison, and from being chained to the stone wall, Gerrard started after Hector with the two women.

Andromeda continued alongside the battered man as he half limped along, and she wondered about the events that had unfolded that had left this champion so injured. But she thought also that perhaps since they were sneaking through tunnels, maybe it wasn't the time or place for any conversation beyond what was absolutely necessary.

And so, the four continued through the tunnel leading out of the chamber. To their great fortune, they went a long while without encountering any of the Order. The tunnel grew darker as they descended deeper. The magical light that had showered the shallower levels was absent, and they were now going only by the light of torches lining the rock walls of the mine. Still, even those were relatively few and far between, and the companions strained their eyes to see in the darkness.

They came at last to a deep chamber in the maze of tunnels. There was a large mobile drill here, sitting silent and stationary. Gerrard recognized it as a relic compared to the more modern technology he was used to working with. It was far from the cleanest, safest, most efficient technology. But that, he supposed, made sense. The Order was surely more concerned with short-term gains and low up-front costs than using the best and safest technology. They were similarly unconcerned, he was sure, about the long-term health risks or environmental impacts of what they were doing and how they were doing it.

The workers were likely a near equivalent of slave labor to the Oranlak. Perhaps they were hopelessly ensnared by the group after having their debts purchased by the ruthless but deep-pocketed organization. Such a practice was far from unheard of for the Order of Oranlak.

Gerrard found himself reflecting on his great dislike for the feeling of being indebted. He had gone to great lengths in his life to not take on debt, or to at least be actively working to rid himself of what debt it had sometimes been necessary for him to take on. That was the sort of radical self-reliance Gerrard had fostered within himself throughout much of his life. He aspired to the maximum level of self-sufficiency. And so, it troubled him now to be in so weakened and vulnerable a state. But he took heart that he felt his steps becoming easier, as his mind and body were gradually overcoming the poison that had struck him down.

His thoughts were interrupted then when he saw Hector pause in front of him.

Hector, unbeknownst to the other three, felt a group of people approaching the chamber they were now in, from one of the deeper tunnels. He motioned to his companions. Then he spoke in a voice barely above a whisper: "Hide behind the drill!"

Hector did his best to blend into the dark, away from the main light at the center of the chamber. The light was apparently another magical emanation, which was successful at illuminating much of the area, but didn't reach as well to the edges of the space. He stuck himself closely to the wall, just to the side of where the tunnel of concern connected to the current chamber the four of them were in.

He watched the workers as they walked out of that tunnel, past him and into the chamber, toward an ascending tunnel on the other side. There were a dozen of them, likely at the end of a long workday.

Is it nightfall already? he wondered. *Will a fresh batch of workers be entering soon from above?*

Some of them held pickaxes, but he knew that didn't make them formidable opponents. Not that he wanted to take on a dozen at once anyway, however useful his three new companions might be in the fight. And more than that, he didn't want any noise to attract the attention of more powerful entities, or to end up putting the entire place on high alert.

One of this group appeared to be a member of the Order. The others were perhaps just essentially Oranlak's slaves. Hector wasn't sure if that one was a shadow-walker, as he knew not all of them could wield that dark magic. Many were just talented with the blade; they had some of the best fighters in Gracyr, shadow magic aside. But even if this one wasn't a shadow magic user, he was still likely up for a fight—even at the end of a long day. That day was likely mostly spent cracking a whip, as opposed to digging or mining, anyway. In any case, engaging him in combat would likely result in an instant call to his superior, subsequently putting the entire mine operation on high alert.

Hector held his breath and hoped they would pass through without noticing him or his companions. Passage would be far smoother if they could go unnoticed as long as possible. The twelve continued on, and with what felt like a great stroke of luck, they exited the chamber—apparently without noticing any of the four companions.

When they had departed, Andromeda quietly remarked to her companions as they rejoined, "I believe that last man in the line has a bounty on him—could be profitable for us to take him out."

Hector responded first, sounding completely uninterested, saying, "What we can find here if we can continue to remain undetected will far surpass whatever bounty is on that man—who is at best a low-ranking member of the Order."

Andromeda looked upon Hector, at first seeming a little disappointed, but then she seemed to rebound quickly with excitement after considering his words.

"Okay, then, let's go on and see what's deeper down," she suggested.

Then Regina chimed in, "You'll have to be explaining, Hector, when we're out of here, about how you know so much about what's going on and what we should be doing."

Hector considered that briefly. He looked the three over and thought about whether they had much potential and how much effort they were worth. A well-known champion, who, despite his recent injury, did seem to be recovering well; and a similarly skilled sword fighter—and Regina, too, with her magic shield. He could tell the shield was also quite powerful.

Yes, the three of them could be rather useful. Purchasing their ongoing interest and support with some cryptic information and insight would likely be worthwhile, and the three of them could likely introduce some further excitement to his adventure—even if he couldn't entirely trust them. It'd be worth slightly tipping his hand and telling them a few things.

"I … understand," he stated simply to Regina, and nodded his acceptance of what she said he would have to do.

The four of them continued for a time after that, guided by the torchlight, spurred on by their need to unlock the secrets of the mine. And not so long a time later, they did come to uncover some of the arcana that saturated the place. In another big chamber deeper down, they came again upon that strange magic illumination, and the group observed something of great interest in that light.

Hector silently looked around, seeing no tunnels to progress further.

Gerrard spoke first. "This is … crimson fluorite, in the walls here." While he had surely seen far greater and richer deposits throughout his past mining jobs, he couldn't help but acknowledge aloud, "Unusual to find so significant a concentration of it. This is likely what the Oranlak is after down here."

"Is it of great value, you think?" Andromeda asked.

"Fluorite is rather common," he responded. "It's unusual to find crimson fluorite, though. A rare combination of impurities gives it its distinctive deep red color. They use it in jewelry sometimes. It can be melted and merged with molten steel to make stronger, lighter weapons, too."

He thought of then, but did not mention, his own weapon—his claymore sword. It had been forged with crimson fluorite, to achieve a powerful steel alloy that was increasingly rare in the modern age. This meant his sword possessed exceptional strength, and that he could swing it far faster than one would expect for so large a weapon. Many opponents had fallen to his blade, it being typical for them to be caught off guard by the speed with which he could brandish it against them.

"Not many still know how to work with the material or make that blend of steel, and anyway, the stuff is so rare, there's not much of a market for it, even for those who have that rare knowledge," he went on—casually, even as he spoke with remarkable authority on a topic few alive in Gracyr could match. He considered going on about the crimson fluorite and describing how it often contained lutetium, a powerful substance that, when properly purified, could have magic extracted from it.

Of more interest to Gerrard personally, though, was its specific use in creating blaster shells. Powerful ammunition for his blaster had always been hard to come by, and it wasn't getting easier in the ever-changing world he lived in—a place increasingly devoid of magic.

He decided against going on like that, though; the group seemed satisfied with what he had already said. And anyway, Andromeda interrupted his internal thoughts then.

"How do you know so much?" she inquired.

"I have worked in the mining field for … many years," Gerrard replied slowly.

Hector silently considered to himself—or at least mostly to himself, as he felt the mental intrusions of Kazahvir—that while this was interesting, it was still not the level of interesting he was really longing for.

There must be more here, he thought.

Then Regina drew him from those thoughts, though not intentionally. The stone wall she was leaning against budged a bit, pressed in by her weight. She attempted to catch herself, but failed, tumbling unceremoniously to the ground.

Hector immediately moved to examine the wall she had been leaning against. It seemed a little unusual, a little smoother than the surrounding rock. He did smile slightly, though he otherwise managed to restrain any outward displays of emotion. He felt over the stone and came to believe he was looking at another doorway. He quickly pulled the emblem-emblazoned shield-like object from his back again and set it against the stone. Orange light suddenly outlined what appeared to be a doorway. The rock collapsed inward in the shape of the door, to Hector's escalating excitement. He stepped inside almost involuntarily, as his need to know what was beyond rapidly overtook him.

He considered a few moments later, though, that perhaps he shouldn't have, as a shadow-walking member of the Oranlak jumped up from his desk, immediately at the ready. An emblem matching the one on the key he'd used to gain entrance to that room was visible on the uniform of this Oranlak fighter, at the man's shoulder. And Hector could sense on a deeper level, through the magic of Kazahvir, the ties this one had to the shadow realm.

Bizarre, he thought, as he considered that he hadn't felt this obvious presence before he entered the room. He could usually feel it through a substance so mundane as a wall of rock. There was something more at work, he was sure, that had been masking this shadow magic user from his sight.

The member of the Order slung out a sleep-poisoned dagger, launching it at Hector, but it narrowly missed him as he dodged to the side. Gerrard stepped swiftly inside, at once understanding the importance of silencing the attacker quickly. He drew his massive blade, though he could feel his nerves, muscles, and joints all flaring up in protest.

Andromeda drew her saber and stepped into the hidden room as well. Regina followed, sword and shield at the ready.

The dark, cloaked figure launched an impossible stream of daggers at the companions, perhaps counting on a quick victory in his outnumbered situation. Then the man, if that was indeed what he still was, shadow-jumped right into the midst of his adversaries. He drew a short sword against Regina, who managed to deflect the strike with her magnificent shield, the magic of it utterly denying the shadow-walker his intended target: her throat. The magic spark show that ensued, and the reciprocated force that was turned back against him, sent him reeling and off balance. And then Gerrard was there, to cleave the head right off the creature—as he knew it now to be, as it had forsaken its mortality for that enticing power from the other world.

Hector marveled momentarily at the efficient dispatch of the creature. *And the force, the speed of that strike from Gerrard!* he thought. It came as all the more impressive to him, too, when he considered the older man's current wounded state. It hadn't been a particularly powerful shadow-walker, but still, so efficient and decisive a victory commanded a degree of admiration and respect—even from the well-seasoned warrior that Hector was.

He brought himself back to the moment, glanced around, and moved expeditiously to the only thing he noticed in the room that seemed to be of any interest. It was the desk the shadow-walker had been sitting at. He rifled through the drawers and dug through the paperwork for something, anything of interest, straining his eyes in the dim torchlight.

Regina noticed his difficulty and willed her shield to glow gently and provide some reading light. Andromeda joined in and scoured through the paperwork in and on the desk as well. Gerrard stood by, looking around and with his guard up.

Hector paused after a few minutes, reading over something slowly and carefully. It was a book, maybe a journal. As he thumbed through it, some pages and old maps fell out. Hector scrutinized the ancient book as best he could and looked over the frayed and faded maps to glean some spark of recognition. It wasn't something the Oranlak was writing or had written; it was something they had found somewhere. Perhaps it had been in one of the old tunnels here, one that predated the newly drilled ones they had made.

The text was in rough shape, much of it barely legible. Still, Hector excitedly read what he could of it. Kazahvir glowed brilliantly with similar excitement for what was unfolding.

Andromeda picked up the dusty papers that had fallen out, and she could see these included some old maps.

Curious, she thought. *What did that book contain that has Hector so enthralled?*

***

A vidscreen's printer light blinked on in a chamber far above the room the four companions occupied in the underground mine network. Ursula looked on with great interest at the message it printed. She recognized the source as being Mercedes's office at the capitol building, a grand edifice known as the Castle. She immediately moved to retrieve the single-page response. Her dark but fiery eyes glowed with anticipation.

Mercedes approved of her proposed course. Ursula could immediately silence the inconvenient prisoner and demolish and self-destruct their mine operation here. She wasn't too surprised; she had felt strongly that Mercedes was going to approve the plan she had suggested. The excerpts she had sent over from the journal they had found in the old mines had been particularly compelling, and much of the information it contained was well substantiated by what the Order already knew. They were looking at a figurative goldmine near the city of Akastair—though in actuality, what they were looking at was even more valuable. And the dwindling, lackluster returns of their operation at Waterfall Ridge had surely aided Mercedes in concluding that their organization should be refocusing its priorities elsewhere.

Ursula immediately set out from her office space to dispatch the prisoner herself and get on with new, more exciting plans.

* * *

She found, upon her arrival to the chamber where the chained man had been left, that he was now gone. Rage boiled within her. This was a rather untimely setback. She glanced around for some clues about what had happened as her thoughts raced to find the optimal course of action. She observed a trail of blood starting from where the man had been chained. He appeared to have set out going the wrong way and had actually proceeded deeper in instead of toward the entrance.

She glanced at her clonra device to check the time. It was already late, and the mining operations for the day were over now. And she had heard what must have been the final group for the day noisily heading back up to the surface some time ago. She could just trigger the self-destruct mechanism of the place and almost certainly terminate the life of that getaway somewhere deeper down in the tunnels—and probably without harming any of her own people. She resolved to do so and be on to grander and more important things. She headed back to her office and spoke briefly over the intercom of the maze network.

"This is Ursula. Our operation here shall immediately cease. Proceed to the exit, or alert me via clonra right now if you are inside and unable; this complex will self-destruct imminently."

She knew everyone was almost certainly out, and actually didn't care much, regardless, even if they weren't—a fact she was considering before she even finished speaking over the intercom. Even so, it wasn't becoming of someone of her station to waste personnel lives, so she knew she should make *some* attempt at not doing such a thing. Still, she acknowledged, she was vastly more concerned with silencing the escapee.

She returned and activated the self-destruct mechanism in her office. Then she jumped through the shadows. She called on her dark powers to expedite her departure, before the trinitrotoluene self-destruct system organized throughout the place could explode and bury her down there.

Ursula stalled then briefly, just after emerging from the mines. Something occurred to her. She glanced at her clonra, which showed barely a minute left until the destruction of the place. She realized that the original journal was likely still down in the mines.

She shrugged it off. Much of it had been copied over and digitized, anyway. It likely wouldn't matter if the original was destroyed. She shadow-jumped a few more times to get a greater distance away from the pending explosions and was quickly gone from that place.

* * *

The companions heard the intercom message. They knew they didn't have time to climb all the way back out of there. In what was quickly growing into a state of panic, Regina examined the walls, hoping she could discover another of the hidden doorways that seemed to exist throughout the place.

There was a section of the wall that appeared inconsistent with the surrounding rock—a little smoother, with the color not quite right. "Over here!" she yelled to her companions, though most specifically to Hector—so he could put to use that key shield thing of his again. Hector instantly understood Regina's intent and was almost as instantly there beside her. He hoped, as did they all, that there was another hidden door here. He placed the shield against the wall repeatedly as the seconds counted down. An artificial voice came onto the intercom system as the count dropped below a half minute, but the companions could scarcely hear it over the sound of their pounding hearts.

What they saw then was almost miraculous to their hope-starved eyes. They saw a light activate—an orange-lit outline of a door emanating from the rock wall. It gave way and opened to the beautiful sound of owls and crickets, the sounds of the night beyond that opened barrier. They ran in quick succession out into the starlit night beyond and continued racing as fast as they could before the explosive *boom* could transpire.

They heard that *boom*, but went on running for a time, until Hector, in the lead, finally halted. He wasn't so much tired as he was just fairly certain they had covered enough distance and enough time had passed that they could probably stop galloping blindly through the dark.

Everyone was severely out of breath, except Hector.

"I feel perhaps … luckier than I have … ever felt before," remarked Andromeda.

"Ditto," agreed Regina, laughing a little between heavy breaths.

"Where … to now?" asked Gerrard, his voice sounding gravelly but focused as he caught his breath.

Hector looked silently to him at first, then replied decisively, "Akastair." And his lips creased in the faintest smile as he thought over the many encouraging things he had read in his new journal.

13

Chapter Thirteen

Akastair was an old city, rich with history. It was an extravagant and wondrous place that nearly all of its citizens still loved—so much so that they rarely dwelt on fantasies of moving elsewhere. Many grandiose edifices towered high into the sky over the city. Many people who visited aspired to visit again. And indeed, many across Makeva dreamt of someday moving to Akastair.

Still, the glamor of the place had faded for some. Regina was one person who did not see so much in the place as she once had. People often didn't really know Akastair at all—they heard about it from others, the media, word of mouth, and so forth—and their imaginations were what truly built so much of the place. It often took a hefty dose of reality, and on a rather lengthy timeline, to bring down the fantasy that their imaginations had built.

Regina had lived there a long time—been born there, even. She had left it finally, a decade or so ago now. Much of the illusion about the place had shattered for her about a decade before that, though.

She had at that time, some two decades ago, won a contest. As the prize, she was afforded a grand opportunity, along with a just small group of others. But that supposed opportunity had turned out to be of quite a different sort than what she expected.

Objectively, the opportunity was to meet an artist, a singer, well known and from Akastair herself, known as Selene. It was not at all uncommon in the city, or in many areas across Makeva, for a person to openly profess their love for this singer, even just in going about one's normal daily activities—say, out and about on the town, or talking with friends or coworkers, or on your favorite vidscreen programming. Selene had incredible influence and wealth, and by extension, considerable power, too. It certainly wasn't entirely undeserved; she was indisputably talented, whether her particular themes or style or lyrics appealed to a certain individual or not. She'd had some lucky breaks in life, sure, and she was gifted, no doubt, but she'd taken many risks even so—and had persevered. She had sacrificed much to accomplish what she had.

Regina had idolized her back then, as many had, though she did not do so to the extent many of Selene's fanatics did. There was one song in particular that spoke to Regina deeply. It had been a favorite called "Saving the World."

Regina had drawn such moving and beautiful ideas in her mind from the lyrics and the music. What a vision she had come to have for the future of Gracyr after hearing that song! She tied so much of herself to it, and her self-image and her view of the world were so connected to this fantasy of a better world that she came to dream of. Her interpretation of the song had spoken to her in a way and at a level that she felt nothing and no one else ever had. So it was with great anticipation that she finally met Selene, with just a small group of other lucky fans.

It had been after the singer's concert at Akastair's Grand Stadium—a place she filled to the brim with a ridiculous number of people. Regina remembered how jaw-droppingly delighted, how starstruck they had all been. After the show and during their meeting, the contest winners had all been asking their favorite singer questions about what it was like to be such a star, various things about some of her songs, and what advice she had for them so they could be more like her.

Regina's questions had to do with her favorite song—the one about saving the world. She asked her about it, about what she meant by some of the lyrics. She asked about what had led her to write it, about what she thought was needed to save the world. Regina had felt so strongly that she and Selene were of so much the same mind; the words of the song had spoken to her too profoundly for that not to be the case. Still, she knew she couldn't justify a belief that they saw things precisely the same. And yet, she did expect something substantially similar—and maybe something more similar than she dared to believe was possible.

The answer, to its credit, had left her every bit as breathless as if that had been the case— but it was so thoroughly in the absolute wrong way. Selene's actual view of saving the world turned out to essentially be Regina's idea of destroying it.

Regina was sure that her suddenly not-so-favorite singer had interpreted her breathlessness and jaw-dropped expression as just her being starstruck. And luckily, anyway, there had been no shortage of questions coming from the others in the small group, and they successfully kept the conversation rolling along. Regina had managed a faint smile to keep the situation pleasant, though in her mind, she distinctly felt her world collapsing around her.

The vision this singer had, in Regina's perspective, was horrifying. She spoke of ideals of a world of powers, forces with incredible control to protect and ensure safety and fairness. A world of no conflict, a world of perpetual peace. It was a centralized, standardized, overreaching abomination that Regina saw as, basically, slavery. It was unquestioned loyalty to a presumed-benevolent behemoth that could not be stopped or have its power limited or controlled.

The truth was that these were ideas that so assailed Regina's beliefs that she could not continue their exchange beyond that faint smile. The person she had just spoken with was one who, given the power to do so, would destroy the world—and would wholeheartedly believe she was saving it in doing so.

The world described to Regina was one she needed to dissect, right then, in those subsequent moments. She needed to reconcile her beliefs, her whole world, with this new, inconsistent information. The true world from the song was hopelessly flawed, and she knew it now at great personal depth—in her soul, if not in her mind—even if she couldn't manage to reason through it all just then. And it was a world that she felt, should it ever actually be realized, would create gargantuan problems that would dwarf the problems the world had now.

A classic case, Regina mentally summarized, *of the cure being worse than the disease.*

Regina hadn't been angry at the revelation. *Disappointed* was a more suitable word. And concerned, though she was concerned primarily with just piecing much of herself back together, having had so much of it shattered in those preceding moments.

Regina knew she could do it, though; she had repaired her reality many times before and built herself back better every time. And that was what so much of the world and life was to Regina. It was all a complicated infrastructure of the mind, a deep and interconnected mental framework. And the solution to life, to the world—she knew it wasn't a straightforward, objective answer. It was a solid foundation of truth and belief, and the mental framework built atop it. And that structure often needed *re*structuring, maintenance, repairs, additions, and updates to continue standing, and to be improved and reinforced to stand against life's ever-harder trials.

The solution was a journey, mental and physical, to shape and build the mind. Someone hearing the answer from another would still not comprehend it without having undertaken the journey themselves; it could not just be told to someone. It was like an advanced equation in mathematics, or reactions of complex chemicals. It couldn't be just looked up; the smaller pieces needed to be understood for you to comprehend the greater solution that you had read or had told to you. Indeed, it would do nothing for you to hear the secrets of the universe; you still wouldn't understand them if you hadn't built the mental framework to be able to comprehend them accurately.

So it was that she ultimately resolved to fixate on that task of adjusting her perspectives and piecing herself back together, for as long as it would take. She did feel a degree of mental anguish, though, in considering all the things in her life she had to get back to after that fateful artist meet and greet was over…

She had been studying to graduate from the academy here in Akåstair, one of the most prestigious in Makeva. And it was finally happening that year. She had been considering what specific route she wanted to pursue after graduation. She thought over further education or skills development, ideas to start building up personal wealth and a livelihood, or just obtaining more life experiences of various sorts, and a more potent understanding of the world.

Regina didn't mind the idea of changing her previous ideas, or really altering any course she had been previously considering. Perhaps most of all, she wanted self-improvement, a better understanding of herself and others. She wanted to come to know more things that still eluded her. Indeed, she valued the attainment of knowledge more so than material wealth. She wanted to understand, to see through the ubiquitous utter lack of transparency of their world. She wanted to unlock channels, unlock conversation and minds and discussion, things that were so central a pillar in the framework of her freedom—at least of her mind, if not her body as well.

She understood, though, that she was a bit distractable. And despite herself, particularly when excited, she was a bit emotional and impulsive. But she could typically control those tendencies—at least well enough to keep herself progressing generally forward. She had many ideas about experiences to have and concepts to figure out. And she had ideas about so many of the things she could see doing with her life. Regina knew she had the potential to excel in a multitude of different areas, though it was certainly true that some things came more easily than others.

She didn't necessarily even want to be doing what she was best at. She didn't want something she loved to become something she despised because she *had* to do it.

Perhaps most important to her back then, after that long-ago concert, had just been the need to settle on a course she could proceed on for at least a moderate length of time into her future—something she had the will to initiate and sufficient passion to maintain. Over the months that followed, she had decided on pursuing a path advocating for particular aspects of the energy industry. She had come to understand much about past and modern energy technologies, as well as about theorized future means of power generation. She was able to learn a lot about these topics through projects at the learning academy she had attended growing up, but much of it came through further research she did by herself in her personal time. She came to care powerfully about practicality and sustainability. And it helped further spur her interest to stay in Akastair—a significant hub for the energy industry in Makeva.

Akastair was located on the short eastern coast of Makeva, which was the country to the northwest of the Ezmondian Empire on the continent of Gracyr. Akastair was like other cities and towns across Makeva in many ways. Its populace was an often sturdy and self-sufficient, hard-working folk, commonly with strong individualist leanings. This was typical for most communities across the country.

They had a unique set of their own laws and regulations in Akastair, as other cities and towns generally did. The development and modification of these laws and regulations was often hotly debated among the people and their representatives, to such an extent that it often appeared not much was being accomplished day to day, politically speaking.

The communities across Makeva were loosely bound together by the Gatekeepers Council of Makeva, headed by the current Grandmaster of the Council. They developed overarching principles and guidelines that maintained some sense of a larger, unified community—though Makeva as a whole rarely operated as such. Perhaps it was more important, though, that the inhabitants of Makeva shared many common values. Indeed, the values and virtues of the people likely did far more to hold the country together than the work of those representatives, the Gatekeepers Council, and the Grandmaster himself combined.

This was in contrast to Ezmondia to the southeast, which operated more as a large community of a single mind under the emperor, with some help from the Elite Council of Ezmondia. And though the empire had comparatively complicated and extensive sets of draconian and byzantine laws, they were often bent and broken at a whim by the overpowered leadership.

Ezmondia generally had a much hotter climate than Makeva, which was rapidly—historically speaking—becoming hotter and drier. And this was very taxing on the hydropower energy systems Ezmondia primarily relied on.

The climate had been changing more subtly in Makeva, but hydropower was still where most of their power was coming from, too, and the systems there were surely being affected as well. The population of Makeva also did not have the single-mindedness that most Ezmondians had, which assured widespread agreement among the people about whatever their leaders deemed to be a solution.

Akastair ran substantially on hydropower, as was typical for cities in Gracyr. And there were abundant concerns among those who lived there about the sustainability of that reliance. As one of the larger cities of Makeva, Akastair's energy needs were considerable. Water levels at its primary hydroelectric plant had been trending at lower levels for years—and though it hadn't reached a clearly critical point yet, there was still growing talk of exploring other, nascent sources of energy. Fortunately, societal horizons were broadening with respect to perceptions of the energy industry and exploring new sources of energy, but the pace was gradual and slow.

So it came to be that Regina settled on the field of energy as a career focus. The need for changes and adaptations in the industry were clear to Regina, and it was a mission, a movement to undertake, from which she came to feel she could extract great personal fulfillment. There was a unique perspective that needed to be brought in to fix the pending energy crisis in Makeva, and the structure of their society called for something different than what had been done in the past or what was being done now elsewhere in Gracyr. In time, she found herself applying for, accepted to, and then excelling at the Future Energy Program at the University of Akastair. She experienced a diversity of perspectives from peers and professors over those years, which drew her interest ever deeper into the field, enriching her own views and captivating her mind throughout her post-secondary education.

The professors there harbored a thought-provoking blend of diverse perspectives. That was important to Regina—to have different views to drive deeper and more intriguing debate, which would hopefully also push her toward some greater ultimate truths about the world. She felt she needed to be around that to develop the sort of education that was truly important to her.

Some people, she readily observed, clung to what was almost a love of hydropower and to what was simultaneously an irrational dedication to a failing enterprise.

The changing climate itself was also often a contested topic. There was skepticism among her professors and peers about how quickly it was happening, whether it was going to continue to happen, and whether it was even happening at all. Would things change again? Would the climate become wetter given more time, perhaps? It was not unusual for her to hear such questions during her time on campus.

Professors taught classes often in line with their proposed solutions, though they were not always solutions widely accepted as viable. For instance, some spoke of harnessing the kinetic energy of falling raindrops ... or some even spoke of harnessing the power of the sun's processes of atomic fusion. Still more ideas abounded, things that were perhaps more realizable, but wholly insufficient—solutions that worked only when the sun was shining or when the wind was blowing. Most ideas struck Regina as unrealistic, for various reasons across the plentiful topics.

Her heart did come to be tugged in one particular, undeniable direction, though. Many of her favorite professors taught in the subject areas of geothermal energy production and geothermal heating. Why exactly those particular topics appealed to her was difficult for her to put into words. Maybe it just had to do with the professors themselves, the way they taught, or the way they made the material so relatable. In any case, she could not deny a certain inner calling during those lectures in particular.

Some of those professors would make connections that seemed brilliant, sometimes even between what appeared to be, at first glance, wildly unrelated matters. They helped her relate to the material and better understand it, and further, to even be entertained by the oftentimes information-dense lectures.

On multiple occasions, she had seen some of her favorite professors challenge prevailing societal perspectives that were widely accepted as accurate, and to many, nearly indisputable. She had seen them challenge the text of the books they were educating the class from—and do it convincingly. And still, they weren't boastful or arrogant about it; they were calm, objective, and matter-of-fact.

She often reflected on them, those professors back at the University of Akastair, especially those in the Geothermal Department. She still took great comfort in the fact that such people existed in the world.

Of course, she was always careful to not make the mistake of trying to dig too much into how those professors might describe their deeper beliefs, especially after the past incident with a certain no-longer-favorite singer of hers. She found she could interpret their words and actions in multiple ways that were sometimes contradictory—and so she came to often just appreciate what was presented to her, and to strive to find what truth she could in their actions and words that resonated best with the truth she already knew in her heart.

She often felt her fellow students at the university, both in and out of the energy programs, were also of highly diverse perspectives. Still, she didn't meet many fellow students that she felt were very much like herself. And it did cause her some trouble. She felt, as perhaps all the young learners on campuses across Gracyr sometimes did, that troubling mental nagging of wanting to feel like part of a group, or to be popular, or some other related but nebulous thing.

She came to be tested by the incredible minds of many professors who taught her—and she excelled, which she took great fulfillment in. That was enough to sustain her, to quiet that mental nagging.

It was still true that she often felt disconnected from other students, though—detached, maybe, from the greater student body at the university.

It was hard for her to engage with a lot of what she saw as the silly motions of campus life. Her peers often led, what seemed to her, distracted, decadent lifestyles.

Their lives seemed distanced from the things that were truly important. She had felt feelings so powerful that she didn't always feel worthy of having felt them. Such a deep appreciation for forces so great was painfully absent in the other students she encountered, so far as she could discern from the demeanor and conversations they persisted with.

To her, what was important were things like seeking deeper connections to and between things and people, understanding how different people saw and experienced the world, and how that changed throughout their lives, edifying oneself about the greater problems of the world and how to solve them. But other students were caught up in transient, superficial love interests, or the gossip of the day, or distracting, addictive games, or dwelling on demotivating, destabilizing emotions, or building personal wealth—an admirable pursuit, perhaps, but they were often doing so without any greater ambitions for putting that wealth to effective use for the benefit of humankind.

Regina held an often singular focus that was set on ideas about advancing humanity, on larger-scale problem-solving, rather than on navigating the chaotic social circles that dominated so much of the world around her.

Anyway, it seemed to her there was always a pathway for her to attain more of a sense of inclusion, if that was, indeed, something she needed or was lacking. And that helped her to not dwell on it, or on how it occasionally troubled her.

She could fit in. She chose not to.

She saw this in how there wasn't any shortage of people interested in talking with her. She was, by most standards, a rather striking young woman, beautiful and with many of the qualities would-be lovers sought. People naturally gravitated toward her. She was clever and quick-witted, but generally found her well-thought-out rebuttals and layers of conversational intrigue lost on those who engaged her in conversation. She made references to history and other topics that seemed to elude her peers.

Still, she kept an open mind, would sometimes humor someone new to see if they might match her cleverness or wit, or just strike her as unique in some other way in the too-typical world that engulfed her.

People didn't seem to be looking to challenge their views, to rebuild themselves—not like her—and at times, they seemed even hopelessly shallow in their perspectives and emotions. She didn't regard such people critically, though, but rather objectively. She wasn't expectant or angry toward them; she was just, perhaps, disappointed with the state the world seemed to be in.

After all, maybe she was just obsessed with self-improvement. Her frequent skepticism about concepts, people, and other things certainly didn't always make her the fastest-working or most productive member on any given team she was on, either. Her way of living was far from proven, in even her own mind, to be an ideal way.

And so, she tended to spend her days thinking about things more along the lines of geothermal heat pumps and steam energy, rather than things like how to become the most efficiently inebriated with the handsomest boy. In fact, she was inclined to just avoid the handsomest ones altogether; they often seemed the most troublesome, they were oftentimes the shallowest in their perspectives, and they generally seemed hopelessly distracted by things profoundly uninteresting to her.

In any case, she dwelled often on the perceived shortfalls of hydropower and the weaknesses of the current energy infrastructure of Gracyr. The current faltering hydropower operations, and the limited number of new ones coming online in recent years, often drew in her thoughts and her hunger for problem-solving. Things like the climate becoming drier, the once-abundant waters that now flowed only weakly, the many bodies of water across Gracyr that never reached the fullness they once regularly contained—these were all items that could command her attention.

In time, she came to be a strong advocate for the solutions she believed in that could fix these problems—particularly steam energy and geothermal pursuits.

She enjoyed learning about heat pumps that could use the constant temperature underground to facilitate a temperature exchange between living spaces in buildings and that of the underground, where temperatures remained largely the same, even across the changing seasons. They could be designed to use water, or other fluids that could carry even more energy, moving through pipes that circulated the temperatures. She saw in such systems great potential to reduce overall energy use and build a more reliable, comfortable, sustainable system for heating and cooling across Makeva—or even all of Gracyr, for that matter.

She also saw in such systems the potential to make a stronger economy—and perhaps more than that, a better availability of more meaningful work for the citizens of Makeva. So much of what people were doing for work, she often lamented, seemed an awful waste of human talents and capabilities. People often toiled away their years essentially just serving to make people with too much power even more powerful.

Regina had what she felt was a natural distaste for holding so much power, but she would often caution herself to not be overconfident. It was perhaps truth that under the right circumstances, anyone was corruptible. And she wasn't going to bank on herself being the sole human exception.

She didn't study in depth the tyrants of the past, or even those of the present day. Although she could surely think of one example: the current emperor of Ezmondia.

Examples of lesser tyrannies, or at least things that seemed to take the world deeper into their grasp, seemed rampant throughout modern society, though. Regina could just look to the merging of behemoths across numerous industries, which ever concentrated power and deceptively stripped away options and choices from consumers, to plainly see the stage being set. And it was happening across so many areas, ranging from farms and ranches to even her chosen field of energy.

Regina understood that much of the pushback against her favored forms of energy was fueled by the titans of her day, by those who drew great wealth and power from the old way of hydroelectric—and she saw how they prioritized continuing that ever-slimming stream of profit over saving lives or improving the world.

Spurred on by such ideas, Regina came in time to give lectures and talks, at the university and beyond, on various energy-related topics. She would speak about modern-day energy problems and geothermal solutions. She had the opportunity to assist some of the professors she had admired greatly, and she networked thoroughly with them and their circles of influence, large and small.

Some of these professors were advocates for various other proposed solutions, such as the use of hydrogen as energy. Many favored enhancing hydrogen systems and infrastructure to expand the hydromagnetic railways.

Previously, there had been concerns about how to produce or where to find the amount of hydrogen needed to make many of the ideas very practical. The answer to that quandary had come largely from bacteria. Bacteria was now grown that could consume garbage and produce hydrogen in the process. That hydrogen was being used for the trains and for general electricity generation, which powered more of Makeva than ever before—more than previously thought possible.

Of course, the hydrogen solutions still hadn't gotten to the point where they were fulfilling a majority of the current energy needs. They were still at a fraction of what they would have to be. The field was still dominated by hydropower—largely rivers and reservoirs across Makeva. And in Ezmondia, it was far worse; hydropower was practically the sole source of energy, and hydrogen systems barely had a presence there at all.

That all seemed well in line with Regina's theory—her theory that those in power in Gracyr, because of the current hydroelectric systems, were working to hold onto it, through maintaining a public perception of its ongoing viability and necessity, and of course, talking up the dangers and drawbacks of any alternatives that threatened them.

She spent a couple years in the city of Akastair after her graduation from the university, advocating for more geothermal energy and less hydropower. But that city had a persistent love for—and faith in—their hydropower systems. Ultimately, she came to largely abandon her efforts in Akastair. She left in favor of the western city of Razora, which was a better environment for her ambitions with geothermal energy.

In the decade or so that had followed since, and leading up to the present year, she had continued to advocate for the changeover to geothermal energy, and she did so with a notable degree of success. She managed to help move some areas significantly away from their overreliance on the slowly failing hydropower systems.

Contrastingly, some areas clung to hydropower energy. And even in the places where geothermal was far more substantially welcomed and developed, Regina knew it was all still coming along far more slowly than it needed to be. The vast amounts of silver and gold poured into public perception by the giants that defined so much of her world were a great impediment to her increasingly tiresome efforts to gain ground in the energy arena.

Even so, as it was in Makeva, the hold of those companies over Ezmondia and its inhabitants was far more absolute. Geothermal energy was practically nonexistent there, and exacerbated fears about it were rampant.

It was probably the case that efforts in Makeva fell short of what was needed to avoid dire catastrophes from failing hydropower systems in the years to come. However, seeing as those catastrophes had not yet come to pass, and life mostly chugged along as it had for so long for the citizens of Makeva, the reality of the situation apparently hadn't taken much of a hold on them.

Still, the situation was far more dire in Ezmondia. It had now come to pass that, in the current year, energy production was going to fall noticeably short of what was required—*very* noticeably. The expenses required to frame public opinion adequately so as to prevent things like riots, protests, and deaths were going to be astronomical.

Of course, Armando, a man still largely unknown to Regina, was quite aware of this reality. But in his sickeningly self-serving way, and especially as he was caught in the throes of what was a disease—though it was disguised as a prize—he could see only the opportunity the situation presented.

14

Chapter Fourteen

The four-member team of Gerrard, Andromeda, Regina, and Hector walked (or perhaps put more accurately, stumbled) through the night some distance before eventually coming to a partial clearing. They determined it was a suitable enough spot to make camp, and they pulled their bedrolls from their travel packs and hunkered down.

Even Hector, so incessantly untrusting of his surroundings, lowered his guard more than usual. His tiredness was weighing on him. But he also had a general sense that he could trust his companions more than he was accustomed to trusting anyone. Maybe something about escaping a self-destructing mine complex together had that effect on him. That wasn't necessarily to say that he was enthusiastic about doing it, though. Still, it did seem they had just gone through a rather radical trust-building exercise of sorts.

"Where to, in the morning?" Andromeda asked uncertainly.

Gerrard answered calmly, despite some frustration that his original plan had gone askew. "I had hoped to get an early start out of Nethereel that I … suspect isn't going to be working out as planned. I'll still be trying to reach Akastair by day's end tomorrow, via the train out of Nethereel. I also have a friend to meet with before I depart … whose patience I hope is holding out."

Regina chimed in optimistically, "I'm sure that, given the circumstances, if ya explain the situation—"

Gerrard cut in with an upturned palm and a smile barely visible in the moonlight. "Yes, yes, I know," he said, and he let out a friendly laugh, if a bit artificial.

"Tomorrow, then," Regina announced to the group. "We're out early for Nethereel. Take a little time for what ya need when we arrive, and meet at the train station after." She sounded confident and made it sound decisive.

The others just nodded. They were exhausted well beyond any wishes they may have had to protest the plan, in any case. And it wasn't much time after that at all that they were all already asleep.

* * *

Gerrard was the first to awaken the next morning, and it was mostly still dark when he opened his eyes. That, of course, wasn't a surprise. He didn't usually sleep as soundly as he had back in his younger years.

He listened to birds and insects and other sounds of the forest as the sun gradually glowed brighter and came up over the horizon. He gave it some time, then eventually pulled himself to his feet and rolled up his bedroll. He took a hearty swig of water from his canteen, then moved to nudge Andromeda awake.

She woke easily and let out a yawn before she greeted him. "Mornin'."

Hector was awake next, after hearing Andromeda, being a rather light sleeper himself. Regina remained sleeping, still catching up on how much of it she'd lost across her college years—or so she would jokingly conclude to herself, upon waking a few minutes later and seeing everyone else already prepared.

When Regina did wake, she yawned and greeted everyone. She noticed they seemed to be waiting on her at that moment. "Hi there. You're all up bright and early. Anyone … have anything to eat?" she asked hopefully.

To her delight, Gerrard tossed her a strip of beef jerky as her stomach growled.

"Any of that for me?" asked Andromeda hungrily a few moments later.

Gerrard smiled a little and handed her a piece of the meaty snack. He also handed Hector some, before he asked. Then he smiled at the group and said, "Best enjoy it, everyone; that's all I have."

"Let's be on our way," suggested Regina between chomps of the jerky.

Hector started off, also munching away, and everyone else followed along.

As they walked on back toward Nethereel, Regina struck up some conversation.

"So, Hector," she said, "I guess you must be feelin' you've found that excitement an' adventure you're looking for, huh?"

Hector answered in his usual lackluster tone. "So far, I won't say I'm disappointed. I do hope there's more to come."

"Is *that* what you're in this for?" asked Andromeda, almost accusingly, though in more of a playful than a mean way.

"Something like that," Hector responded cryptically.

"What were you able to gather from that journal?" asked Gerrard, prodding a bit, trying to extract a more detailed response from the quietest of his new companions.

Hector yielded. "There may be rich veins of crimson fluorite near Akastair, which I'm sure caught the attention of the Oranlak—if they've read the entries I have. There seems to be a new energy source in the area, too, which I expect has garnered their attention as well."

Regina's ears perked up a bit at the mention of a "new energy source," though she remained silent as she listened to the conversation.

"The journal looks to be quite dated," Gerrard observed, a little skeptically, but well-meaning.

"Yes," replied Hector, glaring back—and a little harshly, too, as if he had been challenged. "The shadow-walker we dispatched, or perhaps another, seems to have marked and highlighted some of the entries—particularly those about this new energy. That seems to have been where their attention was focused."

"Very interesting," remarked Regina, almost involuntarily breaking her silence as her intrigue with the situation overflowed. "What else does it say about this mysterious new energy?"

"This may seem far-fetched to you, but apparently there's a vessel that fell from the stars, which is sunken off the coast of Akastair at great depth. There's a vast quantity of this new energy-producing substance aboard that ship. Supposedly, anyway," Hector finished, a little pessimistically.

"That *is* very intriguing," said Gerrard, concurring with Regina. "Returning to Akastair may prove more interesting than expected."

Right then, the outskirts of Nethereel finally came into view out in the distance. And whether it was because of the distraction of that welcome sight, or just genuine unanimity, none of the four disagreed.

* * *

The day had progressed into the early afternoon by the time the group returned to Nethereel. Upon reaching the outer limits of the city's largest marketplace, Gerrard departed from the others, saying, "I'll see you all at the station. Take the time to get yourselves prepared for what's ahead. I'll see you all in about two hours."

The other three split up as well, and all went their separate ways. Of the four of them, Andromeda was probably the least excited to be leaving the group.

It was the way she had always been. She had long favored and tended to thrive in team or group settings. She liked to be in environments that capitalized on her natural ability to connect people to one another and to herself. She liked to tap into their personal strengths and find ways to empower them. And she favored having more perspectives to run ideas through, rather than relying solely on her own. How much more efficient it was, she often marveled, to not have to run her mind through the myriad possible perspectives of things—to have others to divide up that monumental task. She might take days to think of something the way another person might think of it in just moments.

She enjoyed forging connections with people and helping them develop themselves, as well as developing herself. And she wanted their viewpoints to strengthen whatever it was she was working on. Andromeda believed in balancing views, in mediating, and in partnerships and forgiveness. She loved working with others to not only understand them better, but to understand herself better, too.

For the next couple hours, though, she resolved not to dwell on such things. She decided to pick up a few items and replenish her supplies before their group departed for Akastair. She ambled down the main street of Nethereel, a little farther north than where she had been previously. Many local residences and shops for daily staples were in this sector, as opposed to the more tourism-focused section farther south in the city. There were more grocers and food stands here, local farmers selling fruits and vegetables. It reminded her of a scaled-up, larger version of her hometown.

She had to admit, she had, by most standards, lived a rather reclusive, sheltered life. But that made it all the more exciting now to be wandering around amid so many of the sights she might otherwise consider boringly mundane—and she was all but certain that the locals regarded the scenes unfolding around her as just that. Andromeda took notice of how the people around her seemed to be going about their way as if there really was nothing all that amazing or interesting going on. But it was all very interesting to Andromeda. The simple fact that everyone seemed to regard it as so uninteresting amused her. It was intriguing how someone could become so used to something that they could see truly amazing things and think they were not—think nothing of them at all.

She suspected some around her now would think her hopelessly sheltered, perhaps naïve or worthy of their sympathy, to know the life she had lived. They might think her cursed or unfortunate. And yet, to be able to see the wonder of such a bustling place now, of so many people exchanging goods and skills from all across Makeva—to be able to see the beauty of the system that had made such a gargantuan task possible was doubtlessly, to her, a good thing. She might even have held a slight sympathy for those who could not see it as she did now—who perhaps never had.

She purchased a few basic supplies and food items with her tournament winnings. She bought an impressively large apple and a fresh, juicy-looking orange. She purchased some beef jerky, hoping it would be something close to as good as what Gerrard had shared with the group that morning. It all cost very little of the small fortune she had won from placing in the tournament—just a few coppers here, a few coppers there.

The shops seem almost endless, she thought as she racked up a couple more minor purchases in another small but nifty local store. *A couple hours of this won't be difficult at all.*

She smiled, more to herself than the person at the sales counter, and made her way out of the shop and into the next one that caught her eye.

* * *

While Andromeda was, at least initially, the least excited about the time to herself, Hector was probably the most excited. Granted, though, he was never really by himself these days. Not even now. Not since the moment he had first picked up that magic sword of his, that moment when it had first mentally imparted its name to him: *Kazahvir.*

The blade was a masterfully forged weapon, far older than Hector's barely quarter century of life. It was a weapon from times long past, produced by magics and means long lost to the world. The magical sentience the weapon possessed could give its wielder a sense of the life-forms around him or her, could even sometimes scramble the thoughts of the weak-minded nearby. Perhaps the most notable of its abilities, though, was that it could summon a powerful magic scorpion once a day. That scorpion could strike with lethal force, and almost always had. Even if the strike itself failed to bring down an opponent, the potent venom injected would course through its victim's veins and almost certainly finish the job.

There wasn't any antidote for it, or so Hector understood from what the sword had mentally imparted to him. It could, however, be overcome if it was believed by the victim to be what it truly was—an illusion. But you would have to be of strong mind, and either know, or sense, the truth of the poison. No one Hector had ever used that special ability against had survived—and there had been many. He lived in times and around people who—measured against the greater entities across the millennia that Kazahvir had been brought to bear against—were weak and inconsequential, at least so far as the sword was generally concerned. By and large, these people had not an inkling of the power that once existed, which reigned over far more than present-day Gracyr. Kazahvir was a weapon out of time, displaced, but flourishing in a world with so little magic, strength, and force of will to hold it back.

Hector had sought the weapon after listening to his grandfather's stories about it. It wasn't until Hector retrieved the ages-old weapon that he came to realize how little his grandfather had truly even known about it. The venerable man had finally given Hector the map, the key to finding Kazahvir, on his deathbed. The old man had been alive more than a century. His grandfather had been a military man and a high-ranking general for many decades. Over the course of his life, he had come to know many things that were largely unknown to the public at large. Eventually, he had settled in the relatively quiet (at the time) town he ended up raising his family in. His son, Hector's father, had chosen to raise his family there, as well. For as long as Hector could remember, his grandfather told what his father had generally referred to as "tall tales." Nevertheless, Hector had always found them entertaining, regardless of how true they were.

Kazahvir seemed to be something his grandfather opted to keep more of a secret, at least until he had advanced far further in years. He apparently hadn't brought it up for many years after leaving the military, though Hector couldn't be sure if he had not wanted to speak of it, or perhaps had just forgotten about it for a time. Perhaps he had some reservations, some concerns about ever speaking about it again.

Initially, he had vaguely alluded to the existence of the weapon. Perhaps it was Hector's level of interest, the way his younger self's eyes had widened when he had spoken of it just a little, that had spurred his grandfather on to tell more of the story.

Ezmondia, where Hector had grown up and lived at the time, was dedicated to developing in the minds of its youth the importance of its elders. Their experience and knowledge were practically made an object of worship. So, it was to be expected that the youth would listen to and enjoy the stories of those who came before them—if not out of genuine pleasure, then out of that ingrained necessity of demonstrating respect.

His grandfather often had a cautious and concerned tone to his voice when he spoke of the magic sword. He warned Hector not to take it lightly, that it was as serious and real a weapon as perhaps any that remained in the modern world. He said it was a weapon that should only be sought if all hope was lost, only if danger, perhaps unprecedented, threatened the world, and when the spread of that danger could not otherwise be stopped.

And when the dying man had handed him the map to the sword on his deathbed, Hector thought of those long-ago words of warning and imagined that the world must have come to be a rather dark place. Because a rather dark place is what it would have to have been for his grandfather to so willingly ignite the chain of events that would bring Kazahvir's power coursing back into a new age.

The battle of wills that had ensued when Hector first grasped the hilt of that weapon had been incredible. It had been ... as if all the challenges of his life flooded his mind in a single, otherworldly instant. But Hector summoned a strength within himself, drew from the pains of a difficult life that grounded him powerfully, and fiercely defended against those spirit-splintering strikes of Kazahvir's mental assault. The onslaught of painful imagery and burning, destabilizing feelings relentlessly pounded his conscience with everything it seemed to be able to find in his mind—and when that wasn't enough, it had pulled forth even worse from the depths of its own memories, to bring him to his hands and knees.

Hector was a young man of the modern era, not nearly a match for the ancient and powerful weapon. Yet he had apparently held out well enough, demonstrating something worthy to Kazahvir. The young man's life had been riddled with difficulties and challenges, as a human life generally was. But Hector had been something more than what Kazahvir had suspected.

Kazahvir had been buried at a time long ago when the powers of the worlds were already rapidly diminishing. It did not have grand expectations for more glorious exploits than in its past—though the magic of its creation would forever compel it to seek them, regardless.

It could feel and understand the young man's thoughts, and it had a great understanding of the goings-on of much of the world by scanning through them. It knew his grandfather's unusual level of wisdom and Hector's resilience—and it could tell more clearly than he could that he was unique in the modern age. There was an awareness, a mental fortitude, a physical capability that justified the man's use as at least a temporary vessel.

Perhaps more compelling than that justification was to Kazahvir, though, was the simple fact that it very much hungered to be gone from the cave in which Hector had found it, free from that burial place it could not otherwise escape—not for some uncertain and likely vast span of time.

The sword had remained at Hector's side for years now. And it drove him, often at a subconscious level, to seek out new magic—and in general, excitement and adventure. But as a consequence, Hector could no longer find the satisfaction he previously had in many simpler, easier aspects of modern-day living. He needed more than that; it was a hungry fire that burned in his heart, ever fueled by the mysterious and long-ago magic that had forged Kazahvir. In any case, at least Hector had plenty to reflect on and think about in considering such things, and it was an effective means of fighting off the boredom that seemed to plague the general public in these modern times.

So, he didn't look to shopping or people to use up the couple hours he had to fill now. He waded with directness and purpose through the crowds, right to the vicinity of the hydromagnetic train station. But Hector didn't care to wait directly inside or on the grounds, given the debacle the previous day. Someone might conceivably recognize him, especially if he was hanging around there for hours. He went to a small local park not far away and sat on one of the public benches for the next couple hours. He read more of the journal he had swiped from the Order of Oranlak and periodically checked the time on his clonra device.

* * *

Gerrard made his way through the city to his friend Duncan's shop. He was now fully a day overdue for their planned meeting, but he suspected his friend had anticipated he might be delayed. He surely knew Gerrard had no intention of missing the meeting entirely; it was a rare happening for them to get together, after all.

Gerrard had figured Duncan would be working at his shop the following day, too, anyway—he had longstanding workaholic tendencies, and it was uncommon for him not to be there.

It was more than just a simple shop. Duncan made armor and weapons in a back section of the building, and it was all a fairly large operation.

The two had met back at a mining gig they had each signed on for many years ago. It had been a lot of work, but both had found it very rewarding, too. It had been Gerrard's first mining job, the one that got him into pursuing a lot of future work in the field.

Gerrard had been a young man experiencing a lot of challenges around that point in his life. His was a city that had many talented workers across many different fields of work. People typically had specializations and advanced degrees, and those who didn't were often still highly experienced and connected. It had been a tough time and place to be looking for work if you didn't already have a lot of experience, or connections, or something to that effect.

Gerrard had lived an independent life. His parents weren't connected, were anti-social, even, and certainly didn't have a lot of wealth between them. He had spent much of his childhood working, so he couldn't focus much on academics and school, or social circles there, either. Gerrard was gifted, though, in how he did tend to think things through well, and in the way he carefully planned things out. He was actually highly adept at reasoning through difficult situations and creating effective, stepwise solutions.

He was always working hard, and for cheap wages, back then. But the work had generally served him well enough, at least to keep up some semblance of stability in the precarious living situation that defined much of his younger years. He eventually plotted out an escape route for himself, a means to gradually crawl out of that difficult life. That life was incrementally gnawing away at his potential and his prospects in the world—and though it was so often a subtle or numb sort of suffering, he knew his future could not indefinitely endure it.

There were mines not so far from where he was living at the time, which needed new recruits. It was tough, demanding work. It was the kind usually done by young men with few attachments and responsibilities. It was perfect for people with, in a manner of perceiving it, very little in the world, who were hungry to break out of an existence that threatened to define them for the rest of their lives. And perhaps that hunger, so commonly associated with youth, was a further prerequisite for the kind of work it was.

So it came to be that Gerrard put in for a job in the mines. It took him out of the city to more remote, rural areas where the mines were located. The first company he had signed on with actually had quite extensive facilities as encampments for the workers. They were often far more comfortable and pleasant—if not somewhat luxurious, even—in comparison to whatever Gerrard's actual home was at the given time. He had met many interesting and entertaining people, too. A few of them had come to be highly decorated and accomplished figures in society over all the years that had followed since, and some of them he was even still friends with.

The travels to the mine locations brought him, and others like him, out of and away from cities that were almost impossible to compete in. In such cities, like the one Gerrard hailed from, the highest-tier candidates claimed all of the remotely desirable work. Great talent was attracted from all across Makeva to the amenities, resources, and connections those cities could offer. Everyone else outside those top percentages was left scrounging for work they didn't want and wouldn't suffer through keeping for long, even if they were fortunate enough to find it. The difficulty of those jobs was often high, and the pay, generally, could be assumed to be unreasonably low.

Gerrard went out to these mines with groups of other contracted workers. They commonly went for stints of a week or two straight, going hard every single day. They would then return home for usually a week before returning again or proceeding to a new site.

The work he did at the mines was generally for the extraction of rare or valuable elements. This was work Gerrard saw as important. Acquiring these raw materials to build the future of humanity was an admirable pursuit. And sometimes, he could even be compensated for the work with whatever it was that they were extracting, which could even be silver or gold. The coin he earned was vastly better than he would have been making with virtually anything else he figured he could realistically have been doing.

Beyond that, he wasn't ensnared by the sort of job where he had to do work that he found much less meaningful. There was a lot of work out there that Gerrard saw as doing a lot of harm to society and to the people of Gracyr, which he was thankful he did not have to try to stomach actually doing.

The food industry was such a place. The industry had grown over decades to be an overregulated, byzantine mess. It did the job of feeding people, but the quality of the food was ever descending into greater depths of unhealthiness. Unnecessary additives more about profit-making than feeding people; unnatural processed products with major health risks; unsustainable harvesting practices—it all permeated the bloated, overcentralized system that had come to be.

Historically, many citizens of Makeva were highly self-sufficient and self-reliant. Food diversity might have been comparatively low compared to more modern times, but people were generally still getting enough to eat. And anyway, even currently, world hunger was far from eradicated, despite any and all supposed advancements.

There was also intrinsic value, Gerrard felt, in being able to feed yourself, your family, your neighbors—a value in being able to do it without intervention from some vast, overcentralized source you had to rely on. He believed in the virtue of self-reliance and in personal independence. And centralized operations were breeding grounds for corruption and malfeasance that often brought enough harm to a given situation to outweigh whatever good they were purported to be doing.

Such views had led him to pursue potato farming in later years, when he was building a family and establishing a home. And such views had also led him to develop and foster friendships with people like Duncan, whom he was now going to visit—someone who had rekindled the love of swordsmanship and fine weapons, which his father and he had shared.

He, of course, had concerns about the work he did for some mining companies, too. At times, he had been contracted to work for many different companies in a short span of time. Some had certainly not been the best stewards of the land, and some had hazy interpretations of the law, which seemed likely to be legally challenged or to be just downright harmful. Sometimes working under such an entity was a sacrifice Gerrard had to make, though, in his pursuit of a greater good he hoped he was still achieving.

Over time, Gerrard was able to attain jobs more closely aligned with business practices and principles he could get on board with. He was able to be more selective and scrutinizing of employers before taking jobs. He came to largely favor working for those with the most up-to-date, state-of-the-art technology, and those that were most environmentally conscious. And he endeavored still to press those companies further in a sustainable, but realistic, direction. Many, in his view, were not necessarily good or bad but simply had good and bad elements to them, and they could all be nudged one way or another with proper incentives or disincentives.

Gerrard stepped into the weaponsmith's store, where he almost immediately encountered his old friend Duncan, at work forging something of metal.

"Good to see you, old friend," Gerrard greeted Duncan in a relaxed and benevolent tone.

"I know that voice," Duncan responded with his own low, gravelly voice. "How are you, Gerrard? Running a little later than expected, aren't you?"

"Apologies, yes," responded Gerrard. "My day yesterday took a rather interesting turn," he reflected.

Then Gerrard changed his tone, speaking in one that was more challenging and serious. "I trust that I've given you sufficient time, then?" But he flashed his older friend a disarming and genuine smile.

"Ha," laughed Duncan, quickly catching on. "You haven't changed, have you?"

"Perhaps not so much," Gerrard admitted, smiling widely.

Sometimes Gerrard could come off as gruff and more reserved, but not so much around Duncan. Seeing his old friend now had him in too uplifted of a mood to be at all cold or reticent.

"So, let's see it, Duncan. What have you for me?"

Duncan nodded dutifully. "This way." He motioned for Gerrard to follow him to another room of the store. He guided him over to a sizable safe, which Duncan hastily unlocked with palpable excitement. He removed from the safe a small treasure-chest-type box, intricately designed with overlapping gold and blue symbols. Duncan removed a small key from his key chain and handed it to Gerrard, and then handed him the chest, as well.

"You're going to love this," Duncan said, grinning.

Gerrard took the box, inserted the key, and turned it gently. He removed the cloth covering the item inside to reveal what the small box held. It was a blaster bullet, imbued with magic, glowing faintly red.

"One double-A-grade round," declared Duncan as Gerrard set his eyes upon the rare sight. "Not too many of these still around."

"No, sure aren't," Gerrard managed as he marveled at the glowing projectile. "What do … I owe you?" he also managed, after pausing mid-sentence, caught up in his amazement.

"Ahh…" started Duncan, seeming to be almost reconsidering something. "I do believe I still owe you from times past, so … we'll just say we're square after this," he finished, though the words did seem strained.

Gerrard smiled again. He had half expected as much from his old friend. Neither of them really needed the coin. They had built up the means to get along in life just fine. Of note, though, an AA bullet in the modern era was something of great rarity, and it was of incredible value. The hard labor of a person of even considerable means could likely still only afford one after many years of dedicated saving. And that was, of course, supposing you could find one to begin with.

When fired, the shell could destroy powerful defenses—perhaps even top-of-the-line defenses. Gerrard hadn't fired one in years. And he had perhaps only once ever fired one that was stronger. He looked admiringly at it for a few more moments. He wasn't one to dwell often or long on such physical, worldly things of great material value. But he did consider the immense value of the thing then, and considered how few things in the world could command such a price, how few things could be offered up in any semblance of a fair comparison. But then, he had saved the man's life, after all.

This was an additional bullet he could add to the few he had already accumulated, and he placed this one together with those in a case he carried. He could now fully load his six-shot blaster with them. Though he pondered, momentarily, the kind of mission that might necessitate a blaster fully loaded with AA rounds. He briefly entertained that this upcoming venture might be such a mission. Then he laughed aloud and sidelined his paranoia.

"Something amusing, Gerrard?" Duncan asked, smiling slightly.

"Oh, just an old man's needless worries. What of the other matter I had inquired about: news of Lucian?" he asked, to Duncan's quickly subsiding smile.

Lucian had been another old mining friend of theirs, from that same first mining trip Gerrard and Duncan had met on. The trio had become fast friends. Lucian had been at the mining game for quite a few years already before the two of them came along, though. He had also been more theoretical and experimental in his past work in the mining field. Lucian had been more of a scientist, though he lacked a formal education, and so was generally regarded to not be credible. This had the consequence of him becoming more of a general laborer in the mines, which Duncan and Gerrard, in coming to know him well, came to regard as a terrible travesty to the person he could have become. He had had a mind for it—for striving to understand more of the world, what they were doing with the resources they were extracting, and what they could be doing with them. He had even made some important discoveries that he hadn't made widely known.

"So, apparently," Duncan began, "you and I have some rather important knowledge. The last company Lucian was working for found a means of keeping him rather ... permanently quiet, and all his belongings and writings seem to have been confiscated. They may have been successful in snuffing out a source of knowledge they were terrified of the public knowing about."

After pausing a few moments, he went on. "The ensuing technology apparently really could compromise their level of power over Gracyr."

They each silently reflected on the memories they had of the process Lucian had been studying, which he'd said could lead to solving the looming energy crisis. It was a process rarely still known in the modern day, for refining crimson fluorite. In theory, it could lead to achieving the ambitious goal of solving the energy crisis, at least when combined with what Lucian had learned in his experiments. Crimson fluorite, extracted from mines, could be ground down to increase its surface area and prime it for better chemical reactions. An acidic solvent, subsequently added, could be used to separate out lutetium. It would ruin the already valuable crimson fluorite—and so was not a common or favorable process to employ.

The lutetium could be used to channel what was known in Gracyr as magic. That magic could be used to power, strengthen, or create weapons, including blaster bullets. But the grade and yield varied drastically depending on the quality of the crimson fluorite and the lutetium it happened to contain—and, of course, on the skill and proper technique of the processor.

What remained of the crimson fluorite had previously been thought to be useless waste. But Lucian had discovered a new use for that leftover substance known as verium. It was the verium that was of interest to Lucian. And it would have been to any who grasped its world-changing potential. He had discovered that the substance verium, with further refinement, could contain and withstand extremely high temperatures, even millions of degrees.

It very well could be the missing piece of the puzzle that humanity needed to finally harness the kind of power the sun employed: atomic fusion. And the potential for creating renewable, clean energy in Gracyr would be incomprehensibly improved if this knowledge could be made known to those with the means and the will to forge the technology into reality.

The problem was that very few people were investigating and experimenting with developing a means to harness the power of the sun. Those who were publicly doing so were, at least in Lucian's previous opinion, doing so as more of a façade—perhaps not even sincerely believing in or caring about the work. And many might have been awarded grants to fund their research, but even so, they were simultaneously hampered and delayed in that research. That research, Lucian had suspected, was funded to subdue members of the public who might otherwise have voiced outrage that no such research was being funded. But that research was also hindered at the same time to limit, if not halt, its progression. They were presenting an illusory image—to convey that problems were being worked on and addressed, and that future breakthroughs might yet save them from an impending energy disaster—but the true intent was for those orchestrating the grand design of it all to be able to cling to wealth and power for as long as possible.

Perhaps, if they could get this knowledge about the verium to those who would listen, who were sincere, who were not intentionally serving in such capacities, but who still had the necessary means, qualifications, knowledge, will, and access—perhaps then they could get this technology developed and this source of power harnessed.

After what felt like a long time of reflection for the both of them, Duncan decided to move away from the gravity of that weighty, unpleasant situation. He didn't have much more to offer Gerrard on their friend's status or what to do regarding it, and he didn't really want that negativity to define their long-anticipated meeting.

"So, what have you been working on recently, Gerrard?" he inquired, his intent obvious to his old friend, but not unwelcome.

The question drew Gerrard from his reflections. "A lot of interesting things, actually," he replied, his cold countenance rapidly warming.

"Well, do tell!" exclaimed Duncan.

Gerrard went on, "We've been working with these new methods at Old Guard Mining, at our newest worksite, not far from Akastair. We've been using these specially bred plants that can extract minerals and nutrients from the ground—as plants do—but these also absorb certain metals from the ground. They can be used to clean up land that has been contaminated with heavy metals from poor mining practices or other unfortunate situations of the past that have left an area desolate, barren, and dying."

He paused for a couple seconds to see if Duncan's face might display an excitement matching his own on the topic. It was there to some degree, though it was far less pronounced than what Gerrard felt. He continued, "We can then burn the plants that have accumulated those metals, and we can collect that metal from the ashes. We can even mine metals this way that otherwise we never could, because of how spread out and unconcentrated they are under the ground!" He stopped, just as his excitement seemed to hit a crescendo.

Perhaps Duncan just hadn't had time to adequately consider the implications, but he definitely seemed far less enthusiastic about it. Gerrard managed a chuckle to himself. He was a bit disheartened by his friend's response, but he also understood that he, compared to others, spent an uncommon amount of time marveling over such things. He just felt he understood what undeniable potential for the future was there.

Not overly discouraged, he went on talking about other new advancements. "We've also been working with the newest drilling techniques. We're using high-energy beams to penetrate underground, sometimes to unprecedented depths, and there is barely any of the pollution, the contamination, or the toxins that our past practices were associated with. It's incredible!"

Duncan did seem mildly intrigued at that, but he had long been mostly out of the mining scene, and he maintained more of only a passing interest. Contrastingly, Gerrard continued to feel his own excitement welling up inside him as he talked about it.

"That sounds fantastic, Gerrard. It's refreshing to see someone so enthusiastic about their work," responded Duncan, sincerely happy for his old friend. "I've heard of some of these new methods and technologies on my favorite vidscreen channels, but it's still an entirely different animal to hear about it in person from someone—especially you."

"It's all so exhilarating to think about. I'm actually surprising myself a little, with how excited I feel talking through it now," Gerrard said, his smile persisting.

* * *

In another section of the city, Regina waded through the crowds as she moved farther from where the companions had parted ways. She wound up at a predictable place—predictable, at least, to someone who knew what the focus of her studies had been back at the University of Akastair.

She had stumbled upon a local museum. And of course, museums weren't so uncommon. But this one piqued her interest in particular. This museum caught her eye because it was dedicated to a topic important to her: energy and its applications, history, sources, and future. Regina, having studied and being well-read on the topic, could not keep herself from taking a peek inside.

The fee for entry was just a few copper pieces, a small price she happily paid. Inside, some of the first things she saw were displays of what were now archaic, outdated systems. These systems had been abandoned in favor of hydropower, which now dominated energy production in Gracyr.

The development of high-transmission line networks between population-dense areas and large bodies of water had been instrumental. Sometimes, the body of water serving as the source of power was made by humans, and sometimes it was natural, but regardless of the source, the new transmission lines had been a boon to the rising popularity of hydropower in modern times.

Regina walked along a timeline exhibit, reading as she walked and pausing occasionally. It detailed the development of complex multi-lake systems, where lower-elevation water bodies were combined with higher-elevation water bodies to create energy loops.

There were models of manufactured waterfalls and other exceptional feats of engineering. The displays were impressive, and though perhaps they didn't discuss much that Regina hadn't read before, it all got her thinking again about energy systems in the current era, the history of where energy had been, and where the future of energy needed to be headed.

The incredible societal achievement that hydropower represented was clearly evident from the displays. Still, Regina reflected while walking through the museum on how necessary it was that they discover or develop something better. She knew strained and ever-less-sustainable hydropower systems were an escalating threat to the stability of their society and to the health and safety of all the people of Gracyr.

On some level, the portion of the public that was only mildly or moderately concerned fascinated her, as did that portion that was not concerned at all. Crises were already unfolding across Gracyr, but they were sparingly reported. When they were, it was rarely with any real depth or sense of urgency. She knew that was in part because it was all happening so gradually.

The climate was drier, average temperatures were up, and annual rainfall had been consistently decreasing for many years. The bodies of water used as energy systems throughout the continent were becoming less stable—less able to provide the energy needed to sustain the communities across Gracyr. And that was most particularly the case for those in Ezmondia.

The building of hydrogen-generating infrastructure had been helpful in mitigating some energy losses. Hydrogen was being more substantially adopted as a fuel source, sometimes used to produce electricity through hydrogen fuel cells at power plants. Still, developments, even in more hydrogen-friendly Makeva, were not coming along at a sufficient pace. That was something Regina clearly understood and couldn't help but dwell on as she made her way through the museum. She walked by displays of hydrogen combustion engines, something else exciting to see coming into more use, but even taken together, she knew it all far from sufficed.

She thought inevitably of her preferred energy source: geothermal. *Should I go back to that?* she wondered. She had fought for so long to gain such little ground. Despite her stellar performances in so many debates she'd participated in, and her enduring of all the hateful messages, and having had to suffer the pushback and devious propaganda from people corrupted with wealth and power, she still hadn't taken Makeva nearly as far as she knew it needed to go.

She had gone on to try her hand at something else—this sword fighting thing. She had even come into possession of her powerful magic shield. She looked it over then and smiled as she considered it. It had been a gift from her mother—something of a family heirloom, actually, and it had been time for it to be bequeathed to her. She even fancied herself at times as one of the shield maidens of old stories she had read—not that she had really read much about them or their history. But to her, they were courageous and brave and prepared to fight and defend for powerful beliefs and principles, and she could not help but be drawn in by the ideas she had of them.

The shield had been given to her years ago when she graduated from the university. Then she eventually involved herself in the sword fighting thing. She studied some fighting techniques and became fascinated—almost in love—with the idea of participating in and winning the annual sword fighting tournament the city of Nethereel was famous for. At that time, perhaps a decade or so ago, she had rekindled an interest in speaking with her grandfather about the many old stories he used to tell. Her grandfather was pleased to teach her some things and introduce her to other master swordsmen who could show her even more. She had been so grateful for that.

She had learned about Gerrard from her grandfather, too, and even studied him, to some degree. She had rare insight from her grandfather about him, because her grandfather had known Gerrard's father, so he knew the technique and tactics his boy had been trained on.

Regina came to feel strongly that she could defeat Gerrard in the tournament that had made him famous. Maybe it would help that he wasn't getting any younger, and she was perhaps some twenty years younger than him. More so than that, though, she understood his typical attacks and felt she could exploit their weaknesses. He might overbalance on certain strikes he sometimes made if he thought he wasn't going to miss. Or if he assumed the imminent success of the strike was about to end the fight. She knew she could catch him ever so slightly off guard and off balance if she invoked the magic strength of her shield to withstand the blow. She knew that, in such a scenario, she'd have a chance at beating him.

Her shield had even fallen within the parameters for an acceptable shield in the tournament's rules. Of course, that was based just on its physical characteristics. No one expected to see a magically enhanced one, and the means to test for such a thing were exceptionally rare.

But alas, she thought, *it was not meant to be.* She had fallen short in the tournament before ever securing the chance for a showdown with the reigning champion. And now, here she was, practically best friends with the man and having abandoned her aspirations of winning the tournament someday. That was okay by her, though; she could reconcile that with herself. It was far from the first time she had pieced herself back together from the broken fragments of what she had been before.

Regina dragged her mind back to the present moment. She felt so much at home here, thinking about and being surrounded by energy. Perhaps it had made her a bit reflective. The sudden immersion back into a life that she had abandoned had sent her mind reeling back across the years.

Still, she now harbored doubts about whether even the geothermal energy she had raved about was able to salvage Gracyr. Even if it were feasible technically, the will of the people was not there. For the people of Gracyr to be willing to adopt the technology, and to come to harbor the conviction needed for its success, an essential framework needed to be built. And it did not seem that mental infrastructure could be built in time—even if the actual physical infrastructure and the necessary technology could.

Gracians, she felt, needed something more.

* * *

The four companions reconvened at the hydromagnetic train station in Nethereel. Andromeda checked in at the counter with the attendant, about the schedule and pricing.

Trains ran between Akastair and Nethereel all the time, and there were more trains than usual running, given that the tournament had just ended. She purchased one-way tickets on the hydrogen-fueled magnetic train for her and her companions. She offered a ticket to each of them, and they all offered to pay, requesting the price from her.

Andromeda declined to tell them the price or accept their reimbursement, though. She had found some interesting and entertaining travel companions; she could learn much from these people. And perhaps she might even be able to call them actual friends.

The four excitedly boarded the train to Akastair. There was a tangible electricity to that excitement, encompassing and enveloping the air around and between them. It was an energy they all surely felt—though perhaps not one they could fully understand.

15

Chapter Fifteen

Mercedes sat at her desk in front of her blank vidscreen, trying to overcome her feelings of anxiousness. She was thinking through and finalizing the solutions she planned to propose to Armando. She felt she had formulated a reasonable case that she could make to him, and one that he could conceivably accept and go along with. The trouble was that she could also see him not going along with it. She ran through her thoughts and considered how she would deliver her ideas, one step at a time, one more time.

She thought about Armando's predecessor, that man who had been ancient when he died. She thought over his propaganda campaign, which had spanned decades, which had so successfully ingrained in the minds of the people in Ezmondia the importance of the elders. She considered it all in a neutral, objective sense, trying not to assign any inherent rightness or wrongness to any it. She suspected, of course, that there was a great degree of selfishness there, a natural need for self-preservation underlying it all.

Better that he would have just passed on to the next life sooner—open up some space and resources for the young, she thought as she scowled.

Still, she felt that she would not cling to life in such a way, if she ever came to be so advanced in age. In any case, she quickly returned her thoughts to the needs of the moment.

She reflected that she had this system in place that she had to work with. It was a system wherein the people were conditioned to care about—and to some degree, even practically worship—the elderly of their empire. The campaign she would propose to Armando would be to weaponize this framework that was prebuilt in the minds of the people. The campaign would tie this ingrained need to faithfully serve the elderly to what Armando wanted—or at least, to things that would lead to what he wanted.

The elders would need more people being born for them to be taken care of adequately. The current population, it would be conveyed, would not be able to fill that need. They would further convey that, when the subject population themselves entered their elderly years, sufficient human resources would not be available for them to be properly cared for, either. Not without changes. They needed to be reminded on a daily basis of this; it needed to be nearly constant. And further outcomes, which would come by extension, would be the stability of the empire and the preservation and growth of its power.

Vidscreens, program hosts, newsmakers, and beyond would have guidance from the Elite Council, and their messages and reporting would be influenced to convey certain perspectives and details to shift and ease people into the new paradigm of thinking. Some stations would be prompted to more dramatic shifts in messaging than others—some more quickly, some more extremely—but the overwhelming majority would all convey the same essential message.

Some number of dissidents in the media would be tolerated, of course. They would even be intentionally maintained. The people of Ezmondia who might harbor rebellion buried in their hearts would find in such media an outlet—something just enough to get out their frustration, to feel like there was some hope or some fight going on for what they felt. But it would just be there to blunt any thinking that they were backed into a corner—a feeling that might come to elicit more extreme responses, which could be disruptive and damaging to the empire, if not addressed. Movies would be produced, songs would be sung, poetry and books and articles would be written—and they would all be used as tools to achieve the needed outcome.

Mercedes could see it unfolding in beautiful detail, and with potentially amazing success. She couldn't help but grin as she ran her mind through it all. Then, satisfied with the proposal she had formulated, she turned her thoughts to the next solution she needed to present to Emperor Armando.

Her second issue was regarding their energy woes in Ezmondia. And she didn't actually feel that it should be the second issue at all; in her mind, it was the primary one. The current hydropower energy system that the empire relied on was faltering. They were far more dependent on it than even their neighboring country, Makeva, was. Granted, Makeva was far from capable of operating without hydropower, either, since most of its power still came from that source as well.

Ezmondia hadn't embraced geothermal energy and hydrogen fuel as much as the Makevans had, though. Of course, despite their greater embrace of them, there was still only a limited supply of power being generated from those sources, even in Makeva. And what they did produce still remained wholly insufficient overall. But Ezmondia essentially ran off hydropower entirely, plus the state of the climate was far worse in their region. They had perhaps an even greater need to pursue alternatives.

But now, the Empire of Ezmondia had an opportunity—in this alien ship they had discovered, and in the unusual substance they had discovered in and around it. The strange ship, a vessel fallen from the stars in ages past, had an abundance of this new, strange material. Perhaps the colossal ship itself had run on it when it had been functional, or perhaps it had merely been cargo. There were many questions surrounding the ship and the odd rocklike substance it carried.

Mercedes looked over at a sample of it encased in a small glass box on her desk. The scientists studying it had spoken of the incredible potential of that little black rock to provide astronomical amounts of energy. With such potential, they could resolve this escalating problem with the failing power plants and electricity outages across their empire.

The bulk of the supply of the stuff was not overly accessible. The promethium, as they had come to call it, was mostly scattered throughout the sunken ship—hundreds of feet deep in the Eastern Sea. Much of it was also scattered along the ocean floor in a large area surrounding the ship. Trips down to collect the promethium were costly, complicated, and time-consuming. The empire had designed systems to be able to retrieve it, though. And they were rapidly improving the technology and methods to reach more of it faster and more effectively.

Even if what they had already collected was all that they would be able to retrieve, there was some possibly credible speculation that they already had enough to do something to help turn the energy crisis around. But the simple reality was that there was still so much more to be had.

The Ezmondian Empire would have an absolute monopoly on the promethium. It would be perhaps the most profitable endeavor the empire had ever undertaken. It was, to many of the high-ranking elite who ran things under the supreme command of Armando, irresistible.

Mercedes, though, was more interested in the simple fact that it could solve or at least delay some of their problems in Ezmondia. She wanted better security, comfort, reliability, and stability. To have the wealth, and to have the power that wealth could purchase, might be a means to retain and enhance those things—but she still didn't feel it was power itself that was her endgame. At least, not so much as it was for Armando.

Regardless, the elite—and particularly Armando and herself—would have the sole means of saving not just the empire, but all of Gracyr, as hydropower systems continued on their inevitable path toward failure and collapse. Even those fools in Makeva would be on their knees as their systems failed, and they would turn to Armando and Ezmondia for the new energy source—unless, of course, they chose to perish instead.

Armando and she would have all the power they needed to ensure ongoing and improved stability, comfort, security, safety, unity, and peace across Ezmondia. And that peace would be further ensured by the strength of the enhanced army they could far more easily and efficiently build up.

For Armando and Mercedes, for their partners in the Order of Oranlak, and for the Elite Council, it had become all very much a matter of how quickly they could get their hands on as much of the promethium as possible.

Could it be collected quickly? Could it all even be reached?

Mercedes had to continually work on reassuring the ever-impatient Armando that in fact it could—and yes, it could be done quickly—and to do that, surely, she had to believe it herself. And that, in itself, was at times a challenging task.

They had been hard at work planning an underwater facility, and further advancements in relevant technology were constantly being worked on. Mercedes understood that if they devoted a majority of their sizeable available resources to building the underwater facility, which some of their lead scientists and engineers had proposed, that acquiring most—or even all—of the promethium was well within the realm of possibility. Compelling solutions could be put in place to guard against and reverse the energy crisis before it escalated out of their control.

They had efficient builders, a work force well incentivized to serve the empire and its emperor. And they had many people of great means, whether in wealth, knowledge, or skill, who would invest their coin or time in a chance—just a chance—to have a slice of the monopolistic power that was coming into existence, or even just an opportunity to glean some degree of favor with the powerful elites. So, they surely had the resources to carry out what needed to be done, if anyone did.

Mercedes got up from her desk and moved to the door of her office, pausing only momentarily as she considered a slight imperfection that occurred to her. But there was so much to gain, and so much potential—surely, she could justify brushing it aside.

There was a problem with some of the waste products, harmful resultant compounds that were created as a consequence of harnessing the promethium for energy. The "black dust" that was detailed by their scientists arose from the burning of promethium. But it wasn't so compelling, given the data extrapolations showing how unlikely it was to be a problem in the foreseeable future. And of course, it was all very much still under investigation, pending further review.

Endlessly so, perhaps, she thought as she grinned.

She mentally sidelined the imperfection; she did not need such doubt creeping into her mind and holding her back from what she knew had to be done. She moved confidently down that hallway of the Castle that would take her to her scheduled meeting with Emperor Armando.

If she had needed further motivation to strive for success in that meeting, it surely came in the form of another brief episode of flickering lights and fluttering power. It was an increasingly common phenomenon, even in the Castle, as power systems all across Ezmondia strained to meet demand. Mercedes pressed on down the hall. Much was at stake.

She knocked on the door to Armando's grand office with confidence. She heard his booming, deep voice call out in response, "Yes, state your business."

She responded, "It's Mercedes. With updates on those matters of concern you had."

"Yes, come in, Mercedes," came the expected reply.

She entered the large, multiroom office space. She made her way through to where it sounded like Armando's voice had emanated from. She saw him where he most often was when she visited him in his office.

She moved closer, walking past portraits on the walls. They were mostly of accomplished conquerors of ages past. Many were just of Armando's favorite predecessors, of rulers of great notoriety for one reason or another—who had reigned on the throne of Ezmondia at some point throughout its long history. In some cases, the portraits depicted someone who was both.

She walked through the library, which contained a vast collection of texts. She began to ascend the spiral staircase up to a quiet and comfortable area on the platform above, overlooking much of the office suite. Outside the large windows was a beautiful view over the city of Imadazan.

The spiral staircase wrapped around a monstrous skeleton of a bizarre creature unknown to Mercedes. But she couldn't help but regard it with great interest every time she looked upon the long-dead creature, if indeed it had once been living. Perhaps it was artificial, something from Armando's imagination. It was terrifying—even to Mercedes, who had seen so many horrors of the world—to think such a creature might have once been alive.

She had thought to ask about the creature many times, but she also understood how Armando liked to keep conversations short and to the point—unless maybe he wanted to go on about something for the sake of hearing himself talk for a time, which did happen on occasion. But he didn't often go on long tangents. He was, generally, blunt and to the point. He was quite impulsive at times, too, especially considering that he presumably had a lot of knowledge from all the books in his personal library. One would think such knowledge would lead one to be a bit more contemplative, particularly given the millions of lives an emperor's decisions impacted. She suspected that reading just a fraction of the books in the library would cause a person to consider more sides to a matter and to take longer to act than Armando generally seemed to.

Mercedes did appreciate his efficiency, though, and the man certainly kept things progressing. He was assertive and made quick, effective decisions. Maybe he just couldn't keep himself from acting rashly at times, or maybe it was just thrilling to him to be this way. Maybe he just liked occasionally smashing things to pieces so he could put them back together differently than they were before.

Regardless, things in Ezmondia had been coming along well with regard to bringing the empire more completely under his and the Elite Council's control. It all fell ever more so under that overarching umbrella. And they increasingly scrutinized and controlled the lives of those who lived there. This, Mercedes saw as having a great stabilizing effect on their society. Yes, their society truly had come to seem far more stable than one would suspect it to be, if one were just observing Armando's relatively chaotic day-to-day actions.

Fascinatingly, Armando never seemed to convey that he was fearful or worried about … well, anything. It probably helped him that he towered something like a foot over the average Ezmondian. It also made his hotheaded temperament frequently come off as more than just a little intimidating.

"What news, what updates have you, Mercedes?" asked Emperor Armando, in a voice less throaty and impatient than usual. He stood from his desk as Mercedes entered the upstairs area of his office. He seemed more relaxed than usual, calm and almost cheery.

Mercedes let her curiosity get the better of her for the moment, and she asked the long-standing question she'd had on her mind: "Might I ask first, dear Emperor, as I am hopelessly curious: what is the name of the creature this skeleton once belonged to, that your spiral staircase so wonderfully wraps around?" She spoke the words sweetly, carefully complimenting her emperor's taste.

Armando hesitated a moment, but granted her the question, and answered, "It is a beast from another world, though one very real, nonetheless. It is from the shadow realm; it is a monster known as the king of that domain—a shadow dragon." He paused a few seconds. "Now, let's hear what you have for me," and his voice adopted a tone more akin to what was typical for him.

Mercedes nodded appreciatively, then bowed her head slightly. "Emperor, on the matter of building up our military forces for the future..."

"Yes, continue," Armando urged.

"I have determined our best strategy moving forward. We will harness the mental framework that has been ingrained in the public for a generation's time and more, most intensely and recently by your immediate predecessor."

Armando nodded and continued listening.

"We have a public that reveres its elders. We shall devise a campaign to use that truth. We shall take their conditioned need to serve and care for them and intermingle it with the initiatives we want advanced. And as always, it will be done with an appropriate measure of subtlety to guard against any backlash from extreme and sudden changes. The spin will be that the best way we can serve our elders is to ensure there is a large upcoming future generation to provide the workforce needed to care for them. We'll also tie in the need for us to have people to care for those who will be tomorrow's elders—which will of course include many of those we are targeting with this messaging," Mercedes finished.

She paused, trying to remain as concise as possible and trying to measure Armando's reaction, and not push his patience with what he might regard as unnecessary details.

To her satisfaction, Armando responded, "Very good. And what of the other matter?"

Mercedes went on, "We have an increasingly concerning and obvious energy crisis on our hands." She paused a moment as the lights flickered again, then she resumed speaking. "Promethium from the alien vessel has shown promise well beyond expectations. It can be used to generate the electricity we are going to need to keep the power on in Ezmondia. Our empire will be able to run entirely on the energy generated from promethium and can be prepared to do it with plenty of time to spare, even given the most grim and pessimistic projections of our failing energy grid. It is, we can assume with great certainty, a solution to waning hydropower," Mercedes said with confidence and surety.

She continued, "This solution would also have the added benefit of enriching and empowering us in the process, with us being the controllers and sole owners of this new source of energy. We and our Oranlak partners could conceivably, and quite quickly, have an absolute hold over much more than just Ezmondia. The conquest of all Makeva seems within our grasp, should we follow this path, and so too the construction of an empire that dominates all of Gracyr."

Mercedes let the good news sink in a few moments before she continued, "There are, perhaps, a few matters to consider carefully."

"Go on," said Armando sternly, and what was a growing smile on his face now vanished.

"How deep underwater the promethium is continues to present a challenge. It is largely scattered throughout the sunken alien ship. The ship itself is also something of a maze to navigate. The promethium is, as you know, heavy and time-consuming to transport," Mercedes went on, and she took a careful breath before she continued.

"To get to it, divers need to adjust to the pressure at that great depth. They have limitations on how much work they can do within a given time frame and how long they can do it. Safety protocols will be necessary and are going to slow the extraction. They will, however, prevent what would be an unsustainable loss of our people who are performing the work. Extensive amounts of time will also be lost from needing to undergo decompression—a necessary step to return safely to the surface." Mercedes paused, but Armando just stared silently, unblinkingly back at her.

"Undoubtedly, many will still experience adverse symptoms and will need to return to the surface early to avoid costly complications." Mercedes paused again, and she shifted her body nervously as she watched Armando's too-serious face regarding her. "However, we can leverage our recent developments in underwater technologies, so as not to have to waste much time decompressing. With the underwater facility we are planning, we will still need to keep in mind a number of matters, but many concerns are able to be substantially addressed," she stated as confidently as she could, as she continued to observe Armando's splintering patience.

As her discomfort escalated, she moved to finish the too-one-sided conversation. "We can begin construction on this new facility at once, and with sufficient dedication of our considerable resources between our empire and the Order of Oranlak, we can have it up and running in just a matter of months. Workers stationed there will need relatively little training to work out of this facility—"

"Okay," interrupted Armando finally, his patience wearing thin. "Anything else on this?"

"There is a concern also, dear Emperor, about the toxic fumes that the promethium gives off as it is used up. Our scientists are unanimous and firmly confident, however, that any negative consequences to us and the atmosphere from harnessing this energy source will take many years to become a significant problem—if they ever even do. And we will have much time to study and determine solutions to this, if they are needed, in the meantime," Mercedes swiftly answered.

"Good," said Armando as he nodded and sat back down in his chair. "See to these things at once. I've got to get back to planning the eradication of this band of rebels daring to defy us in our northern region."

Mercedes saw his blood beginning to boil then, as it often did. She had known this man for years—had known him even before he had ascended to power. And that was in part how she had come into so much power herself. She appreciated Armando's rashness, his often blood-boiling temperament, which was thoroughly entwined with how successful both of them had become.

She felt it really had gotten him far in life, even if many only saw the negative aspects of such characteristics. She moved closer and placed a gentle hand on the large man's shoulder then—and it did calm him.

"You know you get those awful headaches when you work yourself up like that," she reminded him. She flashed him a suggestive and inviting smile—one which Armando seemed to take as very welcome. She leaned in closer to kiss him, but she hadn't gotten quite halfway to his lips when she felt his connect with hers. She smiled a little as he kissed her; she knew such tactics kept him calmer. Besides, it felt good to kiss him.

She guided him to the extravagant bed in the adjoining room—a room of comfort and luxury to rival any in the city—and she regarded the man she had long held a deep attraction to. She was so excited about the developments they'd made in the first segment of their meeting today that she wasn't immediately certain if the first or second segment was going to bring her the greater pleasure.

No, not immediately. But she was certain very shortly thereafter, as she felt herself melting into the warmth and strength of his body.

16

Chapter Sixteen

After a smooth, uneventful ride, the four companions stepped off the hydromagnetic train and onto the landing platform of the train station in Akastair.

Hector had been buried the entire time in the journal they had found in the mines at Waterfall Ridge. The other three had mostly just made light conversation with one another in their train car. They hadn't wanted to divulge too much information to any potential eavesdroppers about where they were going and what they were doing, so they had opted to keep the conversation that way.

There were many trains coming and going from the station in Akastair. It was a major city and transportation hub in eastern Makeva. A highly prestigious university was based there, with its flagship campus and learning facilities. Many renowned high-class restaurants and a multitude of quick-bite eateries were also popular.

Regina had a weakness for a number of those restaurants. She hoped some of her old favorites were still around. As she walked across the platform, she remembered there was a small place that specialized in burritos. She felt her salivary glands starting up, but she shifted her thoughts so as not to torture herself too much.

Many museums and large businesses were headquartered here. Plays were always going on in the evenings, theater of great quality with actors and actresses of incredible talent. Well-funded and well-maintained public parks were present throughout the city, too. There were lavish gambling establishments, dance clubs, and all manner of other ways to spend your time, if you had the coin. Akastair wasn't generally thought of as a low-cost place to be.

There were virtual reality networks you could plug into relatively inexpensively, though, where you could simultaneously unplug from whatever was bothering you in the real world and immerse yourself in one that was whatever you wanted it to be.

Akastair was also a port city, which had numerous ships always bound for and setting sail from its docks. Sometimes there were cruise liners for vacationers. Most typically, though, ships were there to transport goods between ports along the coastline of Makeva—and more rarely, sometimes also Ezmondia.

Seafood options were in abundance around the docks. There were shops with all kinds of wares—supplies, materials, food, and trinkets from all across Gracyr. There was a rich diversity of people and culture, languages and accents, from the different communities across Makeva. There were few Ezmondians—they were generally a rare sight across Makeva—but some were present. They themselves, being from so vast an empire, could be a diverse group.

Memories flooded back into Regina's mind. She had spent much of her life in Akastair, and it was a little overwhelming to be back now after so many years.

The companions walked outside and continued along, not yet making their way toward anything specific. They crossed a bridge—one of many in Akastair. Often the bridges were built over large hydropower energy sources or related machinery, and this one did not deviate from that trend. The view the bridge afforded them was breathtaking, and the four could not help but pause in admiration. Great volumes of water tumbled over a gargantuan manufactured waterfall and descended down far below. Even Regina couldn't help but stop and stare for a few moments.

There were many rivers, too, and an intricate network of walkways and bridges allowed people to walk over many of them. It was a remarkably well-planned network, and it served well to feed the hydropower energy infrastructure of Akastair. Regina couldn't help but dwell again on those systems she hadn't thought so much about in recent years as she had in years past. It had been so long since she had seen all of this—and though it all seemed largely the same as she remembered, it seemed to impress her anew.

"Regina, where is the police base of operations in the city?" asked Andromeda gently, easing Regina out of the circling memories that seemed to have ensnared her. "You've spent some time here, haven't you?"

"Yes, I have," answered Regina. "The base is a short walk down that way—a mile, perhaps."

"Excellent," responded Andromeda. "I'll go see what I can glean about what the Order of Oranlak may be up to in the vicinity, and where they may be."

Andromeda paused and regarded her companions, her eyes falling on Gerrard. "Gerrard, join me, please?" she asked with a persuasive smile.

Gerrard nodded wordlessly, not seeming to have needed the extra touch of persuasion from Andromeda. Then, though, he did ask their other companions, "Would you two go check out the docks and see what you can find of interest in the area?" Then he lifted his wrist that had his clonra strapped to it, and added, "Message us and keep in touch."

The convenient comm devices could harvest electricity from the air; they generated a charge from floating water molecules to use as a power source.

"Let's synchronize," Gerrard said, referring to the ability the devices had to sync with others to form a chat group. He pulled up the application, tapping hologram keys on a keyboard of light suspended in midair, which was projected by the device. It generated an alphanumeric sync code he read off to his companions, which they all entered to get into their new virtual room together.

A few moments later, everyone had completed the code entry, and Gerrard could see that they were all present in the chat room.

Andromeda nodded to Gerrard, then turned to her other companions. "Good luck at the docks, you two," she said, smiling.

"You two, as well," said Hector plainly, but sincerely.

A more enthusiastic, "Good luck, guys!" followed immediately from Regina.

Then Hector and Regina made their way to the docks, following old paths that Regina knew well. Hector, being originally from far away in Ezmondia, had not explored so much of Makeva as she had, and he was completely new to Akastair. Still, he determined from looking around and from the general feel of the city that there were a lot of exciting things he could involve himself in. But his focus inevitably strayed to thoughts about the woman now traveling alongside him.

Regina was intelligent; most would quickly draw that conclusion about her. Unless maybe you were trying to be quiet and not betray your team's location, Hector had to figure, given his dealings with her back in the forest. Then maybe she didn't seem so smart. When she wasn't being so impulsive, though, her voice had a feel rather like a royal shade of blue. There was a confidence there, with a well-educated and perhaps wealthy vibe to it. She seemed interested in a lot of things that didn't matter, and he got the impression that she hadn't endured the same sort of hardships and starving-to-survive scenarios that had defined much of his own life.

She was inquisitive about all manner of things. And this, as well as her obvious familiarity with the city, led Hector to confidently conclude—even before she came to outright tell him—that she had lived here and been a student here in the past.

Those details of her past made a lot of sense, especially in considering how she came across to him now. She had an analytical, scrutinizing nature, and she asked impressively insightful questions, even working with only the short, bare-bone answers he tended to give her.

It was Hector's way to be like that, though. He was a mysterious person to many, but he preferred it that way. He was often cryptic and not overly informative in his responses.

While he could argue with himself that there were reasonable grounds to trust these new "friends" of his, he still wasn't keen on being trusting of anyone. He had an untrusting, heavily guarded mindset, and was generally—in a word—skeptical. Still, he was typically pleasant and honest when he did speak. After all, he wasn't really looking for enemies either.

A short while after leaving Andromeda and Gerrard, after making their way through more of the city, Hector and Regina came upon the docks. And their arrival there prompted Regina's next question.

"So, how'll we go about this?" asked Regina of her travel companion. "Many merchant companies have their base of ops on the boardwalk here. Surely someone's seen something that'd be of interest."

"Let's go to some of these places along the boardwalk and inquire about finding work. We can see if they'll have us on somewhere. Then, we can chat with coworkers for clues about local goings-on and observe the day-to-day here at the docks," suggested Hector.

"Just some small leads might go a long way toward shedding some light on where Oranlak is and what they're up to," Regina replied, nodding. "I can schmooze with some of the locals; I have plenty to draw from, given all my past experience in this city."

Hector nodded. *This person could be very useful,* he thought. Or perhaps Kazahvir thought it for him; it was sometimes hard to tell.

He moved his thoughts over to considering what sort of work he would seek out. He concluded that his best fortunes would come from marketing himself as just a strong, young, hard-working laborer. Perhaps he could load or unload crates off of and onto ships. After all, he didn't have much of a relevant education or the specialized training to likely find much else very quickly.

Regina harbored some similar thoughts, despite having an extensive education. *What knowledge or skills do I have that I can sell these seafaring types on?* she thought, fruitlessly at first.

She ultimately determined she would focus on those qualities she possessed that could be cross-merchandised across a lot of different types of work. She was organized and responsible, personable, a fast learner, and communicative. These were things she could sell a broad scope of potential employers on, even perhaps without whatever specific experience they might initially be looking for in a candidate.

She announced the overview of this determination to Hector, though he hadn't really asked. They both agreed to go off and sell any potential employers on what aspects of themselves they could and see what they could accomplish over the next couple hours.

Hector walked by a group of people starting to unload a ship that, by the looks of it, had just docked. He addressed one of the men, presumably a crew member, who had just moved a large crate off the vessel. They didn't seem to be a large company or operation; perhaps they would be fairly simple to engage with and get involved with for a short time.

"Excuse me, sir," Hector said respectfully. "I'm looking for some short-term work, perhaps at the docks here—do you need any help?"

"Ahh. See the cap'n about it o'er there… Just maybe we're to be usin' ye," the gruff, older man responded.

Hector glanced in the direction the man indicated, and then looked back to him. "Thank you," he said appreciatively.

The older man had motioned to a space nearby the docked ship, where several people were organizing crates. Hector couldn't be sure which was the captain, but he proceeded to the designated spot. He heard the crew joking lightheartedly as he approached. They seemed a lively and energetic bunch, and Hector found himself intrigued. *Where did they come from, and what are they unloading?* he wondered, against the background din of seagulls, the wind, and the ocean waves.

He halted when he was close enough to speak to them and to have garnered their attention.

"Hello there. Good day," Hector pleasantly greeted them. "Is the captain of this ship among you?"

A woman with golden-blonde hair spoke up in reply, with the short kind of answer he might expect from himself.

"She is," the woman said in a neutral but slightly questioning tone. She stopped her work and regarded him more fully. She saw a strong, muscular young man in his mid-twenties, carrying on his hip a remarkable longsword and standing at a height similar to her own. He had dark and longish hair, though it was well shorter than hers.

The response left Hector wondering where he wanted to take the conversation next. *Is this the captain?* he wondered. He opted to clarify his own position before attempting to understand hers further.

"I'm looking for work," he said. He paused a moment and added, "I'm new to the city."

The woman adjusted her black hat, a type common among privateers and independent sailors of the region, and she regarded Hector again. "What manner of work you lookin' for?" she asked, letting a drop of interest seep into her tone.

"I could do some of this heavy lifting," he returned, gesturing to the crates.

"Grand, that'd be just swell. Crane for unloadin' at our docks, she's busted today, an' we're down a few hands," she replied. "What's yer name, sir?"

"Hector," he answered.

"Right, Hector," she said as she approached him and extended her hand. "We'll see how yer doin' with what we give ya."

Hector shook her hand. He immediately noticed the firm grip of that calloused hand, something that surely helped her in fostering the respect she no doubt commanded in this crew—if she was, indeed, its captain.

She seemed to stare hard at him as they shook hands, as if taking a measure of him. "I'm Cap'n Saoirse. This'll be yer trial. We may be havin' use for ya, if ya can prove yerself."

Hector nodded appreciatively and did his best to come off strong and confident. Then he proceeded to get in line with the crew boarding the ship to remove another round of crates.

After several back-and-forth trips, he stopped a moment to message Regina that he'd landed a job and he would update her again in a few hours. He then recommitted himself to his efforts in transporting the heavy crates off the ship.

After some time of lifting and carrying the heavy crates, he came to consider that he was not sure whether there would be any payment for this "trial" he was going through. His primary concern wasn't even whether he would actually be paid, though; it was more a matter of how he might seem suspicious to the captain and crew if he wasn't worried about it. *Perhaps I should bring payment up,* he thought. But then he thought better of it. Better that he just stay the course and focus on doing his best work.

So, he shrugged it off. And he took this as an opportunity to make an investment of his time and effort, to achieve goals well beyond any monetary gain he might've secured. He needed information. And though he was not opposed to making profit in the meantime, that wasn't a top priority.

The work of moving the crates was simple, though physically demanding. Some of the crates even necessitated him teaming up with a member of the ship's crew to be able to move it off the vessel. Hector thought more than once to start in with some light questioning about recent happenings and goings-on at the docks, and about what the crew had seen in their recent travels to and from here. Ultimately, though, each time he considered it, he talked himself out of it.

So, he kept his remarks light and friendly and as noninvasive as possible. He was building something with this group, something he felt could be of great potential—even though he couldn't be sure it was all going to advance him in the direction he wanted to be going.

Hector's mind wandered as he engaged in that mostly physical work. He found himself reflecting on his persistent hunger to seek adventure and excitement and thrills, and how that was only amplified by the insatiable Kazahvir. He knew he was hungry in a way that many who'd come of age in the same times he had were not.

That hunger did come with pangs of impatience that would echo internally through him at times, but he did well at masking any outward signs of them now to the crew. Kazahvir was constantly pushing to have results and tangible progress—for everything to always be progressing. But such was not always possible, and he did his best to temper the sword.

Fortunately, despite such great and magically imbued feelings in the ancient weapon, the centuries had still shown it the value and necessity of patience. The sword knew to sometimes bide its time and lay out many small steps, inching incrementally closer toward the ultimate ends it sought to achieve.

17

Chapter Seventeen

Gerrard and Andromeda made their way to the base of operations building that housed the authorities of Akastair. It was an immense and beautiful structure, a grand edifice of a building. It was clean and neat and surrounded by fountains and waterworks that, beyond their visual appeal, were also important aspects of the hydropower system that served as its energy source.

It almost imparted to an onlooker a feeling of powerlessness. Who would dare to challenge such a breathtaking and beautiful place? What could stand against the fortified and solid masterpiece that this building was? And what of the body of people capable of running it? Who would defy the law and risk the level of justice they could bring down upon you?

Regardless of such compelling questions, it was of course the case that many still did, and Andromeda and Gerrard understood that. They had been alive long enough and come to understand humanity well enough that they knew that much. But they also had to reason that it must be far fewer than otherwise would, had not that awe-inspiring edifice existed in the heart of the city of Akastair.

Akastair was a shining example, if statistics were adjusted for its massive population, of safety and security in the modern world. The police force was well equipped and well supported to handle crime in the city. And it was highly adept at keeping its citizens out of harm's way—or, if necessary, at bringing accountability to those who transgressed the law.

The duo moved inside the building, admiring the sparkling inner beauty and cleanliness of the place. State-of-the-art technology was evident throughout the main entry chamber. It spanned from the large fountain in the center, which was intricately intertwined with the hydropower energy system the place ran on, to the most updated versions of the best vidscreens currently on the market, which were mounted on the walls.

Behind thick panels of glass, they observed a middle-aged man sitting at a desk in the atrium. They advanced slowly toward him. He reached up a hand and signaled to the pair to approach. They moved a little less cautiously forward.

The spacious room was mostly empty and quiet. There was a slight echo that rang off the middle-aged man's voice when he finally spoke to them. "How may I help you?" he asked. He spoke in a stern, all-business voice.

"May we see the books on current bounties in the area?" Andromeda asked.

The man behind the glass panels motioned to a table off to the side. "You can find those right over there at that table, and we welcome your assistance if you can help us bring some of them to justice. Are you licensed as bounty hunters in our city?"

"We're not," responded Gerrard, "but it does seem like you are doing a rather fine job keeping the city safe without us," he remarked, in reference to the city's top-rated safety profile.

"Well, we appreciate that feedback kindly, sir," responded the officer.

"Any trouble at all around here in particular as of late?" inquired Andromeda.

"Oh, it's all been quite typical, I'd say, miss… in the city here, anyway," he answered.

"Trouble … somewhere close by?" pressed Andromeda, perhaps sounding a little too hopeful.

The officer paused a moment, perhaps catching something odd about the eagerness with which the question had been asked. "Nothing to be too concerned about, I would say. Though there has been an uptick in criminal activity and lethal encounters with law enforcement in our neighboring city of Serazema."

Andromeda and Gerrard glanced at each other. Andromeda looked back to the officer and said, "Thank you, Officer. We'll take a look at your bounty books."

The pair then moved over to the indicated table and began flipping through the books stacked atop it. Gerrard hadn't reviewed the bounties here regularly—not for years now. But he still observed what he took as a typical number of listings, compared to what he had seen in years past. Many of the entries were solved or closed cases, and nothing was striking either of them as extraordinary or very unusual.

It did seem that they might be able to make good coin if they wanted to spend some time bounty hunting over in Serazema, though. They briefly discussed the matter before returning to the officer.

"We'd like to register as bounty hunters in the area. My license is long expired, and I believe Andromeda is new to the profession," Gerrard said, casting a questioning glance over her way.

She nodded.

"Very well, sir," responded the man behind the glass. He slipped paper applications across his desk and under the glass panels to them, then he quoted the necessary fees for licensure.

A short while later, Andromeda and Gerrard walked out of the Akastair Authorities Base of Operations, discussing how to best proceed.

"We can try it a few days, few weeks, see what comes up," offered Gerrard.

"Sounds reasonable enough," agreed Andromeda. "Think it may be best to find quarters here, and just commute to this neighboring city where the action is—this Serazema?"

"Probably better to put up the coin and reside here, yes. I'd prefer to deal with the commute, rather than spend more time in crime-ridden Serazema," replied Gerrard. "Though I suppose it would give us more time for our research and investigations to not be wasting so much of it commuting," he added, challenging the course they were fast settling on.

Andromeda wasn't sold on the idea. "Yes, well, I suppose you can select the location where you'd like to reside and that you think would be best, and I'll just do the same," she teased.

Gerrard felt his lips crease in a slight smile, but didn't otherwise immediately respond. All the saved time in the world wasn't going to help if it got him killed, he reasoned with himself. But his internal deliberations went on for a few moments all the same. He didn't necessarily just want to take the easy way out, either.

Andromeda mused about how he actually seemed to be debating with himself about it. She figured she'd interrupt him so he could just leave it at his original impulse, sparing him from talking himself into risking his life trying to live there.

"This hasn't taken us so long a time. Let's get something to eat," Andromeda said, and flashed a warm smile to restart the stalling conversation. "There seem to be many viable options around. We can do more strategizing before we meet back up with Regina and Hector," she added, hoping she hadn't come across too sharply to her companion.

"Sure," Gerrard agreed, deciding he was thankful for the excuse to halt his internal debate.

They continued on along the walkways of downtown Akastair, over more bridges and past several small, manufactured waterfalls. The mist from nearby waterpower systems sprayed lightly in the air, feeling pleasant on this late summer afternoon in the otherwise dry heat.

"Do you want to pick a good place to eat?" asked Andromeda conversationally.

Gerrard laughed a little. "That is a responsibility I think I can handle."

Andromeda smiled and laughed, too. The feeling faded quickly, though, and she asked, "How do you think Regina and Hector are faring?" as thoughts of them interrupted her mirth.

"They do seem to be highly capable—even taken alone, never mind together," he offered.

"Hopefully, Regina is working on getting Hector to be a little more conversational," Andromeda said, her smile returning.

"I'm sure she's capable of getting him to open up a bit more," Gerrard said reassuringly.

Andromeda stopped suddenly and practically darted into a restaurant that the pair of them nearly walked right by. He followed after her on impulse, and so suddenly, he didn't even think to check the name of the place before he'd jolted inside after her.

* * *

Regina ran through a few basic interview questions she had in her mind, from what felt like a lifetime ago. She meandered around the docks and boardwalk, looking for options as she did so.

She thought through milestones of past projects and jobs, about her education, about instances she'd worked with a team, and about other matters of that ilk.

There were markets selling all kinds of seafood—scallops, crabs, lobsters, haddock, swordfish, and more. Restaurants advertised fresh, delicious seafood. There were business fronts for merchant ship operations, which included large multi-ship enterprises and smaller single-ship entities. There were general stores and farm stands nearby, and a few armorers and swordsmiths littered the greater area, as well.

Regina didn't know much about food preparation or working with seafood. She also didn't know much about sailing, or merchant ships, or their accounting or business operations. She scanned through memories of electives she had taken back at the university, and she momentarily regretted foregoing others that would have been more useful to her at the moment. She wasn't an armorer or weaponsmith, either. And although the work intrigued her, she doubted she would be that effective in those areas, even if she had pursued them earlier in life.

She didn't feel very effective then, as if she had taken incorrect paths, as if she'd not appropriately acted to prepare herself. Her thoughts surged toward the cause of justifying the course she had taken through her life.

Regina reconciled with herself after several minutes of aimlessly pacing around, caught up in those thoughts. She eventually reassured herself that the path she'd taken was the one that harnessed the strengths and innate abilities she had been born with. Still, that was little immediate consolation to her now. She needed to find a job in this place that seemed so far removed from what she had done with her life.

Then Regina came upon something that struck her as a possibility. She halted dead in her tracks on the boardwalk. She contemplated the potential of the place as she read the name of the business again, and she looked over the building and its surrounding location. It was a pub and restaurant called Seaside Sprite. There were other restaurants and pubs around, but the elaborate artwork of the storefront of this one caught her attention, so she found that her thoughts dwelled on this one a little longer than on others. She came to see the opportunity this sort of establishment, which she had been overlooking, could offer. *This is something I can work with,* she thought as her excitement escalated.

Regina figured this one would be as good as any for her purposes, and she headed inside. As she moved through the doorway into the air-conditioned coolness, she continued to consider the opportunities that would be presented to her if she worked here. People would be coming and going all the time from all sorts of places, other ports and places all over Gracyr. A few potent drinks at the bar would surely loosen some lips, too. Yes, she could conceive of the place serving as quite an effective information-gathering operation for her.

Inside, she let her eyes scan the interior. She continued to feel she could learn a lot about the goings-on of the general area from working here. There hadn't been any signs calling for help needed or anything along those lines, but surely, the owner would be of a mind to always want to hire good talent when it came along. And Regina could spin herself, market herself that way.

From the front of the restaurant section, Regina watched the bartender skillfully making some alcoholic concoction for a patron at the bar. She thought about how, while she wasn't highly experienced at complicated drink mixing like that, it wasn't as if she had never done it. She actually questioned if she could even retain her sanity in the modern world without occasionally partaking of something alcoholic, if only to periodically distance herself from the often frustrating reality she lived in.

She was also a fast learner, and she was many of the usual adjectives useful for such a server of customers—friendly, personable, communicative, and outgoing, too, at least when she wanted to be.

Regina looked over at the bar and felt she could envision herself there, doing that work. She ran her hands through her hair and neatened it quickly. The place was impressively clean and seemed either new or recently remodeled. It was bustling with people, and the din of excited customers chattering about all manner of things permeated the place. Servers and waitstaff moved with speed, focus, and efficiency, moving around between tables and the back kitchen.

"Just yourself for the dining room, miss?" came a young woman's voice, interrupting her contemplations.

"Oh, no, thank you. I was actually wondering, is the hiring manager in today?" Regina asked courteously.

"Yes, actually, I believe he is. Let me see if I can fetch him. I'm not sure we're hiring at the present time, though," the hostess replied.

"Ah, I see," Regina said, but then pressed on. "Would you see if he does have a moment, though, all the same?"

"Sure, miss. It may be just a few minutes," the young woman responded, then started off toward the kitchen.

"I'll ... be over at the bar, thank you," Regina said as the hostess left her.

Regina closed in on a seat at the bar. She sat down quietly, taking the measure of her surroundings. The bar looked to have an extensive inventory of liquors, mixers, enhancers, and flavors. So many ingredients were going to make for a vast number of combinations and many different drinks to learn to make.

There were conversations happening between patrons at the bar and all around her, but nothing she heard struck her as immediately interesting.

The bartender also seemed to be keeping quite busy, juggling a few different customers. Regina couldn't help but think how a little time working at this place would certainly afford her the information she was looking for.

The bartender interrupted her thoughts. "Good afternoon. Would you like a food menu, miss?" asked the kind-sounding man, who appeared to be just a little older than her.

"Yes, I'll look one over, thank you," she replied, hesitating a moment as she dragged her thoughts back to the present.

The gentleman promptly handed one to her. "The soup du jour is clam chowder, and we have a few specials written on the blackboard there," he said, indicating a large blackboard hanging on the wall just over the extensive liquor selection. "May I get you anything to drink for now?"

Regina ordered one of the lower-percentage options from the available drafts. She wanted to be pleasant and engaging, but not really intoxicated. The bartender was back with her drink in short order, despite stopping off to capture an order from another customer along the way.

Regina thanked the bartender, then asked him after receiving her drink, "How's working here?" And she flashed him a friendly smile.

"It's a living, miss," he responded simply, though he returned her smile. "I'll check in with you in a bit to see if you would like something else, or feel free to flag me down."

Regina nodded as the bartender moved on to another customer, who appeared about ready for a refill on whatever the dark, frothy drink he was enjoying was.

She looked around to get a better sense of the atmosphere of the establishment. The lighting was on the darker side, but it was comfortable—soothing, even. The lights on and around the bar weren't too bright, either, but still bright enough to see what you were doing as one of the bartenders, she figured. From what she heard around her, the tips seemed to be coming in well enough. The clothing of many of the clientele also suggested a degree of affluence for most of the customer base—but surely there was a diverse blend of people with different backgrounds present.

Regina regarded her clonra device for just a moment, checking the time.

Another person approached her then, an older man with a raspy voice.

"Excuse me. I'm told you wanted to speak with me? I am the hiring manager here at the Seaside Sprite," the man said.

"Yes!" Regina replied, a little more loudly than she had intended. "I mean, yes, thank you," she said more quietly.

"How can I be of service to you?" The man stood on the shorter side for males, though easily still taller than Regina. He was perhaps in his sixties, with a fair amount of gray creeping into his otherwise light brown hair. He reminded Regina slightly of her grandfather.

"This is a lovely establishment you have; I'm really enjoying the atmosphere and the pleasantness of your staff," she started. "I went to the University of Akastair, actually, here in the city, many years ago. I'm finding that I'm really enjoying being back in the city—more so even than I would've expected."

"Many years ago?" the older man interrupted, though with a disarming smile. "I must confess, I do doubt that it was so many years ago, miss." It was an obvious reference to her young age.

Regina accepted the compliment with a knowing smile. "Thank you," she replied. "Anyway, I do appreciate and value your time, and I'm sorry to have gone off on a tangent there with all my banter. The short of it is that I've decided to stay here a little longer than I'd planned, and I'm looking for a short-term employment opportunity around the docks here. In enjoying your bustling operation here this afternoon, I cannot help but think it an ideal place to experience this fine city and its people. Wouldn't you agree?"

She'd backed the hiring manager into something of a corner, as it was a question he could not answer in the negative without criticizing his own workplace. But he also wasn't looking to hire anyone. Regina flashed a convincing smile at the manager.

"Well, I suppose I would have to agree with that much, at least," came his watered-down reply. "We aren't really looking to hire anyone, though."

Regina intentionally let her smile slip, let her countenance slide into something conveying disappointment. And to that, the manager did seem responsive.

"But as you can see, we are keeping quite busy, sometimes struggling a bit to keep up with the demanding influx of customers lately. And I suspect you are experienced in the realm of restaurant work," the manager said.

The young woman's talent at conversation, and seeming comfort with the atmosphere, had guided him to an incorrect assumption. It was so funny, Regina thought then—the assumptions, the poorly connected associations one could be coaxed to make. Leverage a strong talent, and it was amazing how one might think you were an expert on a subject that was so unrelated. To the man's credit, though, he went on with a further question for her.

"Have you worked as a bartender before?" the manager asked.

"Well, no, not so much," replied Regina, honestly. "But," she said, perking up, "I'm quite fast at learning new things, and I'll be a dedicated server of your customers. And I notice your bartender on duty now is quite the multitasker—and I can certainly say the myriad of extracurriculars I juggled with all my classes back at the university were quite effective at molding me into the seasoned multitasker I am today."

"Back at the university, so many years ago?" he joked lightheartedly again.

Regina smiled back knowingly, catching his point. "Not so many years ago," she said, cleverly rephrasing her previous words.

A short while later, an update from Regina appeared in the clonra chat room the companions shared. She had secured gainful employment with a local business, and she was on her way to meet back up with Hector.

18

Chapter Eighteen

Andromeda and Gerrard were just finishing up their meals at a cozy local eatery when the message came through from Regina, with her excited update.

"That was scrumptious," said Andromeda, swallowing the last bite of her meal. "It's perfect timing for Regina to come through with an update, too."

Gerrard nodded. "Let's go meet her and regroup," he said.

The pair departed the restaurant moments later, as the sunlight was fast fading from the western horizon. They made their way back to where their group had split up. Andromeda and Gerrard reconvened with Regina a short while later.

"How did it go?" Regina asked when she saw Andromeda and Gerrard approaching.

"Well, you're looking at two newly licensed bounty hunters!" exclaimed Andromeda.

"Oh, very prestigious, you two!" Regina teased lightly.

Andromeda smiled. It was good to see Regina again; she was growing rather fond of her and her other new companions. She returned Regina's slight teasing. "That's right. And what, may we ask, have you managed to accomplish?" She let a skeptical tone creep into her voice.

Regina couldn't help but break out with a bit of laughter, catching on to Andromeda's obviously fake skepticism and blatant teasing. It proved infectious, as Andromeda started laughing along with her.

Gerrard shook his head, understanding, but not participating. "Just tell us, Regina: what is this new job you're all excited about?"

"I'm sure," Regina said, beginning her announcement, "that you'll both be excited to know, I've landed a job as a bartender at the Seaside Sprite!"

It didn't sound particularly impressive as a means of employment, generally speaking, though neither of them was familiar with the Seaside Sprite. Regina's cause for excitement was mostly lost on them at first. It did sink in a few moments later though: the bartender position would afford her a great opportunity for information gathering. Her excitement did still seem a tad overblown, but it didn't seem so misplaced after considering it in that light.

Regina could tell the two of them weren't sharing in her excitement, but she suspected they'd come around eventually. She shifted gears and turned the conversation over to them. "Any useful leads from the authorities?" she asked.

"Not so much," answered Gerrard.

Andromeda cut in, "No … but we are thinking we'll likely learn some useful information in pursuing our new line of work over in Serazema."

Regina's face sobered a bit at the mention of the crime-ridden place. It had long been dangerous over there, and she could not imagine it had improved much in the years she had been away. "Dangerous place," she stated, "at least, as far as my memory serves."

"We are open to your alternative suggestions, Regina," remarked Gerrard dryly.

Regina smiled. "I'm sure the two of you highly capable fighters will fare just fine, even over there," she said sincerely.

"Glad to have your support," Gerrard responded firmly, his face creasing with a slight smile.

"What of Hector?" Andromeda asked, looking to Regina.

Regina shrugged and offered her empty palms upward. "He was checking the docks and boardwalk for local jobs. The last I heard from him was that same message he sent us all."

Just then, the group's clonra devices indicated the receipt of a new message by sounding a familiar alert tone. It was Hector, who had messaged the group simply, *On my way.*

"Oh, good," remarked Andromeda. "I'll message him back. 'See … you … soon,'" she spoke as she typed the message into the clonra's hologram keyboard.

"We should seek out an area hotel, grab some vacancies somewhere for the evening," said Andromeda when she'd finished typing the message to Hector. "And we should consider what longer-term arrangements we can make regarding our housing situation," she continued.

"We can rent a place!" Regina chimed in suddenly. Some pleasant nostalgia from her dorm room days was coming back to her, and she couldn't help but consider that Andromeda held great potential to be an entertaining roommate.

Andromeda smiled and said, "Yes, we'll have to give that some thought, too, I suppose."

Then Gerrard spoke up. "I saw a place back that way where we could probably get by for a night. Unless maybe you have something else nearby in mind, Regina?"

"I believe you're referring to the Regal Residential Inn," Regina said. "I think that'll be just fine for the evening. Those places have lots of rooms and hardly ever sell out, unless some big music artist or someone is playing the arena."

"Let's head over," said Gerrard. "Could you message Hector and let him know to find us there?"

"On it!" responded Regina.

The trio journeyed over to the Regal Residential Inn. They walked in together, and Gerrard approached the front desk first.

"Do you have any rooms available for tonight? Perhaps a large one for a group of four, or a couple smaller ones?" he asked.

"We have smaller rooms available, each with a bed and a fold-out sofa bed," responded the hotel deskman.

Gerrard looked back at his companions. "I'll grab a couple rooms for us. One you two can share, and one for Hector and me."

"Sounds like a plan!" responded Regina cheerily. "And also, on another note … have you two eaten? I'm starved!"

"We have," said Gerrard, turning back to finish his business with the inn staffer.

"It looks like they do have a small restaurant over there, if you want to grab something," offered Andromeda.

"Yes, I think that's a wonderful idea," said Regina, already salivating as she considered the option.

Gerrard reviewed the particulars with the gentleman manning the desk. He offered his coin card for payment. It was a small, flat, rectangular card linked to one of his accounts. The cards were commonplace in Makeva and could be used to spend one's coin electronically, and more conveniently than carrying satchels of heavy metal with you.

"The payment has processed. Please, everyone, hold up your clonras, and we can link them to your rooms," the man said. Then he scanned the trio's wrists. He offered Andromeda and Regina a five-digit number to enter into their devices to synchronize with their rooms. He provided a different number to Gerrard.

"Upon our friend Hector's arrival, please assist him. He will be in the same room as me," said Gerrard to the staffer, who nodded.

"All right, let's plan to get together over at that restaurant in the morning for breakfast before we head out. We'll meet there at eight a.m. and do some further planning before we depart," suggested Andromeda.

"Sounds good," said Regina.

Gerrard nodded.

With that, Andromeda and Gerrard headed to their respective rooms for the night, and Regina walked over to the restaurant to find some grub to tide her over until morning.

* * *

Hector came along a while later, feeling more exhausted than was usual for him after the day of heavy lifting. He was no stranger to manual labor, but he was thankful the day was behind him all the same. He stopped at the front desk for his clonra sync and to get some direction from the staffer.

He was pleased to learn that the charges for the rooms had been covered, as he wasn't any richer since his job hadn't paid him anything yet. At least they had invited him back in the morning. *Though I'm not sure I even want that invitation,* he thought to himself as he considered his sore and tired body.

He headed up to the room. He found Gerrard still awake inside, flipping through channels on the vidscreen.

"Trouble deciding ... what to watch?" asked Hector, between pangs he felt from his aching body.

"Oh, it all just seems a bit repetitive and gloomy to me lately. There isn't much new material these days that I take as being very uplifting, I suppose," admitted Gerrard.

Hector nodded. He didn't disagree with Gerrard's appraisal. Uplifting and empowering programming was not on the rise in Gracyr. Such programming did not serve the ends of those who controlled the content, of those who clung pathetically to their undeserved power over the common people. Uplifting programming—things that taught about what was beyond the moment, beyond the material—was dangerous to those puppeteers. After all, a person could be far more easily controlled when all they cared about was worldly, physical things, and when they only cared about what was happening to them right then.

In Makeva, it was far and away better than what Hector had seen back in Ezmondia, though. Makeva was a long way from being so hopelessly lost. Just not as far as it used to be. Really, it probably worked against them there in Makeva, he figured. To be able to so easily point to somewhere where it was so much worse—it seemed to Hector it was demotivating to the Makevans. Though, of course, many were naïve to conditions in Ezmondia, anyway. But so often it was that very fact—that it was so much worse somewhere else—that defeated the argument that action needed to be taken to fix what was going wrong in Makeva.

Hector wondered if Gerrard harbored such a transcontinental understanding. It was surely a rarity in Makeva. Not many born in Ezmondia ever got out. Either way, he could appreciate that Gerrard possessed a longer memory than him. Granted, of course, he had some fragmented memories of many things before his time—courtesy of Kazahvir.

Gerrard was perhaps twice Hector's age, and Hector could easily entertain that there was value in the fact this companion could offer a much longer timeline of experience than his own lifespan could.

It got him thinking about those long-lost virtues of yesterday, like self-reliance. And about personal independence. And about how the individual character of the common person had been so regrettably devalued in these dark times. He suspected the public of many yesterdays past had such things ingrained in them—that they were taught to value them on a level not typically seen in the modern era. So many of the things of yesterday were now, at best, transmogrified, twisted abominations of what they once had been.

Hector easily imagined an eventuality wherein Gracians would destroy themselves, in all the ways that truly mattered. But he harbored doubt in his heart that it could all truly come to pass—that the forces he sometimes felt spurring him on to fight against it could ever possibly be defeated. And even given all the dark places his mind had been, having suffered the pain of struggles spanning centuries untold through Kazahvir's sentience, this eventuality was a place of darkness his heart could not reach.

"How's the job?" Gerrard asked suddenly, and Hector was drawn rapidly from his deep contemplation.

"Job," Hector echoed, and scoffed at that definition of what he had been doing all day. "Well, suffice it to say, maybe I shouldn't call it that yet."

Gerrard interrupted his channel flipping, looked over at Hector, and raised an eyebrow. "I was hopeful Regina might have made some progress in addressing that cryptic manner of speaking you have," he remarked.

Hector consciously considered it for a moment, and then did grant him a smile. "They just haven't paid me yet is all. Doesn't make me feel like the employment is too official yet," he clarified.

Gerrard continued to regard the younger man curiously. "It doesn't look to me like you performed any shortage of work this afternoon," he observed, clearly in reference to Hector's obvious tiredness and dirty, sweat-stained clothing.

"Yes…" Hector conceded. He felt he was likely to be chided by the older Gerrard, but to his surprise, Gerrard responded differently.

"You know how to make a short-term investment for a longer-term gain. That's admirable," the older man said.

Hector thought that assessment of his particular situation a little gracious, perhaps overly kind, and thought to scan Gerrard's mind with Kazahvir for some hidden intent. He thought better of it, though. Such an action would spur him further down his usual avenue of distrust and dislike for people, and he had decided he was going to try to like and trust his new companions, at least as far as he could convince himself was reasonable. Such a scan wouldn't afford Hector anything at the depth of really reading Gerrard's mind in any case. It would more so yield ideas of general intent or potent emotions. Besides, maybe Gerrard would even be able to detect such an attempt from Hector. He couldn't see that scenario playing out particularly well, and it wouldn't serve as much of a trust-building exercise, either. Plus, Gerrard was essentially a living legend of the sword and the arena; he wielded a large, powerful, magnificent sword, and by all accounts, he did so exceptionally well.

No, he resolved with himself. He moved to take a shower and get some sleep, though he also silently berated himself for not thinking to grab something to eat before he headed up to the hotel room. *No matter,* he thought. *I'll be asleep soon anyway, and won't notice the pangs of hunger in my stomach for very long.*

And he accepted that solution readily, it already being one he had employed countless times before.

***

In a nearby room, Andromeda and Regina excitedly shared stories of past exploits. Andromeda found herself often enthralled by the stories and accomplishments of the younger woman, who had lived a life perhaps fully ten years shorter than her own. Regina detailed her years at the University of Akastair. She talked about countless speeches she had given, generally advocating for harnessing new or underused technologies in the energy sector.

Andromeda appreciated Regina's visions for the future, how the gears of her mind rapidly turned with thoughts of the possibilities of tomorrow. And Andromeda reveled in her own thoughts about how she might further unlock and enhance the capabilities of that brilliant mind and set them loose upon the world. She was fascinated with how Regina challenged what she saw and believed, almost constantly. She seemed to have come to rebuild herself anew many times over, over many years across a relatively short life.

"This way you have of always challenging yourself and what you think you know—that's admirable in a world where people so often spend their lives believing things they never challenge," said Andromeda at one point.

"I appreciate that," Regina responded, "but I also have appreciation for those who are trusting in things all throughout their life, who don't sway from them erratically, like I feel I do sometimes."

"Well said," Andromeda replied, "but it strikes me as just as important to challenge things, to strengthen those beliefs."

"Sure," Regina acknowledged. But with insight reaching well beyond her years, she went on, "You would save yourself so much trouble and effort to just believe or trust from the start, though, to not waste all that time and energy questioning whatever it is." And in so saying, she did seem to be criticizing, of all people, herself.

"I suppose, so long as what you believed in at the start was entirely right," Andromeda noted.

Regina smiled and seemed to concede the point. "So, what's the plan moving forward?" she asked, trying to bring them back to the matter at hand. "Not going to be letting the guys decide it all, are we?" she said, smiling and challenging her female friend.

“I think we can lay out some ideas,” answered Andromeda. “We could look into renting a house here in Akastair, maybe on the side of the city closer to Serazema.”

“Yeah, that’ll work!” responded Regina, thoroughly thrilled with the idea of having roommates again. Memories of humorous misadventures from her old university days were flowing back to her. “Within the city limits, we’ll still be under the protection of the authorities here, and it’s much less expensive in that area than in a lot of others.”

Regina excitedly went over to the vidscreen and flipped it on. She scanned through the channels until she settled on a familiar and relevant one. “They detail a lot of the local real estate on this channel,” she said, turning the volume up. Vidscreens were highly interactive devices, and Regina checked and swiped through many options on the touchscreen. The different options were essentially channels within that primary channel. She was seeking one that would provide the specific material she was looking for—material maximally relevant to their current situation. Then the two watched the eventual subchannel she landed on for a brief while, one which showed houses to rent or buy in the segment of the city they were interested in. They saved several listings as notes in their clonras, to investigate them further and to pitch them to the guys sometime soon.

* * *

The four companions got back together at the ground-level restaurant the following morning.

“G’ morning, everyone!” Regina greeted them.

“Good morning,” repeated Hector, less emotionally.

Andromeda looked skeptically to Regina then and inquired, “I thought you said you were working on him?”

Regina flashed a knowing smile, and they both laughed. Hector looked to Gerrard, who offered him a shrug.

"Let's just get something to eat," Gerrard said. And that did sound good to Hector; he was still hungry from the missed meal last night.

Midway through breakfast, Andromeda began her pitch to the team. "So, everyone, I don't think any of us aspire to spend any great amount of time living out of hotel rooms. If all goes well today, we should look into more sustainable and comfortable arrangements, for a longer-term basis," she suggested. She tapped on her clonra a few times and brought up a detailed, three-dimensional hologram of one of the promising rentals she and Regina had found the night before.

"Nice place, isn't it, everyone?" asked Regina.

"It looks a touch lavish for our needs, I think..." remarked Gerrard, drawing a slight but playful scowl from Andromeda. Gerrard caught on after a few moments that he was being teased—but he also understood it was being done with an undertone of seriousness.

He then continued his sentence—though he hadn't initially intended to, ending it with, "... But it certainly appears worth a look."

Andromeda's frown turned into an approving smile. It was intentional, though. It wasn't so much reflexive or involuntary as it was a purposeful game of conversation. She sought more to have an interesting and spirited, intriguing talk with her companions than to force her ideas or view about this particular rental. She couldn't be sure any of the others were really aware of her game, though. And that was okay. She was used to playing such games in her mind, and mostly with herself, anyway.

Andromeda laughed a little, disarmingly, to try and help her friends interpret her playfulness for what it was. It seemed to work fine, save for perhaps with Hector—but he might not care, even if she really were just being mean. He seemed like he was on a mission and would work with them, the companions he had fallen in with, even if he truly didn't like them—if only for their usefulness in accomplishing his mission. He also seemed more preoccupied with filling up his stomach, perhaps in preparation for another day of hard labor at the docks.

"So, anyway," Andromeda continued, "Regina tells me places like this don't tend to last long on the market. We should go check some places out after our workday today. Or at least, those of us who are available by a reasonable time should," she said, casting a sidelong glance Hector's way. But it was a joke he didn't seem to catch, or pay any attention to.

"I'll put in for a couple appointments for us to go see some places later," Andromeda advised after a brief pause.

"Sound good, team?" Regina asked.

Gerrard and Hector both nodded.

"It's settled, then," Andromeda announced triumphantly, clapping her hands together.

Then they finished up their breakfast, and each of them contributed some coin to cover the meal.

"Gerrard and I will message you two when we're headed to the address for the first place we're going to be looking at. It'll be out near the city limits, close to the city line between Akastair and Serazema," Andromeda informed Hector and Regina, already having a couple places in mind.

"Sounds good," and "Okay," were the responses that came back, and Andromeda was pleased to hear the team was so well aligned for the day ahead.

* * *

Andromeda and Gerrard made their way to the hydromagnetic train station close to their inn. The trains were the primary mode of transport throughout Akastair, and also in Makeva and most of Gracyr. The hovering, magnetized, near-frictionless train car systems glided over the railways with great speed and efficiency all across the continent. The elaborate network burned hydrogen as fuel, emitting only heat and water vapor as exhaust. Andromeda hadn't spent much time traveling on the wondrous things, having spent so much of her life just in her small town, and the idea of being able to ride on them more regularly was not an unpleasant one to her.

The two of them purchased a pair of tickets and boarded a train bound for the city center of Serazema. When they arrived, they could connect with the Authorities Ops Base nearby, and hopefully, there'd be challenge, excitement, and coin aplenty to track down from there. And also of course, hopefully, there'd be leads that would take them to the Order of Oranlak.

Meanwhile, Hector and Regina headed out together in the direction of the boardwalk. Regina chatted excitedly along the way, mostly to herself, about her hopes for her new position as a bartender at the Seaside Sprite.

By Regina's estimation, Hector was far less enthused about her bartending gig. And he seemed equally unenthusiastic about his own new job. Maybe it wasn't so much that he was unexcited, though, as that he was just being his usual overly restrained self. It was interesting for her to observe such a person, one so apparently determined to express as little emotion as possible. She couldn't help but wonder how much was natural and to what extent he consciously worked toward being that way.

In any case, the two of them split ways as they neared the Seaside Sprite, and she let him know she would message later on. Hector continued on toward the docks.

Regina walked in and made her way to the barstool she had sat at the previous day. She did not see the manager she had spoken with yesterday, and it was also a different bartender on shift.

It was a few minutes before the designated arrival time she had been given, and the place was a ghost town. There were no customers currently at the bar, and only a few at the booths and tables, mostly enjoying coffee and breakfast.

She was greeted by the friendly man bartending.

"Mornin' to ya there! What may I get my first customer this day?" the bartender asked.

"Oh, apologies. Actually not here as a customer; I have a meeting with the hiring manager. My first day on the job, actually," Regina replied in her silvery voice. She extended her hand professionally and said courteously, "I'm Regina. It's a pleasure to meet ya."

"Ahh, nice to meet ya, too! He mentioned you'd be along, asked me to show ya the ropes! I'm afraid, see, that he has been involuntarily detained by one of his other business operations this mornin' and may well not be joinin' us 'ere," the man informed Regina.

"Okay, no worries, I'll be flexible. And I appreciate ya making yourself available on such short notice," said Regina in a friendly fashion. "What shall I call ya?"

"Name's Blaine. Pleasure be mine meetin' ya, and no trouble at all. Glad to have the help. We had an employee leavin' on short notice some while back, and management never sought to be replacin' him. Not once they were seein' us chuggin' along okay with less help and fewer draws on the payroll. But it's been a lot, miss, and we're sure glad to be seein' someone new along now!"

"Oh, isn't that always the way of it! But glad to be welcome, and glad to be helping, Blaine!" Regina replied, sharing a smile and a laugh with her new coworker.

* * *

Hector made his way back to the ship from yesterday and its crew and his new captain. He didn't immediately notice Captain Saoirse as he was approaching the vessel, but he did notice one of the crew members he had worked with the previous day.

"*Oi*, Hector, back for more, eh? Good to see ye got some fight left in ye!" the man spiritedly said, laughing heartily.

Hector let his face crease with a weak smile, and though he did verbalize a reply, it was more under his breath and to himself. "Got fight left in me yet, to be sure."

"Glad to hear it," came an unexpected, firm female voice coming up beside him. It was Captain Saoirse. "Thought perhaps we'd seen the last of ya. Not everyone's always takin' well to a first day like the one you weathered. Not when we're bein' understaffed and overworked like that."

Hector responded formally and in an all-business sort of way. "Where do you need me today, Captain?"

Saoirse seemed to appreciate that. "We're loadin' up supplies to be settin' out again soon—tomorrow, maybe. Not to be much of a layover for the lot of us this go-round. Have a few clients who've hired us who'll be coming by this day to pick up crates we spent yesterday unloadin'. The red an' blue paint on the crates ya saw marks the client they're for. Blue's for the ship comin' into dock ten in 'bout an hour, and in 'bout three hours, another ship's comin' into dock eight for the red 'ns. And we be, of course, docked here at nine. So, in the meantime, we're loadin' the crates that're over thar—which're supplies for our next trip—onto our ship here. Start with those 'ns 'til the first client arrives. The other crew will guide ya and give ya whatever further direction yer needin'."

Hector then lifted the first of what would be many crates that day. He carried it up the ramp and onto Saoirse's ship, which he noted—judging from the words on the side—was named *Liberty's Reach*.

* * *

The hydromagnetic train glided along the tracks from the station in Akastair over to neighboring Serazema. It was just a short ride before the train was already arriving at the platform there, coming to a gentle stop at Serazema's Center City Station.

"Not a bad commute," observed Andromeda upon their arrival.

Gerrard shrugged. He could still see the lost time mounting up, even given the short commute. But he was already mostly decided on living in Akastair over Serazema anyway. He did wonder, though, if the commute they were experiencing was consistently how that commute was, or whether it varied a lot with the day of the week or other such things. He also wondered if the stroll the two of them were now about to embark on would hold any surprises.

"Come on. Let's see if the rest of the commute is as smooth as the first part," he offered his companion.

He started out from the landing platform and led the way from there, briefly stopping to consider a map of the city they happened by—one depicted on a large vidscreen near the entrance to Center City Station. Then the two of them walked out onto the streets of Serazema.

It was bustling with activity outside, and they could already feel the temperature taking a blistering turn for the day. The area around the station did not seem particularly dangerous. The building exteriors looked relatively clean and updated and mostly graffiti-free. There were many people rushing this way and that, and there were food vendors with various quick-bite options available. A few merchants were also littered about, selling random trinkets and inexpensive giftable items.

"Come on, this way," said Gerrard to Andromeda after they had taken a moment to look around the area. They made their way the short distance from there to the Authorities Ops Base. Moving at an efficient pace, they made the base in just a few minutes.

Security was tight at the building. Various detectors were stationed at the entrance, which scanned for various things of potential concern. Andromeda and Gerrard presented their weapons and noteworthy possessions, along with their new bounty hunter licenses, up front at the entrance.

One of the guards remarked upon the beauty of Gerrard's claymore, and how incredibly light the weapon was for its massive size. The crimson fluorite that had gone into the creation of the sword had enhanced its strength and reduced its weight. Not that the guards questioned it so deeply; they spared the time for just a passing compliment.

The blasters struck the guards as more unusual and raised more eyebrows. These were a rare sight in the modern day. Fewer and fewer were being made—if, in fact, any even still were—and ammunition wasn't easy to come by, either. It was very unusual for the guards to see one here in Serazema, let alone two. Andromeda's, of course, was archaic in appearance, and one of the guards remarked that he wasn't sure it would even still fire.

Her vicious-looking saber also caught their eyes, and it scored a few compliments among the guards as well. The pair of them also presented the ammunition they carried, though Gerrard held back on showing some—his case of AA-grade blaster bullets. The case was imbued with a magic that was likely to prevent its detection by the guards and their scanners. And even if they did find it, there was a reasonable chance Gerrard could apologize and claim he had forgotten, perhaps seeking some recognition from them of who he was to draw a measure of leniency. It was worth the risk. He truly didn't like to unveil that he carried on him something of such rarity and value, and which was so blatantly powerful.

There were detectors to find common magics, weapons, and items, and a spectrum of other potentially concerning things. But the pair, save for the one exception from Gerrard, made their sincerest efforts to be transparent and not make any bad first impressions at this new place.

A short while later, they managed to move through the scanners and other security measures just fine, though they had to leave many possessions—particularly their weapons—checked in at the front with the guards. They were, at least, permitted to keep their clonras. The pair continued into the spacious lobby area, where they were greeted by a guard behind a large glass panel—not so unlike the setup they had observed back in Akastair at the base for the authorities there.

"Hello," greeted the guard, a middle-aged, stern-voiced woman. "What business have you here today?"

"We are hoping to be of help to you, actually. We possess some skill with the blade, and we'd like to put that particular skill to use—to assist in maintaining the law and order around here," replied Andromeda. She looked into the guard's eyes, and her voice sounded sincere.

"More bounty hunters," the guard behind the glass panel remarked, as if the thought left a bad taste in her mouth. "You're all always thinking you're going to hit it big, make some big difference in the world or something," she criticized.

With a judgmental shake of her head and an exasperated sigh, the guard directed the pair to a different section across the room. "The vidscreen over there was updated with a treasure trove of information this morning, which I'm sure you'll find interesting. Feel free to use your clonras to save and store whatever information you find pertinent," she said.

Andromeda and Gerrard made their way to the vidscreen. There was a plethora of bounties and related information. They each copied the files they wanted and stored them in their clonras. Many of the bounties were on small-time offenders, but there were also many more dangerous-seeming ones, which often held longer-standing bounties. They reviewed known associations and accomplices, and the backgrounds of the top bounties in particular. Andromeda and Gerrard could easily imagine some of them having significant ties to the Order of Oranlak. But of course, such direct associations—and references to the criminal band at all—were entirely absent from the records. The Oranlak paid good coin to remain as intangible and mysterious as possible. As a consequence, the reality was that many people of the common public felt its very existence was a tall tale, a hoax, an impossibility.

Andromeda scoured through histories of bounties claimed, and through numerous records of likely minimal significance, trying to find something promising. Gerrard fared no better in finding anything. But they did think it peculiar that there had been a recent drop-off in claimed bounties that started some months back. It seemed unusual, an incongruent deviation out of touch with what was otherwise a significant history of consistent precedent.

"Something's amiss here," Gerrard said, verbalizing what the two of them were seeing.

Andromeda nodded in wholehearted agreement.

"We can reflect on this matter more later," Gerrard continued, not wanting to go where he suspected this conversation would—not in the place they were standing right now. Indeed, possible internal corruption would be better discussed elsewhere.

"I think we have the information we need to get started," said Andromeda.

Gerrard nodded.

They headed back toward the front entrance. They paused to sign back out and pick up their possessions at the front security checkpoint, then they bid the guards a good day. They were back out onto the street and into the still-escalating heat of the summer day in short order.

"Something other than inside corruption could have caused those irregularities we observed in their recent records," Gerrard said, in large part just wanting to test how the words sounded to him when he spoke them aloud.

"True," responded Andromeda. "Perhaps some high-performing bounty hunter moved on to greener pastures—or was taken down," she suggested, with a degree of dramatic emphasis on the latter part.

"I would think there are enough skilled ones around that the loss of some still wouldn't have so dramatic an impact as we saw with the numbers we were just reviewing. And there aren't likely any bounty hunters so skilled that the loss of a single one would make such a difference—not in such a large population of them. Anyway, there was no such exceptional hunter contributing to the monthly claimed bounties before the numbers dropped off like that," Gerrard challenged.

"So, something larger has been going on for many months," Andromeda stated.

Gerrard nodded. "Something seismic, I suspect."

"The Oranlak always hold a degree of influence, essentially everywhere, to keep themselves as unseen ghosts to the general public," Gerrard went on. "I suspect the drop in bounties collected to be a consequence of their high interest in this area. More chaos, crime, and fewer collected bounties all serve to create more lawlessness, a state of affairs that often suits their needs well. It will facilitate them getting away with all sorts of shady dealings in the area."

"Where do you think we should go next, given what we've found so far?" asked Andromeda, searching for where his points were taking them.

"Let's go where there is a lot of casual conversation—maybe a place akin to the one Regina was talking about, where she's landed a job," suggested Gerrard.

"A place with a lot of people and a lot going on, where no one will be likely to pay much attention to us, where we'll be safer out in public," Andromeda agreed.

"All right. But let's make it a place that some of these bounties we're after have ties to," Gerrard suggested.

He stepped aside on the busy street and began typing into his clonra. He searched through the files they had acquired from the authorities' base.

"There's a place on the other side of the city that looks promising. We can head back to the station and catch a train over there and probably arrive within the hour. It's called The Bleeding Dragon. Rough place to get along in, by the sound of it, though," Gerrard finished.

"Sounds like as good a place as any to delve into this compendium of information we've already collected this morning, even if nothing else is going on there. Let's head back to the center station and get over there," Andromeda said, already picking back up the pace.

19

Chapter Nineteen

"Okay, and this next one is called a Blue Monster. It's another potent one," warned Blaine, rattling off another silly drink name that Regina half suspected he had made up.

Regina laughed a little over some of the names. "How many of these names have you made up yourself, do you think?" She was doing her best to come across as humorous and personable, in what she partly still took as an extension of her job interview. She almost couldn't see them not hiring her at this point, though, even if judging just from how likable Blaine seemed to find her. She was also making great progress at memorizing recipes for all manner of alcoholic concoctions, which were apparently all very common at the Seaside Sprite. She had heard of only a scarce few of them before, but Blaine seemed genuinely impressed with the progress she had already made.

Regina's greatest strength seemed to be in how she engaged with the customers, how she made small talk to keep them conversing and interested in being there. And it didn't seem to be a drag on her efficiency at fulfilling orders, either; her multitasking skills seemed well developed from her time at college. She was also confident that her appearance inclined some of the customers to perceive her as more engaging. Held to most any standard, she would be considered beautiful. Today, she had worn a red ribbon, intricately interwoven with her long hair, which had already earned her many compliments. And her shapely and sharply defined feminine form tended to catch a person's notice almost as quickly as her impossibly clear blue eyes and her pretty, angular face.

Not one patron so far had given Regina a very hard time, but she was confident she could manage more difficult customers should any turn up. Blaine seemed to categorize one fellow who had stopped by as difficult, but she hadn't seen much from that man to justify it. Maybe she had dealt with too much to be so easily bothered as Blaine was. Or maybe the man had just been having an unusually good day.

In any case, she felt she was getting a very helpful and interesting feel for the mannerisms, the views, and the interests of the clientele that frequented the place. Many of them were regulars Blaine knew by name, and Regina knew she would be outmatched by the seasoned bartender, even if she'd had a similar number of years of experience, just because of the rapport he had already built with so many of them. Still, it was her sense that she could quickly establish a sufficient connection with the general customer population here to do quite well, both in terms of heightened earnings potential through tips, which was where she understood her pay potential substantially came from, and in terms of the information she could gather about possible Order of Oranlak operations in the area.

At one point, she moved to prepare one of the more complicated mixed drinks and nearly added a wrong ingredient. Fortunately, Blaine was there to catch her mistake before it was made. And while not greatly discouraged, she did let out a slight sigh after she finished making that drink. It was still going to take some work to be proficient and independent at this. But going through this training and holding this job would afford her an opportunity to advance her greater mission, and she was committed to staying that course. And anyway, she couldn't deny that at least a modicum of personal satisfaction came from this work she was doing at the Seaside Sprite. She might even actually be enjoying herself, she thought.

The work didn't require the depth of thought generally necessary in much of the work she had done post-college. Granted, of course, she still found herself attributing deeper thoughts than were probably necessary to her drink-making and her conversations. Still, it was nice to know that it wasn't really necessary.

"Something wrong, Regina?" asked Blaine, catching her sigh.

"Not at all," she said, returning his concern with a smile.

Then, to shift the conversation away from what she had really been thinking, she pulled a relevant memory from her past. She didn't care to be getting into the truth of all that was on her mind at that moment.

"There's a drink I remember trying back at my university that this experience is reminding me of, but I can't for the life of me remember whatever it was," she said, feigning frustration.

"No worries, Regina! I know quite a few more I can still teach you; I'm sure we'll stumble on it sooner or later," said Blaine reassuringly.

"Thanks, Blaine. Appreciate it," she said, with a mostly sincere smile.

They did, indeed, go through many more, joined also by a thorough run-through of a cornucopia of food specials and various menu options, combinations, and available substitutions for orders. They carried on with her training that way through the afternoon and well into the evening.

* * *

Not so far away, Hector continued his work, carrying crates back and forth throughout the day. That work wasn't so challenging. What *was* challenging, however, was simultaneously advancing his broader goal of acquiring information from the crew members of *Liberty's Reach*. He was rather far over on the introverted side of the communication spectrum, but as he understood the need to communicate with the crew to get the information he wanted about what was going on in the area, he made multiple attempts to mingle.

It didn't help that the crew was not overly conversational—but perhaps that was just because of how new he was to them. The crew seemed a tough lot, a little rough around the edges, perhaps, but stoic and uncomplaining about things. Hector generally felt he rather liked the lot of them. Maybe they didn't talk all that much, but he didn't feel he was the right person to be critical of such a thing, being the introvert he usually was and all.

The crew weren't particularly well-read or studious, or concerned about technicalities or theories related to their work. They were practical and applied general common sense. They seemed to abide by an internal code that generally governed their actions and their approach to things. And they were certainly an interesting bunch to be around and scrutinize.

Hector counted about a dozen crew members in addition to the captain. They were mostly men, but there were at least two women, too. He found he liked the ship's name, *Liberty's Reach*, in particular, perhaps because it reminded him of Scorpion's Reach, a place back where he was from in Ezmondia.

Eventually, Hector placed the final crate on the second client's ship. Feeling a measure of accomplishment, he returned to *Liberty's Reach* to continue the work of loading that vessel up for its next journey. Upon his arrival, though, Captain Saoirse halted him—and at the end of a sword, no less.

Saoirse's sword was a razor-sharp, wickedly curved cutlass, and she brandished it at him with no words of warning.

I have been foolish to trust any of them, Hector thought. Perhaps his tiredness had affected his judgment, eased him into letting his guard down. He knew he should have been more vigilant, and he silently berated himself. Perhaps he should have been scanning minds around him with Kazahvir's magic. But it was mentally exhausting to keep doing that, and he could see why he hadn't had that idea at the forefront of his mind while laboring the day away, lugging all those boxes around.

Hector considered retaliating. Perhaps he should unleash Kazahvir's scorpion attack on Saoirse and lay her low. He could not detect any magic about her now, or in the immediate area, for that matter. He doubted she would survive. Of course, given his current predicament at the end of her sword, she might get him first. She certainly looked practiced and capable with her weapon as she stared him down. And he didn't care to flush away all the effort he had just poured into cultivating something with this ship and its crew. He also didn't really want to kill her.

So, he thought better of trying to. He tried simply asking a question before things escalated further. "What's this about, Captain?" Hector asked, as respectfully as he could manage.

"Ya know what this is about, sugar," Saoirse flatly stated.

Even given the sharp and deadly edge to her voice, that matched that of her sword, Hector couldn't dissuade himself; there seemed a persisting pleasantness to hearing her speak that he couldn't help but note.

"Actually ... I'm confident I don't. Perhaps if you'd clarify..." Hector said firmly, and he let his words hang in the air between them.

Saoirse's face remained unchanged. "That las' crate ya loaded onto that client's ship, it arrived there a tad lighter than it left our ship last night, didn't it? What's that about?" she demanded.

"If you think I know about some missing contents, or pilfered them for myself or some such thing, you are mistaken, Captain," Hector confidently stated. He was careful and sure to respectfully use Saoirse's title.

Saoirse continued to seem unmoved by the statement; she was unflinching and intrepid and did not lower her blade.

She's probably going to make an attempt on my life, Hector grimly considered.

"If you're missing something, check me first for this thing before you bury your blade in my chest," Hector suggested.

"Ya probably stole from us las' night, thought we wouldn't be noticin'," she reasoned.

"I don't think I would have come back if I had," Hector pointed out.

"Perhaps ya couldn't help yerself," Saoirse said, narrowing her eyes.

Hector sighed audibly this time. He called upon Kazahvir and scanned the minds of the crew around him and aboard the ship. The number of minds he immediately felt, through Kazahvir, was short by one. He mentally searched, imploring his sentient sword to reach as far as it could. Then he located him—someone that was distanced from the rest. Hector couldn't read their minds, but through the ancient magic of his sword, he felt basic impressions and feelings and the presence of others around him. He came to a hopeful but plausible solution a few moments later and spoke out.

"Captain, hold on. Isn't someone missing here right now?" Hector said.

Saoirse didn't move her eyes from him, but did call for one of her crew to determine what Hector was going on about.

"Aiden's not among us. He's the only one not accounted for, Cap'n," said one of the crew.

"Well . . . find him!" she commanded.

Immediately, most of the crew scattered to search the ship and surrounding area for the missing man.

Hector considered what he should do next. He wasn't keen on tipping his hand too much, didn't want to give out any premature impressions that he had magic in his arsenal. But he knew this Aiden was below deck, down in his quarters. He considered whether making the suggestion to search below deck might be helpful, or whether it might allude to too much or make him seem suspicious.

Saoirse took a step back and let Hector breathe a little, but she didn't otherwise let up. Her gaze remained fixed on him. He was thinking that she still might have let her guard down enough that he could manage a successful attack and escape—but he had a sense, magically, that this mystery was about to be as good as solved. He also found over the course of the ensuing few minutes that he was rather enjoying having Saoirse's dedicated attention on him. Granted, he did wish it was under better circumstances.

A few minutes later, the crew members who had been searching below deck returned with Aiden.

"Found him below deck, Captain—and he was counting these," said one of the crewmen. He tossed a couple pouches over to Saoirse, which landed on the ground and partially spilled out their contents—silver coins.

Saoirse lowered her cutlass from its threatening position pointed at Hector's throat. She looked down for a moment and breathed a sigh of what seemed to be disappointment, presumably with this Aiden character. She shook her head slightly, then looked back up at Hector. She didn't speak to him, but instead moved her attention over to Aiden.

"Aiden." She spoke his name as she drew closer, cutlass held ominously out in front of her. "I trust that ya don't think it'd be wise to cross us, or *me*, again, would that be right?"

The young man, perhaps just barely into his twenties, nodded his head vigorously. Sweat was visibly forming on his forehead and face.

Saoirse let the moment drag on a while, maybe to let a little suspense build up among the crew. Maybe she just liked seeing the guy sweat. In any case, it would strike Hector as awfully gracious if that was all the young man suffered as a consequence of his theft.

"Be gone with ya," she said finally. "And know that yer gamblin' yer life away if ya come 'round here again." She looked to her crew that held him, and she instructed them, "Release him."

Aiden blinked in disbelief. But once the crewmen released him, he immediately took off. So far as any of them could tell, he was bound for somewhere well beyond the docks, and at an impressively rapid pace.

Saoirse glanced back to Hector once Aiden had gone, and she spoke to him again. "Don't think, Hector, that I'll be so forgivin' toward someone like yerself, who's already had a few more years than Aiden to be straightenin' yerself out."

Hector nodded solemnly.

Captain Saoirse held his stare a moment longer, then called out, "All o' ya! Back to work!" Then she broke off her stare, and without any further words, went back to loading crates, too. She was eager to be done with the work—ever more so because the resupply of *Liberty's Reach* was now nearly complete. They could be out on the ocean again tomorrow, and that was very much where the seasoned captain preferred to be.

* * *

Andromeda and Gerrard sat down at a vacant table in the back of The

Bleeding Dragon. There was another open table nearer to the front, but the pair took the opportunity to walk a little more around the place and take a seat where they could more fully immerse themselves in the experience of being there.

After sitting down, they each activated their clonras. A couple button presses initiated the hologram keyboard and the generation of the visual display, aspects of the technology that were only visible to the user and those the user opted to share them with. They each began skimming through the database of files they copied over from the Ops Base. They maintained an awareness of the happenings and conversations unfolding around them, but their attention fluctuated between those external events and what they were reading about.

The Bleeding Dragon wasn't a large place, but it was nearly filled to capacity. Dozens and dozens of patrons were enjoying drinks in what was apparently an early start to their weekend. There was talk about local events and live music, which was apparently going to be performed later on. There was some excited chatter about various upcoming sports events. Still, there was nothing that seemed of any immediate interest to the two visiting bounty hunters.

After a time, Andromeda broke the silence between them and mentioned that no one had come around to offer a menu or drinks to them yet. "Strange," she said. "The sign at the entrance directed us to seat ourselves, right? Didn't it say they'd be right with us?"

"Yes, it did," Gerrard affirmed, not lifting his eyes from the display of his clonra. After a few moments, he added, "I was looking forward to a beverage of some sort or another, too."

"I'll go over to the bar, see if I can order something or expedite the service," offered Andromeda.

"No worries, Andromeda, I'll go check what's going on," Gerrard said, already standing up. He rose from his wooden chair at the small round table he and Andromeda were sitting at and began making his way the short distance over to the bar.

He was already back just a minute or two later, and he said to Andromeda,

"The barkeep assured me they'll be right with us."

That sounded typical and not overly promising to her.

She then had the idea to make a playful presumption and attempt to understand her new ally a little better. "Don't like to have people doing too much for you, do you?" she asked, referencing how he had declined to let her be the one to resolve the issue with the drinks and menus taking too long.

Gerrard conceded that much, responding, "I suppose there is a measure of truth to that. I do favor a sense of … self-sufficiency."

"I can understand and appreciate that. It's good to be independent and self-reliant, for sure. Also good to be part of a team sometimes, though."

Gerrard shrugged and didn't offer any challenges to the statement.

A few moments later, a waitress approached their table. "What would you like, you two?" she asked, sounding a bit rushed. She had skipped the pleasantries and any conversational formalities. Making up for lost time, Andromeda lightheartedly supposed.

"I'll have one of your stouts. Whatever's popular," said Gerrard.

"Okay, and you?" the waitress asked, turning to Andromeda.

"What do you like to drink here? What's good?" Andromeda asked her, trying to stir up a little conversation.

The waitress's response came mostly in the form of a suddenly irritated and overworked expression on her face.

Andromeda, taking the hint, quickly added, "I'll have an ale, please. Anything's fine. And is that a menu in your apron there? Could I have a look at that, as well?"

The waitress actually rolled her eyes slightly, but she did remove the menu from her apron pocket and laid it on the table. Then she was immediately off to get in their drink order. She apparently hadn't paused to consider that Andromeda's companion might also want to look over a menu.

"Having a tough day, maybe," Andromeda remarked when she had gone. It was an understanding, empathetic tone, Gerrard couldn't help but notice. "Probably not everyone here is going to have time for much questioning from us about whatever's going on in Serazema these days."

"Perhaps it won't come to us having to question many people," Gerrard offered.

Andromeda nodded, seeing that as hopeful, but accepting the possibility.

"So," she said, changing the subject, "I'd like to know more about my new ally. Why does a man of such popularity and means continue to slave away for the mining companies? Trying to set a good example for your children, perhaps?"

Gerrard considered her questions for a few moments. He wasn't accustomed to answering many personal questions, or generally talking about himself. He did see himself as more of a head-down, work-focused sort of person. But he recognized the potential benefits of going down that road with his new teammate. Building more of a relationship with Andromeda could be helpful in terms of them achieving their goals. If they understood each other better, they could work together more effectively and be more likely to succeed at uncovering whatever Oranlak was up to, finding the sunken spaceship, and so forth.

"Well, you see," Gerrard began, "I'm not exactly feeling that I'm saving the world, fighting in these tournaments. And sure, there are many who would pay me all kinds of coin to say I support what they want me to support, so they can sell more of whatever they're trying to sell. But I don't generally find it to be for the greater good for me to help such people accomplish such things."

Gerrard paused a moment to let her digest the words and to reflect on how he felt himself. He didn't often try to verbalize his thoughts, which he simply acted on, almost as if they were instinct.

"I enjoy the fighting in the arena and the swordsmanship, and meeting others sometimes, too—perhaps such as yourself—and I suppose I do just enjoy doing something I'm good at," Gerrard went on. "But I find my work with Old Guard Mining more … meaningful. Though of course, I don't exactly endorse everything they've ever done or are currently doing, either."

Gerrard took a moment and sighed, evidently reflecting on some particulars he wasn't verbalizing. "But at least they're better than most. And their work and mission are important to finding the materials we need to build a better tomorrow. My work with them in recent years has afforded me the opportunity to help with state-of-the-art technologies for the sustainable and responsible extraction of elements, metals, and minerals that are surely needed for the world we need to be building."

He saw that Andromeda's interest persisted, so he continued. "This company uses some of the least invasive mining techniques, like underground mapping, using the most minimal and unharmful seismic waves possible."

Andromeda nodded, acutely interested and accepting that response as wholly adequate … to her first question. Then she reiterated her second. "Kids?"

Gerrard smiled a little. "I have one daughter. She's grown-up now… We're mostly out of touch these days," he answered. "She lives with her mother still, on the potato farm we used to run back when we were together. I see her sometimes, but her mother and I had a lot of issues in the past, and it's been many years since we were together. And I'm so consumed with everything else in my life and the world nowadays."

Andromeda nodded again, intrigued. She didn't want to pry on a potentially sensitive matter like that, though, so she resolved to change the subject.

Before she could, Gerrard spoke again. "Suppose I might be quitting the mining gig soon, though—at least if we have any success with what we're doing now. I'll probably have to make that call soon; I can't be much more overdue in getting back. But I do question that they wouldn't take me back, regardless, given all the years I've given them at this point," Gerrard finished.

Andromeda nodded again and went on to speak about herself a little. "I have one kid," she said. "He's not really a kid anymore, though; he's grown, too. He has a desire for that feeling of self-reliance, like you. Not sure he picked that up from me, but…" She paused and laughed a little, then continued. "He's awfully distracted these days. I have siblings with children who are roughly his age, and they're all—along with my parents, who are still going strong—back home running our cattle ranch. There are other operations we're in, but that's our mainstay. They've long been telling me I need to be out in the world, though, not confined to the day-to-day back there. So, here I am, to put it on a very basic level—out here in the world, forging connections and looking for whatever it is I'm supposed to take back home with me."

She paused, thinking over likely questions Gerrard might have in mind, even if he wasn't immediately voicing them. "You're probably thinking about the swordplay. Apparently, I do have a fair measure of skill with that. My father showed me a lot of that when I was younger. I'm not sure I'm going to achieve the stardom you have, but it could be useful if I did. Maybe I could make some coin to bring back or send some business to our operations back home. I wore our ranch's name on my uniform during the tournament—just trying to get us out there and noticed a little more. It hasn't … been easy times, exactly, for family-run ranches."

"True that," said Gerrard, just as the waitress returned with their drinks. She actually placed the ale in front of Gerrard, and the stout in front of Andromeda, so they needed to do a swap after the glasses were down on the table. They waited until the waitress left them again.

"True that," Gerrard repeated, and he took a thirsty swig of his stout. "It's probably intertwined with a lot of the other problems going on in our society nowadays—under, of course, one bigger overarching one."

"The elites who essentially control us, who we're scarcely even aware of, you mean?" Andromeda asked.

Gerrard regarded her silently a moment, genuinely interested in that question—and the mind that put it together just then. "What would you say a big problem we have in our society today would be?" he asked.

Andromeda seemed to consider a few options, then answered, "Excessive and unnecessary over-centralization."

Gerrard smiled a little wider than usual, except perhaps for when he was among his closest friends. "You know, it really doesn't make a lot of sense to have all your resources allocated to one place. Something happens to that one place, you can be out of luck."

Andromeda smiled, too. She was sincerely thrilled to hear that someone not even in the realm of cattle ranching had some understanding of the critical issue their society was facing and what she and her family were going through. "If the smaller operations like ours go under, and all we have are a few different companies to get our beef from, where do you think that'll leave us when something happens to one of the few producers left?" she asked, though the question was rhetorical; she knew they saw eye to eye.

Just then, a clamor started up over at the bar. Some shouting rapidly ensued. Then a blaster shot went off. A few bar patrons went tumbling, and one was launched across the bar, slamming into the bartender.

Andromeda and Gerrard looked at each other, then stood up instantly. They activated their clonras and scanned the person who seemed to be the primary offender.

"He's on our list!" Gerrard shouted, pulling his claymore off his back.

Andromeda regarded the figure as he continued to shout at several others with whom he had apparently entered a squabble.

Then she shouted herself, in warning to Gerrard, "All caution! It's Lorcan! He's near the top of the list!"

She scrutinized the man and considered what weapon would be best to employ against him. He was a massive hulk of muscle who towered over Gerrard, who was probably half a foot taller than her. And her shouts had apparently drawn the behemoth's fiery gaze. The giant's eyes fell over Andromeda and Gerrard as he was probably taking note that they were bounty hunters. The large man could likely have scanned Andromeda and Gerrard and unveiled them to be as such with his clonra, if he had doubts or wanted to be sure.

In any case, the simple fact that the two of them were a couple of the very few that weren't fast making for the exit of the place was compelling evidence.

"Thought the lot of you had run scared from Serazema months ago!" the angry man shouted at them, apparently well aware of their bounty hunter status. Then he erupted in maniacal laughter.

The towering man regarded Gerrard, who was fast closing in on him and brandishing his oversized sword.

"I'm shocked to see you pull a blaster; don't see too many of those around," Gerrard yelled, halting not far out of range. He paused for a few moments to take measure of his opponent. "Nice to meet you," he said calmly, controlling his voice masterfully in the face of an intimidating adversary. "I'm Gerrard. My friend and I here are actually new in town, and we'd like to extend our appreciation for the warm welcome." Gerrard watched his enemy carefully. "We see that bounty on your head. We'd love to take you in quietly, without any more damage to this property or more people getting hurt—including yourself," he said honestly.

The behemoth scoffed at the thought. "Let's see what you've got, Gerrard," he challenged, lifting his blaster.

He fired it just a quickened heartbeat later, and the D-class round barreled toward Gerrard's chest. Spiraling lights emanated from the potent magic as the distance instantly closed.

Gerrard brought up his blade in what would have seemed an impossible defense. It glowed faintly with a defiant crimson hue as the bullet struck the sword and ricocheted harmlessly away from him. Particles of fragmented energy showered the area in front of Gerrard after the well-timed collision.

The blowback toward Lorcan nearly knocked him over—though it was more than the mere physical force that did so. Witnessing the fantastic defensive maneuver already had him off balance.

Gerrard moved to quickly close the remaining distance between them as Lorcan hastily reloaded his blaster. He was efficient at doing this, and Gerrard had to dodge to the side to avoid being shot after the rapid reload. Gerrard still would have had him, but Lorcan pulled forth a secondary, smaller blaster from within his long trench coat. Lorcan had long thought of this secondary blaster as overplanning on his part, an overcautious insurance policy that was incredibly unlikely to be needed. His skills, strength, and reputation were all well earned, and the additional safety net of a secondary blaster had seemed unnecessary to him for a long time.

Gerrard considered for a moment that he might have made a fatal mistake. Lorcan's gun whirred and glowed with a potent energy he had not seen in ages. It was the distinctive glow of a blaster unloading a nigh-impossible-to-defeat AA-grade round.

But another bullet was fired off an instant sooner, and it went rocketing past Gerrard, having originated from somewhere behind him. Waves of energy enveloped each of the bullets as they tore through the air on a collision course. The room came alight with green, crackling energy as they smashed together. The shot emanating from behind Gerrard hungrily consumed the energy of the other, but it didn't stop there. It seemed to extract everything it could reach. The space immediately around Lorcan was immersed in brilliant shades of fiery red and green light.

Then an orb of energy darted right back toward the origin of the vampiric bullet—Andromeda and her archaic blaster. She flinched and even dropped her blaster as the orb made impact. Then the light and pyrotechnics quickly subsided, and Andromeda recovered enough to look back at the target she had fired on and the blaster she had dropped to the ground. The blaster appeared perfectly okay, though the same could not be said of her target—the man was a smoking husk of lifeless charred remains.

Gerrard moved back closer to Andromeda, and they both regarded the dropped blaster. To their amazement, what they viewed was not a broken or even just old and dated weapon, but one that appeared newer and in vastly better shape than it had just moments ago. Gerrard looked up at Andromeda, having moved over to her to thank her for her timely intervention, and found himself in that moment consumed by a more pressing, overriding question.

"What did you just do?" he asked of his unexpected savior, his mouth hanging slightly agape.

Andromeda held her hands out and patted the air in front of her as she verbalized her response. "I have ... absolutely no idea," she admitted.

"Something seems a touch vampiric about this thing," Gerrard observed.

"You know, now that I think about it... I was tipped off by someone that a weaponsmith in Akastair might have some answers about this old blaster," Andromeda recollected.

Gerrard looked on the floor, then back to Andromeda. "I'd say that's worth pursuing," he commented. "What type of round did you just fire?"

he asked.

"Low-level, D class," she replied.

"There's something very odd about a situation where a D-class round overtakes an AA round like that. It must have to do with the weapon it was fired from. That AA round was eaten up like it was nothing, and apparently the blaster has absorbed the energy to restore itself," Gerrard said.

They let their thoughts settle for a few seconds. Then Gerrard walked back over to their table, lifted his glass, and drained the rest of his drink. "We sure picked the right place to have an interesting day here in Serazema," he reflected.

Andromeda took a moment to look around the battered wreckage of the establishment. "You don't think all the bars today in Serazema are having days like this?" Andromeda jested, smiling a little at the absurdity of her own question. She moved over to the table and had a sip of what was left of her own drink. "How long until the authorities arrive here, do you think?"

"By the sound of the state of affairs in this city, it might be a bit," answered Gerrard. "Let's review more of the files while we wait here for them; I don't really care to drag the remains of our bounty back to the Authorities Ops Base, anyway."

Andromeda nodded. Then they both spent about fifteen minutes reviewing more information on bounties they had obtained from the vidscreen back at the base.

Those minutes were not the most productive, though, as Andromeda couldn't help but reflect on how curious and ecstatic she felt over her blaster and the new potential she now recognized in it. And her excitement over the impressive bounty that they, two novice bounty hunters, had just secured was also something she couldn't help but let get the better of her.

* * *

The pair walked out of the Ops Base several hours later. They were both surprised about the ridiculous amount of time they'd had to spend waiting on the paperwork to be processed, just so they could claim their bounty. It had taken significantly longer than it had taken them to dispatch the assailant to begin with.

"Too bad we didn't take him alive; the coin would've been even better!" Andromeda reflected, as the two of them walked down the many steps descending to the street.

"That's your fault," accused Gerrard jokingly. He even went so far as to narrow his eyes in something of a bid to replicate Andromeda's usual conversation tactics. It elicited an amused laugh from Andromeda, as she recognized it as the sort of tactic she herself would employ. She was glad Gerrard was apparently catching on.

"You sure have your entertaining moments," she said, "for someone who doesn't talk so much."

"Thank you…?" said Gerrard, in what was his attempt at just a slightly questioning tone. They both shared a laugh.

The pair went on afterward to spend much of the remaining couple hours of their afternoon reviewing other bounties and leads from the information they had gathered so far.

* * *

"So, do you think you'll be retiring from this mining thing, at least for now?" asked Andromeda at one point later that afternoon.

"I do feel I've found a new calling in this different line of work—one I expect I won't be denying," Gerrard answered, to Andromeda's seeming satisfaction.

A short while after that, they headed back to the hydromagnetic train station for the commute back to Akastair. Andromeda messaged the group their estimated time back, as well as the address of the place she and Gerrard determined was the most practical and had the most promise as a more permanent living situation.

The train ride back was as smooth as the ride in had been. Andromeda and Gerrard realized most people actually traveled from Serazema to Akastair in the morning, and so were traveling back to Serazema in the afternoon—the opposite of what the two of them were doing. It made sense—Akastair was where the economy was stronger and jobs were more abundant and of better quality, and housing was much less expensive in neighboring Serazema.

If these experiences on their first day in Serazema were at all representative of things to come, the two of them couldn't help but reflect that it seemed they had come into a remarkable stroke of good fortune.

20

Chapter Twenty

The four companions met at the address of the place that was most promising, for their scheduled appointment with the property owner.

"This place is beautiful!" Regina praised, in deep appreciation of the selection Andromeda and Gerrard had made.

"It does still seem a bit lavish, even in person," responded Gerrard.

Andromeda scowled a bit at that. "You don't take praise very well, do you? We did agree on this place probably being the best, you know." She followed her words up with a playful and disarming smile, easing the slight tension.

Hector cut in a few moments later, having just arrived. "This the place?" he inquired of the group.

"Well, I'm certainly hoping so!" exclaimed Regina. "It's gorgeous!"

It was a six-gabled Victorian-style affair that exuded beauty. It was the sort of house that in times past was considered commonplace, but which was now a great rarity in a world of more modern, reduced-size works. It was likely owned by someone who had held onto and cared for it a very long time, and it was undoubtedly worth mountains more coin now than it was back then.

The property owner arrived, then approached the front door to unlock it. She beckoned to the four companions to follow her inside. The companions entered the home, and they took a few moments to gather their first impressions.

Andromeda and Gerrard, who had owned properties in the past and were familiar with the kinds of problems that came up and what to look out for, were particularly inquisitive.

The owner took the group through what seemed a practiced and typical walk-through of the home. During the course of the walk-through, Gerrard in particular seemed very questioning. He asked questions that struck the group—particularly Andromeda—as probably going beyond the scope of what renters needed to even be concerned about. Nevertheless, the owner had answered his questions, and seemingly to his satisfaction.

The line of questioning was clearer to Andromeda at the end of the walk-through, though, when Gerrard asked an even less expected one.

"How much to purchase this property from you?" Gerrard asked.

The property owner seemed particularly struck by that question. "Well, I'm not really looking to sell it," she responded. "I'm sort of looking forward to just the steady rental income for a while."

Gerrard put his hand to his chin. "I see," he said.

Andromeda cut in then. "You did say you have several properties, and it's been a little challenging to keep up with them all."

"And how the city's changing regulations have been so bothersome and not favorable at all for people like you renting out places within the city limits," added Regina.

"Surely, fewer renters to worry about is not an entirely unpleasant thought…" Andromeda said, trying to persuade the woman a little more.

The property owner smiled over the team effort and their collective persuasiveness. She quoted Gerrard a slightly inflated estimation of what she believed a fair price would be.

"Straight coin, though. I don't care to tie the place up in a mess of financing. Do you have it?" she asked.

In Gerrard's estimation, the price sounded high. If she had held the property for as long as he suspected, she stood to make a fortune by the sale, even with a much lower price tag.

Even so, the coin wasn't so much for Gerrard. He had more than he was ever likely to spend. And even if he spent it all, his name recognition alone would grant him the pathway to earn all of it back, so long as he was willing to say a lot of things and do a lot of things he didn't particularly care to. The thought was comforting, especially considering all the coin he was thinking about spending now. And it was far from a matter of him spending all his coin anyway; he could buy that house many times over if he wanted to.

"Deal," he simply stated.

The property owner regarded him with a fair degree of surprise, but shrugged and punched a few buttons on her clonra. The appropriate documentation and paperwork generated digitally and instantly. She swapped some credentials with Gerrard, and he reviewed the documents on his own clonra device. The largely automatic technology scanned the documents for possible concerns, irregularities, unusual clauses—things potentially not in Gerrard's best interest. He sat down at the table in the spacious kitchen, which was beautifully redone and had luxuriously high ceilings. He took some time and reviewed the information intensively.

Andromeda and Regina, in particular, moved back through the house again, chatting excitedly about how they might possibly have a more permanent living arrangement there. Homeownership and a sense of housing security, while still highly typical in Makeva, were far from the heights at which they'd once been. Renters and giant corporations that bought up and controlled apartment dwellings were ever more commonplace—and they, of course, all but controlled the housing situation to the southeast, in Ezmondia.

Eventually, after a number of pages and scans, passwords, and signatures, Gerrard transferred the necessary funds for the transaction and closed the deal.

The previous property owner provided keys and other details of the place, and she left the companions to their new home not long after.

"Well, that was certainly efficient," remarked Andromeda.

Gerrard offered a shrug in response. He had amassed a lot of wealth in past years and rarely bought much of anything he didn't need—he lived a rather frugal life for someone of such means. The worldly, the material—they didn't usually do much to slake his desires. In any case, real estate was a reasonable place to store some of one's wealth, if he didn't care to frame the purchase as a personal splurge.

More than that, though, he was just very moved by the potential importance of what he and his companions could accomplish. He was prepared to take a gamble, if that's what it was, and throw down some coin to advance what the four of them were doing.

* * *

It was a four-bedroom house with high ceilings and spacious rooms throughout. The rooms were only lightly furnished, but the house still had what was necessary to suit the companions' immediate needs.

"There's a small restaurant I know, around the corner," said Regina after their excitement had died down a little. "They're always makin' the most scrumptious sandwiches. Would you all like to put in the group chat what your preference would be for something to eat? If everyone's feeling interested, I'd go and pick up dinner for us!"

"Splendid idea, Regina!" said Andromeda, already keying her preference into the group chat via her clonra. Gerrard and Hector followed suit. Then the companions sat down at the basic, round wooden table in the kitchen—except for Regina, who left to get the food for everyone.

"How was it today, Hector?" asked Andromeda. "What's the work like over at the docks?"

"I've come to ... to like the idea of being part of that privateer vessel I've stumbled on," Hector replied. "It's a ship called *Liberty's Reach,* captained by a woman named Saoirse."

"That ship's name sounds familiar," commented Gerrard. "Not sure about the captain's name, though... Know the ship's history at all?"

"Not so much," Hector admitted.

"How do you spell the name?" Gerrard inquired.

"That would be S-A-O-I-R-S-E, even though it's pronounced *ser-sha,* apparently," answered Hector.

"Maybe I have heard your captain's name before," said Gerrard. "I know that ship's been around for some time though; I've read of it over the years. Its crew has built quite a reputation, working many successful commissions from the Gatekeepers Council of Makeva. *Liberty's Reach* has intercepted valuables, silver, and gold. It's also served in retaliating against some of the more problematic factions of Ezmondia when they have committed hostilities against Akastair and other communities here in Makeva."

"Yes," Hector responded, "that all sounds much in line with what I've heard."

Andromeda's eyes lit up then. "It sounds like such an enthralling opportunity to be part of a ship like that! I'm sure this experience is going to be fascinating for you, regardless of whether it earns us leads on the Order of Oranlak. You absolutely must get better at sharing stories, so we can hear about your exploits aboard that ship!"

Hector granted Andromeda a slight intentional smile.

"Excellent!" exclaimed Andromeda, optimistically presuming Hector was agreeable to this.

"We're planning to intercept some ships over the coming weeks," he divulged. "We're actually planning to head out tomorrow. Not sure how immediately promising it's going to be in terms of uncovering more about the Oranlak's operations around here, but … I'll see what I can find. You all probably wouldn't find the crew to be much more talkative than I am, but I'll engage them where I can."

"You should probably leave the journal behind, since you'll be in this new environment with all these new people," Gerrard suggested.

Andromeda chimed in there, as well. "Yes, that'd be wise, I think. Maybe some of us back here can make progress with the thing while you're away. Where are we with our understanding of it? What have you found out?"

Hector thought a moment before replying. "That's probably a good idea," he said, before pausing another moment. "Basically, we know the Oranlak found this old journal they were researching, scrutinizing. There were many associated papers when I found it, which are now lost, given the self-destruction of their operation near the waterfall. But the fact that they existed is a testament to Oranlak's great interest in the contents of this journal."

He went on, speaking more of the journal itself. "Someone or some group penned this journal a long time ago—perhaps centuries ago. It details the crash of a spaceship that landed near present-day Akastair. Part of the ship has been exhumed from the ground near Akastair and researched and discussed extensively. The vast majority of the vessel, though, is apparently sunken off the coast, but still not far from Akastair."

Hector watched his companions and could see they listened intently and with great interest. He went on. "*Liberty's Reach* likely plots courses that will bring me near—if not right over—where it seems to me this sunken spaceship must be. I can seek further confirmation of the location and monitor for any potential Oranlak activity in the vicinity."

Thoughts about what seemed most important from what he had read circulated through his mind. "There is wreckage described in the journal, of strange machinery and technology. There were also some limited quantities of a substance recovered. This substance is described as a powerful energy source. It seems to be the case that there is a vast sum of it, sunken at depth with the rest of the spaceship. At the time of this journal's writing, though, the technology did not exist in Gracyr to reach the wreck so deep beneath the waves. And that's ... pretty much what I know."

"I've gone through much of the journal," Hector finished, "and it's not clear to me that we'll be getting all that much more from it. Much of the rest is not legible."

"We can safely assume that new, advanced technologies in the hands of the Oranlak will not bode well for us and society at large," said Gerrard, concern creeping into his tone.

"It's good to know where we stand, though," said Andromeda. "And what an opportunity this all presents to us."

Hector nodded, far from disagreeing with that assessment.

"So, anyway..." Hector said, "how was today for the two of you?"

"Oh, thanks for asking," said Andromeda first. She sounded a bit surprised, undoubtedly from hearing such a question coming from Hector. "We had an eventful first day as bounty hunters, I would say," she started, casting a glance Gerrard's way. "We collected a treasure trove of information on local bounties and leads—though not much we can tie with certainty to Oranlak ... yet. But we're hopeful and did bring in a sizable bounty today. It was someone the authorities have been trying to capture—well, supposedly, anyway—for quite some time. The guy actually had two blasters. Now, that's a rare sight nowadays!"

Hector seemed interested, but didn't say anything. Gerrard didn't bring anything up, so she went on a little more.

"I also learned this blaster I've recently acquired has more to it than I suspected. I'm planning to have the gunsmith on the other side of the city—the one who does historical and antique appraisals—take a look at it tomorrow morning," she said.

Just then, Regina returned with the food. "I'm back, everyone! Who's hungry?" she asked, coming in through the front door. "Did ya all keep entertained okay without me? What'd I miss?"

Regina pulled the jumbo sandwiches out of the large to-go bag and handed them out.

"Hector was talking about the journal and about his day at work, mostly," answered Andromeda. "I was talking a little about the day that Gerrard and I had, too. Did you want to add anything, Gerrard?"

Andromeda looked over to Gerrard. He began talking as he unwrapped a toasted turkey and cheese sandwich.

"We'll probably have to fill you in on some of that update from Hector, but I want to ask you something, Regina," Gerrard started.

Regina's ears perked up.

"What was your major at the University of Akastair? Andromeda mentioned you attended it."

"Well, basically, energy," Regina answered.

Gerrard dug deeper. "Any particular focus?"

"Mostly geothermal applications, though I also did a fair amount of work with hydrogen—both combustion and fuel cells," she said, her curiosity as to why he was asking creeping into her countenance.

"It seems like hydropower has been a more popular area to study in that field for many years," Gerrard reflected, accurately.

"Yes," Regina said. She reflexively flashed him a smile, pleased to encounter someone who also had interest in the subject. "That's just like me, I s'pose—going against the grain."

She considered that for a moment. Could she make the course her life had taken sound reasonable to Gerrard? Did he already think it was?

Regina went on. "I've had concerns about the long-term sustainability of our society's obsession with hydropower. My understanding—and I recognize that I'm easily in the minority—is that we should be turning our eyes elsewhere, to other, more viable future sources of energy."

"There are other sources of energy, too, that were apparently absent from your studies at the university," Gerrard observed.

"My impression is that, given the span of time we've had to work with since I came into the field, any others you could be referring to are not realistic," Regina responded. "There one in particular you're interested in?" she asked, genuinely curious.

"Nuclear, harnessing the power of the sun," responded Gerrard.

"Ah, yes, atomic fusion, sure," Regina said, sounding intrigued. "It could be promising at some distant point in the future. It is impractical for now, though. Maintaining the conditions needed, and sustaining the reaction, is—to put it mildly—difficult."

Gerrard's look of interest did not fade, so she continued. "Plasma—that is, the superheated fourth state of matter—needs to be maintained at temperatures of millions of degrees in a very precise environment."

"What if, theoretically, you had a material that could handle that heat, that could contain the plasma?" Gerrard proposed. "What if you had a material that provided ... an environment that did not allow the superheated components of the plasma to cool at different rates? Something that ... could maintain a consistent temperature and sustain the reaction?"

The insightful question had her a little surprised. "Well… I suppose such a material would hold great promise for the advancement of atomic fusion as a viable energy source," Regina replied, sounding more impressed now as well as intrigued.

"I'm far from an expert in that type of energy, though," Regina admitted. "And I wouldn't know who to bring such a material to, even if I possessed it. People doing research on that are almost unheard of these days, and the large publishers don't tend to even look at papers submitted in that area. The energy journal publishing world is very biased, and it prioritizes developments, modifications, and advancements in the hydropower sector."

"Are you familiar with crimson fluorite?" Gerrard inquired, asking a seemingly unrelated question. He was thinking it might be better to keep more of his present thoughts to himself, but he saw how intrigued Regina was, and he felt something within himself urging him to trust Regina just a little more.

"Yes, of course," Regina responded, not missing a beat.

"I have heard that after you remove lutetium from crimson fluorite, the compound that remains, verium, is … theorized to have potential to advance atomic fusion," Gerrard stated, pretending to be a little unsure. He knew, of course, that it was more than theory, so far as his late friend, Lucian, had been concerned.

"That does sound interesting, Gerrard," said Regina. "I'm not the one to test it out, though, and we're not likely to find anyone much more qualified, unfortunately. I'll scour my memory banks and keep my eyes open for an opportunity to be exploring this further, though."

Her face turned sterner then—a little cold, even. "I would…" she started, but then hesitated. After a pause, she continued, "Caution all of ya, though." And she looked around at her companions. "Many of the energy moguls of our day don't take so well to ideas about changing the current order and way of things in the energy sector. I would suggest ya take great care in going against that current, and even in who ya choose to discuss things of this nature with. True progress toward shifting the balance of power is not likely to be met kindly by the powerful in our society."

Regina let her words hang dramatically in the air for a few moments.

"Okay, enough seriousness, everyone!" she then proclaimed lightheartedly. "Take a breath. Let's eat more o' this delicious food, which I'm dearly missing from my university days!"

The four managed to keep the conversation relatively light for the remainder of the meal and into the evening. It was a nice departure from the unrelenting seriousness that often plagued them lately.

They didn't have beds yet in their rooms, but their bedrolls were fine. They each went to sleep that night, contented with full stomachs, and hopeful and excited for what they knew their future could bring.

21

Chapter Twenty-One

The following morning, all four of the companions awoke reenergized and were up and ready to start out early. But perhaps Andromeda was particularly so. She was eager to get to this renowned weaponsmith and to see what she could learn about her blaster. Apparently, it altered or enhanced the ammunition fired from it and had what were at least vaguely vampiric attributes. She held it in her hands and marveled at its new, unblemished appearance. She could almost see her reflection in the silvery finish of the weapon.

Gerrard thought to go along with Andromeda. They could learn what they could about the blaster together, before another day of researching and hunting bounties, which would hopefully lead them to the Oranlak. He ultimately decided against it, though, determining he would just get a head start over in Serazema.

Regina headed to the Seaside Sprite for another day on the job, and Hector departed for the docks and *Liberty's Reach*, and for his several-weeks-long journey. He copied some of the maps and descriptions from the journal into his clonra's memory, and he was hopeful they would assist him in zeroing in on the area he should scrutinize while out at sea.

Andromeda made it over to the weaponsmith shortly after the shop opened that morning. Longswords, short swords, sabers, and a cutlass were displayed. Some claymores were on display, too, though none struck her as being as magnificent as Gerrard's.

There were many maces and battle-axes, too. Also available were many varieties of shields and armor. Tower shields, bucklers, plate mail, and chain mail armor were for sale. There were a few blasters, though they were prohibitively expensive. A sign on one of the counters stated, *Limited class D rounds now available.*

Andromeda yelled from the front customer area out to the back section for employees, where she assumed someone who could help her must be. "Excuse me, anyone here?" she called.

"Yes, be right out, thank you!" came a venerable, strong male voice from the back.

A minute or two later, an elderly man appeared through the door. He regarded Andromeda briefly and asked, "How may I be of service to you, miss?"

"I have something, a blaster, that I'd like you to take a look at," she replied hopefully.

"Certainly," he said. "What seems to be the trouble with it?"

"Oh, no trouble, really, sir. I'm actually just quite curious about it. I haven't owned many blasters, but I picked this one up recently, and it just seems rather unusual."

"Very well. Let me take a look at it, then," the man said.

Andromeda handed him the weapon.

He took it, sat down, and looked it over. The interest in his eyes seemed to escalate quickly. "Where did you come by this, miss?" he asked, fascinated.

"A shop in Nethereel—though it looks much nicer now than it did in the condition I found it in," she replied.

"What do you mean?" the weaponsmith inquired.

"It seems to ... have a way of restoring itself when it's used. And the bullets it fires seem to be ... a bit more damaging and effective than expected," Andromeda responded haltingly, struggling to describe what was going on with the peculiar blaster.

The man's eyes widened a bit at that. "Very interesting. Let me look into this a little," he said. "Feel free to browse around my shop; this may take a few minutes." With that, he started typing something into the clonra attached to his wrist, apparently looking something up.

A few minutes passed, and then he left the blaster on his counter and went out back again. He returned shortly after, with several large texts. He proceeded to open and flip through them, referring repeatedly to various pages over the following minutes.

"I've never seen one of these before, not in all my years..." the seasoned weaponsmith said finally, sounding astounded. "Don't waste any high-level rounds in this blaster; they will all work the same fired from its chamber. It changes the ammo you load into it to create its own special rounds."

His old eyes turned to the far younger Andromeda, standing across the counter from him. He went on, "These blasters are legendary; you can't possibly know what you hold. I wasn't even sure until this very moment the fantastical things existed. A shot fired from it absorbs the energy in the immediate area of where the bullet hits something. It drains a person's life force in what I can only imagine is a horrific demise."

The old weaponsmith broke his gaze from her and looked down at the floor, shaking his head in disbelief. "This is a true treasure. Its power may well surpass any other magic of this world."

"It doesn't seem to have fully restored itself yet," Andromeda remarked. "What happens to the energy it captures after it has completed its restoration? I would think it's just another shot or two away from being completely restored."

The man shrugged. "That, I am afraid, I do not know for certain. It's put to some other use, perhaps," he theorized.

Andromeda nodded, then asked, "May I purchase some blaster bullets from you? Just low-level rounds will do, I suppose."

"I have only a few in stock, but they're yours if you've got the coin," replied the weaponsmith.

A few minutes later, Andromeda was exiting the shop with her small pouch of blaster bullets. She felt empowered from the ammo boost and with the information she had acquired from the old historian and weaponsmith.

She also felt herself becoming quite thrilled with this new line of work she had fallen into.

She returned to the train station she and Gerrard had departed from yesterday, and she boarded one of the hydromagnetic trains back to Serazema. She would meet up with Gerrard, and hopefully, they could still secure another large bounty today. *Or even better,* she thought, *maybe we can catch a lead on the Oranlak's operations in the area.*

But even just the idea of learning more about this vampiric blaster of hers had her plenty excited enough to be practically running back to Serazema.

* * *

Regina arrived a little early to her workplace, but she didn't mind. She chatted with Blaine enthusiastically, almost as if they were already old friends. She felt she could remember well the recipes and processes he had shown her to make many of the exotic drinks routinely requested at the bar.

Regina was pleased to see she was still capable of memorizing large amounts of information efficiently. It brought her back to her university days, when the need to do so had been second nature. And this work at Seaside Sprite was not stressing her out nearly the way a lot of exams did back then—exams she had sometimes even perceived as potentially life-destroying at the time.

She remembered much of the menu in remarkable detail, though hadn't mastered all of it yet. She was also getting a sense of what people in the area liked, becoming familiar with popular tastes and with the various accents of the many people who visited the establishment. She had even made some rather successful meal suggestions to a number of appreciative customers.

The day progressed smoothly, and it was even easier than her previous day had been. Strikingly few of the customers gave her any trouble at all, though certainly some were more difficult to please than others—but

Regina understood that was just an inescapable reality of the customer service world.

* * *

Hector arrived at *Liberty's Reach* right at the instructed time. He would have been slightly early, but he had been briefly distracted by someone in one of the crowds. The person wore a cloak that looked to be—at least at a glance—that of the Order. But he lost the person in the massive crowd. He scolded himself not so much for that, though, as for just wasting time being so foolish as to think a member of the Oranlak would openly wear a cloak designating themselves as a member in public—especially in a heavily guarded and vigilant city like Akastair.

The group prided themselves on being intangible, mysterious—ghostlike, even—and in more ways than one. He could not seriously entertain, upon reflection, that this person had been one of them.

"He's back for more again, Captain!" shouted one of the crew as Hector approached.

Hector released a slight smile. He was coming to like this band of swashbucklers a little more than he had expected. Not that he was terribly keen on letting his guard down regardless, though.

Captain Saoirse just looked over at him momentarily, gave him a nod, and beckoned him to join the rest aboard the ship.

Hector felt an almost electric thrill welling up within him in thinking about the possibilities ahead. He felt the nerves of his extremities tingling with excitement, though the feeling was likely amplified by Kazahvir's influence. In any case, he couldn't deny it: it felt good.

He continued on with his crash course in sailing and expectations aboard the ship. They set out shortly thereafter—out to sea, and then southward, toward the empire of Ezmondia.

* * *

And so, this work continued on for some time for the four companions. Regina became greatly familiar with not just the menu and drink offerings at the Seaside Sprite, but also with the other staff and with many of the regular customers. She listened in to local stories and gossip whenever she could, scanning for anything useful that might take her and her team closer to wherever the Oranlak was. When possible, she even engaged the customers directly, though lightly, for any mysterious or concerning local goings-on.

Many of the crowd that visited the place were tourists just passing through. This wasn't always helpful to Regina, as they were generally less plugged in to local happenings. She found the locals more promising, at least in terms of finding leads about the Order. Though it also became noteworthy that the tourists passing through didn't tip as well as her regulars.

Still, it was interesting to talk to people often from distant cities and towns on the other side of Makeva. It did add to her enjoyment of working there. But even so, the work was exhausting sometimes, and the experiences, while she fought to spin them in a positive light to herself, were sometimes quite negative.

The simplicity of the work, though—there was a beauty to it, something that was missing from the more technical, academic world she had dwelled in much of her life.

Andromeda and Gerrard continued to enjoy great success in their bounty hunting endeavors. They came to be a team with a fair degree of notoriety in Serazema, by securing numerous large bounties in a relatively short time frame.

Gerrard, in time, came to be more conversational and open about his views on things with Andromeda. He also came to be a little more willing to depend on her, and he sometimes found that he had to, given their new line of work. His radical sense of and need for self-reliance certainly persisted, but it was substantially lessened by her presence.

Andromeda came to learn that her energy-absorbing blaster was even more vampiric than she thought. After restoring itself fully—as she suspected, with just a couple more firings—it began to restore Andromeda. It reinvigorated her, bringing bursts of youthful energy she had thought hopelessly lost to her.

The companions furnished their house over time, but they mostly let Andromeda and Regina take the reins on that front—and those two seemed to delight in fulfilling that task.

Hector was often away for long stretches, out on some voyage on *Liberty's Reach*. But it was exciting to hear of his travels when he came back, and he did become progressively better at sharing them.

Andromeda came to find comfort in the arrangement the companions had. Though it did trouble her, as it did all of them, that it was difficult to discern how much progress they were really making, at least toward finding out more about the Order of Oranlak and what they were up to near Akastair. Still, even if all their efforts were truly not advancing them toward those goals, there was so much more they were gaining from the experiences they were having. Andromeda knew it wouldn't be appropriate at all to measure everything they were doing simply in terms of how much progress they were making finding some criminal gang. And she found that these feelings of comfort and contentedness often catapulted her mind back many years, to a past time when she had felt so similarly.

22

Chapter Twenty-Two

After several months of generally adhering to this routine, Andromeda fell ill. It wasn't a particularly debilitating illness, but still, it made her feel drained of energy.

On one day in particular in the midst of this illness, Andromeda considered going out anyway, pushing through the sickness. She suspected she would bounce back quickly, and maybe especially if she had the opportunity to put her vampiric blaster to use. But the years had taught her that sometimes it was a good thing to just take the day off work, or whatever it was, when you needed it. A day of reflection or of recovery—it could sometimes help a person reassess things about their life. This was something she had not known so well in terms of how or when to do it in years past—but surely, it was a concept she could appreciate now.

On this particular day of recovery and reflection, she found herself thinking back over her life. She was in her mid-forties now, and with likely decades of life still ahead of her, but she couldn't help but feel she had already known and experienced so much. And she could not help but see how even the awful things that had come into her life over the years had ultimately brought her to where she was now, feeling the mental and physical contentedness that she was. Andromeda felt she could see with crystalline clarity how even the bad had helped guide and shape her into the person she was now—a person she respected and appreciated deeply.

And yet, even in reflecting how so many circumstances molded and shaped her in what was such a lengthy process, over such a long period of time, she couldn't help but feel a deep connection between what she had come to believe and value in the present and what she always remembered valuing and believing in. For certain, these values and beliefs were now more refined, and she could more eloquently and confidently convey them, but they were still so much the same as they always had been.

During this illness, Andromeda came to reflect on her youth, growing up with her siblings. She thought about the ranch with her parents. She remembered how often her grandparents, uncles, and aunts were around. There was a ... sense of security back then, even though she was so young. There was a certain stability to her life then, which seemed now so important to have in one's youth. And in remembering it now, she greatly appreciated having had it. So many of the young in present-day Gracyr did not have such an environment to depend on and to thrive in. The times had taken an objectively dark turn, with the failing power systems that threatened to define them, the excessive centralization of wealth and power, and the rise of a more aggressive empire of Ezmondia.

She thought about how it was for them back then, growing up. She thought of how typical and expected it was that a child would follow in whatever line of work his or her family happened to be involved in. For Andromeda, that work had been the cattle ranch. She had been tasked from a young age with seeing to the needs of the place and helping to ensure its longevity.

Andromeda recalled a time when, as she neared the end of her public education, at just eighteen years of age, she had come to entertain doing something very different with her life. It wasn't really just her age at the time contributing to those ideas though; the ideas were something that came about as a result of many entangled happenings and circumstances. In any case, she came to harbor different sorts of thoughts and aspirations that deviated from those the rest of her family held. To their credit though, they still had been supportive of her voicing her thoughts about a different course for her life. They listened to her, helping her afford going to the university, even.

And then, fortunately for her, they welcomed her back ... when she ended up returning. They hadn't agreed with or been happy about the path she had pursued in going to the university in the first place, and she understood them not being pleased about it not working out and her not seeing it through. But they welcomed her back all the same, and she had always appreciated that. When she returned home, she had essentially determined that she just wanted to do what her family had long been doing.

None of that was to say that she felt it was entirely a waste to have gone, though. Not in retrospect, not in the grand scheme of things. Though perhaps she did feel that way for a brief time when she first returned home. She had studied many subjects and taken a multitude of different classes. Perhaps part of the reason for that was just that she had not been sure what exactly it was she wanted. She craved broader perspective, heightened awareness—a deeper understanding of people, things, and the world as a whole. And there had been so much for her young mind to dig into to gain ground in such pursuits back in those early years.

Those four years in higher education had gone quickly. She was twenty-two years old and graduating before she knew it. She had studied literature, biology, physics, law, history, communications, and chemistry, among what seemed countless other subjects. She had met professors and fellow students who had moved her profoundly, and she had delighted in working with and getting to know many of them. It had been a matchless pleasure to have connected and communicated with so many inspiring people of such broad perspectives and experiences. At times, it even seemed the most fascinating things she was learning—things that struck her as so profoundly critical and fundamental to being human—were things she was not learning in the classroom at all. That is to say, they weren't even strictly the things she was spending all that coin to be educated on.

Andromeda came to have a deep appreciation for the world, their beautiful Gracyr, and what made it so special and incredible—physically, biologically, environmentally, and beyond. The way the atoms, the elements made things up. The forces of nature. The physics of the world and the universe. The human mind and body. There was so much to admire—at such amazing depth—and though she felt that over those years she learned and came to understand much, she knew even more confidently that in the grand scheme of everything, she still knew nothing. And that thought continued to move her. After all, she had been one of the top students at her university every year she attended. There were not many who could have claimed to have outperformed her. And still, the case could be made that what she knew had amounted to nothing.

It was around that age that Andromeda had come to reject some of the commonly agreed-upon theories of her time—those about certain things in Gracyr, and those about certain things, essentially, even in the greater universe. It seemed to her an impossibility that things had just spontaneously come into existence at some distant previous point in time. Or that things could have progressed along as they did over nigh-immeasurable spans of time, in what seemed to her to be such incredible perfection.

In any case, she was not entirely convinced herself, particularly back in those earlier years, whether she could be confident at all in challenging so many of the things that were ubiquitously taught to everyone. But she could not deny to herself that there were things she was taught that … never felt right to her. So it was, she supposed in reflection, that she had come to believe some things that, apparently, everyone else did not.

On one occasion in particular back at the university, she had come upon a very compelling and memorable story. It had been in an old, dusty text buried in the historic grand library. The library was a gorgeous place, with vast high ceilings, ancient statues that were impossible works of art, and stained-glass windows of a forgotten era. History hadn't been one of the most popular majors at school while she attended, and it hadn't been for a long time before when she was there. So, it had made sense to her that the text was coated in a thick layer of dust. And she felt confident that that section of the library at the time had been almost entirely forgotten. To this day, she still clearly remembered removing the cobwebs off the thing.

She read in that archaic, ages-old book of the beliefs and teachings of a past empire. It was one largely lost to time and forgotten about by the modern-day population of Gracyr. The tome detailed massive, otherworldly battles, almost incomprehensible in scale. There were discussions of galaxy-destroying weaponry, and of the insuperable speed and strength possessed by entities surpassing human imaginations. It also spoke of profound darkness, and of planet-swallowing monsters that fought in epic conflicts spanning universes.

But it also referenced great goodness, and the incredible and beautiful purity of other entities. It spoke of an intelligence and power that dwarfed even the forces of such planet-devastating warfare. And of an entity that had also created Gracyr.

She read on that these entities walked even across the voids between planes of existence—voids between planes such as those between Andromeda's world and the shadow realm.

She read of one such entity that this fallen empire had revered particularly greatly. This entity, according to the descriptions, had laid down its power, sacrificing itself. The story claimed it had even done this for the sake of humanity. And there had been many similarly compelling stories about others that sacrificed, or conquered, or overcame all manner of mind-boggling obstacles and adversaries.

To put it mildly, in Andromeda's view, it had not been her experience in life to see that degree of selflessness often. And there were so many other admirable characters described in the old stories, and they made a joke of so many of the supposed leaders of her mortal world, though she did sincerely feel she had witnessed many great and beautiful things in humanity. Any—or even all—humans she had ever met or heard of, though, had nothing compared to what this greater entity that sacrificed itself had to lose. Yet it had laid it all down for the sake of the preservation of humanity, and essentially for the sake of even Andromeda herself. The idea that this being, before Andromeda had ever even been born, and not even having known her, had cared enough to do such a thing fascinated her.

Still, it was her natural reaction to question it. But even so, the stories had dwelled ever since in her memory. Over time, she came to consider in depth that she rather liked the idea of it all being true. She came to align her thoughts and actions with the idea that it was. And she felt keenly that her life was the better for it. It was a theoretical structure to her, of how to rationalize and understand the world as well as the human mind could—and she came to find in that structure a degree of guidance and self-empowerment, which strengthened her as an individual, and did infinitely more to guard her from the darkness that lurked in her modern world than anything else she could find.

There was value, she felt, in having a solid foundation like that to stand on. The stories she read of that day in the grand library were old, as time-tested as anything she had ever read. And still they had spoken to her, moved her deeply. If the untold number of centuries or even millennia that had passed since they had been written had failed to strip them of their power, she wasn't sure anything could.

Andromeda came to wed shortly after she returned home to her previous life on her family's cattle ranch. Not so long a time later, she also had a son. And her life was quickly filled with many distractions and the chaos of having so much to do and so little time to do it. But the groundwork she had laid while at the university was something that held strong for her. Though her life experiences piled up atop that mental foundation, it still lent her a steadiness of mind that she carried with her through the chaos and trials of the ensuing years. Though that foundation seemed to occasionally crack or fracture, it never gave way, and it always survived ultimately stronger.

Andromeda only had one child, which was a drastic departure from the large number of children her own parents had—what people for generations past generally had. Times were different now, though. There were complexities in Andromeda's childbearing years that were not present, or were substantially less so, in her parents' time. And Andromeda had also spent years working on other pursuits instead of having children—years she could not reclaim.

In having and raising even just that one child, though, Andromeda couldn't help but think about the value of the sacrifice and how important it had been in her life for her to invest in something like her son. He represented something so much greater than she herself did.

She couldn't bear to see herself dwelling in selfish, self-serving ends and pursuits. Such things brought her a hollow, empty feeling, which did nothing to satisfy her desire for a greater sense of fulfillment. The effort she poured into her child, through motherhood, was something she took very seriously.

She had done her best to give what guidance she could to her son when he was young. She always knew he would grow up to be a product of the unfortunate times in which he was coming of age. It was a reality that concerned her immensely, considering so many of the atrocities she already saw unfolding around the time of his birth.

Andromeda found it to be immeasurably frustrating. She knew things in her mind—things so clear, so strongly reinforced and defendable. But they lost so much of their meaning when put into words. Words were loosely interpreted between individuals, holding different meanings and associations. And they formed concepts that varied even more intensely between different people, who often didn't even hold a consistent interpretation of concepts throughout the entirety of their own lives. Such interpretations were inevitably altered by their surroundings and changing perspectives as they aged.

She tried to convey to her son, Lucas, the stories she remembered, back in the grand library of her university. She gave him what she felt to be hard-earned and valuable advice. Andromeda told him about how she felt indebted to the sacrifice of this greater entity, of how she held in her mind to an agreement wherein she lived her life as admirably as she could, to honor the sacrifice of the entity that had given its own for her. She knew it was with this understanding, with this mental framework and theory of their world and beyond, that a person could best hope to navigate it. Andromeda believed it at a level she knew she could not accurately put into words.

Her words to her son often seemed to fall upon deaf ears. And Andromeda came to realize that a person needed to go through a life of building mental pathways to their own understanding—that her son could not simply have the truth she already knew spoken to him and automatically understand.

Still, sometimes despite herself, she found herself determined to try.

She spoke to her son of the importance of such concepts as hope and love. About how to put value in such unseen and undying things was to take control of one's life. She cautioned him how the external, the material, and the moment could be seized and used against a person—such as by a tyrant vying for control of an empire. But that to believe in things such as hope and love—that was to defy and weaken the control-hungry monsters that some people in society always inevitably became.

But the people of Gracyr, their thoughts were made to dwell—by the influential and powerful—ever more so on the present moment. In the empire of Ezmondia in particular, people's minds were conditioned to linger on things that could be controlled. And Andromeda could see how they were poisoned, not just by the low quality of their food, but by the decadent and self-destructive content so increasingly ubiquitous in the ever-expanding, vast network of vidscreen programming.

Over the course of her present illness, Andromeda thought about a long-ago time when someone dear to her had also been ill—though he had been significantly more so. Her late husband, the father of her son, had been defeated by that malady. It had been difficult on the family, but perhaps most particularly on the son they had together. She remembered how Lucas had expressed emotions that had been, up to that point, rare for him. In time, his emotions came to settle better under his control—but perhaps it was true that they were never fully the same again. The trials of that period had left something of a lasting tension between the boy and his family, even between him and his mother.

Andromeda had loved her husband deeply. She had been invested in the man and what they had built together. She had been pleased with what their efforts had wrought and the relationship they had built; she even took it as irreplaceable. He had been a strong-willed man, committed and devoted to her—and these were things she deeply valued. She had barely wasted her thoughts on ideas about what could have been better or was lacking about him. And beyond such things, they worked toward many of the same ends and goals, and they were committed to advancing those ends and goals together, even if they could not maintain their mutual love for each other.

Her husband ultimately had died of a terrible cancerous affliction. They were vigilant about his health and had detected it quickly, but not quickly enough. It hadn't made life on the ranch easier for her surviving family members who lived and worked on the ranch, and especially not for Andromeda and her son. It still wasn't easy for Andromeda to leave years later when she had embarked on her current mission.

Yet she knew she had to. She recognized something it seemed the rest of her family hadn't seen as clearly as she had.

Andromeda understood that the situation at their ranch was deteriorating, and the rest of them knew at least that much, as well. But they lacked the urgency she possessed. The greater context of their situation was that they were on an unsustainable road to ruin, and this point seemed to be lost on the rest of her family. They plugged along day to day, the same as they always had, apparently coasting on some nebulous belief that things would go on forever, that they would somehow work out if they just kept pouring their lives into the fading family enterprise.

But the reality was that larger operations were buying out great swaths of cattle ranches, which were often smaller, family-run operations like theirs. And in so doing, the giants of the industry were coming to control a greater majority of it. Andromeda had perceived a darkness on the horizon that those she loved most in the world simply could not.

So it was that she came to understand that she had to leave. The tournament in Nethereel had been the gamble she was willing to take. It was the key to unlocking the door to a way out for her and her loved ones, something that could turn the tide of the all-encompassing waves gradually overtaking them. She seized her past skill with the blade—that she had picked up from her father—and sharpened it to what extent had been possible for her. And she took the bejeweled saber he had left her when he died. Off she had gone to Nethereel, and ultimately to the situation she found herself in now.

Andromeda also thought about one of her last conversations with Lucas. He had been upset over a matter at school—something he thought at the time was unfair, that he thought of as an obstacle he could not hope to overcome. He had a teacher that he took as not liking him so much, and indeed, Andromeda's observations tended to make her inclined to believe it was true. Her son had a test coming up in the subject this teacher taught—something in mathematics. The teacher had apparently conveyed to the class some things about the test that had not made Lucas feel confident, that had actually worried him greatly.

Andromeda recalled speaking to her son, trying to offer words of advice applicable to his troubles. Of course, it was also advice she was sure she had given him many times previously.

"My son," she recollected telling him, "what is in your mind will defeat you, or empower you, far more than any external force ever could."

Andromeda suspected that the boy felt she put too much weight on such things—ideas about the importance of finding inspiration or shifting mental perspectives. But she knew the power of inspiration and a positive frame of mind. She felt on that last occasion that maybe she had finally gotten through to him.

She remembered speaking to him again the following day. He still had that test coming up—it was something like a week away still. But the next day, he hadn't been in such a state of despair anymore; he had his mind on other things. Maybe it had been that the weekend was arriving or had nearly arrived, or maybe he'd had a date with a girl at school or something of that nature.

Regardless, Andromeda recalled remarking to her son about his relatively sudden change in outlook. Lucas hadn't had much to say in response to her questioning it, though he acknowledged the change in his mood. She remembered saying to him then how the world was the same place it had been the day prior, when he had been so upset with it. And she observed and lightly expressed to him how his view of it was now so dramatically different. She told him how nothing had significantly changed about the greater world over the course of that past day.

Andromeda had taken the opportunity to try to explain to him how such small happenings—and the views, perceptions, and context that *he alone* chose to focus on, along with the particular light he decided to cast them in—could reframe his reality to be anything he chose. She had told him, "You live in the world that you want to live in—you have the power to change it. The world will be as you believe it to be."

23

Chapter Twenty-Three

Most of a year passed by. Andromeda and Gerrard came to build up greater notoriety locally for their bounty hunting successes. Sometimes they split up and worked on separate hunts, but they came to find they were more effective working as a team.

Some gangs and criminal organizations even pulled out of the city in time, finding it no longer profitable, and many others scaled down their operations in Serazema. The authorities in the city were also better able to manage the crime now, and many people living and working in the city came to be of the opinion that conditions in Serazema had dramatically improved. And no small portion of that credit was attributed to Andromeda and Gerrard, who were also commonly known as the top two finalists from the last tournament in Nethereel.

But not everyone felt so positively about the two of them.

* * *

"I'll ask you. One. More. Time," offered the second-in-command of the Ezmondian Empire, in a tone harsher than usual. "And Ursula, do not fill up your answer with extraneous, irrelevant information to distract me from your incompetence," Mercedes warned. "Do not complicate your response to hide the truth," she scolded her underling, despite how powerful that underling was. "Now, what is going on with our operations in and around Serazema?"

Mercedes was shorter on patience than usual that morning. Circumstances had necessitated an unexpected in-person meeting with several of her direct reports that day, and she already had a full schedule as it was.

The black-market mining project, as well as its associated dealings operating out of Serazema and its outskirts, which had not so long ago been flourishing, had become troubled some months back. Slight problems and minor setbacks had escalated, and now, the diminishing returns to the empire from that area had even caught the attention of Armando—who had not so subtly brought up his displeasure about the situation to Mercedes that morning.

The rich veins of crimson fluorite in the area had been a boon for them and the Order of Oranlak with whom they were in partnership. They had loaded up their coffers considerably from the lucrative business they had built up there in recent years. Of course, they had skipped out on obtaining the time-consuming work authorizations and regulatory approvals, so they could conduct their business, and they had instead purchased the cheaper blinded eyes of the authorities tasked with finding such illegal operations in the area.

Troubling, though, was that some of the local authorities—those not purchased in such a way—had recently been poking around, getting alarmingly close to their empire's crimson fluorite and their black-market dealings.

It didn't help that they were working in a limited time window. The dated, unsafe mining practices they used to mine the crimson fluorite were helping them do it with great efficiency and minimal expense—but it was also polluting the area. Underground charges were causing cracks in the foundations of some houses in the woods on the outskirts of Serazema. And the water pollution was an issue in particular, as a major nearby river was becoming quite blatantly affected. The local groundwater aquifers surely had pollution seeping into them by now, as well.

It might still be some time before the greater public really caught on to the problems, and it would be longer still before it could be traced back to the mining operation causing it. And even then, of course, Armando and Mercedes, the empire, and the Oranlak were thoroughly shielded and distanced from the mining operation there, which would just publicly be deemed some renegade operation. They remained supremely confident that it would not significantly be tied back to them. Too much of the media the public consumed masked such unpleasant associations, with many people working tirelessly to prop up the empire and cast it in the most positive light possible. And in the case of the Order, references to them would even be entirely omitted. Still, they did not want their profits from their operations to halt, or even slow, for that matter.

To add further tension to the situation, there was another disappointment frustrating Armando recently. The media campaigns the empire ran, though effective, could sometimes be slow to bear fruit, and the initiatives to persuade its people to produce more offspring were catching on too slowly for Armando's liking. As a consequence, they had enacted new laws to incentivize the public further. Of course, they were all adding to the already draconian compilation of laws they had in their empire. Mercedes could see how all the technical, complicated, poorly researched, and weakly understood laws they passed often seemed to cause more problems than they solved—and it was as apparent to her now as it had ever been.

But the phenomenon could even be observed with the mining industry in Makeva. All the countless authorizations necessitated by laws did arguably more to restrict and harm that country than they did good—though surely it was true that elements of some were advisable and good to have in place.

Mercedes found her mind continuing to trail off now as Ursula unsurprisingly hesitated again to answer her question.

Ursula had been reluctant to detail the situation in Serazema very thoroughly for her superior. She had asked for and been granted this new assignment not even a year ago, and it had been running successfully for many years prior to her coming on board. It wasn't a good look for her at all that it was failing now.

She had, of course, done the digging to get to what was going on with their business interests there, which did remain an important opportunity for her, and one she held substantial interest in maintaining.

Their Order—and by extension, the empire—had lost some key people involved with the mining initiatives they had in the area. Members of the Order of Oranlak mostly had whitewashed records and were usually absent from reports retrievable by the authorities. But it wasn't a perfect system for them. Some of their members inevitably had past offenses that got them put on bounty lists, so they could sometimes become targets for bounty hunters.

Many of the key figures in the chain that made their operation in and around Serazema function had now been hunted down by a pair of new bounty hunters. The authorities had also captured some, particularly now that they were getting a grasp on the chaos in the area, with fewer criminals running amok. The chaos had favored the Oranlak in the area. And more order, less chaos was a not-so-hospitable environment for what they were trying to achieve.

Of course, they bought off and bribed most of the higher ranks of the authorities. They were variously corrupted and instructed to do some things or not to do others, depending on what the Oranlak or the empire needed.

The authorities' lower ranks might have had the good they were doing often overruled or ignored by superiors, but it wasn't possible to stop some of the criminal band from being caught and imprisoned when there were still so many non-corrupt agents in the enforcement system.

Ursula's digging had revealed to her that the bounty hunters responsible for turning this colossal tide back in the favor of law and order were the very same pair who had won first and second place in the last Nethereelan sword fighting tournament. And to her persistent frustration, one of them was that very same Gerrard who had slipped through her fingers back at her previous assignment at Waterfall Ridge.

It had been careless of her, she reflected, to have just triggered the self-destruct mechanism. She should have hunted down the fool and done him in then, directly. Now, he had lived to cause her an ongoing series of escalating headaches.

In any case, she wasn't in a hurry to relay to Mercedes the name of this person causing the mischief, as she might well remember that name—the name of a certain person Ursula should have ensured was no longer among the living a long time ago. She had hoped it had been something of a fluke, or that Gerrard and this female bounty hunter, Andromeda, would just hunt down a few bounties and head to greener pastures—make some coin for a bit and move on to something else. But they hadn't. Months had passed, and they were staying put. She couldn't afford to not take action anymore.

"The loss of a number of critical people important in running aspects of the operation in Serazema has caused the delays, the backups, the breakdowns," Ursula advised, finally answering Mercedes. "These people were all brought down by the same duo of newly minted bounty hunters originating in Akastair. They are unusually skilled and well equipped. They do not seem to be targeting our people in particular, but engage with any local bounties, with a possible favoritism for the higher-paying ones. They have been making a lot of coin and have become well known in the region these past months."

Ursula's voice sounded even more ghoulish than usual, and it was a little off-putting, even to Mercedes, someone who was almost unmatched in her position of power in Gracyr.

"Better," Mercedes managed, repositioning herself mentally to try to sound stronger and undaunted. Then she narrowed her eyes dangerously, utilizing her frustration and anger at her own perceived weakness. "And what are you doing to rectify this situation?"

"I am going to track them down and deal with the matter personally," Ursula replied. She knew well—or at least justifiably suspected—that any lesser answer would not go over well with her. Mercedes was, after all, in all likelihood actively considering trying to bash her face in with that menacing mace she carried.

"See to it at once. I expect results soon," Mercedes stated. Then she muttered, "I have enough going on already, and I'm late to my next meeting about the fertility crisis." She regarded Ursula for a moment. "You seem to have some skill with buying yourself more time. What do you think I should do about that situation?"

Ursula considered it for a moment. "I understand some are saying the present campaign to drive up these numbers is worsening the situation, and it seems that our sudden obsession with this problem is exacerbating it. Perhaps consider creating an environment that indirectly incentivizes the people to do your will, rather than relying on these new laws essentially forcing their compliance. Ezmondians don't seem to be taking well to new laws. It seems even those slaves to the empire have their limits... Perhaps endeavor to guide them to think that the idea you want them to have is their own," she suggested.

Mercedes considered Ursula's response for a moment. She could relate to this concept of there being too many laws, causing more problems. Maybe she should lay off that particular tactic they'd recently been leaning into. And surely, while they could force many things effectively, it was usually easier to get their subjects to do something when they believed it was their own idea.

Maybe she shouldn't be so quick to entertain these thoughts of bashing Ursula's skull in after all.

"Be gone with you," Mercedes snapped, waving dismissively, which was as good of a response as Ursula could have hoped for.

* * *

On the way to her next meeting at the Castle, Mercedes took some time to run through in her mind other outstanding concerns for the day ahead. She landed on one matter in particular. She hadn't judged it to be a major problem yet, but after recent events, she could appreciate why it was sticking in her mind now.

Their operation to collect the promethium and bring it to the surface had been a resounding success. They were generating electricity from burning the substance, and they were hooking more of the empire up to that power source every day. Lights flickering and power failures were starting to feel like a distant memory at the Castle and in many other places across Ezmondia, even for commoners. Just months prior, they had dealt with such things on an almost daily basis. And now they were making a lot of profit, as it was incredibly lucrative. They had already brought up enough promethium to keep things running in Ezmondia for a long time.

There was, of course, the pollution that some were trying to raise alarms about—but the greater public really hadn't caught on. And it was doubtful that they would, given the overwhelming information dominance the Elite Council and their ilk enjoyed.

Even media aside, the eyes of the public were too fixated on the multitudinous benefits of the power source to dwell on any proposed negatives, anyway. Their minds were on the life-sustaining energy, the continued availability of heating and cooling systems and electricity necessary to life as they knew it. Even the supposedly higher morals of those few who advocated for environmental sustainability to the exclusion of so much else still utterly collapsed in the face of their own imminent deaths.

Such heavier concerns also conveniently distracted the commoners of the Ezmondian Empire from the vast amounts of wealth she and Armando, the Oranlak, and the Elite Council were generating for themselves. And for that matter, they distracted them from thinking about any long-term costs at all, whatever they might be for Gracyr or the planet. So much of it all was coming along rather smoothly, really.

But still, the blemish her mind settled on now was one she could see escalating and threatening what had been so beautifully orchestrated of a plan.

Their operation had hit something of a snag. They'd had to pause their work at the underwater facility they had built after some disturbances and a few personnel going missing.

Strange circumstances surrounded the whole scenario. The ground-breaking facility constructed to help in the extraction of the promethium had been built on a never-before-seen scale underwater. It had also been built in a miraculously short period of time. But they had come to learn that time was actually moving differently down there, around the sunken spaceship where the promethium was. And the time fluctuations didn't seem consistent, either. Weeks or sometimes even months passed by for people down in the facility and around the spaceship, while just days passed back in Gracyr. This state of affairs had enabled them to build the place with great speed. They had already been collecting promethium for months, when they were initially projected to still be building the facility at this time.

But now, this past week, there had been more disappearances. Their workers on the ground, so to speak, were rightfully spooked, and she could no longer explain away the circumstances without further action being taken.

It was already a claustrophobic and unnerving setting down there, and they surely didn't need the added stress of these recent unexplained events. The workers described things going on that had given even the hardened Mercedes chills. She had done her best to chalk it up to the delusions of overworked employees in an intense environment. Perhaps these were symptoms of decompression sickness affecting their minds. Despite her explanations to herself, though, these things had lingered in her thoughts, and now had come to nag at her more demandingly.

At this point, they had been forced to pause their work in the underwater facility and investigate further. Fortunately, they had already gathered so much promethium that Mercedes wasn't immediately worried. They had time to figure things out. But she also understood that it could be deceptive, how time could make you feel more shielded from a crisis than you actually were.

Some of the other high-ranking members of the Elite Council were more worried, though. She thought of Ursula, too, for a moment. She wondered, even if just fleetingly, what Ursula's thoughts on this matter were.

Mercedes shoved thoughts of this matter aside as she came upon the room of her next meeting. She sighed a little, then put her hand to the doorknob and turned it, easing the door open.

One issue at a time, she thought.

* * *

Regina arrived right on time to open up the Seaside Sprite on another warm summer day. There was a light breeze in the air that late morning, which was perfect to keep a person still relatively cool with the hot sun blazing. She wondered if the breeze would persist through the day, or if it would be another long scorcher of a day like yesterday. If it would be another day with temperatures like yesterday, she fully expected a jam-packed and busy day ahead of her, as more people would be seeking comfortable places like the Seaside Sprite to spend some time in.

To her delight, the Seaside Sprite had recently installed a geothermal heat pump. Regina had been the most enthusiastic of any in attendance during the installation. She loved chatting about it with any willing customers, and sometimes even brought it up to any patrons just looking to strike up some manner of small talk.

She had developed a fair understanding of the customer base at the Seaside Sprite. For example, she knew the general hobbies, lines of work, and perspectives of those who frequented the place or tended to visit, as well as their sensitivity to extreme temperatures.

Regina unlocked the front door and flipped on the switch inside to light the place up. She made sure the open sign was lit and welcoming.

She had perfected what she thought of as "the art of being right on time." She liked to plan things out that way and to see them come together just as planned. She was not one to be late—and sometimes, for certain, measures had to be taken to ensure she would not be. But she didn't like to be too early; she saw it as wasted time that could have been put to use doing something else productive. When she was right on time, she felt like she was maximizing her potential and getting the most out of her day. It was sort of a silly game she played with herself, she knew. But then, she suspected everyone played such silly games with themselves.

In any case, in walking through the door of her workplace that day, she entered what she fully expected to be another plainly typical workday, albeit perhaps a busy one. She was beginning to become restless with the work. She certainly still appreciated the simplicity of it, talking to people so lightheartedly most of the time, but it was becoming a bit bland and repetitive. Plus, too many of the customers were a little too frequent regulars. She felt like she understood them now too well, and she was consequently losing interest. People had been such a mystery to her at the start; they were from some background or line of work she wasn't familiar with, and she wanted to dig in and learn about it. But she had learned much of what she took to be interesting in a rather short time. And now, the people around here were starting to seem too typical.

She also wasn't picking up any tips about the Order of Oranlak operating in the area or about any long-lost, sunken spaceship.

Anyway, Regina's workday started off typically enough, and it went on as expected. Then, after what had been a day of catering mostly to her regulars, a man sat down at the bar in the midafternoon whom she hadn't seen before. The restaurant and bar were almost at capacity on this busy, increasingly hot summer day. Still, she noticed this man in particular. Perhaps it was because of the person he was accompanied by, an apparent friend of his who looked familiar. Regina had overheard the man recommending that the pair of them grab some open seats at the bar, rather than waiting for a booth or table in the main restaurant.

"Excuse me, miss," the man said, hailing Regina as they sat down. "Is the full menu available at the bar here?"

"Ya, sure is!" Regina cheerily responded, already placing a couple menus in front of them. "Be with ya in just a moment."

Regina continued on to the end of the bar to deliver a drink order to a couple who had sat down a couple minutes prior, skillfully recalling their names as she delivered the drinks. She rattled off a few specials before asking what they'd like to order.

She returned to her newest customers a few moments later. "What may I get ya to drink, friends?" she kindly asked.

"Well, you see, miss," said the one she didn't find familiar, "I'm new to your city, and this is my first time in your fine establishment. My friend is a local to the city, but I'm afraid he doesn't go out to eat terribly often—so while he has been an excellent guide to so much in Akastair, I'm afraid he can't help me much in this present situation. Would it be okay, do you think, for me to presume you can offer us some guidance in what's good here?"

The lengthy response suggested to Regina that the man either had exceedingly high expectations of her, or that he was just blind to how busy she was at that moment. But Blaine was on at the bar with her, and they had been keeping up with orders okay, so she figured she'd spare a minute for this older gentleman and indulge the situation.

"Well, the steaks are top notch; I like the rib eye, personally. The loaded baked potato and grilled asparagus are faves among the usual crowd. I'll bring ya each a glass of my favorite ale, if ya think you'd like to be givin' that a try," Regina offered.

"Very good. So glad to have your guidance, miss..." he said, in such a way that Regina understood he was asking her name.

"Regina," she stated. "My pleasure to be assisting ya."

"My name is Viktor, and we'll each try a baked potato and a rib eye, and we thank you kindly. It is likewise a pleasure to meet you."

Regina nodded and smiled at the older gentlemen, then she moved off to relay the food orders to the kitchen and to pour their drinks.

Viktor continued to be highly conversational, and though it was tricky for Regina to fit much extra into her busy day, she did endeavor to talk with the man a little more than she might have ordinarily been inclined to. She knew she could juggle just a little more than she was, and there was something about the pair that she wanted to understand. Maybe she just wanted to unveil why the quieter one seemed so darn familiar.

Viktor's work experiences came up a few times, and Regina learned that he was the retired captain of a fishing vessel. His more interesting work, so far as she was concerned, though, was what he described doing prior to falling into all that. He had apparently served in the armed forces and had significant experience aboard submarines. Someone of that experience struck her as a rare sort of person to have the opportunity to encounter.

Still, she did not immediately realize the usefulness the man might present for the mission she and her companions were on. He did happen to mention that he was just visiting for a time and was from the other side of the continent, where perhaps, she supposed, this line of work and sort of experience might be more common. He also had mentioned he was staying with his friend there, Cid, until the man had to leave on his next fishing trip. When she finally heard him mention his friend's name, she regarded the quieter man for a lasting moment. And then it occurred to her where she recognized his face from. Cid walked by her some mornings when she was going to work, always headed in the opposite direction. He probably hadn't been a customer here, as she had initially suspected.

In any case, the two friends moved along from the Seaside Sprite just shortly after she finally had that realization. And the whole exchange quickly blurred into the rest of Regina's chaotic workday, fading quite thoroughly in her memory as the tidal wave of new customers and the overflow of new orders came pouring in.

* * *

Hector's day had mostly been smooth sailing. After another successful mission plundering Ezmondian merchant vessels off the coast of Ezmondia, he was bound with Captain Saoirse and the rest of the crew of *Liberty's Reach* for the port of Akastair.

Their actions were, of course, perfectly legal. They even held what many considered to be fairly prestigious positions. This crew of *Liberty's Reach,* just a dozen people, actually fancied—even romanticized—themselves to be swashbucklers.

The exact membership had varied a little over Hector's relatively short time with them, because it was dangerous work, and sometimes, they did lose someone. But apparently, the perception that people in and around Akastair had of them and of the work they did was highly favorable to recruiting new candidates. Many locals had apparently grown up on fantastic and sensationalized versions of what they actually did. *Liberty's Reach* was apparently even a symbol to many of them—a symbol of things its crew did not even outwardly advocate for. Many people aspired to the glamor they perceived in what their crew did, regardless of the real truth of it.

But then, who is to say what the real truth of it all is, anyway? Hector couldn't help but ponder, at least from time to time.

He had come to find it entertaining to interact with people who learned his title as first mate of *Liberty's Reach.* They were privateers—corsairs, even—with official authorization in the form of a letter from the Grandmaster of the Gatekeepers Council. They had authority to take, commandeer, usurp, and plunder Ezmondian ships. They took many ships hostage and took possession of many rare and valuable inventories. Ezmondia had been deemed indebted to Makeva by the Gatekeepers Council, as a result of years of theft, pillaging, and other atrocities they had committed and not answered for to the satisfaction of that ruling council of Makeva. It was a debt the Gatekeepers Council had determined Ezmondia would repay one way or another. Seeing as Ezmondia had openly refused for many years to hold any serious talks or gatherings to mediate—and it continued to commit hostilities against the country of Makeva—the Makevans had been driven to extract compensation by more forceful means.

There was specific guidance that *Liberty's Reach* and its crew had to follow, of course. There were laws to abide by and practices and protocols to adhere to. Not all ships and cargo were subject to raids by privateer ships like *Liberty's Reach*. Ships with cargo essentially consisting of medicine or medical supplies were an example of ships that ought not to be attacked.

On one occasion, Hector and the other crewmen had come upon a vessel waving a flag that was supposed to signal that it was immune to privateer attacks, as per the order of the Gatekeepers Council. It was then that Hector had learned the process of boarding a vessel with this purported immunity. They had the Makevan legal right to inspect the claim of the vessel, and it was the guidance of the Gatekeepers Council that such a ship invoking this protection was subject to confirmation of its immunity. It was important to keep to the guidelines in this matter, Hector learned, as the stability of their ongoing employment depended on it. And of course, the integrity of their profession also demanded it. They could, if violating the laws around such circumstances, be stripped of their authorizing letter from the Grandmaster and would no longer be able to practice in the profession. Any transgressions might need to be subsequently determined to be willfully, knowingly, or recklessly done—but it was best to take care to act as lawfully as possible, since, as Hector came to understand, it was all taken very seriously.

Unfortunately, it had apparently been the case that sometimes ships invoked the protection to try to catch privateers off guard, to obtain the first strike and gain an advantage in a battle that was going to happen for them anyway. As a result of such incidents in the past, measures had been taken to better assure the safety of those privateers confirming such claims. The crew of a commandeered ship would often have their lives spared by Makeva, but if they falsely invoked these protections, that crew would face a near certain—and generally quite painful—death.

In the single instance Hector had witnessed, their crew had confirmed the invocation to be legitimate, and the vessel had simply been allowed to continue on its way. But it prompted the explanation and lesson about it all—by Captain Saoirse, no less—who seemed to have taken to him rather fondly since he had joined her crew.

Hector had just intended to lend some muscle to justify his presence among them, but it seemed he had been able to be of greater use to Saoirse and her efforts. He even had some relevant knowledge of Ezmondian ports and shipping routes from his time growing up in Ezmondia.

It was unusual, Saoirse had remarked upon first learning of his upbringing in Ezmondia, to encounter someone who had escaped from the place. Even someone who got out was more likely let out for some insidious espionage mission in Makeva than any other reason. And even those who might be able to physically escape were so seldom able to find freedom from the chains that bound their minds. Such conditioning as one suffered in the empire was not easily undone.

There was a certain ease of life in Ezmondia that didn't really exist in Makeva. The northwestern segment of the continent of Gracyr that was Makeva was more substantially defined by harsher weather conditions and various hardships—hardships that, in some ways, just made life more difficult than in Ezmondia. In Ezmondia, it was more just a matter of being provided for—albeit meagerly—and falling in line. There was less worry about figuring out how to solve your own problems, and more reassurance that others would figure them out for you.

Perhaps part of Saoirse's draw to me is where I'm from, Hector thought. She was looking for someone ... different than the usual sort of person she was accustomed to encountering in Makeva. There was no shortage of charming, chivalrous, charismatic men among the ranks of privateers around the docks of Akastair. But perhaps the glamor of such men had long since faded for the more worldly Saoirse.

She certainly seemed to have greater ambitions than most people he had encountered. But then, it wasn't so long ago that he had lived his entire life surrounded by people eager to submit to the will of a tyrant, for scraps of satisfaction that were wholly insufficient for him. She was looking for something more, or something different. Hector figured he was an oddity in her world, however well traveled she might be.

Regardless, Hector was glad to be whatever he was to her. He wanted, of course, the opportunity to stay aboard *Liberty's Reach* to locate some clues to finding the Oranlak. But it was more than that, he knew. Saoirse was certainly attractive, though it was in a dangerous and stormy sort of way.

Maybe she wasn't so obviously ravishing as someone like Regina, whom he estimated to be not many years past Saoirse's age, but there was a deeper, more meaningful beauty that he saw in her.

Hector was too consumed by other needs—achieving grand exploits and adventures—to dwell at length on any fantasy of a longstanding relationship with Saoirse. But he had to wonder to what degree that might be because of the mental manipulations of a certain sentient sword. In any case, he knew that on a very personal level, he distrusted any deeper connection like the one he felt himself gravitating toward with Saoirse. He had reservations about opening up to others, or letting his guard down with those who might seize the opportunity such a crack in his defenses would present. And the whole thing would serve as a distraction from things that were more important. Indeed, he longed for compelling opportunities to make a difference, and so intensely that he knew he would lay down his life if a suitable enough opportunity presented itself to him. And he suspected it would feel amazingly good to die for such a cause. That, he knew, was surely amplified—if not created entirely—by Kazahvir.

Hector recognized that his occasional distractedness by Saoirse irritated the sentient weapon. They had shared a bed on several occasions now, and he sensed how it would tolerate and entertain her as a means to an end—but it didn't derive its own satisfaction from or see any goals that it personally harbored as being achievable through any deep connection with this person.

He endeavored not to reach the point of having to engage in mental battles with Kazahvir. It was not an outcome he could be confident in. He needed often, if not always, to reason out with the ancient sentience that its greater ambitions were being served by actions Hector was taking.

Hector suspected, though he couldn't be certain, that Kazahvir entertained ideas about severing ties with him and seeking someone more easily dominated. He had wondered on a number of occasions why it didn't do just that. He supposed it wanted someone mentally strong, who was up to the tasks it saw as necessary—whatever those were—and it was apparently willing to accept that it would have to give ground, compromise, and sacrifice some aspects of what it might otherwise prefer to have in such a wielder.

This trip *Liberty's Reach* was now returning from had been a particularly interesting one. That was, in part, because Saoirse had pursued a deeper line of questioning than usual in one of the conversations he'd had with her, shortly after their last successful raid. But Kazahvir had interrupted that conversation and conveyed a great sense of alarm to Hector. The sentience had essentially screamed in his mind about the importance of him silencing himself and not talking so much to her; it apparently saw great vulnerability in his doing so. *Sometimes your greatest friends in one moment become your greatest enemies in the next,* it had imparted to him. And it had done so with such emphatic force that it actually caused Hector to lose where he was, mid-sentence, in his conversation with Saoirse.

He hadn't denied the sword's reasoning, though, and he went on to end the conversation with Saoirse almost immediately after. Granted, he just ended it by moving their conversation expediently to actions that were more passionate and intimate.

Still, he knew Saoirse undoubtedly saw him as having high mental walls to overcome and as a heavily self-guarded individual. Whether that appealed to her or not was something of an ongoing question in Hector's mind.

This trip, though, was particularly interesting for other reasons, too. Hector observed at one point, through Captain Saoirse's spyglass, a small boat off in the distance. Its size was suitable to accommodating just a few people. It struck him as unusual, being that it seemed to be alone and was a few hours offshore, and it lingered around a seemingly random spot in the open ocean.

"See that?" Captain Saoirse had asked Hector after handing the portable telescope to him.

"What are they doing? Who are they?" he asked in return.

She had hesitated for a few moments. When Hector finally looked back at the small boat, she whispered to him in response. Hector was unsure, but he considered that she might have whispered so as to prevent any upstirring from her crew.

"I've been noticin' other sim'lar boats, with divers just like that, 'round recently," she said quietly. "Think it's been pretty much 'bout that exact spot, too. Odd but fancy divin' gear to boot. I'm suspectin' they may be with the Order," she finished, her words taking a serious tone.

Hector's eyes had widened at that. *This is it,* he thought. *The sunken spaceship!*

Or at least, he thought, reeling himself in a bit, there was promising evidence for it. He had moved to mark down the coordinates on his personal map as quickly as possible.

Normally, after arriving back at the port of Akastair, Hector would have been most interested in sharing some personal time with Saoirse, and then in returning to his three companions back at the house. He determined, though, that for this return to port, he should reprioritize.

It was not without a degree of coaxing from Kazahvir, but he understood he should be off to his companions as soon as possible after any outstanding official duties, like starting to unload or resupply the ship.

He was most enthused to finally report something of consequence and to have finally made some headway, after all these months of effort, in finding what they had been searching for.

24

Chapter Twenty-Four

Andromeda and Gerrard had just secured another bounty, out past the edge of Serazema. The two had been making their way down remote and isolated trails, moving deeper into the forest that lined the city's outskirts, when they happened to run into a rare pair of fellow travelers. These travelers were two men heading in the opposite direction, back toward the city. They were aboard a large wooden wagon, pulled along by a pair of mechanical steeds. A few friendly words in greeting from Andromeda and Gerrard had given way to a line of light questioning. The two men seemed to go from slightly uncomfortable to blatantly nervous in the span of a minute or so.

The one whom they subsequently recognized to have a bounty on him had lunged at Andromeda shortly thereafter, though she had swiftly and easily dispatched the attacker with that razor-edged saber of hers. The other had similarly come at Gerrard, though he was in a state of what had to be heightened desperation, as he perceived his chances of escape dwindling. Gerrard had made quick work of him, actually succeeding in cleaving the man in half with his massive claymore.

When the fight was over, Gerrard moved to take a closer look at the wagon, as Andromeda found herself briefly distracted and fascinated by the wondrous mechanical horses. They were, for sure, wonders of modern technology. They were known in the area for their advanced hydrogen fuel cell technology and their groundbreaking efficiency and strength.

"I bet Regina would be so intrigued by these machines if she were here!" Andromeda remarked excitedly, perhaps similarly intrigued herself.

Gerrard smiled a little, not contesting the likelihood of that at all. He retained his focus on the covered wagon, though, as he moved toward it. Then he lifted the large tarp covering what it contained. Underneath, Gerrard's eyes beheld the greatest amassed quantity of extracted crimson fluorite he had ever seen.

"Well, don't you think she would be?" Andromeda asked when she didn't hear any response from Gerrard. But she was too captivated by the robotic steeds to immediately turn her eyes away from them. "Hey, don't go all tough and silent on me again. I thought we were finally past all that," she jokingly warned him.

She finally looked over when he still didn't respond, and then she instantly understood the reason for the delay in his response.

The two of them stood there, both enthralled by the sight their eyes beheld. The dazzling reflection of the rare and beauteous substance sparkled in their eyes.

"It looks to be of an impressive quality, too," managed Gerrard after a time.

"Yes," Andromeda said, mesmerized and nodding in agreement.

"It wasn't apparent these men had ties to an operation of this magnitude. Only one seems to have a bounty on him, and not for anything I'd expect would have led us to something like this," Andromeda reflected.

"There are no active mines licensed anywhere near here. This crimson fluorite was probably mined at an illegal operation, one sourcing crimson fluorite for black-market deals in Akastair or even across Gracyr," Gerrard stated grimly.

"This amounts to a lot of coin to be handing over to the shady authorities of Serazema. We should probably take it to Akastair," suggested Andromeda.

"I don't think we should act too hastily here," Gerrard replied.

"Oh?" responded Andromeda, tilting her head slightly, though in a lighthearted, cartoonish sort of way.

Is my friend proposing we go rogue or something? she wondered. *Does he want to steal the crimson fluorite and keep it for personal gain?* It didn't seem to her that Gerrard really needed the coin. Maybe she did a bit more than him, but even then, they were both getting by just fine as things were—especially with all the bounties they had been bringing in together for some time now. She wasn't feeling nearly financially squeezed enough to break the law. Was Gerrard needing a new thrill or something, or having some sort of later-life crisis she didn't understand? She was years younger, after all, and she supposed such a thing was possible.

He might consider spicing up our barely existent romantic relationship, before turning to thrills from breaking the law, she jokingly criticized him in her mind.

He finally spoke up and explained himself another few moments later.

"We can do a lot with this supply of crimson fluorite," he said. "So, let's think this over. First, we turn these guys in with details of where we found them, and so forth. The authorities, assuming they're on the level, are going to be hot on the trail of those involved with whatever is going on here, and in all likelihood will find and shut down the illegal mine in short order. And all this is going to get some rather dangerous eyes on us and on what is going on around here."

Andromeda cut in before he could continue. "The great Gerrard, fearful of something?" she asked teasingly. "And with an ally of my caliber at his side?" she complimented herself facetiously.

Gerrard gave her a slight smile. But he seemed to pause, perhaps deep in thought. Maybe he was scrutinizing the plan he was still formulating, testing its weak points and trying to reinforce them before pitching the rest to his partner. "Let's just consider pausing for a moment on the way to the authorities of Akastair ... for a short and much-needed break... You know, unload some of the weight we have on us," he suggested, haltingly and with obvious innuendo.

Catching on, Andromeda replied simply, "Oh, okay... Got it," even going so far as to give him a wink when she finished.

Gerrard had to laugh a little, but mostly he just looked down, shaking his head. He was sincerely glad his companion was apparently willing to go along with his controversial plan. Maybe she was just looking forward to cashing in on the likely ensuing bounty he was going to end up with on his own head. The thought occurred to him initially as a joke, but he ended up expending a fair degree of effort reconciling with himself that it was unlikely she had any such intention.

"All right… Let's get these bodies wrapped up," Gerrard eventually suggested.

These days, the pair kept a few body bags on hand in their travel packs. Their numerous successes had justified the additional inventory.

They got the bulk of the remains of the two bodies bagged up, then tossed them into the wagon with the crimson fluorite. Then they covered everything back up with the large tarp. Andromeda and Gerrard were just about to board themselves, then embark on their first ever mechanical horse-drawn wagon ride, when something suddenly lunged at Gerrard.

Ursula had watched them for a few minutes after she arrived on the scene, before engaging them. She had mostly just observed them bagging up more bodies of her men, though, and then, of course, them tossing them into the wagon. She knew the wagon carried weeks' worth of mined crimson fluorite. She had come upon these frustrating bounty hunters just as they had landed a bounty that could, in all likelihood, lead to the end of the Oranlak's mining operation here. The responsibility for that failure would fall greatly on her. She was currently in charge of this area. And she was witnessing what was for her a potentially career-ending, if not life-ending chain of events.

It was with a fair degree of desperation that Ursula determined she needed to act immediately. She understood the notorious exploits of these two bounty hunters and the many notable circumstances of their past histories. And even in watching them briefly just now, she understood clearly from the way they carried themselves that they were formidable.

It didn't matter. Every inch these two, their bounties, and that wagon made toward Serazema was another nail in her coffin. The risk to her life was escalating exponentially as the moments passed. And it wasn't like they really had all that far to go to get to the authorities in Serazema.

Even though a number of authorities in Serazema had been bought, bribed, or otherwise compromised by the Oranlak or its associates, there were limits to what could be concealed. There were conceivable situations that would take them beyond what any amount of coin could keep from the public's knowledge. Plus, with a wagon carrying so much of the precious and sought-after substance, all bets might be off, regardless. She could not gamble everything on how well-bought a corrupt officer was when that officer was about to be presented with a scenario wherein they could make vastly more coin. Indeed, even though that officer would have to undertake significant risk to get away with it, Ursula was far from comfortable with this state of affairs. So, this chain of events had to cease now.

Ursula called upon her ability to jump through shadows, dissolving into one nearby in the bushes. She drew a dagger in one hand and her sword in the other. She would catch Gerrard unawares, then quickly move to kill the female, as well—before she would have time to mount any countermeasures against the sneak attack.

Ursula wanted to be done with the matter as efficiently as possible, though she of course doubted—however long this fight ended up running—that the pair could bring her down. She was a high-ranking member of the Order of Oranlak. Ursula could shadow-jump some of the longest distances of anyone in the Order, could even hover in the void between worlds. And she could call upon many of her powers as frequently as she wished. The less trained, less knowledgeable among their ranks had greater limitations on what they could do and how often they could do it, in regards to the shadow arts. And even Ursula's few superiors within the Order answered to the same leader she did: Mercedes, who was not of their order, but was the second-in-command of all of Ezmondia.

These two bounty hunters might be a formidable duo, but they surely could not throw down with the likes of someone who had risen to the levels of power that Ursula had. Those were levels of power that transcended even the limits of her previous humanity, and these two were undoubtedly still bound by those limitations. Countless fools had come against her and had only served to bolster her own confidence and drive up her personal body count.

Ursula glided out of the shadows beside the wagon, her dagger closing in rapidly on Gerrard's throat. She knew she had transported soundlessly to Gerrard's side; he wasn't even looking in her direction. He would be easy to slay, she thought, and her face cracked in a vicious smile.

But suddenly, Gerrard launched forcefully forward. He hadn't been positioned to initiate a strong forward move like that—he had even been leaning backward slightly—and Ursula's mind reeled from the unexpected turn of events. Gerrard continued to tumble forward and fell to the ground in a heartbeat. Ursula then regarded the cause, and as she did so, she felt rage welling up within her at the one who had denied her that sweet moment of satiation.

Andromeda stared back at Ursula, with a first panicking but then quickly clearing countenance. Andromeda had her blaster almost instantaneously in position, with what seemed to Ursula to be inhuman speed. And there was something else peculiar about this female—something that had Ursula more on her guard than she had expected to be.

As one who practiced the shadow arts, Ursula was well attuned to forces beyond the realm of humanity. She could feel entities of other realms near to the divide of the worlds, could feel others that were only partially or had once been human. And she could feel vividly that there was something off about this female—something otherworldly. She wasn't like Ursula, not a shadow-skilled member of the Order, but there was still something dark—and darkening—about her. Taken together, it was all enough for Ursula to be discouraged from continuing her planned strike. She drew back and away and slipped back into the comfort of her shadows. She managed this just as Andromeda got the barrel of her blaster in position.

Andromeda held that barrel and glanced around frantically for some indication of where this human or this creature had gone. Was it running, having missed its chance at an easy kill? Was it waiting nearby for another chance at her or Gerrard's throat?

Gerrard quickly regained his footing and darted his eyes around while he spoke to his companion. "Thanks for ... getting me out of harm's way," he said. "Think you might've done it a little less painfully, though?"

"I'm sure you'd rather have a few bruises than a sliced throat," came the response, "or should I take a few extra moments to consider that next time?" Andromeda shot back, though with the flash of a smile still.

Andromeda had surprised even herself with the speed with which she had fended off the assault. It was well in line, though, with how she had been acting and feeling lately. She seemed to be picking up on things she didn't used to notice, and her reflexes seemed dramatically faster in recent months. She usually told herself it was just all the practice and experience she was getting lately—but she knew on a deeper level that there was something more going on. She felt so powerful, especially when she was out hunting, and more particularly when she was bringing down a bounty. She almost felt a measure of addiction to the experience and to the sensations that seemed to be associated with it lately. She sometimes felt like she couldn't even stop herself. There were times that the day had come and gone, and night had fallen, and she felt still that she wanted to go on, that she wanted more and didn't need to stop and rest at all.

Gerrard had seemed to pick up that something was amiss, but he hadn't pressed her much with any questions about what was happening to her. It was not like he could complain much about the results. And perhaps that all applied most especially now, when she had so clearly saved his life.

Just then, a dagger flew from somewhere deep in the shadows. It struck and penetrated deep into the seat of the wagon, just missing Andromeda. The magical black dagger dissolved almost immediately after it plunged into that seat, back into the shadows from which it was created.

A sword came at Andromeda then, from her other side, but this time Gerrard was there to deflect the blow. The force of his claymore smacked aside the smaller sword and put Ursula momentarily off balance, but she rapidly regained it and slipped away. Gerrard's counterstrike against the shadow-jumper sliced harmlessly through the air.

Ursula again could not help but be surprised by this unlikely pair of bounty hunters. Gerrard wielded that massive sword with impossible speed—so much so that he had just come close to actually landing a strike against her. And yet still, she felt nothing to indicate that this person was not entirely human.

Ursula understood clearly that she'd had enough surprises from these two and rather wished to quickly end this fight. She reached into the depths of her shadow-infused magic arsenal to summon her most powerful ally from the shadow realm. She expended enough magic to command a strike from that legendary creature, that horror that lurked in the nightmares of even the most powerful adventurers. She carved a portal between the worlds—one meant to persist for a few seconds. And the titanic monster—a shadow dragon—emerged and lunged at Andromeda with mighty, fiery jaws.

The gargantuan shadow creature stole Andromeda's and Gerrard's breath as completely as anything ever had. Those jaws zeroed in on Andromeda, appearing to lock down on her decisively. The creature's jaw then clenched, and it pulled back and vigorously thrust its head back and forth while it chomped on … nothing. It circled around, taking flight, and came back at them with a secondary attack. Its teeth and claws caught one of the mechanical steeds, and scrap metal went flying, along with a gargling, static neighing noise.

"Again!" Ursula screamed in escalating desperation at the flying colossus, knowing full well she was now overstepping her limits. Her magic could compel the creature from the shadow realm into their world briefly, but the strain was great to accomplish it, and it heightened exponentially over mounting seconds.

The dragon disregarded the ridiculous command from the lesser being, barely more than mortal, and yet it found itself still bound to this other world. Ursula's plea was powerful; the magic held, in what was perhaps an unprecedented feat. The beast roared in defiance, but was bound all the same to the spell and by the woman's sheer force of will as she poured even her life force into the effort. The dragon channeled the full weight of its rage into an additional strike, and this time it selected Gerrard as its target.

Raging flames spewed forth from its maw, seeming to set the air around them on fire. Green-tinged acid accompanied those flames as they reached out for Gerrard in a deadly stream. He held up his blaster in what he knew was his only chance. The massive area being immolated by the attack was too large to escape from; he could only stand and fight.

He fired a blaster shot—one he had saved for many years. It was the final bullet of its kind that he knew of, and that final Quadri-A blast was expelled from the blaster's chamber in a blinding explosion of magic. Then the powerful projectile shot into the acid-infused firestorm that was making its way right for him.

For perhaps the span of just one of Gerrard's hastened heartbeats, time seemed to hover frozen around them all. It was as if the laws that bound reality could not settle on what should happen next.

After the Quadri-A bullet was propelled into that acidic, fiery stream, the fabric of the world seemed to tear. Fragments of energy, stray flames, and splashes of acid spilled out erratically in all directions. Andromeda and Gerrard took cover on the far side of the wagon. The dragon roared as stray streaks of energy shot like lightning bolts into its breast. Ursula was struck even harder, acid burning into her arms as she tried to shield her face from the acidic flames. They tinged her hair and scorched her body as her screaming amplified.

She lost her grip on the portal, and then the dragon was quickly gone from their world. A few remnant streaks of crackling energy fizzled and faded where the mighty blasts had collided, as Ursula dropped to her knees in the greatest torment she had ever known.

Andromeda and Gerrard, mostly uninjured, looked to each other. Acting quickly, they jumped out, prepared to finish—or at least neutralize—their assailant. They moved swiftly to Ursula, but she was so distracted from the pain, her mind barely registered their approach. Andromeda brought her saber to bear, holding it close to Ursula's throat, her other hand gripping her blaster.

Gerrard leveled his own blaster at Ursula, and though it was now loaded with a less-powerful bullet, he bluffed, "Want another blast from this?"

Andromeda's eyes widened at that threat. She resolved with herself that her companion would not be so foolish as to fire another shot like that so close.

Ursula hissed as she grasped one of her arms. It was hopelessly burned and appeared useless.

"Anything you can tell us that may make me inclined to spare your life?" Gerrard offered the dying shadow-walker.

"What is your name? Why did you attack us?" Andromeda pressed.

Ursula groaned in pain and could barely string together a meaningful response. She swallowed hard and pushed through it, knowing she needed to mend her scrambled thoughts enough to buy herself an escape route, if she were to have any chance of surviving at all.

"My name is Ursula, and the two of you have been..." she started to say, before the pain interrupted her. Then she released a slight strained chuckle, and she pressed on with her sentence. "... causing me some headaches with all of our people you have been hunting down."

She winced, not just from the physical pain, but also from the realization that they probably didn't know any of them were from the Oranlak—not before now. These two needed to be dead, she knew, or *she* certainly would be—even if her present wounds weren't the cause.

"You cover your tracks well. We weren't aware we were so close, or that we were taking down so many of the Order," remarked Andromeda. "Of course, it was clear to us, given your repertoire of shadow abilities, that you're with them."

"We're curious about this underwater spaceship that your lot has taken recent interest in," Gerrard said, cutting in. "So, maybe we could spare your life for some information about that," he bartered.

"What ... do you want ... to know?" Ursula managed to ask, fuming with anger, but too limited in options to protest.

"Where is it, exactly?" Andromeda asked.

"I don't—" Ursula started before Andromeda inched her blade closer to her throat, causing her to reconsider her response. But then she continued, and she completed the statement defiantly. "I don't have ... that information.

It's not something my … position requires … me to know!" she managed to respond, but her syllables dragged out, and she groaned between words.

Thinking quickly with what scrambled thoughts she had, she realized she had to give these two something that would buy her some time—something that would afford her an opportunity to escape.

But what does it matter? she thought. She had no great love of Mercedes or Ezmondia, or even her Order. It was—they were—all just means to greater ends of self-enrichment: greater power, more influence, enhanced wealth. Ursula understood that as it was, she was already dead if these two were not slain this very day. It didn't matter if she told them something that would make it even more necessary that they die; they already had to die, regardless. So, she answered them.

"There is an energy … source on the sunken ship. It seems to be from another … world. We have built systems that can harness that energy source and provide … power to grids across Ezmondia," Ursula said, forcing aside her pain so she could answer. "It appears that in the short term, at least, this will … solve the energy woes plaguing Ezmondia, if not all of Gracyr."

Then she groaned through several long pangs that scattered her thoughts. Her usual eerie, echoing voice was made all the more unnerving by the way it seemed to slip uncontrollably between the worlds of the living and the dead.

"An underwater facility… has been constructed to facilitate the extraction of the substance," Ursula managed, finding herself again. "The substance, promethium, is littered throughout the spacecraft, which is … located well beneath the waves at a great … depth," she continued. "Efforts, however, have been … paused for now. Mysterious circumstances and disappearances are … being investigated before the extraction operations are resumed," Ursula finished. Then she took a few painful gasps, trying to steady her failing body and strained mind.

"What concerns are being investigated? What of these disappearances?" pressed Gerrard.

"Kill me if you must!" Ursula howled at him. "I'm no … threat to you now. Look at me. And I don't know … the information you're seeking. What I told you ... is all I know."

Ursula lied about how much she knew, but she truly didn't have all the answers she was being asked for. She hoped the truths she had already conveyed would suffice to get these two to take their leave of her, to leave her to her likely fatal wounds.

Maybe it doesn't matter, anyway, she thought. She was expecting to die from her wounds, regardless. And a quick death, which perhaps they could grant her, didn't even sound so awful anymore.

Gerrard looked to Andromeda, who just offered him a shrug. Then he turned his eyes back to Ursula, appearing to think carefully about what should be done with her.

"Go," he said decidedly. But then he warned, "We'll be quick to finish the job we've started here today if you cross us again." His words rang with a coldness of tone that would have been impressive even amid the heartless ranks of the Order of Oranlak.

Ursula slowly rose from her knees, stepped back, and started limping toward the tree line. Small residual flames fought to survive as they burned in several of the trees around there, as well as on a few of the limbs that had fallen during the encounter. She made her way around them, thoroughly beaten and exhausted, but still thrilled that Gerrard had been foolish enough to actually let her walk away.

She clenched her teeth and pushed on, feeling the eyes of the duo following her. A few moments later, she slipped back into the realm of shadows. She could shadow-jump now, over some great distance, and be well gone from this wretched place. She'd be hunted down by her own, though, if she didn't report soon.

She thought through her options—as much as the incessant pangs coursing through her aching body would permit. Perhaps she could throw herself to the mercy of the Order, or at the feet of Mercedes, if she could even stomach such a thing. She supposed that would probably earn her a quicker death, if that was her wish. She sighed a little, and she drew a final breath before settling on the course she felt to be her most likely path for survival.

Ursula jumped through the shadows, instantaneously transporting herself to right beside Gerrard. Then she smacked his blaster out of his hand and immediately sank back into the shadows. She reappeared and came at him from a new angle an instant later, wielding her dagger to bury it deep in the man's throat.

Something happened to her before she could finish that strike, though—something that had never happened to her before. Something she would have sworn was not possible. A blaster bullet penetrated the shadow she had just jumped through. It followed her through the path she took through the shadow realm, and she felt its magic now impacting her, unraveling her existence. This was a dark magic, indeed. Ursula was hateful, and filled with rage and defiance, but still—even despite the imminent threat to her life—she could not help but feel intrigued in that last moment.

The life-sucking, magic-infused blaster round Andromeda had just fired made short work of the shadow-walker. Her last scream came echoing back from somewhere between the realms—and the two companions knew Ursula was no more.

***

Shortly thereafter, the two boarded the wagon again and started for Akastair, pulled along by the one remaining mechanical horse. The wagon struck a steady and gradual pace, the sole robotic steed struggling a bit with the weight, but not tiring.

Andromeda and Gerrard were largely silent for much of the long trek back. After they finally passed back into Akastair, Gerrard spoke.

"Okay, this is the place, down this way," he informed Andromeda. "This might be a slight detour on our path to the Authorities Ops Base, but at this time of day—with the traffic and all—it might actually turn out to be a shortcut, anyway."

Gerrard guided the horse by the reins down a quieter side street, and after they had proceeded down that street for a short time, he cued it to stop in front of one of the houses.

"This should be it, I think," Gerrard said.

"You could be a little more reassuring in your tone, you know," remarked Andromeda.

Gerrard offered her one of his usual slight smiles before he got down from his seat next to her at the front of the wagon. He made his way over to the front door of the residence.

Andromeda saw another man, about Gerrard's age, come to the door.

"Gerrard!" the man exclaimed, greeting him warmly, actually throwing his arms around him.

"Okay, okay, Carmine. It's good to see you, too, old friend," said Gerrard, trying to extricate himself from the embrace. "How's business coming along in Akastair since you've arrived?" he inquired. "Been a few months now, is that right?"

Andromeda reasoned that he was warming his old friend up with some friendly banter before dropping the bombshell of the situation they were in on him.

"Oh, you know me. It's all coming along a little slow for my tastes. But in time, we'll grow our new operation here to be as profitable as our others. Just you wait and see!" Carmine said confidently.

"I understand you're doing some smelting, forging, and weaponsmithing over here?" Gerrard asked.

"Yes, that's correct," answered Carmine, curious.

"I have some … raw materials … that I have come by, which I would like refined and processed. I thought we might enlist our mutual friend, Duncan, as well, to assist with this project," Gerrard said.

"Interesting," remarked Carmine, bringing a hand up to his chin as he contemplated what could be brewing in his old friend's mind. "I don't keep much for materials or tools here, though. I also don't commonly take shipments of materials here, either," he said.

"This shop you have set up—I understand it's on the other side of the city. My friend Andromeda here and I are a bit pressed for time at the moment,"

Gerrard explained.

"Oh?" Carmine responded, looking past Gerrard to the mechanical horse-drawn wagon, and his friend Andromeda.

Andromeda offered Carmine a friendly—though somewhat comical, given the circumstances—wave of her hand. *What a scene we are so randomly presenting to this person,* she thought.

"New love interest?" Carmine asked of his friend.

"Come on, Carmine," Gerrard pressed a little more insistently. "You know I wouldn't waste your time. This is an unprecedented moment for you to seize the kind of lucrative business opportunity that could propel you to even grander heights."

The pitch seemed to have some effect, though Carmine apparently remained reluctant. "I do suspect, I'm afraid, that you are embellishing a touch here," he replied skeptically.

Gerrard waved the contrary thoughts away dismissively. "Take the materials for now, and I will be in contact with you soon for further discussion and planning," he said.

Carmine stared hard at his old friend for a few moments. "Okay, Gerrard," he said finally, though his skeptical look didn't diminish much.

It did fade, though, another few moments later, when Carmine burst out in warmhearted laughter. He even patted a heavy hand on Gerrard's back. Apparently, as far as Andromeda could tell, he had been holding that look more to get Gerrard going than to accomplish anything else.

"You seem a bit worn down, you know—like you've been out slaying dragons or something," Carmine said, then laughed. "But it is good to see you, old friend. I'll hold onto your stuff, and we can talk more later."

Gerrard nodded. "Thank you, Carmine."

He returned to the wagon and confirmed to Andromeda that they were proceeding with partially unloading the wagon here at Carmine's place. Gerrard then ran around behind the house to Carmine's backyard shed, as he had instructed him to, and retrieved his wheelbarrow.

Andromeda moved the wagon as close to the shed as she could, and they set to work unloading it. They transported much of the crimson fluorite into that back shed, and then after a time, Carmine came over with a shovel to assist. Upon joining them, Carmine was astounded to find that the "raw material" in question was a massive load of crimson fluorite.

"Gerrard!" he shouted, a little louder than he intended. "What are you getting me into? I told you before that I'm done with all the shady business dealings!"

Gerrard attempted to disarm him with a smile and by patting the air with his hands. "Simmer down. It's not illegal ... clearly," he said.

From Gerrard's wording, Carmine wasn't sure if he meant the situation was obviously not illegal, or that the situation just couldn't be viewed as being *clearly* illegal. He shook his head and smiled in a sort of frustrated defeat, knowing he couldn't go back on telling one of his oldest friends that he would help him—not when he seemed to be in such extreme need of his assistance. He was also just too thoroughly intrigued by the scenario that saw one of his oldest, most accomplished and remarkable friends taking what seemed to be an unjustified, mysterious gamble like this.

The three worked quickly. A few people happened by while they did so, either walking down the street or riding on a mechanical horse similar to the model that had pulled Andromeda and Gerrard's wagon. They did their best to cover up what they could when people went by.

Eventually, the shed was pretty well filled with crimson fluorite. A majority of it had been removed from the wagon, though a large share still remained. Andromeda and Gerrard determined they needed to move on to their next stop, so they packed up and prepared to get back on the road. Gerrard took a few moments to even out the piles of crimson fluorite that remained in the wagon, so it didn't appear like a massive chunk had been removed.

They reboarded the wagon and continued on the rest of the way to the Authorities Ops Base in Akastair.

When they arrived, the pair answered what questions the officers had for them, but they didn't offer what they saw as any unnecessary additional information. They also collected their handsome bounty. The officers, as expected, were highly interested in the wagon and any details the pair had about it. The location where it was found was also a particular point of interest for them, naturally.

Andromeda and Gerrard breathed a mutual sigh of relief as they left the building and started down the steps to get back to the street. The sun had mostly fallen below the horizon, and it was getting dark quickly. The pair wasn't far from home now, though, so they wouldn't be too late.

"Hector was due back today," Andromeda recalled. "Should make for some interesting dinner conversation this evening."

"I suspect we had plenty of excitement today ourselves to keep the conversation at dinner moving along just fine," Gerrard said.

"I'm not arguing that," responded Andromeda, laughing a little, considering who might have the more impressive updates to share with the group.

On the walk back home, Gerrard turned to Andromeda at one point and asked, "So, do you know how that shadow dragon missed you?"

"I figured … it must have just missed…" Andromeda answered, though she was far from convinced of that herself.

"That blaster of yours—I don't know much about it," Gerrard admitted. "But I recognize it is a powerful relic from another time—a time of potent magic now mostly lost to the modern world. I feel its power … is changing you Andromeda, and I must admit, I am a bit concerned. I see it has done us some good, but I suppose I just feel that I need to know that … that I expressed some concern to you about it. I don't think you should plan to continue using that thing indefinitely. I think it's doing things that may not be so good for you, and that you should probably cease using it soon."

Andromeda nodded as her friend spoke. She liked the weapon, but she also knew that she had been harboring many similar thoughts herself as of late and had concerns similar to Gerrard's. But she also recognized that the thing had probably saved her from a rather agonizing death that afternoon.

"Soon," she said to her companion, agreeing.

With that, the pair continued on the short rest of the way home to meet with Hector and Regina, for what they were sure would be a dinner with some most interesting table conversation.

25

Chapter Twenty-Five

Hector finished up his remaining tasks unloading *Liberty's Reach*. The crew had all stayed after docking to unload the goods and the spoils from their latest trip before they departed for some much-needed rest and relaxation. He let the last of the crew on site know that everything else was done. Then he headed down the docks and to the streets beyond.

Hector knew he wasn't far from Saoirse's place. And he also knew she'd be expecting him, as he always dropped by when they got back from their trips lately. He agonized over whether he should, or if he should just go straight home. His thoughts also lingered for a while on how long he should stay if he *did* go by her place.

Ultimately, he found himself knocking on her door.

She opened the door, and they exchanged a few words, chatting briefly. He ended up inside, almost unthinkingly, and then they were fast at work removing each other's clothes in no time at all. It was almost reflexive, and even with all that was on his mind, Hector found himself hard-pressed to deny her—or to halt himself from pursuing her further that way.

It's such a beautiful thing, Hector thought, *to have such space, and privacy, and time for the two of us.* He could see Saoirse was similarly pleased, and they found it mutually very exciting to have so much of each other's rare, undivided attention—for whatever fleeting amount of time they had.

Indeed, for the two lovers, the next couple hours went by faster than either of them wanted. And the relativity of time for them then was as real as it ever had been. Those couple hours later, they found themselves lying in Saoirse's bed together, exhausted from more than just the day's work. It was then that it finally occurred to Hector again that he needed to be getting home. He gave serious consideration to staying the night, but he knew he couldn't. He was on a mission that he needed to hold above his immediate desires. And besides, Kazahvir's protests were quickly escalating as he persisted in those more personal fantasies.

Saoirse was just nodding off to sleep when he finally spoke up. "Hey, love, I need to get back and meet up with housemates back home. We had a meeting planned for tonight I shouldn't miss," he said, uncharacteristically softly for him.

Saoirse's eyelids lifted, and she set her best bedroom eyes on him for a few seconds. She was impressed when he didn't retract or amend his statement, but she also grew quickly frustrated.

"Whatever," she said, breaking her pleasant look and rolling her eyes.

It was, to a degree, a heart-shattering change of tone. And Hector, perhaps, wasn't so susceptible as many were—but he still recognized that he didn't like what was happening, that he did care and wanted to stay here with her, but that it was necessary that he go. Saoirse seemed to be interpreting his words to mean he didn't care, and so apparently was expressing that she didn't care herself.

"Why do you have to be so uncaring?" he asked her plainly.

Saoirse got up from the bed, which prompted him to, as well. She stood there, staring back at him for a few moments. Her rich blonde locks tumbled down her naked frame, partially covering her breasts, but still leaving so little to his imagination. She had to know that was affecting him, but he couldn't be sure. The scene was like an intangible dagger held to his heart—but that dagger was as real a blade as any Hector had ever crossed swords with.

She sighed then, after regarding her lover just a little longer. "Not uncarin'," she stated resolutely. Then she let a few more silent moments pass by. She sighed again, deeper this time, as if in great disappointment. "I'm understandin' I'll be the person you perceive me to be, but the person you're perceivin' me to be—that's *not* the person I am," she said, almost to herself, as if bringing herself to terms with some inevitability about the situation or the world.

Hector paused as he considered her words. And then he felt their meaning take hold of him. He thought then that, if he desired, he could make this beautiful person out to be entirely different or even contradictory things compared to what he saw now. Was she a wicked, vile creature that reveled in causing such pain in his heart? Or was she a being of purity and goodness, a gift, and his salvation?

He understood how, in his mind, and so to significant extent in reality, she would be whatever he perceived her to be, whatever he imagined her to be. But he also understood how, whatever that personal perception, it was far from any universally cast-in-stone, absolute truth about what she really was.

The woman's words nearly knocked him over, and he chose to let his feelings about her being uncaring melt away. They held each other in a warm embrace, wordlessly resolving their conflict. Then they found themselves subsequently, and quite quickly, back under the covers for a short while.

A few minutes later, Hector rested there in the bed they shared, caressing her gently. She again started to nod off to sleep.

"Have a good night … sweetheart," he told her, the term of endearment coming a little awkwardly to someone so ill-practiced in using them throughout his life.

"You, too, my love," Saoirse said. She smiled a little and didn't protest, understanding that he felt he had to go, and resolving to let him.

Hector gave her a kiss on the forehead. Then he arose from the bed, clothed himself, and taking care to make sure he locked the door behind him, walked out into the night.

* * *

It was a bit past the companions' usual dinner time when Hector arrived back at the house. He walked in and found them all—Andromeda, Gerrard, and Regina—as he expected them, mostly done eating, but still at the table talking.

"Hector, good to see you! I was beginning to get worried. Join us!" Andromeda invited him, pulling out a chair for him. "I baked some giant potatoes, and there's plenty of sour cream and grilled chicken left if you want to grab some before you sit down."

Hector grabbed an oversized potato, the last of the steamed asparagus, and a serving of chicken and sat down with his friends. Once he was seated, Andromeda got him up to speed.

"So, Gerrard and I procured some promising information today, in the course of our bounty hunting work," Andromeda began. "We have learned that the Order has had an operation going on at a newly constructed underwater facility near here. The sunken spaceship is real, as is a substance, the power source they are calling promethium. The underwater facility was built so they could collect it more easily from the sunken ship."

Andromeda looked to Gerrard, trying to gauge whether her words were on par with his own understanding from their earlier conversation with the shadow-jumping woman. Nothing about his expression indicated anything to the contrary to her.

"It seems they are generating electricity from their use of promethium, seeing it as a solution to the ongoing and worsening hydropower crisis that all Gracians are dealing with. There seem to be some issues with the promethium or the operation, but the details are not clear. I suppose it's at least worth noting that they are already using this substance, despite how likely it is that they have no real understanding of it at all," Andromeda said.

"Doubtless they have designs to scale up promethium-harnessing infrastructure and expand its use greatly," Gerrard cut in. "Certainly, they are also aware of the astronomical wealth they can generate for themselves and their associates in the process. It's quite easy for me to entertain that the Oranlak is in league with the empire of Ezmondia to accomplish these designs. But we've seen no indication these new systems are in use here in Makeva, or that the Gatekeepers Council is even aware."

Regina chimed in next. "Has something gone awry with their underwater facility?" she asked. "Ya mentioned ... issues?"

"The Oranlakian we fought today mentioned some mysterious happenings, some sort of disappearances that have troubled them recently," Andromeda answered. Her mind whirred with ideas about what Regina was thinking. Judging from the seeming excitement in her tone when she asked, Andromeda considered that maybe she liked the idea of having a mystery to solve.

"Regina also encountered a couple people of interest having lunch today at the bar she's been working at," said Gerrard to Hector. "One of them sounds to be someone I know, an old friend of mine. He may be able to help us."

He paused a moment before continuing. He seemed to hold the undivided attention of all his companions, and he reflected briefly then on how thankful he was to be working with a team that seemed to care so much about whatever it was they were all ultimately working toward together.

They all seemed pulled along to him, guided or impelled to action for the sake of internal forces none of them fully understood. He had at least some nebulous sense himself, though, surely. Gerrard knew his life had been lacking something, that he was feeling a greater fulfillment in the work he and his companions were now doing than he had felt in years—maybe since his daughter had been young. But it was something almost impossibly difficult to even momentarily grasp—and something beyond his ability to clearly define.

He pulled himself back to the moment and the conversation at hand. "Perhaps more important in this matter, though, is the person my old friend was with," Gerrard continued. "He has knowledge and experience we may find most useful. I'm sure I can track down my old friend Cid, who himself may be of assistance to us, but likely, more critically, he could connect us with his friend who he had lunch with today at the Seaside Sprite. He is someone I suspect can get us to that spacecraft."

Gerrard stopped speaking again for a few seconds. Then he changed gears.

"On another note, we have secured a large quantity of crimson fluorite, and I'm about to make a call to another friend who can help us refine it and produce some high-power ammunition. And it does sound like there's a compelling case to be made that we're going to need it, especially if we're going up against forces like the Order and the empire … and the kind of tyrants that reign over them."

Andromeda could not help but pick up on a tinge of… What was it? Something like pain, or a sentimental scar, or a poorly healed wound tearing open again. There was something like that in Gerrard's tone as he spoke those last few words.

"We do still need to find the actual location of this spacecraft, though," Gerrard finished, looking hopefully to his companions for any further leads on that front.

Hector smiled despite himself then, as Gerrard's eyes fell upon him. Hector had taken to more frequent expressions like this of late, and he was also vastly more emotional with his responses with his friends nowadays than he had been in the past. That was not to say he was all that expressive or emotional in general, but certainly, any of his companions could detect the change in him since they'd first met. In any case, Gerrard took the smile as reassuring and listened attentively for what the younger man would say next.

Hector intentionally let their anticipation levels surge for a few moments, and then finally laid out for them what he had learned about probable Oranlak members, or at least their associates, diving from a small boat at a very particular spot off the coast of Akastair.

* * *

Andromeda was the first to awake the next morning. Then she went and woke up her friends without too much difficulty.

Hector was half awake already; he was ever-vigilant, so that had been easy.

Regina seemed to be on the verge of waking up, too, from what sounded like a nightmare she was having. It apparently had something to do with a big test the following day—though it did seem strange to Andromeda that Regina would be having nightmares about such a thing, so many years removed from school. Andromeda certainly didn't envy her having gone through whatever class it was that was still plaguing her with nightmares a decade later.

Gerrard was more difficult to awaken. He had been up talking with Carmine on his clonra until some late hour. Andromeda had caught bits of their conversation. They were discussing a plan for moving forward. And after that, he had contacted his other friend, Duncan, and they had a similar talk themselves.

It had been quite interesting, in Andromeda's view, to hear someone so radically self-reliant at times appealing so hard to others for help. Gerrard was always striving to do things himself. He'd more often just go without help he could easily secure, even if he was not going to be able to do the task as well, just for the sake of being able to do it himself. Such extenuating circumstances as they were in, Andromeda supposed, must have driven him to be willing to lean on a few people. Granted, they were still some of his oldest and best friends in the world, so far as she understood.

It was also striking to her to hear the way he laid the groundwork for his plans with his friends Carmine and Duncan. The steps, the process, the probable outcomes, the things to be wary of and watch out for... It seemed to Andromeda that he had considered so many angles and perspectives of his plans already.

In any case, despite seemingly having much of it mapped out, these conversations had run long into the night. Essentially, though, as far as Andromeda could tell, things were falling into place as Gerrard was envisioning. Carmine and Duncan were going to be working on smelting and refining the crimson fluorite Andromeda and Gerrard had supplied yesterday. They would derive the sought-after lutetium from that raw material, with which they would set to work making blaster bullets.

It unnerved Andromeda to consider the kind of destruction that might ensue if they were talking about making rounds like the one Gerrard had fired at the shadow dragon. But she also was far from convinced that having such power at their disposal was not going to be necessary.

She also didn't miss the fact that there was going to be considerable profit in this for Gerrard's friends, but Gerrard hadn't dwelled on that point more than seemed necessary to convince them to do the work and take on the risk.

Andromeda understood from their conversations that this was all going to be a process for them, that it was going to take some time, and that Gerrard was going to have to give them a while to build and to gather the other necessary resources to produce the product he was after.

Gerrard had also gotten in touch with Cid the previous night. He had arranged, she overheard, for the four of them to meet up with Cid today. Hence, she had understood the importance of getting everyone up and ready to head over to Cid's place early. And to Gerrard's delight, she was sure, apparently Cid's friend Viktor was also going to be at the meeting.

* * *

Later, the four companions arrived at Cid's place at approximately the agreed-upon time. This was an impressive feat to Andromeda, who hadn't thought they'd make it in time, despite her best efforts. There had been a late arrival of the hydrogen fuel supply for the train that morning, which had held them up at the station.

The train engines combusted the hydrogen to operate. The other component of their fuel supply was just oxygen—something of incredible abundance that was readily extracted from the air wherever the train went.

The hydrogen, though, needed to still be produced and delivered—and apparently the infrastructure and supply lines of even the illustrious city of Akastair could use improvements.

That aside, after the train could refuel, it had been a smooth ride aboard the magnetically levitated train over to where Cid lived on the other side of the city.

When the four arrived and Cid let them into his house, he guided them directly to his living room. It was an enormous house. The living room itself was quite extravagant. The high ceiling featured beautiful, historically authentic artwork painted over it. Expensive paintings and various items were displayed in glass casing that almost gave the place the atmosphere of a museum. The wall-mounted vidscreen was one of the largest any of them had ever seen, and it was surely one of the latest, most state-of-the-art models.

In making some preliminary small talk with Cid, Regina learned his children were all grown into adulthood now, but he still enjoyed regular visits from them and his grandchildren. That was good, she figured, since it seemed too large a space for just one person to be occupying. Although, he did have a sizable and perhaps a little overly friendly dog.

Cid had made his fortune in fishing, going out on sometimes months-long voyages to catch various sea-dwelling creatures for food markets up and down the coast of Makeva. He had even owned and operated, by the sounds of it, a very successful fishing company for a time.

Even so, Regina had to figure that the man had purchased this mansion—as she felt it could be accurately defined—in easier times. The building itself was quite grand on its own, never mind the locale of being in one of the nicest neighborhoods of one of the most popular cities in the country. It was surely worth many times over whatever he had paid for it.

In Regina's past years living in the city, particularly back when she was a student, she had come to learn that residential dwellings there were usually overpriced rental units owned by shady, oversized, bloated megacorporations. And as she understood it, the situation had only worsened in her years away. She suspected even owning your own space, however small it was in comparison to the mansion she was in now, was probably a relatively rarity in Akastair by now. Houses like Cid's were bought up and demolished to build new compact and more efficient units. Or possibly, they were divided up into such small units directly—and those who came to live in those units likely paid more for them than Cid had ever had to, and he actually owned the whole place.

But then Regina realized she was reflecting a bit more deeply than intended on how troubling that whole scenario was to her. An increasing lack of private ownership in their society was another topic of the modern day she could get lost in, particularly as it was one that had so strongly impacted her generation.

Fortunately, she was drawn from her contemplation by a nudge from Andromeda, who seemed to pick up on her friend getting caught up in distressing thoughts.

Regina heard Gerrard speaking. He was talking to Cid about the battle he and Andromeda had been engaged in the previous day with the shadow-walker and the dragon from another realm. A few seconds later, she heard Hector's voice come through, and by then, she felt back in the present moment again.

Hector seized on a brief pause in the conversation to cut in, feeling that enough time had been spent on formalities and pleasantries. Viktor had finally entered the room, too, although he had mostly just been listening to the conversation already going on. Hector addressed the old fisherman and submariner directly.

"Viktor, this is the spot here," Hector said, unfolding the map and handing it to the older man. "This is where I believe the Oranlak, or an associate group, is diving out of a small boat, to perhaps plunge down to their new underwater facility and the sunken spacecraft."

Hector paused to let Viktor look over the map and familiarize himself with it before continuing. "They have peculiar-looking, perhaps highly advanced gear. I could tell that even from the long distance I viewed them from," he said.

"None of us have much in the way of a means to get down to it, though, or any diving experience, for that matter," added Andromeda.

Viktor nodded. "Indeed, the gear would have to be highly advanced. That is, if it's truly permitting them to actually just descend down to an underwater facility from the surface. I suspect they have some sort of midway point they dive down to, or perhaps a covert submarine that picks them up. In any case though, I've been looking for a new challenge … and something of a new adventure, too, I suppose. And it has been too long since I've had one." He grinned mischievously at Cid. "I'm not much for standing around and just waiting for death to come for me either—not while awful organizations like the Order of Oranlak are becoming nearly invincible."

"There is a base," Viktor went on, "that we could swindle a submarine from. I reckon I could call in a few favors, get a team together to take us down."

"We're not going to have to actually … *steal* it, are we?" asked Andromeda, a little skeptical, and a little concerned in tone. She matched her eyes with the man's to try to gauge where he was coming from.

Viktor regarded her for a few silent moments. Then he looked back at the group as a whole. "We *are* prepared to go to whatever lengths necessary, *aren't we*, team?" he asked. "I'm not much either for asking a person to lay their life on the line—not if they're really not up to the task," he stated firmly.

Hector found the man's words inspiring, and it seemed to tug even on Kazahvir's metaphorical heartstrings. He couldn't help but voice his strong agreement with the sentiment that Viktor's statement had just captured. "Aye! We're with you!" he suddenly exclaimed, feeling a touch of his recent swashbuckling lifestyle spilling over into the moment.

His three companions felt the power of the emotions stirring within them, too, and they could not disagree with Hector.

Viktor laughed heartily at the young man's response. He wanted to believe in this group, and he would not let that desire be defeated by his worldly skepticism and his generally pessimistic outlook on the state of modern-day Gracyr.

"I'm just trying to be a little dramatic for y'all," Viktor said to the group, but then let his eyes fall on Hector for a few silent seconds. "But I appreciate the spirit," he said to him.

Hector nodded in gratitude for what he decided was a compliment.

Viktor seemed then to be thinking quickly in the moment, but also to be drawing on plans he had been working on for some time—perhaps well before the companions had even arrived at Cid's house that day. He described how he would arrange a tour for them—his "close friends"—and he'd even arrange for them to be taken out in one of the submarines to do some exploring out in the ocean. And when they were out there, they would just maybe take it a little further with the exploring bit than they would initially let on.

"That really going to work?" Regina asked, raising some doubts among the group and prompting Viktor to look the young woman over for a few seconds.

"Well, you've come here to get help for what would seem to me to be some rather ambitious goals," Viktor replied. "And I suspect you don't have other solutions in mind that are any more realistic. So … relax and trust me; it sounds like you're going to have to."

Regina crossed her arms, but nodded in understanding and backed down from her challenge. Viktor nodded, too—in respect and appreciation for her accepting his judgment.

"I'll make the arrangements and get the team together," Viktor went on. "We'll plan to borrow one of the smaller subs, but we'll still need at least a couple dozen people. I'm certain we can recruit much of my old team."

"Why so many?" Andromeda asked.

"We'll need people to steer, to man the sonar, a navigator, engineers, and others. I'll make some calls and get us set up for our 'tour' soon," Viktor answered without hesitation, sounding as sharp now as Andromeda imagined he could've been even well back before he retired.

"You all go on and head out, and I'll get to work on this. Gerrard, I'll be in touch the day after tomorrow," Viktor said, sounding both motivated and confident.

* * *

The four companions departed from Cid's house, bound for home.

Viktor activated his clonra and started sending messages and making calls. He felt—for the first time in a very long time—a great sense of purpose. He felt he had a new mission—one potentially of great importance. It felt good to have that again.

He almost didn't even care if it ended up being a lot of effort and risk for what turned out to be a lost cause. It felt good to be going on a mission, to again feel others' need for him, to harbor the empowering thought that there was someone he could not let down.

* * *

The day after next, as promised, Viktor called up Gerrard on his clonra and laid out the plan. In a few days' time, they would all gather near Akastair at the submarine base on the coast for a scheduled tour of the facility. They would then be allowed aboard a small submarine operating with a skeleton crew of about two dozen people. They would go out for a three-day trip on a predetermined course, and there, they would have the rare opportunity as civilians to get a feel for life aboard a submarine.

The course would not quite take them to the X mark on the map Hector had shown Viktor, which he said indicated where the Oranlak was presumably diving down to the underwater facility from, but it would come close—at about the midway point on the chartered course.

So far as Viktor could glean, no one at the base was aware of the existence of this underwater facility. They would have to dive to an unknown depth below the indicated spot on the map and hope they could pick up the place on sonar. It wasn't a perfect plan, but it gave them a chance.

Viktor was able to recruit a number of crew members that were old friends, and he knew he could bend the rules and push the limits of what would normally be permissible. The submarine would take an unexpected detour along its chartered course to drop off the companions at the underwater facility. Then, the sub would resume its expected course. At the end of the preplanned course, they would turn around and head back to base, as expected. But they would detour again on the way back, to pick up the companions from the underwater facility. They could buy the four companions twenty-four hours to investigate before they would have to be picked up again.

They would relay to Command Control back at the base that some obscure difficulty or another had taken them off course temporarily. They would subsequently respond, with confidence, that all systems were now green. Then they would push forward to complete the planned tour.

Their story would be that one of the tourists aboard had seized the opportunity to don some of the diving gear and left the sub during the temporary hiccup. They would say they needed to suddenly detour again to save him, upon learning of his absence on the way back to base. After they detoured to pick up the companions on the alleged rescue mission, they would head straight back to base.

Gerrard accepted the plan, more because he knew he didn't have an alternative to go with than because he thought it was foolproof.

Viktor knew it was flimsy. But he also knew many of those who would be involved, and that he could push the story through long enough to at least get through the mission. They might even be able to maintain the secrecy of the underwater facility and whatever was going on down there, if they chose to. He did have to accept, though, that it was possible that he, the four companions, and potentially others were going to end up in a lot of trouble over this whole thing. That was a gamble he would just have to take—and that he would have to sell others on.

Some who would be on board had had their lives saved by him. Some considered themselves in his debt, beyond even what they could ever hope to repay. All of them respected him and understood he would not ask of them something that would endanger them if it was not necessary. And if he played it correctly, with a little luck, very few would need to take on much risk. And for him personally, that was a consequence not so difficult to accept. He wasn't getting any younger, anyway, and besides, it was all such a thrill, to be playing the game again.

Viktor was playing a game that he used to play with himself in his younger years in the armed forces. It was a game wherein the fate of the world hung in the balance, and the outcome would define the future of Makeva, if not all Gracyr, for generations to come. And it all hinged on what he and his team could accomplish on this sole mission—as if it all came down to that. He would align his actions accordingly with that degree of importance, to make certain that what was needed to be done would be done. His role was to get those four to that facility and circle back to them in twenty-four hours for the retrieval, and then get them home. And he determined he would complete that mission at any cost.

Viktor couldn't be sure he should really gamble his life and reputation on this endeavor, but someone needed him again, and he had the means to help them. It was a clarion call he could no more deny than he could deny his need to breathe.

He felt, in those moments as he considered all this after speaking with Gerrard, a void long empty within him now being filled. And even if it cost him his life, he knew that for what it was affording him, it was still as grand a bargain as any he could imagine.

26

Chapter Twenty-Six

The four companions returned once to Cid's place in the following days leading up the start of their submarine mission.

That morning, Regina and Hector had informed their employers that they would be on hiatus for a few days. Naturally, it wasn't guaranteed that their positions would be held, but they both suspected they would be if they were only gone a few days. Andromeda and Gerrard's line of work, of course, didn't require such notice, since they worked whatever hours they wished. So, with that, the four companions found themselves nearly prepared and ready.

The four made their way later that morning over to Cid's. As they were walking the remaining mile or so after the train ride that took them to the other side of the city, they noticed a new contraption making its way slowly down the road in the opposite direction. It rolled along amid the morning foot traffic and mechanical horses, picking up and emptying garbage receptacles lining the roadway.

The hefty vehicle had a gradual but steady pace. It used large robotic arms for much of the work of emptying the receptacles—though two men traded off driving it and assisting with the trash collection as well.

"What is that?" asked Andromeda, not having seen one before and genuinely curious.

"It looks like they've finally rolled out the new garbage vehicles they've been raving about forever," responded Regina, looking quite interested herself. "Special bacteria break down the garbage. This specialized type of bacteria produces hydrogen from that breakdown, which is used to power the hydrogen combustion engine the vehicle runs on."

"That's fascinating," remarked Andromeda. "A top-notch idea! Leave it to a city so grand as Akastair to spearhead technology like that."

Regina appreciated the remark, though she wasn't as enamored with the prestigious city as she once had been.

"You would think we would be seeing more of these around, in these modern times and all," Andromeda observed.

"Yes, I believe that'd be a good thing," responded Regina. "There are, however, those who cling to the past. Or perhaps it would be more accurate to say, there are those who cling to the power and wealth the things of the past have brought them, and so they actively pursue the persistence of dated and failing systems to maintain that power and wealth."

In hearing the way Regina spoke of people who clung to power and wealth like that, Hector couldn't help but get lost in his thoughts about a past life. Still, this time he maintained his typical reserved silence, despite the strong feelings he felt on the topic. And anyway, they had arrived at Cid's house.

The four companions went over some particulars of the plan with Viktor and Cid. Viktor was also determined to convey some information he felt important for them all to know. One of those items was just about being down so deep in an underwater facility like the one the companions were telling him about. Viktor spoke of the "psychologically demanding" situation he anticipated that this facility would present.

Hector listened particularly intently. He couldn't help but wonder how he would hold up. The feelings of confinement and isolation being described did not move him. But then, it was a very different thing, he knew, to experience something firsthand, as compared to just being told about it. He wondered how well the experiences of his past had prepared him for what was ahead, and he was intrigued by the idea of being tested.

* * *

The rest of the day passed quickly for them all, and before they knew it, the next morning had come, and they were all gathered outside the gates of the submarine base. Viktor pressed the buzzer, then spoke briefly with the guard through the intercom device. The gates activated and opened for them. A young woman greeted their group when they walked into the compound. She introduced herself and cheerfully explained that she would have the pleasure of being their guide.

It was all new to the four companions, and much of it even to Cid. Viktor, of course, was quite familiar with the place, having worked there years ago. The place had apparently not changed much.

Viktor answered their tour guide's trivia questions easily and lightheartedly, trying to keep things interesting and moving along smoothly. His answers actually delighted the guide, and they seemed to be even more detailed than those she had intended to give herself.

"Our submarines nowadays are built with a double hull, to better withstand the pressure at great depths," she explained, as some of the largest subs at the base underwent maintenance behind her. "The outer hull is composed of a heavier metal, and the inner hull a lighter one, for extra support. If the structural integrity of the hull is compromised, an implosion could occur."

They moved on to view the newest models, and the tour guide continued to educate them. "Air quality is another thing we must be aware of," she went on. "We consume oxygen, which must be replenished. Fortunately, our systems can generate oxygen while we are aboard to replenish the supply. We also need to remove carbon dioxide, which we exhale, and we need to remove the moisture we also breathe out. The moisture can be taken care of by dehumidifiers aboard the submarine. We have various filters to further improve and maintain the air quality for those on board. And on these models here, we have desalination systems to provide drinking water for the crew."

Gerrard and Hector were mostly silent, taking in some of the information, but mostly too focused on the greater mission to be engaged. Regina asked a few things, but Andromeda was the main questioner. She was pleasant, inquisitive, and sincerely curious, and she did make their entire group seem much more engaging and authentic.

When they finally came to the submarine they were to embark on, another new model, Regina started being more inquisitive, even out-asking Andromeda. Her questions were more pointed, and she seemed to follow deeper and more insightful lines of questioning—something surely made possible by her more technical understanding of the energy systems the subs used.

Not that Andromeda got very competitive about it. If anything, she was just more intrigued with how Regina's background was suddenly bubbling to the surface in this environment. She even learned a lot from hearing her speak with the tour guide and some of the staff and crew members.

Electricity generated from atomic fusion was apparently used aboard the subs. The fusion process gave off heat, which changed water to steam, and that steam was used to turn turbines that generated the electricity for various things on the sub. The heat was also used to keep the temperature comfortable for the crew when they were in the coldness of the deep ocean.

This atomic fusion—though apparently small and limited in its application here—seemed to fascinate Regina. She voiced ideas about scaling the system up and using it for other purposes, and with a technical level of understanding that the guide herself could not match. Andromeda knew she was thinking of how to use such a system to replace current hydropower systems, which were in broader use throughout Gracyr. Some members of the crew, who were more knowledgeable about the atomic fusion systems aboard, repeatedly dismissed the direction Regina's mind was going, though. They reviewed various technical limitations with her, which came up when trying to apply it at the larger scale Regina was suggesting.

It seemed in Andromeda's more rudimentary understanding of it all that they were only missing a few key pieces of the puzzle to make such advancements possible. And she could not help but take an interest in the way Regina advocated for the technology, now that she had seen what was already operating here so successfully.

This is a person, she thought, *who is very driven to create a better tomorrow.*

She wondered what Gerrard was thinking and how confident he remained in the future of some of the ideas he had spoken of before—those that were on this very same topic: atomic fusion.

At that moment, of the several crew members who had addressed them, Gerrard was thinking about one in particular. This particular person seemed to seriously entertain Regina's ideas, and Gerrard took mental note of her name: Rhoda. As far as it appeared to him, she was more willing to entertain the potential of scaling up atomic fusion. Perhaps she felt as he did—that it could be made to be a more accessible and widely available source of power for more applications across Gracyr.

Gerrard knew his thoughts were hopeful, but Rhoda seemed to believe that better-controlled, longer-sustained atomic fusion reactions were entirely feasible in the near future, and that larger and longer outputs of energy were not so far out of reach. She also seemed legitimately interested in the conversation. Rhoda didn't seem to harbor the view that it was all just for a job, a means to a paycheck or some such thing. She was actually invested in the discussion she had with Regina, apparently just for the sake of advancing a small piece of the puzzle that would bring widespread power through atomic fusion a little closer to reality.

They had a stint where they were talking about drilling into magma—an idea Gerrard hadn't even heard of before, even having worked in the business of drilling for years. He was quite intrigued to listen to that part of the conversation, too.

Rhoda spoke of how unlocking the immense heat energy could make the field of geothermal heat energy vastly better. She talked about how the concept had just come along in the past few years, and Regina did appear to have some vague prior knowledge of it. Apparently, so far as Gerrard could tell, she had dismissed it at some point shortly after hearing of it, having been preoccupied with other ideas she found more enticing.

He drew a remarkable optimism from the conversation that surprised even himself. He considered that he might be harboring what was genuine hope for the world in that moment.

Shortly after, the announcement came that they were preparing to board and submerge. The four companions, along with Cid and Viktor, boarded, along with the rest of the crew. Not long after they boarded, the ballast tanks of the submarine filled with water to adjust the buoyancy, and they all began their dive.

The crew continued to be focused and mostly quiet as they submerged, but they were friendly and open to questions about what they were doing. Cid asked the sonar personnel about various matters and chatted lightheartedly with them. Viktor talked more to the four companions about all kinds of things relating to the sub—pressure, on-board systems—and was basically reinforcing his reputation with them as a walking encyclopedic guide for the world they were entering.

Midway through the tour, as planned, things were stirred up when several of the higher-ranking crew directed the team off the designated, preplanned course. Higher command had apparently been notified of something necessitating a change of plans. There seemed to be a general sense of surprise among the lower ranks of personnel, but there was no real questioning or significant challenging of the new orders.

What has this Viktor fellow managed to pull off? Gerrard found himself wondering.

Viktor smiled slightly on noticing the surprise apparent on the four companions' faces. Maybe it wasn't observable so much on Hector's, but surely, he could see the shock of the others.

It was going smoothly so far. He knew there would likely be a reckoning, though. Some of what was really happening would probably be found out eventually.

He had called in a few favors to get this detour—and the unusual tour itself, for that matter—but those people probably wouldn't have to take much of a fall for him. If things went sour, Viktor's abuse of his connections and his past command would be the epicenter of it all. He, possibly Cid, and the four companions would bear the brunt of it.

Viktor had plotted out a secret rescue mission that was more or less real to almost everyone on board—and only a select few contacts higher up the chain of command knew it was a ruse. But given the way he had aligned the pieces of his plan, the higher ranks that were in on the plot would likely be able to maintain their plausible deniability. That wouldn't spare him, Cid, or the four companions from any adverse consequences, but it seemed to Viktor that they were prepared for the possible costs associated with what they knew they had to do, regardless. In any case, he knew *he* was. And essentially, it seemed it could truly turn into a rescue mission. Whatever had caused these disturbances and disappearances that the Oranlak had experienced might well make it a real one. There might even be abandoned workers or contractors down in the underwater facility, genuinely needing rescue.

The submarine dove to ever-darkening depths. There was no sight of any underwater facility for some time, despite them plunging hundreds of feet deep.

Then they picked something up on sonar. But given its sudden proximity, it should have been detected well in advance of when it had been.

Some sort of shielding, perhaps? was all Viktor could wonder as the crew went on alert. They continued on, their systems scanning the facility. There was an entry chamber at the highest point of the structure. The lights were dim, likely running on auxiliary power. The facility was still mostly dark, with no sign of people or other life anywhere around.

The captain of the sub instructed his crew to maneuver and position the sub's side door to be aligned and connected with the entryway at the top of the facility. External cameras on the submarine assisted the crew in guiding the sub to that entrance, which was a short tunnel of sorts, protruding above the top of the facility. Fortunately, they observed and confirmed that this newly built underwater edifice had the current industry-standard connector port that the submarines of recent years could easily attach to. After maneuvering into position, they initiated the latching mechanism to connect the sub to the facility.

High-powered magnets helped guide the attachment, and the connection was made. The side door of the submarine had slight depressions that gently spun in a circular motion and aligned with the corresponding protrusions on the door to the entry tunnel.

The exterior side door on the sub had behind it a currently empty interior room, which was sealed off from the rest of the vessel. When the connection with the entryway of the facility was secure, two sliding metal plates that made up that exterior door slid open in unison with the automatic door of the underwater facility. Behind those plates, small sensors began gathering and analyzing information about the air inside the underwater facility, including the pressure. The process was completed quickly.

Viktor reviewed this data from the sensors, seeming very familiar with the process. He spoke briefly to the captain, then turned to the companions.

"We've completed the analysis of the air in the facility and confirmed the pressure within," Viktor said to the four of them. "You can now enter the Rescue Room, as they call it. I'll take you down myself."

He led them down to the room, which they could now use to gain entry to the underwater facility.

"You must remain in this room until I give you the go-ahead over the intercom. And please note, if you haven't noticed already, your clonras will not function well, if at all, while you're down here," he advised them.

Viktor handed Gerrard a wristband with a simple timer device on it. "Use this to keep track of how much time you have," Viktor said to him. Then he turned to all four of them. "The doors that lead from this room back to the rest of the sub can only be opened from this side. But you want to stay in that room, anyway, once you're in it. And do not open the door to the underwater facility until I give the go-ahead."

He paused to make sure the important instructions set in with them. Then he continued, "In that room, your bodies will be gradually and appropriately acclimated to the internal environment in the underwater facility, so that you can enter safely and without incident, and with a minimized risk of any adverse effects. We will use our analysis of the air and the pressure in the facility to facilitate this."

With that, Viktor opened the door to the Rescue Room, let them in, and secured the door again behind them. Then it was a waiting game while the acclimation process was completed. When it finally finished, they heard Viktor's voice again over the intercom.

"Okay, you're ready. I'm opening the door in a few seconds," came Viktor's voice over the system. "You have twenty-four hours, and you must return to where you are entering the facility now to be able to be picked up at that time. We will depart and finish the preplanned course, but we will be back for you in twenty-four hours. We will detour again for you on the way back. Start the countdown on the timer I gave you, Gerrard. And don't be late."

One of the crew, upon overhearing this from Viktor, confronted him, apparently perceiving something amiss about the unusual scenario. The captain, an old friend of Viktor's, quieted the crew member, though, with a rather stern voice, and the man fell back in line. It was a reminder to Viktor, though, that a number of questions were sure to follow this mission, if not even before its completion. Inconsistencies in this, the best plan that he could put together, would inevitably come to light, however impressive their efforts might prove to keep the true mission under wraps.

The crew had been as carefully selected as possible and had been briefed to varying degrees. Their general understanding was that they were to rescue some unspecified persons at a top-secret underwater facility. But those in the control room back at base simply understood this to be a tour for some friendly submarine enthusiasts who were Viktor's friends.

The captain of the submarine owed a debt to his old friend Viktor, and he was more largely aware of the truth of what was going on than most aboard. He would maintain appearances—at least, as well as he could. He would do so, Viktor knew, even at great risk to himself. But he sincerely hoped no significant harm would befall his old friend.

And he was confident—*mostly* confident—that it wasn't going to come to that.

27

Chapter Twenty-Seven

The companions walked into the entry chamber, relieved that they all still felt fine, and that they didn't implode from some catastrophic failure in the systems or technology they were relying on. The entry door closed behind them, and they all turned on their headlamps. It was dark inside; there was barely enough light to see the corridor in front of them. Eeriness and dead silence permeated the place.

"Kinda like bein' in a horror movie or something, huh, guys?" Regina managed. But a bit of nervousness crept into her strained laugh.

"You're not really scared, are you?" Hector asked, picking up on that and glancing over at her for a moment.

"You're already grasping your sword there, Hector. Nervous a little yourself?" Andromeda quipped.

"Ha," came Hector's response. He scoffed at how ludicrous it was that Andromeda had misconstrued such an appropriate measure of preparedness as him being nervous. He didn't engage with a comeback or defense, though, just focused his eyes ahead.

Then Gerrard removed a high-powered flashlight from his travel pack. The corridor, though relatively spacious for what it was, still seemed to hold the cramped, claustrophobic atmosphere that would be expected of an underwater facility.

The four moved down the corridor for a short time. Then Regina spoke up. "There's … an intersection up ahead!" she said, too loudly. As she immediately realized she was shouting, she made a mental note to tone it down.

"There's a map on the wall," observed Hector. Their eyes all fell upon it.

"Where should we head to?" asked Andromeda.

"If we find any survivors down here, they could probably fill us in on whatever happened," suggested Gerrard.

"Gosh, is that the point we're at now?" interjected Regina. "'Any survivors'?"

"Maybe it is a grim presumption about the circumstances so far," conceded Gerrard. "Probably not unwarranted or far off base, though."

"Agreed," said Hector.

"Great… Well, any thoughts, anyone, on which direction we should proceed in, to have the best chance of finding someone?" asked Regina.

"Living quarters," answered Andromeda, pointing to the location on the map. "Let's have a look over there—I think we can make it that far, and it sounds at least as promising as anywhere else on this map."

"It still looks like it is a bit of a trek over to that area, though, and there's a place or two along the way we should probably check in on," cut in Hector.

"Sounds reasonable," said Gerrard, looking over the path to the area marked LIVING QUARTERS.

"Let's take this slight detour here," said Hector, indicating a place along the route with his index finger. "Over to the laboratory, then return to our main route, but stop over here, at communications, before we continue on to the living quarters."

"Can we stop here, too?" asked Regina, pointing to another spot, a bit more out of the way.

"The kitchen?!" Andromeda blurted out, a little louder than she meant to. She quieted herself quickly, though, and continued. "I don't think this is the time, Regina."

Regina flashed the older woman a defeated smile. "Okay, yes, yes, you're right. I was so … worked up about the plan and getting down here, I didn't think to eat as much before we left as I should've," she admitted. "Ya know there might be someone over there, too, though," she went on, pressing a little.

"Let's see what we turn up at these other places," offered Gerrard.

Regina nodded, accepting the path forward.

The four continued on uneventfully, farther down the corridor. Upon eventually reaching the split they'd observed on the map, they took the smaller walkway off the larger main hall. There were miscellaneous items scattered around as they approached the lab, as well as spills of unidentifiable liquids. Then the companions made more alarming observations: broken chairs, tattered clothing. There was broken glass equipment, like flasks and beakers.

Regina paused, which prompted them all to do so, as they came upon the entrance to the laboratory, which was marked by a broken, barely legible sign. It had once been lit up, but in its current state, a few remaining segments just flickered momentarily every few seconds.

"That's a touch ominous," remarked Regina.

Hector didn't respond much, other than to be the first to resume walking. He could feel the excitement of Kazahvir effectively shouting through his mind, and whatever Regina was saying at that moment came across as far less compelling to him.

Regina let her shoulders dip and her arms fall to her sides in defeat as the others shrugged and continued on, too. "I don't think solving this mystery is going to be as thrilling as I thought." She sighed, knowing she was mostly speaking to herself.

Gerrard flashed his bright light around the lab as they entered. A dripping noise echoed through the room. The space appeared devoid of any life, though there was surely an abundance of broken, expensive-looking glassware. There were benches and worktables, ventilation hoods, and an array of chemicals in labeled bottles lining shelves on one side of the room. The group shined their lights through the windows in the doors of some of the breakout rooms that branched off from the main, larger central room.

"Not much here but a lot of broken equipment," noted Gerrard.

"What is that maddening dripping noise?" asked Andromeda.

"Not sure," replied Gerrard.

Regina noticed a puddle on the floor as she was walking around and trying to trace the sound's origin. Then she saw a drop of something fall into that puddle. She took a few more steps to come up next to the dark, slowly enlarging puddle. It still wasn't clear to her what it was. Then she turned her eyes upward.

A leaking pipe in the ceiling or something? she wondered.

Then she let out a scream—one which quickly caught the attention of her companions, and, unfortunately, something else as well.

* * *

There was a smaller room, back off the main hall, that had been locked from the outside. The large metal doors of that room did little to block the sound of Regina's sudden scream, though, and the creature within could easily hear her terror. And it wasn't even that it just heard it; it was at least equally accurate to say that, simultaneously, it *felt* it. And if the strange creature had had the capacity to do so, it would have even salivated over the sensations it felt then, in feeling her terror.

It had no real mouth—at least, not as humans did. Its large, bulbous head consisted primarily of just three hugely oversized eyes. It was standing upright, as it usually did, when that scream had found it.

It was the height of a typical human male. Possessing a vaguely humanoid neck and chest, it had four long, tentacled arms that protruded from it. Two arms erupted from each side, from the general area arms would usually originate on a human's body. Small spikes and thorns lined those tentacles, some of which secreted what was to humans a painful and paralyzing toxin. But even the ones that were not poisonous were as sharp as razors. The creature's body was held upright by many lower tentacles, which it used to slither around the room.

Just then, feeling a renewed hunger, it slithered over onto the final unconsumed remains of a dead human. It lowered its torso as the room filled with the flesh-shredding, bone-grinding din of it feasting through the hole at the center of its lower tentacles. It wasn't so loud as Regina's scream was, though. The blood-stained walls of the room and the distance that it was from the lab sufficed to limit the noise, and the companions heard none of it.

* * *

Back in the laboratory, Regina quickly calmed herself from the shock of what she saw hanging above her. There was a man—or what looked to have once been a man. He was mangled, disfigured, and stuck to the ceiling with a cement-like, oozy, slimy substance. The stuff was spread out over much of the ceiling, seeming to emanate from where the disfigured remains had been stuck.

"Well, that's gruesome," remarked Hector unemotionally.

Regina looked over to him and immediately recognized him as the one who had suggested the detour to the laboratory.

"Yes..." Regina agreed, glaring at him. "Perhaps we should've stayed on the direct path to the living quarters."

Andromeda detected a degree of accusation in her tone, perhaps for the near heart-stopping shock she had just experienced. She spoke up, hoping to deescalate things. "That is ... rather unsightly... Yes... I still don't see anyone alive down here, though," she managed. "I don't think the lab continues on farther from here, and I don't see that we need to dwell on this section any longer. Let's all fall back to the main hall and continue on toward the living quarters. Sound like a plan, team?"

Andromeda looked in particular to Gerrard for his input, hoping he would support her suggestion.

"I think..." Gerrard started as he scrutinized more closely the horror adhered to the ceiling. "… that would be advisable."

The others nodded in acquiescence, and they all started back toward the lab's entrance. Then they made their way back to the main hallway without further excitement, continuing onward, as planned, toward the communications room.

Soon after, they were all in front of the door to that room, which appeared to be far smaller. The sign indicating the room's title was partially covered in more of that slimy, oozy substance, but it was legible enough that they knew they had arrived at their next stop.

Hector, feeling more eager than the others, and certainly more ecstatic than terrified, was first to stand in front of the door. It seemed as though it had been designed to be automatic, but it didn't open.

"Limitations of the backup power system the facility is running on, perhaps," suggested Gerrard. "Anyone experienced with technology like this?" he asked, not being so technically savvy with such matters.

Hector silently considered the panel beside the door. He didn't really have the experience Gerrard was calling for, but he had the will to try, anyway. He felt Kazahvir's urging pounding in his head, and he felt strongly the anticipation it had for uncovering whatever the room held. Normally, Kazahvir would have indicated to Hector the degree of danger it also felt. After all, it truly didn't want to harm the exceptional human—at least, not before it had a suitable replacement lined up. The sentient sword continually reassessed and reappraised the young man, and it often reached out its magical detection to find someone somewhere within reach who might be a better wielder for it. But ever since this human had awakened it, it had not encountered any person it took as clearly more promising.

But what Kazahvir needed now was to feel itself slicing through flesh and bone, experiencing new adventures and heights of excitement and fulfillment. This young man, Hector, had unusually high potential, in spite of the fairly dull times it had been awakened into. Unfortunately for him, though, the sentient sword also hungered for a sense of danger and the thrill of being in it.

Hector was a brave sort, and Kazahvir didn't generally need to worry about whether the exceptional human was up for facing any given enemy. It did now, though. And so, it did not provide any information to its wielder about the true horror that awaited him inside. It couldn't risk him avoiding the encounter. It desired the experience that the life-form within could present.

Kazahvir scanned the creature's thoughts, but it didn't detect a higher order of thinking—not like the humans had. It seemed more of just an intelligent animal—though not so intelligent that it didn't also seem consumed by a voracious hunger to feed, spread its kind, and expand its domain. The sentient weapon stopped short of a deeper analysis, though. It sensed something within that creature's mind beyond its own brain. It was as if it were not alone—as if it were mentally connected to something far more colossal, or at least to many other creatures of similar size. Perhaps even both.

After a few minutes of Hector pressing seemingly random buttons on the panel and on the flickering display, the doors finally shuddered and ground open. Disfigured metal that was bent slightly out of place scraped along the length of the opening doors, but they opened all the same. More lights inside the room strained to activate, though some burnt out permanently in their attempt to do so. Still, the place went from almost perfect darkness to dimly lit.

As they stepped into the room, Hector's mind immediately began to fill with what Kazahvir had been sensing. His magically enhanced blade was careful not to overwhelm his mind—but it imparted what it knew, as efficiently as it felt the man could handle. Hector stumbled back a step as his eyes darted around the room, searching for the monster in here with them.

Gerrard regarded Hector curiously as he took note of the backstep—an unusual action for someone who seemed to usually favor plunging forward into things.

"What is—" Gerrard started to say, as he stopped walking suddenly and Andromeda bumped into him from behind. The unexpected impact startled him, and he jumped forward and to the side, glancing around and drawing his mighty claymore from his back. Andromeda jolted backward a few steps herself, her own saber at the ready.

Instantly thereafter, a tentacled mass came flying at them, apparently having launched itself into a jump at Gerrard. It smashed down harmlessly to the floor where Gerrard had just been standing. Its bubbling, gurgling noises were unnerving, to say nothing of the hideous look of the octopus-like humanoid monster.

A pair of arm tentacles reached out for Gerrard then, undeterred by its missed first strike. It slimed and slithered nearer to him, closing in fast. One of those arms shot out suddenly for him, but then Regina was there with her shield. Gerrard stood in shock while the spiky tentacle struck that shield with great force, but the magical enhancement of her shield held and deflected the powerful blow. The creature seemed to hiss in rage at that, at these weak humans who did not immediately fall prey to its physical superiority. The predator shot a toxic barb from one of its tentacles at Andromeda, and it penetrated the floor an instant after she narrowly dodged out of the way.

The creature was caught off guard by what followed—a flurry of mental energy waves that scattered its primitive thoughts. Its focus fell away from any specific target as it tried to force its thoughts back to the needs of the moment. It hadn't the luxury of such time, though, as Kazahvir struck and was driven deep into its torso.

Toxic fluid oozed out from the injury, a caustic substance that would have quickly corroded most lesser weapons. But Kazahvir held strong—though surely it felt that bite back from its strike against the creature. Hector thrust the blade deeper before retracting the sword and dealing another slashing blow, which unnecessarily severed the head of the thing and sent it tumbling unceremoniously across the room.

Its body crumpled lifelessly to the floor—but not before the monster, through its mental link to others of its kind, imparted a final transmission of what had just transpired. Kazahvir detected the presence and the strength of that outgoing signal, and it noted that this defeated creature seemed to be weak compared to the one receiving it. Still, it was more interested in the rush of having just felled the disgusting, gurgling monster, and it wasn't immediately opposed to more of them coming, anyway.

"Well done, Hector!" cheered Regina approvingly.

Hector let his face crack into a satisfied smile. But he understood through the magic of Kazahvir that a blaringly loud mental signal had just gone out—and he was careful to temper his enthusiasm.

"Okay," Andromeda cut into the outburst of jubilation. "Let's make our way out of here," she said as she looked around at the macabre scene of monster and human remains everywhere.

The others nodded. They didn't need a second glance around the place to feel confident this was the right course of action.

Back in the main hallway, Gerrard led them onward. They continued on without further incident, right up to the doors of the living quarters. The large, metal double doors were banged up and dented, such that the group couldn't be sure they'd even still function. The panel to the side of the door was brightly lit and appeared functional, though.

The group's presence in front of the doors did not activate them, though the doors did appear to have originally been automatic. Gerrard tried a few buttons on the side panel.

Hector stepped forward and did more or less what he had done with the communications doors, which brought up a message flashing on the screen of the panel.

Password needed. Door lock engaged.

Hector looked at Gerrard, then shrugged. "Could try and break it down," he offered.

Gerrard looked at him doubtfully, glancing at the dents in the metal doors, then back again at Hector. "It would appear bigger things than us have already tried," he said skeptically.

Right then, through Kazahvir's magic, Hector sensed a person inside—just behind the doors. He couldn't say that, of course, so he adjusted his message a bit.

"Maybe there're people inside who might open up for their rescuers?" proposed Hector.

Regina stepped closer to the doors and nearer to Gerrard and Hector, and then took up Hector's idea. She announced their group to anyone who might be inside listening. "Hello there! We're … with the rescue party! Anyone left inside?" Regina asked boldly. She did do her best to sound sincere, friendly, unthreatening.

The companions all waited in suspense for a response.

A few moments later, someone inside responded. "Thank goodness!" said a man's voice. "Wonderful to hear another voice, particularly after such a terribly long time."

"How long have you … been locked in there?" Regina asked, trying to continue sounding pleasant and concerned.

"It's been nearly two months now. So good to finally hear from someone!" came the voice again.

That voice from behind the living quarters doors belonged to a man of roughly Gerrard's age, who was now considering his new predicament. Did he want to trust this woman on the other side of those doors—doors that had been his primary defense against the monsters? And what of her team, the supposed rescue party?

But what was his alternative if he didn't? He had not been expecting to survive much longer, anyway—not with supplies, and his sanity level, running so dangerously low. Maybe this was his last opportunity to escape the place.

He knew his fellow scientist, also trapped in here, was in the other section of the living quarters at the moment. She would probably have seized the opportunity to welcome in the alleged rescue team already. After all, they had both concluded weeks ago that the facility had been abandoned for the foreseeable future.

"What's your name?" the pleasant-sounding woman's voice came again, drawing him out of his thoughts.

"Malcolm," he responded. "I'm … going to open the doors now. Stand clear!"

Malcolm entered his password into the door panel, and the doors slid open, with just minor grinding and difficulty.

Malcolm looked at the rescue team—if that was truly what they were. He regarded them to be quite a sight.

There was an average-height, fairly gruff-looking man of about Malcolm's own age. He had a blaster, an unusual sight, strapped to one hip. On his back was a massive two-handed sword.

The one with whom he believed he had been speaking had a far softer appearance. She wielded a sword of her own, though, and had a remarkable—if not magical—shield on her person, too. She was beautiful and youthful, perhaps two decades younger than he was.

The other woman was older, though still perhaps a decade younger than Malcolm. She had a more hardened appearance than the other woman, and a far more dazzling blade—a saber, strapped to one hip. And on the other, of all things, was another blaster.

The final of the four was a much younger man. He seemed quieter and more reserved, standing at the edge of the shadows. He had a longsword—another incredible and deadly-looking weapon.

The four didn't seem to have much in common. They held themselves differently, their body language across the spectrum. They barely seemed to have any commonalities in clothing or style at all. And they did not seem to be an organized force of any similar training or background.

"You don't look like a rescue team," Malcolm observed. "Who sent you?"

"I would think you'd be satisfied enough just to see other humans, regardless of what they look like," Gerrard replied.

"Especially after what we've seen since being here..." Andromeda added, a bit warmer in tone.

"Everyone—could we maybe have this conversation inside?" Regina asked.

Malcolm beckoned for them all to enter. He wasn't so put off by the unusual appearance of the rescue team that he was going to do otherwise. When they were all safely inside, he closed and locked the doors again.

"Okay," said Malcolm. "So, you're an unusual-looking group, and it doesn't seem to me that you were sent by anyone who would've sent a rescue team here. You don't have any uniforms or obvious identification about you. What gives?"

"You're very observant," said Regina. "You alone here?"

Malcolm sighed. Then he repeated his previous question, a little more determinedly. "Who sent you?" he asked.

Andromeda stepped forward toward him. "It's nice to meet you, Malcolm," she said, kindly. "My name is Andromeda. This is Gerrard, Hector, and Regina. We're bounty hunters and adventurers who came to learn of this place and thought it worth … looking into further," she went on. Then she turned and looked over her companions, and then smiled back at Malcolm. "Perhaps we've been guided here by forces we don't quite fully understand. But we're sorry to see the sort of troubles you've all fallen into down here. I do also apologize for the deception; we didn't want to scare you unnecessarily, and we thought you'd be more welcoming to a rescue team. And anyway, we may yet be that very thing for you."

"That's gravely unfortunate for you, I'd say, that you stumbled into a place like this," Malcolm responded.

"What happened here?" Hector asked.

"Well, I would hope you can all appreciate and understand that there is a certain sensitivity to what is being done and has been worked on down here…" Malcolm started. "But … seeing as how I value my life being saved from this place more than I value holding onto any such secrets … I'll tell you about it. I'll tell you all you want to know, and repay you all I can—just promise to get me out of here!"

"We promise," agreed Andromeda.

Malcolm paused, accepting that he was going to have to trust them.

"I have to figure that you already know about the spaceship that sank down and landed right next to where we built this facility. Is that right?" Malcolm asked the companions. Seeing the nods from his four rescuers, he went on. "So, of course, we were collecting the promethium. It was scattered throughout the ship and even spread out across the seafloor in the surrounding area—actually out to a considerable distance. And there's still a lot more out there yet to be found, though we have collected a great quantity already," he said, then paused, assessing how much more he wanted to divulge at that moment.

A thought occurred to him, and he couldn't stop himself from going on a little longer. He hadn't had many people to talk to for so long now, and it felt good just to be speaking to them.

"Funny," he said, and he laughed a little. "Some people actually think the promethium might save the world."

"I take it you are not one of them?" asked Andromeda, intrigued.

"Some of us are more skeptical," Malcolm acknowledged. "Some of us have been studying this substance intensively—this strange material that is presumed to have come from another world. I've been involved with the project here almost since the beginning—and I was a lot more hopeful about it all back then, before I knew so much."

He paused, seeming to reflect regretfully on acquiring whatever knowledge he had. A few seconds passed, then he spoke again.

"Anyway, there's been a whole mess of strange happenings," Malcolm continued. "Since we first broke ground on this project, we've learned that time moves differently down here. It's moving faster than at the surface. It seems to have something to do with the spaceship, or something in the wreckage of what's left of it, anyway. Maybe we activated something, switched something on while we were exploring and gathering. But time does seem to normalize as you move farther away from the ship."

"This sounds problematic," said Regina.

"It actually allowed the construction of this whole facility in what seemed to be an incredibly short amount of time," Malcolm continued. "The speed with which time is passing doesn't seem to be staying consistent, though. It's always moving faster here than after some certain distance away from the ship, but the relativity of time here to time there still varies. Weeks may pass here in the facility, while mere days up there do, or sometimes even as just hours on the surface do. And the variance appears to be quite unpredictable."

"That's amazing … and sort of terrifying," Andromeda cut in.

"It's how we were able to build this state-of-the-art, unprecedented underwater facility so fast," said Malcolm. "It had largely all been an incredible success—though we've since learned that promethium is more dangerous and harmful than we realized. Even so, the Elites running Ezmondia will undoubtedly go on utilizing it. It is a solution for now, even if just a temporary one. It does seem likely that it's going to lead to bigger problems for the world of tomorrow than if we just accepted the consequences of our failing energy systems today. That, of course, is not to say that those aren't quite catastrophic themselves."

Malcolm couldn't help but consider how focused and attentive the four of them were to his words. They seemed to be absorbing everything. They certainly seemed to place great value on what he was saying.

"In any case," Malcolm said, moving on, "there's also a lot of coin involved. So, maybe the promethium solution to our energy troubles—and everything else going on here—is just secondary to that one important truth."

He couldn't help but momentarily agonize over humanity's obsession with wealth and what an impedance it was to true problem-solving. But he pushed through it quickly, wanting to move on to more immediately relevant details.

"More recently, we've also had these ... *things* popping up. We've been calling them octotors," Malcolm said, elaborating on the creatures lurking throughout the facility. "They have venomous spikes on their arm tentacles, and eyes that seem to penetrate darkness quite effectively. The slime their leg tentacles secrete is also highly toxic. They have an array of razor-sharp, spinning teeth that line their—for lack of a better term—mouths, which are underneath their torsos. They can grind up a human body very efficiently ... and thoroughly, and horrifically. You don't want to suffer the misfortune of being alive when they set to work doing that to you. And the smaller ones, they're tiny—a first form of theirs, maybe—they might be even worse. They'll dig holes in your flesh, squeeze their way in, and consume you from the inside out."

Malcolm shook his head, as if fighting to repel some grotesque, haunting memory.

"These creatures all seem to be staying close to their sunken ship. I assume it must be their ship, though they do seem too animalistic to really pilot the thing. Maybe they're angry about what we've been taking from them—the promethium. Or maybe they're just hungry or bloodthirsty. Regardless, I wouldn't risk trying to reason with the things. Those I've witnessed trying have not fared well."

Malcolm's head shook back and forth, and his body seemed to shudder. He grabbed his arms, struggling to stop himself. Emotion was increasingly and involuntarily spilling into his voice as he spoke, as he mentally fought through the traumatic occurrences of these past weeks.

"Fear," said Malcolm. "They are reactive to fear; it's provocative to them. They'll come at you … more fiercely and more aggressively if you're scared. They can even find us with it, as if they're tracking us by that fear. And each seems to have a mental link with the others—and I suspect also to another, smarter type of them. Or maybe even to some mastermind entity. And if you encounter one of them, the other ones all know about that encounter. Fortunately, they do seem to have some trouble sensing or finding us here in our living quarters. Something in the reinforced walls of this place, maybe—some material of its construction. Many mysteries remain."

Malcolm stopped speaking, beginning to feel like he was spending too much valuable time supplying all these details.

"We can't remain here much longer," he said. Then his eyes caught something on Gerrard's wrist. "What is that clock that's counting down on your wrist?" Malcolm asked Gerrard.

"We have to be back at the designated place for our pickup from this facility before this clock runs down," answered Gerrard.

"I hope your … *our* ride isn't going too far from the facility, or they'll be caught in the time fluctuations, and who knows how long it'll be before they get back to us then?" replied Malcolm grimly.

"I was worrying 'bout the same thing…" Regina said.

Gerrard thought on the matter for a moment. "We're just going to have to hope their path doesn't take them outside the same … time zone, I guess we'll call it … that we are in. We'll just have to be at the designated place at the planned time, and we'll hold out as long as we can and hope for the best."

"Not much else to be done," reasoned Hector, grinning inside at the thought of an epic slaughter of the things, in something of a last-stand scenario that Kazahvir was conveying and glorifying to him.

Malcolm let out a defeated, hopeless sort of laugh. "All the time I've spent working on calculations and experiments of exactness and precision, and yet here I am, reduced to going along with plans like this now..." he lamented.

Just then, a voice came from just outside the main room of the living quarters.

"Hello there," said the voice cautiously.

The five of them turned to regard the source.

It was a woman, perhaps Andromeda's age, with long black hair, wearing a white lab coat. She returned their stares. "Is everything okay, Malcolm?" she asked timidly. Then she inquired an instant later with what was a more critical question, judging from her excited tone: "Are we finally getting out of here?!"

"That would ... seem to be the case," replied Malcolm, looking hopefully again at the four companions.

The woman's countenance brightened considerably with that answer. She almost couldn't control herself as she ran over to wrap up the closest of them, Andromeda and Gerrard, in a huge hug. "Thank you, thank you!" she exclaimed. Then she ran right to Malcolm and did the same thing. "We finally have a shot at getting out of here, Malcolm!" she excitedly went on, holding him tightly and appreciatively.

Having been caught off guard by the woman's sudden expression of gratitude, Andromeda composed herself. "We're so glad to have found someone still alive down here," she managed to say.

"Probably not as glad as we are to see you," Malcolm assured her. "This is my long-time lab partner, Mariana. Mariana, this is Andromeda, Gerrard, Hector, and Regina."

"A pleasure to meet you all," replied Mariana with great sincerity.

"May I ask," Regina said, "what ya were planning to go do before ya noticed us just now? Looks like you're working, like this is a normal workday or something for ya."

Mariana smiled at her observant rescuer. "Malcolm and I have still been working, actually," she admitted. "It's had a way of keeping us going, keeping our minds occupied. Though we've certainly been more limited now in what we've been able to do."

"What sorta work have ya been involved in? What have ya been working on down here?" Regina asked.

Mariana looked over to Malcolm, who nodded at her. "I told them some things," he said. "I told them I'd tell them what they wanted to know about this place if they would just get us out of here. This could be our last hope, Mariana," he said to her.

Mariana hesitated a moment, but then appeared to accept the reasoning and proceeded to answer Regina's question. "Well, while confined to our smaller lab in one of the side rooms over there," she began, "we've been working on refining and improving electrolyzer technology."

"Electrolyzer technology?" echoed Andromeda.

Mariana nodded. "We're trying to produce hydrogen more efficiently and sustainably, by splitting water molecules with the electrolyzer technology," she said. "We've been experimenting with materials to try and enhance current systems. If we can find faster, less expensive means of producing hydrogen fuel, it would be a boon for all of Gracian civilization."

"Sure, if you could get them to embrace the new technology," Hector cut in, sounding skeptical.

"If we can show people the results and prove the viability and potential of the technology, show it to be safe and effective, why would anyone deny or push back against what we could accomplish?" asked Mariana.

"Power," answered Hector, almost angrily.

The scientists regarded Hector quizzically.

"Friends, we'll submit our work for publishing in the most respected journals; we'll get the word out to everyone, and everyone will want to know more and work toward what we'll prove is possible," Malcolm said.

"I admire your optimistic view of the world," complimented Gerrard honestly. "I believe if your work is rock solid, if your methods are compelling, if the results are undeniable, then perhaps a reality that is close to the one you describe could come to pass."

"Your journals are not going to be so keen as you think on publishing any breakthroughs that upend the current power balance of this world. Or the enterprises of people who derive their power from the way things are now," Hector said.

"What sort of work have you done in the past, before working down here?" Andromeda asked then, trying to bring the conversation into less tense territory.

"We both have a background in atomic fusion technology," Malcolm responded.

"Interesting. Tell us a little more?" requested Andromeda, who then looked at Gerrard, suspecting he would be intrigued.

And indeed, Gerrard couldn't help his ears perking up, nor could Regina help hers, though Hector's face remained unchanged.

"When the nuclei of two atoms merge, they release a lot of energy," Malcolm responded, rightly assuming Andromeda didn't have much knowledge in the specialized area. "It's the same process harnessed by our sun. It's fascinating. On our planet, we can create a fourth state of matter—plasma—to help us reach this incredible energy. But we need temperatures of millions of degrees and almost inconceivable pressure and magnetic strength. With these things, we could control the plasma and force atoms together, combining them and releasing massive energy. You could rightly regard such energy as millions of times better than what we can produce with current systems—and Gracyr has such an abundance of the essential resources we would need that the systems could persist sustainably for millions of years."

"That sounds very good," Gerrard remarked simply, managing and masking his excitement about meeting such a pair as these two.

Mariana smiled. "There are challenges, though," she admitted. "The high-heat and high-pressure conditions needed make it difficult to control the plasma and the reaction for very long. Experimental systems—what few there have been—have tended to need vast amounts of energy. And those systems run for extraordinarily short periods of time, within which they cannot produce the energy needed to make them practical."

"Some modern-day submarines use them," Gerrard said.

Mariana looked to him, intrigued. "Powering a submarine for a short spurt of time has occasionally been made feasible in some settings for some applications, yes," she agreed. "But powering society at large, on greater scales and sustainably, with bigger and longer reactions—that is going to require fresh perspectives, new materials, or old materials used in new ways … further developments in general."

"We were researching materials we found down here," Malcolm said, "on the seafloor; some truly promising ones are found at these great depths. But our fusion work is all over in the main lab, which has been wrecked and—for all intents and purposes, I'm sure—entirely lost. Still, the work with the electrolyzer has been keeping us going."

"Before we were overrun down here," Mariana added, "we were even looking at harnessing the energy of some nearby underwater thermal vents, to power our electrolyzer!"

"Cool!" came Regina's voice in an excited outburst—a rather nerdy one she couldn't have helped if she tried.

"It is all very interesting," agreed Malcolm, nodding amusedly.

Andromeda, Gerrard, and Regina continued to seem engaged in the conversation with the two scientists, but Hector was increasingly less so. His mind was so captivated by thoughts of this monster he had killed, and by ideas of learning more about them and fighting more of them, that he hardly even noticed how quiet he was being.

"So, I suppose you're always on the lookout for new materials to make reactions happen … more effectively, more … practically. Would that be a fair assessment?" Gerrard asked Malcolm and Mariana.

They looked to each other, then back at Gerrard, and responded together affirmatively.

Andromeda slid back into the conversation again then. "We have a fair amount of time before we need to make our way back to the entrance for our rendezvous with the sub, and by the sound of it, we're probably safest here," she said. "It seems we should wait the clock out a bit here," she reasoned.

"That sounds logical," said Hector, finally joining the conversation again.

Hector had been mentally battling against Kazahvir's invasive ideas of just slaying more octotors. He had finally managed to quell them after doing his best to impart to Kazahvir that such ideas of glory and victory were going to lead to him getting slaughtered, as well as to it being abandoned and lost down here forever.

"I'll stand guard at the doors here a while," suggested Hector. "You all can get some sleep or get on with your work or whatever."

The group didn't offer any protests, and Malcolm showed the rest of them to some rooms they could rest in. There were beds and showers and even some limited food options still available, which Malcolm said they could help themselves to if they wished.

28

Chapter Twenty-Eight

Hector was still too adrenalized from the previous battle to sleep. He stared at the doors, lost in thought for a time, and he made several rounds walking about the area. He remained awake and on guard, and he examined the main chamber of the living quarters section of the facility in excruciating detail.

Some hours passed by uneventfully, and then Regina eventually came and relieved him, saying she couldn't sleep anymore. Hector reluctantly let her take over, and he went to seek an available bed. It had been a long time since he had slept, so when he found one, sleep came to him easily.

After falling asleep, Hector's mind fell back and circled around the world he had lived in many years ago. He dreamed of being a teenager again, growing up in an Ezmondian city.

It had been a hard upbringing for Hector. His parents had never been together—not going back as far as his memory could, anyway. And the two of them seemed to go back and forth in terms of who was the more stable and capable parent. He sporadically spent most of his time with one or the other over the years, and consequently, he'd had a chaotic youth. Regardless of which he was with, though, Hector generally had little parental oversight, or anyone worrying too much about him. His parents were distracted—though in his view, justifiably so. They worried about just finding something to eat, having a place to live, and even their general safety, amid the uprising of many powerful gangs around that time.

The schools, as he came to see them around those tumultuous years, were primarily centers for indoctrination. They were mostly concerned with molding his mind this way or that to suit the ends of whatever the emperor wanted that day, week, or year. He was educated on what the elites thought would be most profitable to them for him to be educated on. But unlike many of his classmates at the time, his mind railed against these pressures and injustices he perceived. He became rebellious in those younger years and strived to be as independent as possible. He didn't like counting on unreliable people, which in his view was basically everyone.

He was always thinking about how things could go amiss in situations, and about what he would say or do to extricate himself from imagined threats and difficulties that, most often, never came to pass. He was that way about things—arguably paranoid, but ready to defend or counter many situations that could conceivably present themselves. He was guarded, and it made him feel secure. He guarded his thoughts, emotions, motivations, and—perhaps particularly—his weaknesses, with great intensity.

Hector often found himself astonished at his peers. It was peculiar to him how they all seemed so willingly—or so unknowingly—pulled along on strings by the master puppeteers of their society. He could, on some level, see that those peers did have a sense of the state of affairs of their world, though. But it was bizarre how often their actions did not reflect any real understanding of it all. Acquaintances, even friends—as he might loosely call a select few—seemed to him too overwhelmed by emotion and impulse. And they were blind to the reason and logic he believed he had guiding him. Others could not control themselves. And so, he continually strived to be better, to conquer himself.

He wondered—as even the older adults and his own parents exhibited such blind behavior—whether this fabled concept of free will even existed. People seemed so machinelike to him—mindless automatons edified by vidscreens and mesmerized by the addictiveness of their programming. The media of the empire was endlessly consumed by its inhabitants, and it was incrementally forming them into what they were, he knew. Others could not see the transmogrification of their human selves into depraved beings, utterly lacking in the fundamental things that seemed, to Hector, to make a person human. But he was determined to be different.

It all seemed to be a silly game to the younger Hector. He was actually prone, despite his general lack of emotion, to occasional outbursts of seemingly random laughter. Others might not always perceive the appropriateness of the reaction, but it was so abundantly clear to Hector how ridiculous people could be. That relatively rare laughter helped him, though. It felt good to laugh at the preposterousness of it all. And it helped him experience some enjoyment in what was so often a bleak existence. It kept him interested in talking to people. At least they might say something he could take a measure of amusement in. And he was always on the lookout for someone who might seem to him to harbor some vaguely similar views about their world. Not that anyone ever did. Still, he could derive more understanding from talking to people and experiencing more things, so he resolved to go on doing so. He had to play the game, so he might as well enjoy it as much as he could.

As he came of age in his home city in Ezmondia—the name of which he didn't care to recall—the world did seem to make more sense to him. Years of working toward a greater understanding of why things were the way they were seemed to be paying off. Hector came to take great interest in understanding and analyzing the motivations of those around him. The people in his home city of Ezmondia were creatures of self-interest who perceived or adopted realities in line with that self-interest. They were committed to the material and the moment, not to the immaterial or the future.

He had, many times over the years, tried to gently guide or test others. He would take a neutral stance or adopt an adversarial position to see if he could encourage them to second-guess what they believed. By and large, though, there was an obstinance he could not overcome. There was a reality they knew, and any incongruous facts were simply reperceived to align with what they knew.

A bothersome aspect of this was the fixation on the moment that others around him had. He could plainly see how for a person to be made to care nearly entirely about just the present moment was an effective means for bad actors to control them. Those bad actors—though he would not openly admit it, because it would constitute heresy—were clearly those largely unseen, unreachable elites that sought to control the lives and minds of the people of the empire.

The distractions were another pain point for him. There was a cornucopia of information available and always flowing about countless topics. An incredible range of personal interests across the population could be entertained with all the different media that was available to them. There was plenty of stimulating material to keep people thinking about things other than unpleasantries like how they were being indoctrinated and controlled.

Hector couldn't help but reason that it was all some grand scheme, some disgraceful design that was manipulating even him, a fool who thought he could push back against something so titanic and elaborate.

To him, people seemed hopelessly emotional. And impulsive. And vulnerable to tribalism and class warfare. So many of the programs, and so much of the media—articles and vidscreen shows, messages carried on radio waves—were blatantly stoking the flames of those weaknesses. They were encouraging it, amplifying it.

Though, of course, it was fascinating how a shift in perception could make it all something entirely different. And one aspect that stood out in particular amid all these things was that it was clear that the people involved in creating much of this harmful media were substantially unaware, and in fact well meaning, despite the damage they were doing.

So, in time, Hector came to understand these things, and he came to understand how the empire of Ezmondia was as it was. He saw why those rulers of theirs, largely unseen, acted as they did. He saw how they could do things he readily perceived as indefensible and horrific, yet how those same things could still be comprehended by the public as glorious and exemplary. Those rulers were creatures of self-interest, too. They lived in the moment and cared about material things—and in that way, they were not so different from the people Hector had met and come to know throughout his young life. Those elites were not so different from the poor and downtrodden, regardless of whether they were born into or came into that state of high living. The corrupting influence of great wealth and power could, over time, curse and change them all into something so similar, so substantially the same, regardless of who they were or where they came from. Indeed, it seemed to Hector that at a minimum, a great majority of humanity was susceptible to being as corrupt as their current rulers—just given some time and the right string of events happening in their lives and their world.

He still could not, however, convince himself that everyone could be defeated by that lust for power and wealth. He had known several people who had struck him as different. And they had almost all been people who had so little in the world. They were the ones who seemed to more sincerely believe in things like hope, faith, and love—in virtues or concepts Hector saw as admirable to believe in. He knew such things lived invisibly and eternally in humanity to such extent that the rulers of Ezmondia, though of great power, were a comparative joke.

Hector, of course, had to conduct himself appropriately in Ezmondian society. He was a low-born laborer, a poor class of citizen not taken as much above a slave. Granted, he felt in many ways that he *was* a slave. He harbored a quiet rebellion as he came of age, just in his mind, but things escalated in his late teenage years.

His father eventually became relatively prosperous, and some of Hector's final years before reaching adulthood were spent with him. He was able to eat higher-quality food and get a sense of how those of a higher class of citizenry generally lived. One thing in particular he remembered of the time, which his dreams brought back to him now, was how the food tasted.

The food accessible by the more well-to-do of their society, by means of their deeper pockets, was better. It was better in taste and appearance, and it was, it plainly seemed, better for you. And after a time consuming such higher-quality food, Hector eventually revisited a staple of his past diet. The food nauseated him and caused him to retch.

And even with the food he now enjoyed daily, he felt he could taste the fakeness, the falseness of it. How the manufactured, processed nature of it artificially triggered pleasure pathways of his brain to convince him he was eating something good. He often tasted food that only seemed to make him hungrier the more he ate. And what a profitable tactic that could be, he considered many times, to those who made their coin off selling the food to him in the first place.

For a time after that, Hector grew his own food. It was frowned upon and discouraged, but not outright illegal in the empire. He suspected that the draconian Ezmondian laws would see to that at some point, after wearing the public down on the topic over some number of years.

So far as Hector could tell, it was by disincentivizing it that the elites would ultimately kill the desire in people to grow their own food. Growing one's own food seemed to establish more of a sense of self-reliance and independence in the person. At least, that's what it seemed to do for him. And the elites would accomplish their ends of greater public control far more effectively by guiding people away from activities that led to developing things like self-reliance and personal independence. It was better for the elites that the common people felt reliant on some overarching, overpowered entity to take care of them. But the elites had to be doing it incrementally, rather than by outright banning it. Put people in a corner, and they would fight. Always give them an easier path, and they would just keep choosing the one that hurt a little less than the alternative.

The insidious and harmful aspects of the food industry in Ezmondia were far from limited to being within the brains of the consumers, though. Hector suspected it was even making them all physically sicker and weaker. He felt stronger and healthier while eating the more expensive, better-quality food. He even lost weight without even trying to—not that he was very overweight to begin with. There was something wrong with the food; he knew it at a level he could not fully convey in words. But he would talk to people about that low-quality poison they ate, and they would regard him as if he were out of his mind. To them, they ate it, they went on eating it, and they weren't dropping dead suddenly or anything. At least, not the ones still alive that he could ask.

It was fascinating, Hector marveled. It was fascinating how effectively something could be killing a person, and how they would doubt it simply because it hadn't done the job of killing them yet. And it was even more moving how much of the vast enterprise of pharmaceuticals in Ezmondia profited from those poisons people ate as food. To Hector, it was a punchline worthy of an occasional, seemingly random burst of laughter.

He knew the true solution for many problems was to address the root cause, to stop the problem from ever happening—not to condemn a person to a life of dependence that would foster a lack of belief in the virtue of self-reliance.

Early in his twenties, Hector came to be sufficiently inspired to finally break out of that place—Ezmondia, with all its trappings—that threatened to ensnare him forever. Most directly, that was probably because he ended being there with his grandfather when the old man was on his deathbed, and because that ancient man had gifted him something at that time.

A map.

The venerable man had said Hector could use it to find something that could be of great consequence to him and Gracyr. But he had warned that he should only ever seek it out if circumstances were particularly dire, that it was a map to something that could condemn him at least as surely as it could save him.

He told this to Hector alone. And Hector sincerely believed that, in all likelihood, his grandfather had not entrusted the information ever before to anyone else. Hector had been the only child his troubled parents had ever had, so he figured his grandfather's options were limited, and that probably necessitated Hector being the one to receive it. The old man probably couldn't bear to see something of such great value just be lost forever, and he knew he had to entrust the thing to *someone*.

Hector had reached a point where he was prepared to take a gamble with his life—if the stakes were right. That whole thing with his grandfather seemed unlikely to be true. He had even considered that it might have all just been the mad rattling of a deteriorating mind, without merit, and baseless. But he had that hunger of youth and had nothing like the risk aversion commonly harbored by the older adults as they aged. He was prepared to risk it all for a shot at the escape velocity that could get him out of the trap of a destitute life that, on a daily basis, threatened to swallow him up forever.

So, he followed that map. He followed the path out to a mountain called Scorpion's Reach. Despite having taken all the preparative measures he could, he had held significant doubt that he was going to make it back. It was a treacherous journey into a desolate and unpopulated area. He pushed himself hard to get there—to his limits, he knew—and he also knew before starting out that he could well just collapse and die from exhaustion and exposure when he finally reached the thing. But if reaching it was within the bounds of what he could achieve with the full effort of his life force, he was going to see it through.

In his dreams now, he revisited that scene, from when he reached that final destination. In the chest he'd exhumed from the ground, he saw the aged, dusty, horrendously dirty-looking thing. It had been a sword—*his* sword.

He pulled it from its rediscovered tomb, the prison that had held it for so long, and he felt it come alive in his hands. Invigorating energy coursed through it and him, and a dim glow encompassed him and the weapon. It shed the dirt and rust of what must have been centuries. Hector's mind flooded with answers about how to get out of the place and back to civilization, and the sword surged the confidence through him that he needed to get out. Hector instantly sensed tribes of nomadic people that weren't so far away, and he had knowledge of old outposts, and he sensed the animals and not-too-distant travelers, as well as naturally occurring things he could consume to stay alive.

And then the powerful Kazahvir had challenged him to what was the greatest battle of wills of his life. Hector heard again that old laugh echoing manically through his mind, from that very moment—that moment when it had threatened that it would enslave him forever.

29

Chapter Twenty-Nine

Lights flickered deep inside the sunken spaceship. No one was around to hear the strained whirring of the damaged systems or to see the blinking auxiliary lights that sporadically came back online. The vessel was damaged well past the point of proper functioning. Still, those systems built to last for millennia, on the timelines of planets and stars and the universe, refused to die.

The warp drive engines sputtered and malfunctioned their way to some degree of partial activation, as they had been intermittently managing to do for some time. The engines disrupted communications from the surface world in the vicinity and periodically overloaded electronics and electrical systems nearby.

Of more severe consequence, however, the warp drive was altering the flow of time itself around it. The result was that time moved faster, and sporadically faster still, within the range of a large bubble of space surrounding the ship, as compared to the rest of the planet outside that space. Time slipped off and on and occasionally a little faster or slower as the engines labored to do what they had been designed to do. And they would continue, so well as they could, so long as fuel still remained.

It was alarming to the crew of the Makevan submarine not so far away—the same that had been tasked with taking Viktor's friends on their supposed tour—that at one point their communication systems went down entirely. Of course, it was relieving to have them suddenly come back online just a couple hours later, but their inability to determine the cause surely unnerved them. Upon getting their comm systems back, the submarine's crew immediately reached out to Command Control again, though even they could not provide much in the way of an answer as to why it happened.

The captain of the submarine was Desmond, a longstanding friend of Viktor's. He was the member of the crew with the fullest understanding of the circumstances and details of the true mission they were on, and he was the one to communicate with Command Control now. He did so in the company of Cid and Viktor and several of his officers.

Captain Desmond had expected Command to be a little concerned about them going dark down there, with the communications systems briefly offline.

"Captain Desmond," came the voice of the man speaking over the vidscreen transmission from Command Control. "Report. We have been most alarmed in not hearing from you and have been searching for you unceasingly."

"All systems green now, sir," Desmond responded. "We had some trouble with our comms for approximately two hours, but we're glad to be back and are actively investigating the matter."

The officer's face on the vidscreen showed him to be at a momentary loss for words. His face went ashen, even. "Captain, you have been missing for nearly two days, without a trace. We have just deployed another vessel to try to discover what happened to you. We need you to report back to base, posthaste."

"Unable to comply, Command," Desmond returned. "We have unfortunately had a member of our tour group get a bit adventurous and go out in some of the specialized deep-sea diving gear. We must track this person down prior to our return," Desmond lied.

"Not acceptable, Captain," the voice responded. "We are not getting a clear read on your location. Send us your location information since you deployed, and where this person is believed to be now. We can utilize another vessel for the rescue. You are to return to base."

Desmond weighed the consequences of the diverging paths before him. He had a debt to repay to his old friend, but he knew it would cost him greatly to stay the course he had resolved to follow. But he felt thankful for the opportunity to repay what he owed, regardless of what it ultimately ended up costing him.

"Command," the old captain said. "Command, we are losing you." Tears welled in his eyes as he fabricated the transmission failure. But the tears weren't over thoughts and worries of what this was all going to cost him; they were in profound gratitude for this chance to repay his debt to Viktor. No monetary value could be placed on that debt; it surpassed any semblance of that. His old friend, all those years ago, had saved his family's lives.

The weathered old captain clenched his jaw with reinforced resolve and cut the transmission feed. Then he activated the intercom system and followed up with his orders to the crew. "Captain here. Turn it around, team; we're headed back immediately for the pickup!"

Viktor looked to him then. "Thank you, old friend."

Desmond managed a nod and a slight smile, drawing on the strength of a life in the armed forces to steel himself against what he knew would be coming for him.

One of Desmond's officers approached him then, questioning his defiance of Command Control's direct order.

"We have a task before us that must be completed," Desmond firmly stated, "at any cost." Then he paused for just a moment. "You follow my orders; I'll worry about the consequences."

The high-ranking officer, a younger woman named Violeta, certainly thought to challenge why he was lying to and defying Command, but she ultimately just swallowed hard and stood down. She had been with this captain for years, and she held deep respect and appreciation for him. Even though she couldn't understand his actions now, she resolved to trust him—if just this one final time.

"Strange that they… they think we've been gone so much longer than we actually have," Desmond reflected to the now-silent group. "They'll be coming after us soon, and they'll probably find us and perhaps even the underwater facility before too long. We should be as quick with completing this mission as possible."

Cid and Viktor agreed.

Their submarine dove deeper again, back to the depths of the underwater facility.

* * *

Although Cid, Viktor, and the crew were not aware, within the bubble of space around that old, sunken spaceship, time was fluctuating again.

But something was different this time. The dying engines of the spaceship groaned in protest as they consumed the little remaining fuel. And sounds of grinding machinery rang out, as the systems defiantly repowered to run just a little longer. But in their broken state, the engines now caused time to decelerate, including for those on board the submarine and those within the underwater facility. Great spans of time were now passing by outside this bubble, while only short amounts of time lapsed inside.

The world was leaving them behind.

* * *

The search for the submarine was conducted, but it did not manage to locate them. If Command had pressed just a little further, gone a little deeper, they might have stumbled upon the underwater facility, though.

But the understanding of the Makevan base that the submarine had deployed from was that the region beyond their search area was carved out by Ezmondia. It was reviewed and determined by the base, and even the Gatekeepers Council, that the conflict that would arise from pursuing the search was not worth the monumental risk to foreign relations and the ire of the often-hostile empire and its emperor, Armando.

Desmond and his crew and tour group were deemed extremely likely to already be deceased, and such tours were explicitly forbidden henceforth by the base. And of course, new laws and regulations came about to further demonstrate that corrective measures had been appropriately taken.

While this occurred, and the world essentially left the companions, the submarine crew, and Cid and Viktor behind, there were highly consequential events unfolding back in Ezmondia. Time passed such that months stretched into over a year in the world above, while it slowed down dramatically deep beneath the waves. In the Ezmondian Empire, new generator plants were constructed to generate electricity from the collected promethium. Failing hydropower systems were efficiently replaced with the promethium-burning plants, which generated vastly more energy. The ruling Elite Council of Ezmondia profited astronomically, as did the Order of Oranlak that was in league with them. It all brought Armando and his ilk an unprecedented ability to fund their population-influencing schemes and media campaigns, to direct and guide public discourse, and to finance ambitious population-wide deceptions. As expected, the inhabitants of Ezmondia quickly developed a dependence on the energy security that Armando and his circle could provide.

Unpleasant details that gradually came to light about the new power source—and the disputed negative consequences of its continued use—were vaguely known to Armando. But such information was scarcely known by or made available to the public. And Armando's circle fought and paid great amounts of coin to keep it that way. Naysayers were flagged as making unsubstantiated claims and were generally silenced with a significant degree of permanence. Or sometimes just harsh legal ramifications followed such blasphemy.

Cast in a certain light, such intolerance was barely necessary, though. Overall, the residents of Ezmondia had been conditioned to think fondly of their emperor, and they usually had little doubt about the elites acting in their best interest. And this was true even though these same elites were secretly in league with a vast darkness-dealing criminal organization spreading all manner of atrocities throughout the continent.

But life did improve for Ezmondians, those subjects of the empire. There were no longer power failures, and those pesky flickering lights became a thing of the past. Life continued to be filled with many pleasant distractions and comforts to keep them sufficiently satiated.

This was in contrast to how many in Makeva fared. And indeed, in Ezmondia, they were routinely reminded of the deteriorating conditions in that country to the northwest of them. They were reminded of how they often still labored until premature death and sometimes even died of exposure. The Ezmondians were distracted with constant flows of information and ease of access to a plethora of cheap pleasantries, and they rarely, if ever, developed much of a sense of skepticism for those who ruled over them. Without such skepticism, without a greater public that called for things that would come as at least an inconvenience to Armando and the Elite Council—things like more transparency or accountability—he and his circle were largely left to their unscrupulous designs.

On a further promising front for Armando and his empire, the campaign for more births was increasingly becoming a success. The passage of time and the influx of more and more coin to fund the campaign were greatly supporting their efforts.

Ezmondians were also successfully being made ever more disconnected from one another. The bonds of family and friends were actively being weakened in what was a new push—one to establish Armando as the one true father figure in their lives. He had, after all, restored light and warmth and solved the hydropower crisis. It came to appear overwhelmingly likely that, in the coming years, he would have the kind of army he dreamed of—a military force that would be profoundly loyal to the empire, and even more so to him. Especially as he had also come to be known as the great savior of those now called the sages, which was the rebranded name for the elders in Ezmondia.

Armando was responsible, the media relayed, for ensuring that the all-important sages of their society were seen to and looked after. And indeed, they were taken care of, though they floundered in hopeless, fruitless pursuits, were often drowning in despair, and clung ever more tightly to a life clock ever faster descending to zero.

Armando even drafted long-term, far-reaching plans with his generals that saw him and the Elites of Ezmondia invading and eventually overtaking Makeva. Makeva represented a larger area of land than Ezmondia, but it was wilder and less civilized. And the many different communities of the country were generally only loosely bound to one another, by the Gatekeepers Council. As a consequence, no great enough number of the independent-minded Makevans would likely ever align effectively—not against a renewed, solidified, and single-minded Ezmondian army coming against them.

Not against the kind of Ezmondian army that was being built now.

30

Chapter Thirty

"Hector, Hector! Wake up!" Regina repeated as she shook the younger man's shoulder.

Hector finally opened his eyes.

"Guess you were more tired than you thought, huh?" Andromeda asked him.

"What's … the situation?" Hector asked, wiping the sleep from his eyes.

"Well," answered Regina, "that wristband Gerrard is wearing? Yeah, it's getting close to zero. We should be heading out of the living quarters now and making our escape from this place."

She gave Hector a moment to attune to the present circumstances.

"Hopefully the time change doesn't throw us too far out of alignment with the rescue sub," she continued. "Not entirely sure how many of those monsters we can fend off while waiting for its return. But come on. Malcolm and Mariana are waitin' for us in the main chamber of the living quarters, and we're all anxious to be outta here."

Hector got up quickly then, and it did help that he felt the excitement welling up within him—the excitement to slay more octotors. He hadn't bothered to undress before going to bed, so he just donned his boots, grabbed Kazahvir, and was ready to go.

Gerrard nodded to them when he saw the two women returning with

Hector.

"All right, ready?" Gerrard asked the gathered group. "Let's go—I've had enough of this place."

"That makes two of us," Andromeda agreed.

"Three," joined Regina.

Andromeda took note that Hector was unresponsive to that remark. *Something more he's looking for down here?* she wondered. They had certainly gotten a good dose of adventure already, she felt. But she also wasn't being tugged along by the same sort of blind fulfillment-seeking that seemed to propel Hector sometimes. She was intrigued and all, but she wasn't sure risking her life here any longer was really going to help her family back home, either.

For a moment then, she found herself also considering Regina. And Andromeda recognized that she could more easily rationalize how her female companion, and her desire to bring some sort of energy reform to Gracyr, was served by being here.

Are these two scientists the answer to any of our problems? she found herself reflecting.

Andromeda thought of her family's ranch back home and wondered how everyone was holding up. She wondered if all her efforts were going to ultimately add up to anything significant. Her current adventure out into the world really hadn't taken her as far as she knew she had to go. But it wasn't just about how far she needed to go for them, she knew. While she was there so much for her family, she was also there for herself and her own sense of purpose.

Regina, beyond her relative obsession with energy, seemed to be on something of a personal journey to find more purpose, too. Was she going to find it in the form of this arguable suicide mission they were currently engaged in, though?

Gerrard seemed to have accomplished so much in his longer life. He seemed to have reached a point where he had hit a wall, though, no longer moving along at the pace of advancement and personal development that he had in the past. And he also seemed pulled along, as in varying ways they all did, by some things they did not understand.

And then there was Hector, with his darker, more mysterious persona; he was surely the most guarded and difficult to dissect of them all.

What interesting companions I have found myself in the company of, she marveled. *As suitable a group as any to be marching off to my likely death with, I suppose,* she then thought more grimly.

Her contemplations about her companions were interrupted then. The double doors slid open, revealing the foreboding, dimly lit corridor beyond. Hector and Regina headed up the front, with Malcolm and Mariana falling in behind them, backed up by Andromeda and Gerrard.

The main hallway in front of them looked as it had before, eerie and dark, and it was unnervingly quiet. They all made their way back through, past the communications room and the smaller hallway that had taken them down to the main science lab. They'd almost come back to the point of the large intersection again before they heard much of anything at all.

What they heard then was a distressed woman's scream. It was reverberating off the walls of the corridor, echoing its way to the intersection from a different direction than the one back to the entrance of the facility.

"Someone needs help," Regina stated, looking to the others, who all seemed to hesitate.

"Some rescue team you are!" she challenged. Then she started moving swiftly down the corridor toward the origin of the scream.

A reflexive grin creased Hector's face as he felt the presence of more octotors in the same direction. "Let's go!" he yelled back to the others as he quickly moved ahead of them.

They all moved down the hallway toward the ruckus, and more yells and screams followed as they got closer. As they gained ground, the din of clashing metal contributed to that loudness. And then they heard the quieter but even more unsettling gurgling noises again, just like those the octotors they had faced before emitted.

Hector, the farthest along, paused up ahead. He stood before the door to the room the nerve-wracking symphony seemed to be emanating from. Regina caught up moments after, pausing next to him in front of the door.

"What's that room up ahead there that Hector and Regina have stopped in front of?" Gerrard asked Malcolm and Mariana.

"Recreation area. It has a pool, weightlifting, games, lockers, that sort of thing," answered Malcolm as they caught up to Hector and Regina.

Mariana pressed a finger to the door panel, and the door slid up and open. Inside, they saw what was causing all the noise.

A woman with a soldier or mercenary look about her was armed with a broadsword and facing off against an octotor. She was badly injured by the look of her, with one arm bleeding from multiple deep gashes. Her body was bruised, and her clothes were torn.

The companions spread out and advanced quickly but cautiously, with the exception of Hector, who plunged in to join the fray more aggressively. He saw the woman's mighty sword disintegrating as he moved closer. It had been soaked in the blood of those monsters—blood that ate away at its metal like acid.

A tentacle jolted for her, which she barely managed to parry, and the deflection broke her deteriorating sword and left her without any clear defense. Hector grinned in anticipation, knowing Kazahvir could finish what she had started and still survive the strike against the octotor. He drove his sentient weapon deep into its upper torso. It hissed and squirmed and lurched forward violently, trying to reach Hector before death took it. But then it fell back and collapsed into a withering mass on the floor.

Kazahvir delighted in the terrors that had rung out from its mind, a final mental call for aid to others of its kind. And how it delighted even more in knowing that more such pleasurable encounters might soon be presenting themselves.

The room quieted after the thing's death.

"Good to ... good to meet you all," the injured mercenary woman managed to say, looking around at the group.

"How'd you end up here by yourself?" Regina asked.

"We were ... the final line..." the woman said with obvious difficulty.

"What do you mean? What's your name?" Andromeda asked the injured warrior.

"She's one of the security personnel here. I had actually thought them all already lost or otherwise gone by now," Mariana responded.

The woman nodded. "My name is Natalia. A small group of us have been gradually fighting our way back through to the living quarters," she said, seeming to recover a little of her strength.

"Good to meet you, Natalia," said Mariana. "We're just coming from the living quarters, actually—and we have a chance to escape now. A submarine is headed here to come and pull us out of here. Entrance A, up the hall just outside this room."

"Well … that's great to hear," Natalia said. But then she doubled over and grasped her injured arm, as if in sudden pain.

"She's been hit with one of the poison barbs from the creatures!" said Malcolm.

"She … going to be okay?" asked Regina.

"She might find it takes … quite a measure of fortitude to overcome that poison… I hope she can," offered Malcolm.

"Ah, she's tough. You can do this, Natalia!" said Mariana in an attempt at lifting the group's spirits.

Natalia managed a smile in appreciation, then responded, "I'll feel better, I think … when we're moving closer to the exit."

The group nodded in agreement, then took their leave of the room and headed back into the corridor.

Outside the room, a loud chittering, accompanied by that same unsettling gurgling, filled their ears. The group shined their lights farther down the hall to see a small army of little creatures hurriedly scampering toward them. They were crab-like little things with small claws. They had legs like creeping spiders, but also had tentacles, and their bodies were almost jellyfish-like.

"Those are what I was warning you about!" Malcolm yelled. "Don't let them get on you; they'll dig into your flesh, consume you from the inside out!"

Malcolm was already headed in the opposite direction, fast moving for their exit out of the facility. The rest of the group followed immediately behind, Gerrard and Mariana helping Natalia limp as fast as possible alongside them.

"Hold!" yelled Natalia suddenly.

Gerrard and Mariana halted.

"Hold here a moment," she reiterated, adjusting her tone to be a little less commanding. "I'll buy us time."

She inched herself closer to a panel on the wall and began tapping buttons on the digital display. Then a large metal door came down in the corridor, blocking off the tiny creatures from reaching them.

The group breathed a momentary sigh of relief.

"They can still get through this door, faster than you'd expect. We must press on quickly!" warned Mariana.

By the time she had finished speaking, that chittering noise had risen to a roaring one. They could hear a wave of the small creatures crawling all over the other side. And an ooze-like substance, similar to what they had found on the ceiling of the main laboratory, was leaking through small holes beginning to burn through the door, as well as from underneath it. The slime seemed to be rapidly corroding the metal door, which started to bulge inward toward the group, apparently from the mounting pressure of so many of the things pressing on the other side.

Their group pushed forward in a frenzied haste.

"There's a main panel up ahead … just past the intersection!" yelled Natalia over the noise of metal scraping and bending. "I can engage it and seal all the doors behind us as we move through the corridor; we just have to make sure we keep moving … all the way to… *Aah!*" Natalia finished with a grimace of pain as she clutched the spot where the poison barb had gotten her. She felt her consciousness fading as the venom took hold. She wondered then if she could even keep her wits about her long enough to make it to the panel. She limped and struggled along as quickly as she could with the aid of Gerrard and Mariana.

"This the panel?" asked Gerrard.

"Yes!" Natalia yelled.

They helped get her right up to it, and she set to work pressing buttons.

Then she held her more functional hand against the panel, feeling a wave of adrenaline bringing her momentarily back from the brink of death. The system needed a few seconds, she knew, to scan her palm. She just hoped she had that much left in her.

The thing seemed to be malfunctioning, or maybe there was too much blood on her hand for it to read her palm accurately. Frustrated, she found strength she didn't know she had left and shoved Gerrard and Mariana off of her.

"Go!" she demanded. "I've got this. Get yourself up ahead and past those next doors!"

They hesitated, reluctant and stunned at Natalia's sudden strength.

"I can do this, but the thing's malfunctioning, and it's going to take a minute. There's no sense in all of us dying!" Natalia shouted.

Gerrard and Mariana looked at each other for a moment, then looked back and nodded at her. They turned and ran with all the speed they could to make it to that next section.

Hector, who had paused with the others by the panel, sensed many more octotors now—the bigger, more mature ones. There were a few toward the front of the wave, just beyond the closed but buckling door. But there were vastly more of them not far behind.

He saw the hesitation all of them had for leaving Natalia by the panel. But he urged them on, as Natalia was trying to.

"Go!" Hector yelled with uncharacteristic emotionality. "You don't see what's coming for us. Go!" he warned emphatically.

Andromeda and Regina came up next to Natalia, and they tried to support her as Gerrard and Mariana had, hoping they would somehow dissuade her from throwing her life away. But Natalia had laid out a mission in her mind, and she was going to see it through to its end. "No!" she yelled at them. She moved to shake them off—and in doing so, she noticed Andromeda's vicious-looking blaster. She reached her good hand to Andromeda's side and grasped the thing, snatching it away as she threw the two of them off of her with unexpected ferocity.

"Get to that next set of doors up ahead. I'm right behind you!" she shouted at them.

The door down the hall gave way then, and the creatures started pouring through the broken barrier, countless in number.

Natalia turned back to the panel, desperately trying to get it to read her palm correctly. The others of the group hesitated just another moment before turning and running to make it to the next section of the corridor.

Hector was last, feeling slowed by that persistent need in him to slay more of the monsters. How he wanted to feel Kazahvir sink into another one of them and slice it wickedly or eviscerate the thing. But he knew falling into that oncoming mob, which was about to overtake the hall, would spell certain death.

Then an octotor unexpectedly dropped from the ventilation system ducts over his head. It crashed down right in front of him.

Kazahvir attempted to scatter the thoughts of the thing, animalistic though they were, trying to buy its wielder the opportunity to get in the first strike. Hector drove the hungry sword deep into the heart of the creature—or at least, where he presumed the heart of the otherworldly thing would be. The octotor fell limp, and Hector retracted the blade from its blood-gushing carcass.

The encounter had slowed him too much now, and more were pouring out of the ducts above him, quickly surrounding him. He found himself defending furiously against their swiping tentacle arms. He made his way slowly while defending, edging persistently closer to the next metal doors, which he knew would be closing imminently. Or so he presumed as he took note of a similarly overrun Natalia forcing her way through the fray, already nearly beside him.

Has she engaged the system? Are the doors going to be sealing more sections of the corridor and buying us more time?

Then another octotor drew his full attention back to defending himself.

Natalia felt life-sustaining adrenaline burning through her. Still the poison affected her, though, and she felt new barbs injecting her with more of it. Her consciousness continued to slip, and she came to a deeper degree of acceptance of what she already knew was going to happen—that she was going to perish there.

No matter, she thought. She had finally gotten the system to initiate, and it would buy the rest of them some time. Maybe it would give them a fighting chance. She had accomplished her final mission, so far as she saw it, and she took comfort in that and knew she could accept the grave.

A dozen of the octotors were violently grasping at her limbs now, but she partially broke free—enough to slam her broken body into an octotor next to Hector.

She screamed a final time, "Get past those doors!"

Hector honored the command, and he pushed on through the path she had temporarily opened up for him.

As he rushed to try to make it to the threshold in time, a robotic voice warned over the intercom system that the facility was going under lockdown imminently.

As her final action, Natalia lifted her surviving arm, which held Andromeda's fantastic blaster. She leveled it with the unfortunate octotor's face right in front of her.

She squeezed the trigger.

The corridor came furiously alight from the blast. It went off just as Hector made it past the doors, and just before that section of the corridor was sealed. The shot was formidable; it sealed the fate of every one of the cursed things that surrounded her.

The blast exploded right as a greater mass of the swarm was overtaking the area all around her. And though that mass of monsters ended her valiant last stand, a countless number of them were slain in the process.

On the other side of that next set of doors, the rejoined group listened to the now more distant-sounding doom the creatures were bringing their way. The intercom system continued to robotically warn about the impending facility lockdown.

"The doors ahead of us, all down the corridor, will be closing in quick succession now," explained Mariana soberly. "We must keep moving."

Red lights flashed all along the path ahead of them, part of the facility's emergency alert system. The group raced for the next one as quickly as they could manage. They didn't need further motivation, but that familiar chittering noise surely didn't slow them any. They could already hear the sounds of the doors that had just closed behind them starting to break down.

They sprinted on through multiple sets of closing doors and made it to the entrance, hearts pounding out of their chests. They all caught their breath over the following few minutes, their minds racing to catch up with all they had just been through.

Malcolm checked to see if a submarine was docked.

"Nothing yet," he said, disappointment evident in his tone. "They ... likely exited the time bubble, for lack of a better term, and that will probably result in delaying their return. But with the way the time difference fluctuates, we can't know by how much."

"Let's hope they weren't outside the bubble for very long if they did exit it, or that time for us wasn't moving too quickly while they were away," added Mariana.

Gerrard stared, as the others did, at the closed doors they had just barely made it through. "Hopefully, these doors hold back the octotors for a while," he remarked.

"Wonder how long we'll have," Regina said.

But all their group could do was shrug and hope it was longer than seemed likely. They heard that now incessant chittering and the sound of buckling doors drawing ever closer.

* * *

Captain Desmond and his crew, along with Cid and Viktor, made their way defiantly back to the depths of the underwater facility. The gloomy darkness of the deep ocean enveloped them as their submarine plunged deeper.

"What were they on about?" Cid asked the captain. "Saying we've been gone for so long when we haven't been?"

"I'm not sure," said Captain Desmond. "We were gone just a matter of hours."

"In all my years and trips out on the ocean, I've never found myself in so bizarre a situation," reflected Cid. The captain and Viktor, standing next to him, could not disagree.

"We have the underwater facility again up ahead on sonar now, Captain," said one of the officers.

"Very good, thank you," responded Desmond.

"There's ... something else, sir," the officer went on. "Something gigantic, although it's much farther away from us now. It appears to be moving, though."

"A whale, a squid, or some such thing?" inquired the captain.

"Seems too big, sir," another officer answered.

"Let's focus on docking at the facility again, getting our people, and getting out of here," decided Captain Desmond. "Do let me know, though, if it's getting significantly closer to us."

"Aye, Captain," responded the officers in unison.

Their submarine came up to the facility to dock as it had before, and the crew attached it again to the entrance.

Desmond attempted to get a message through to the dock inside the underwater facility.

"Hello, Gerrard, anyone, can you hear me?" Desmond asked over the communications system.

"Yes, we're still here!" Gerrard's voice practically yelled back over the speakers.

Desmond's message was coming through just in time. The octotors had broken through almost all the way to them. The creatures had gotten to the last set of doors that separated them from their next meal. And the enticing, potent fear the creatures felt mounting on the other side of those doors only spurred them on more ravenously.

"We are pressurizing the entry room on the sub for you to come aboard; we'll open the doors when it's safe," Desmond advised them over the comms system.

"Time is running short for us here, Captain; please do what you can," requested Gerrard.

"Ya know, ya might've sounded a little more urgent in your tone there, Gerrard," criticized Regina.

"I've got it, Gerrard—understood," came Desmond's voice again over the speaker.

Their group stood by silently then. They waited there in the small space between the final, buckling doors, which held back their doom, and the doors in front of them that were their salvation.

"Why did we have to come here?" Andromeda asked rhetorically, and more to herself than anyone else.

Regina looked to the older woman, her friend, and wished she could offer something.

Hector looked back at Regina. He was having a feeling that she was looking at him for some reason, as if he should answer this question from Andromeda. He let out an exasperated sigh. He wasn't sure whether the answer he had was really going to help the situation, but since he was quite potentially about to die, he figured he'd just go ahead and say what was on his mind.

"If we can't handle going to the brink of our own ruin—and if necessary, beyond—for the sake of our salvation, then we don't deserve it," he stated, with a tone that was matter-of-fact seriousness.

Andromeda's expression softened as his words seemed to gradually strike a chord in her. Hector had taken the question a little more seriously than she had really meant it, but she appreciated that input from him just now. His words spoke to her of pushing yourself to the limit, of giving it all you had, of having faith and confidence, and how otherwise you were not worthy of what you desired. And it made for a compelling case to the older Andromeda, who was surely impressed to hear such a thing from a young man something like half her age.

A few long minutes later, as the creatures just started to become visible through the enlarging holes in the damaged doors, the other doors to the rescue sub finally slid open.

The group quickly rushed in. Then the vidscreen in the rescue room aboard the sub flashed on when they were inside. Desmond appeared and spoke to them.

"Please remain in this room while we gradually acclimate you to be able to enter the rest of the sub," Desmond requested.

"We're going to want to detach and head back to the surface as soon as possible, Captain!" shouted Regina at the vidscreen, which acted as a two-way communicator. By her estimation, they weren't nearly far enough away from the oncoming onslaught they had just narrowly escaped.

Just then, the officer monitoring the sonar spoke up, and their group watched Captain Desmond on the screen turn his head to regard the man.

"Captain, the creature, whatever it is, just started closing in on us!" the man watching the sonar yelled.

"Sounds like we have multiple reasons to get out of here quickly! Full speed back to base!" Captain Desmond ordered.

The submarine was run expediently through its mostly automatic detachment process, and they were off with great haste. They were gone with such speed they didn't get much of a look at whatever that leviathan of a creature was that was making its way toward them. But maybe they were better off for that. And anyway, there certainly wasn't much regret among the ranks on the submarine on the matter.

* * *

The behemoth creature watched them escape. Its emerald-colored alien eyes pierced the darkness of those waters even more easily than it had those of its home world. But even more keenly than it saw them did it feel the fear among them.

Its brood of underlings had mentally imparted much to their mother about the inferior humans. And it was fortunate for the humans that they hadn't lagged a few more minutes. The size of this leviathan, and of its razor-sharp teeth and massive jaws, would have easily sufficed to chomp the sub in half and decisively end the lives of all aboard. The creature did not attempt to pursue, though. Perhaps it could have still caught them, perhaps not, but the creature, more intelligent by far than its underlings, knew it had more pressing matters to attend to. It had a larger nest and swarm to build up, so it could more comprehensively conquer these pitiful human creatures.

* * *

The submarine headed straight back to base—or rather, it headed straight back to where the base once *was.* Where it had been, there were now ruins, damaged equipment, partially standing buildings, and no people at all.

All those aboard the sub disembarked, then journeyed out and into those ruins. They moved about the place in a state of horror and disbelief.

In one of the partially standing buildings, Regina found a calendar. The year was a year that, as far as any of them knew, was another five years into the future. It all seemed to be out of line with the particular sort of time disturbance Malcolm and Mariana had described to them. Apparently, time had moved faster above the waves than below, and their world had left them all behind. The questions and the mystery of it all persisted.

Cid offered Malcolm and Mariana a safe place to stay at his home, which fortunately was found to still exist, in an abandoned state. The four companions also accompanied them back there. Viktor departed from them for his own home shortly after, hoping it wasn't in a similar state to the old submarine base.

Gerrard expressed that he needed to go check in with Duncan and Carmine on the project he had left them with, and he asked for one of them to tag along with him. Andromeda happily signed on, excited about the idea of being alone again with someone who now felt like a close partner and best friend.

Hector noticed that eagerness in Andromeda, and he couldn't help but think of Saoirse. *Is she alive? Does she think about me, miss me?* he wondered. He also had the thought that she could be a great resource to reach out to, to shed some light on what had been happening for apparently the last five years. And even for Kazahvir, that was a satisfactory reason to search her out.

Hector announced to his companions and friends that he was going to meet his own contact and see what information he could uncover about what had transpired in the past few years. Then Regina laid out a similar plan to everyone, too, after she subsequently decided to try her own luck back at the Seaside Sprite. And of course, the thought of seeing Blaine again was not an unpleasant one, either.

So, the four of them went out for the remainder of that day to learn what they could of what had happened, of what had left so much of the world they knew in disarray.

31

Chapter Thirty-One

Late that night, after reconvening back at Cid's house, the companions put together a rather interesting, if fairly horrifying, picture of what had happened in Gracyr while they were away, and of the circumstances they now found themselves in.

Ezmondia was even more thoroughly in the grasp of Emperor Armando than it had been before. The Elite Council of Ezmondia had been largely dismantled and stripped of most of its power, and Armando had risen up as an even clearer supreme ruler—as an even more uncontested and all-powerful leader. He was now working openly with the Order of Oranlak. He controlled the energy and was the richest person in the history of Gracyr. It was, however, not clear to what extent history had been rewritten by media campaigns to make that present-day fact a reality.

Emperor Armando had also amassed greater military might, and his soldiers were often more dedicated to him than to their own families and hometowns. His newfound levels of wealth afforded him vastly greater influence than he'd had before—and as the years continued to roll on, it was widely believed by the subjects of the empire that he was only going to become increasingly unstoppable.

It had also come to pass that essentially all of the Ezmondian Empire had come to rely on burning promethium as its primary power source.

Apparently, some people had spoken out against the new power plants, and against Armando, too, over the past few years. There had even been a few small rebellions, by some of those who believed there were harmful effects resulting from the use of the alien energy source. Regardless, such insurrections were becoming fewer and weaker. After all, Armando could just order power shut off at a person's home and so rob them of what they needed to live in the modern age—of what they were hopelessly dependent on. People helping those who defied Armando could be similarly punished. And if the hot-headed tyrant was having an off day, the penalties could be even more severe.

By the estimation of the four companions, and that of many others across Makeva, it had all come to be a colossal mess. While they took a degree of comfort in the fact that they resided in Makeva rather than in Ezmondia, where Armando reigned supreme, there had been reports of attacks recently even in Makeva—from his increasingly bold forces. Circumstances like those they had witnessed upon their fateful return to the submarine base were the unfortunate result.

Hector, perhaps in particular, knew this tyrant was a great problem—but also that he was far from the sole cause or contributor. He knew many could have served the same role he had—that he was just the one who had stepped up at the opportune time.

His companions agreed that Armando, while not the entirety of the problem, was a rather large component of it all. And regardless of how they may have disagreed on particulars or exact aspects of the disaster they were in, they all agreed the tyrant had to be struck down.

And another development offered something Gerrard knew might prove helpful in accomplishing that very task. On the matter of the lutetium processing, and the crimson fluorite he had left his friends Carmine and Duncan with, there had been a stroke of incredible success. Gerrard added many powerful blaster bullets to his arsenal as a result. They were potent Triple-A rounds, enhanced with special qualities.

After some deliberation, the four companions were able to concoct a plan they felt could conceivably set right the disastrous path that Gracyr had gone down the past few years.

They contacted via clonra the woman from the submarine base, Rhoda, and asked her to come work with Malcolm and Mariana, the scientists from the underwater facility. The three then set to working together on the material, verium, that Gerrard had talked about. There was plenty of that substance, too, as much of it was left over from the work Carmine and Duncan had been doing separating out lutetium from the crimson fluorite.

To their amazement, verium did indeed seem to hold great potential in controlling fusion reactions. Gerrard had pitched to them that the material could help by means of its ability to withstand the incredibly hot temperatures of the plasma, and as their testing went on, the trio were finding that to be increasingly likely to be true. Further testing and refinements seemed entirely likely to lead to practical, large-scale energy generators, on a vastly shortened timescale compared to what was previously thought possible.

They had leaned on contacts elsewhere in Makeva to find a suitable location for their work, and they were now working out of an underground lab on what they hoped was the future of energy. They needed something that could counteract what had spread across all of Ezmondia—the promethium power plants, which were now starting to spread into Makeva. And that was, of course, serving to further empower Armando, as well as to hasten and escalate the environmental damage to their beautiful country.

While Malcolm, Mariana, and Rhoda worked on their part of the energy crisis and its solution, the companions determined that they would work on another aspect of the predicament Gracyr was in. And that was dealing more directly with Emperor Armando himself.

Hector's past love interest, Saoirse, was able to provide a connection to get the companions close to him—or at least into his Castle headquarters. Hector had employed no shortage of effort, persuasiveness, or appeals for forgiveness after those years he'd been mysteriously gone, and Saoirse had eventually become willing to discuss with him how she might be able to help.

She had an old friend who was now a privateer taking on contract work for the empire. The two of them weren't friends to the same extent they had been in years past, but she described how they had once been quite close. At the present time, though, their conflicting contracts with the two entities hostile toward each other, Makeva and Ezmondia, could even conceivably put them in a sea battle against each other. Still, Saoirse suspected—and subsequently had those suspicions confirmed—that the woman, her old friend Cara, would be agreeable to hearing Hector out.

So, for a rather large sum of coin, Cara became agreeable to transporting the companions to the Castle where Armando resided. The Castle had a port, and with the local contract work she had been frequently doing, her ship was not an uncommon sight over there. Even more fortunate, she was due back there soon to turn over the spoils of a recent ship her band had captured.

Yes, despite the profit Ezmondia had brought her, she had no great love for what was going on there, or for the empire's future designs for Gracyr. So, she affirmed she could get them in—though that was only on the further condition that Hector promise her that he and his companions would not fail.

Before Andromeda, Gerrard, Hector, and Regina departed on this mission, a couple more measures were also taken to plant seeds they hoped would grow and solve other problems of their world.

Gerrard contacted his previous employer, Old Guard Mining, and tipped them off to the crimson fluorite mining operation outside Serazema. He knew his previous employer—an advanced and environmentally conscious but practical and massive mining company—could feasibly and sustainably extract the crimson fluorite from the site. He was fortunate enough to reach someone he knew there who remembered him, who even confirmed what he had suspected: that Old Guard Mining was unaware of the site previously being exploited illegally by the Order of Oranlak. Perhaps Old Guard's competing interests could even have some pushback effect on the increasingly wealthy, powerful, and invasive Ezmondian Empire.

Gerrard, though, wasn't certain of the current state of that mining operation—not after Andromeda and he had turned that wagon they found in the wilderness over to the Akastairian authorities what was now years ago. But he acted on what was in him to act on, and he held hope that something helpful might come of it all somewhere down the line.

Regina also took personal action to plant seeds for the future. She went to serve as an alumnus guest speaker for an event at her past university, the University of Akastair. She did her best there to refire the forge. She spoke on the topic of geothermal energy, with the aim of spurring on the imaginations of the current generation of students. She was well received and seemed to generate some interest, but still, she had hoped for a more consequential impact there than the one she seemed to have made.

But *patience,* she told her frustrated self. The years had shown her that it so often was not any one single action that led to achieving goals on the scale to which she aspired. It was a culmination of so many actions from countless others as well—or if only her own, she knew it would have to be her actions spanning across a very long timeline.

* * *

The companions boarded Cara's ship and headed down below deck. Then they remained there, silent and out of sight, as she and her crew sailed uneventfully into Ezmondia's capital—right into the Castle of the empire.

Cara carried on, as if it were business as usual. She directed her crew to unload the cargo from the ship they had recently captured. Then she moved off her ship soon after they docked, to go sign all the typical necessary paperwork. As was usual for them, they were there and gone with great efficiency. But within some of the boxes they left behind on the docks, the four companions were hidden.

Gerrard peeked out first, a little while after they were unloaded, as Cara had instructed him to do. And the scene was as she had informed them it would be: deserted. It was late enough in the day at the time of Cara's arrival that by the time all the boxes were unloaded onto the docks, no one was too interested in staying around longer to unpack their contents.

After a short while waiting, for caution's sake, Gerrard climbed out of his large crate. Then he moved to help Andromeda out of hers. They then moved to assist Hector and Regina out of theirs, knowing exactly which crates they were in because of the markings Cara had had her crew paint on only those the four of them would be hiding in.

The main gate for ships down there, leading out to the open ocean, was long closed now. It barred any ship from leaving or entering. It wasn't clear, of course, how deep the bars extended beneath the water, so perhaps it would still be possible to swim out underneath them. Gerrard jogged over to them for a closer look. Standing on the docks beside where the bars had come down, he saw that they penetrated only slightly into the water, so they could all swim out by this route—should the situation necessitate it.

The four then ascended the stone steps that led up to the doors out of that large room, which was at the lowest level of the capitol. Further steps they took spiraled upward into the main building areas—the offices, cafeteria, living and recreational areas, meeting rooms, personal rooms, libraries, and more. The interior layout was to a great extent a mystery to those not regularly here, so they were largely going in blind.

Gerrard carried his claymore and blaster with him; Regina her longsword and magic shield; Andromeda her remaining weapon—the saber bequeathed to her by her father; and Hector, of course, wielded the sentient sword, Kazahvir.

Andromeda did feel an empty void and a pang of disappointment at the loss of the ages-old, powerful blaster. But she accepted the loss of her secondary weapon back in the underwater facility as a small price to pay for having gotten out safely. And she knew well the vampiric thing had been having some rather disturbing influences on her psyche, anyway.

Even with that loss, the companions represented a formidable force moving through the Castle now. And with Gerrard having his new blaster rounds at the ready, their resolve was only strengthened. Still, they knew they needed to maintain secrecy and stealth as long as possible if they were to maximize their chances of getting to that tyrant, the notorious Emperor

Armando.

They made their way steadily through the complex, the headquarters of the Ezmondian Empire. The mazelike layout of the place did not make navigation easy. Though the place was largely quiet at the present hour, they were nearly discovered multiple times by unwitting staff throughout the building. Somehow, Hector always seemed to know when they were dangerously close to being seen. Whenever they needed to pause or to make a sudden move, he seemed to know. That was, of course, because Hector had the magical abilities of Kazahvir at his relative disposal, and because he could feel the life force of all the people in the Castle. Without its guidance and perceptive capabilities, they surely all would have been found and captured.

Hector felt Kazahvir was primed for an epic fight. It even faintly glowed with hungry anticipation. And how he could feel the electric excitement of the thing lighting up his mind!

He knew his friends were having more questions arise in their minds about him. He knew too much, too many times—about how they needed to stop and wait a few seconds, or how they had to start again at a precise moment. They seemed willing to put off any inquisition about his mysterious insight for the present moment, but Hector knew if they survived this ordeal, there would be many more questions forthcoming from them. That was fine, though. There was a decent chance he wouldn't survive, anyway, and even if he did—well, he would cross that bridge when he came to it.

He felt the presence of two particularly powerful individuals in the building. They weren't far from each other at all. He was having trouble distinguishing which was stronger, and which was their intended target, but he knew it had to be one of them. He kept their group moving in the direction of the two of them.

The companions kept patient and quiet, sometimes having to dodge into an empty room or just silently wait for someone to pass. Eventually, the four companions came to the hall that contained the rooms with those two ultra-strong forces. There was nothing about either door or what was around them to indicate clearly that one was more promising than the other. So, they chose one randomly.

Hector knocked a couple times on the wooden barrier. He didn't wait for a response from whoever was inside, though. He looked to his friends for a moment, and then he nodded to them and barged right in, Kazahvir in hand.

A woman inside the room was sitting at a desk, and she regarded the intruders with an unsettling calmness. Hector swallowed hard. They had selected the incorrect room; they had not chosen the one with the emperor inside.

"Intruders? In the Castle? I'm impressed you made it so far!" said Mercedes, practically congratulating them as she rose from her seat.

The four companions regarded the woman curiously, for her odd demeanor and response. She stood up to her full height, which was fairly tall for a female; she was not much shorter than Gerrard.

Hector's mind raced about how they would not be able to ensnare Armando now, and how the emperor could be getting away right this instant. And his heart sank, though Kazahvir still seemed intrigued by the duel it could have with the adversary they had found.

The woman continued staring back at the surprised bunch that had just rudely interrupted her evening. *How curious,* she thought, *that they barged in on me, and yet they look so surprised.*

The companions continued to look the woman over. She was older in appearance than Regina, though probably younger than Andromeda. She had an average build, not particularly muscular or strong-looking, though she had a menacing-looking weapon at her side.

Hector considered that Kazahvir might be losing its keen magic senses, leading him to someone who did not strike him as very formidable. But then the woman brought up that menacing weapon—her mace—and Hector reconsidered that notion. She drew it out with unsettling confidence and an even more unsettling grin. The idea of having a bit of a dustup with some rebel band apparently excited her.

And indeed, it did; paperwork was far from thrilling or fulfilling to her lately. She even hesitated before she triggered the silent alarm system. She knew she had to though; it would have been irresponsible to do otherwise. And she wasn't bent on getting her next thrill quite like Armando was. So, Mercedes expected that an exceedingly large number of guards would be barreling through her doors in short order. But she still figured that, maybe, she could have a little fun before they came around.

Just then, Regina darted at Mercedes, trying to catch her off guard. But Mercedes easily deflected the strikes from her sword, and the older woman tossed Regina aside with unexpected ease.

Andromeda and Hector lunged at once, Andromeda's bejeweled saber alongside Hector's Kazahvir. Andromeda went low with her slash, and Hector went higher with his own strike.

Mercedes dodged and tossed up her whole desk, sending it flipping over right into Andromeda. An instant later, Mercedes's mace smacked Kazahvir harmlessly aside. But how she felt the potency and power of that wicked blade!

Her thoughts quickly refocused, though, as Gerrard came forth with a downward slash of his deadly claymore. She braced herself with her mace out defensively in front of her, holding it horizontally with both hands. To Gerrard's amazement, she caught his strike and halted it. The mace vibrated violently from the force of the downward assault, and Mercedes felt a tingling momentary numbness creeping into her hands and arms.

What power! she thought. She actually thought for a second that her mace, wrought of the highest-quality materials and workmanship, might fail to stop the giant sword's momentum. *What a delight this group is!* She hadn't felt so challenged in so long a time.

Just then, the guards came funneling though the doorway into the room. Gerrard quickly disengaged with Mercedes and fell back to his companions, drawing his blaster. He fired off a blast without another thought—one of his new Triple-A bullets. And it truly was a momentous occasion; it was almost assuredly the first of them to be shot anywhere in Gracyr in a very long time.

The richest, most vibrant shade of violet poured forth, magic sparks exploding from the blaster's first chamber. The bullet spiraled toward the guards, and that violet light enveloped the lot of them.

A silent explosion ensued.

It didn't seem to affect anything nonliving at all. The furniture and the walls remained intact, seemingly unaffected. But the people caught up in that blast were gone in an instant. Where the guards had stood just a moment earlier, there were now only skeletons. And those skeletons were just momentarily still standing before they quickly collapsed into a heap of ash and dust.

The companions themselves—all thoroughly shocked at the impressive but horrific display—felt their jaws drop. But Gerrard retained the presence of mind to bring his blaster almost immediately in line with Mercedes, pointing it directly at her.

She, similarly in awe, then considered for a few fleeting moments that she might be done for, as well.

Right then, though, their scuffle was interrupted by the sound of hands clapping.

"Astonishing," came a compliment from a booming, strong male voice.

The companions turned their eyes to what seemed to them to be a literal giant.

There stood Emperor Armando. Hector knew it was him from his power level, which Kazahvir imparted to him, as well as the levity and confidence of his demeanor, not to mention his towering physique.

Armando stood closer to seven feet tall than six. The sight of his powerful, muscular frame, with hands that appeared capable of crushing a man's skull, was unnerving to all of them.

"I suppose you must all be here for an audience with me, then, eh?" asked the giant man, ending his clapping and taking a more serious tone. "Please, though, let's not do this here and mess up my place like this," he said, regarding Mercedes's overturned desk and the piles of ash and bones. "Let's take this to my arena downstairs," he suggested.

Seeing an opportunity, without warning, Gerrard then let loose another bullet from his blaster, right at Armando.

But a light lit up on the gauntlet the emperor had equipped on his forearm and hand, and Gerrard's bullet was redirected toward it as if by great gravitational force. The Triple-A blast dissolved into small magical fragments that were then sucked harmlessly into the glowing orb on the gauntlet.

Instantly and with impossible agility, Armando was then right in front of Gerrard, holding him up with one arm, so high that his head touched the ceiling of the place. Gerrard dropped his blaster and grasped at his throat as Armando throttled him.

"I said, *downstairs*," Armando warned with dangerous finality in his voice. "Or would you rather just perish here and now?"

Armando dropped Gerrard to the floor, assuming his answer to what was clearly a rhetorical question. Anyway, he didn't want to throw away what might actually be an opportunity for a halfway-challenging fight.

Armando immediately fell back, and he turned an open palm and an extended arm back toward the door of Mercedes's office. Then, with a sinister smile, he said to the companions, "Shall we?"

And with the exception of Mercedes, who knew him very well already, they all regarded the towering emperor in a state of persistent unease and shock.

The four reluctantly began to move hesitantly toward the door. More guards spilled into the room as they approached it, and they were quickly surrounded. It seemed even more of them were still waiting outside the room.

"Let's peacefully make our way to a more suitable location for this quarrel of ours," Armando advised. "No one is going to lay a hand on you, so long as you don't try anything out of line. Come, let's have a civil discussion and get a little more acquainted on our walk down. After all, you're all going to be far from the land of the living in not so long a time at all."

Armando seemed greatly at ease as they walked on. It seemed as though he was fairly vulnerable to attack, but he had shown himself to be someone who should be taken seriously. And of course, his reputation preceded him. Plus, that was all to say nothing of the two dozen or so guards now enveloping them. It seemed they didn't have much choice but to engage in this ridiculous farce of civility he was putting forward and just go along for the walk. At least they were apparently going to have a chance at what they wanted at the end of it.

They all walked on past the adjacent office, which presumably was Armando's. The door had been left ajar, and there was a clear view of a section of his grand library. Andromeda happened to glance inside as they passed by—and she saw what she felt she could not possibly have seen. There was a thick tome on one of the eye-level shelves that looked just like the long-ago book she had found in the library back at her university. They seemed to match; the color of the book, the familiar font (though the text was too far away to read), the apparent thickness, and the symbol etched into it—they were all reminiscent of it, if they were not the very same.

"Emperor Armando," Andromeda said, respectfully, "that isn't a copy of the book *Of Universes and Humanity* on the shelf in your library back there, is it?"

The emperor actually halted for a second, bringing the entire group to a momentary stop. And then he turned his face toward her and regarded her carefully, and he started walking again alongside her. They all resumed walking again with him, the guards and the four companions alike. He towered over Andromeda, but his expression was not so much threatening as one of surprise and curiosity.

"Surprised you caught that, and that you know that particular text," he responded. "I doubt it very much that many alive in Gracyr today know anything about it."

"You know of the stories in that book?" Andromeda asked, not bothering to hide her shock that he possessed a copy.

"Yes, of course. I know as close to everything, actually, as anyone you're ever going to meet," he boasted, though the companions were too preoccupied with other thoughts to dwell on the blatant display of narcissism.

"Why do so few know about it?" Andromeda asked.

Armando considered a few things before he answered. But perhaps most importantly among the things he considered was the belief he held that this person asking him was going to die very shortly anyway. As were the other three trespassers. And he considered that all others in attendance were essentially mindless loyalists, who lacked the capacity to interpret what his answer would be to the woman anyway, at least in any adverse, meaningful way. That was, of course, with the exception of Mercedes, but that didn't matter. She already more or less knew the answer to the question, anyway.

"The stories are problematic for people to know," the emperor answered.

"Are they true?" Andromeda immediately asked.

Armando shrugged. "Seems doubtful to me. Who cares?"

"Then why keep it a secret?" Andromeda pressed.

Armando paused for a moment, apparently considering the follow-up question a little more deeply, perhaps considering how he might begin to get it across to someone he viewed as a lesser being.

"It's as if the stories are ... a guidebook, or a codebook, if you like. A manual of sorts. Instructions ... or a blueprint," Armando said, jumping through words as if trying to find the one that fit. Then, conceding for the moment, he went on to a longer description. "They are a means of building up the mental framework of the human mind so that a person can achieve greater fulfillment, greater empowerment. In a sense, it is a means by which a person can come to accomplish anything, to maximize their potential, to attain whatever their heart's desire. A person's belief in these stories can serve as a key for them. Yes, *the key*—to unlocking the heights of their human potential. To believe in the stories of that book ... is to empower yourself, as an individual; it is to take control of your life."

He paused, wondering to what extent it was all setting in with the woman.

"I don't need a population of slaves being so empowered. Such a state of affairs would cause me worry over the ... long-term sustainability of my power," he elaborated. "It's quite amusing, actually," the emperor went on, unable to stop himself now. "It's not some all-powerful entity, like you read about in those stories, that I'm worried is ever going to end my reign. No—I'm worried about the simple *belief* in those stories by the people, and how they could then consequently find within *themselves* the power to break my hold over their minds. They don't need some supreme, super powerful entity—not to save them from me—but they do need the belief in such an entity, if they are to be able to do that. And so, in effect, they have the power to save themselves, and yet, they are too blind to see it."

There was a silent pause for a time after that. But Armando continued to paint himself as a rather dark creature, removed from his humanity at a level all of the four companions found increasingly revolting.

The four of them considered a surprise attack on the tyrant many times as he guided them down to a lower-level indoor fighting arena. Of the four, Hector came closest to that action. But even with the hungry urgency of Kazahvir permeating his mind, he decided against it.

He's going to give us the showdown—the fight for the world, as it were, Hector reasoned. Or that was the situation at least as far as Kazahvir and he had romanticized it to be, anyway. And there wasn't much point in muddying up that opportunity. They were going to have their chance, and Hector felt strongly the confidence of his magic blade, that they could annihilate this fool who actually thought he could throw down with the timeless, ancient power that was Kazahvir.

"I really must protest," Mercedes said when they were all gathered down in the arena. She was finally feeling too overwhelmed by Armando's poor judgment; she could not remain silent. Not that he seemed to pay any heed to her comment.

Many of the remaining staff had been relieved of their evening duties so they could come to the arena for the show—and, of course, to serve as an audience for their egotistical emperor. The seating was still largely empty, but Armando needed at least some kind of an audience. There were even some invitations out to staff who had gone home, and others nearby, so they could build up the audience for the impromptu battle.

There were sparring matches that happened there, stomach-turning displays of brutality and death, and other such spectacles—and the events were aired with great regularity over the radio waves and across the vast network of vidscreen programs in Gracyr. This would be an unusual event, though, for the Emperor Armando himself was to be a primary entertainer.

32

Chapter Thirty-Two

"I cannot support this course, Emperor. I'm not sure you should go through with what you're planning here," Mercedes stated as respectfully as she could manage, but with a clear tone of concern spilling into her voice. She knew that however capable he might be, he should not be taking such an unnecessary risk. But she also understood that he was hopelessly prone to letting his overconfidence get the better of him, and it wouldn't matter much what she said. Of course, it was hard to hold it against him—not just because of who he was and how powerful he was, but because she understood everyone around him was also perpetually telling him how great a ruler and fighter he was.

Mercedes also couldn't deny she had been similarly drawn in. She, too, had been intrigued by these four people who had come against them, had been excited for the thrill and the challenge they could present. But she wasn't the leader of the empire like Armando was. Not so much rested on her life as it did on his.

Armando, to some extent, actually did appreciate and consider Mercedes's concerns. Still, he was too enthralled by the excitement of having a worthwhile group of challengers—and he was looking forward to a more riveting and stimulating battle than he had experienced in far too long a time.

It wasn't long before a suitable-enough number of onlookers had filed into the arena seats. Armando waited there a few more dramatic moments, preparing to announce the start of the battle.

The arena was a massive space. They were on the ground floor of the headquarters, and beneath their feet was wide-open dirt. The arena walls were high so that no one in the arena could reach up and pull themselves out—not even Armando. There were entryways, one on either side of the arena, which were generally barred off during events—to prevent any runaways. The open space was surrounded by seating that wrapped around the entirety of the place.

Emperor Armando then collected, from an underling running it out to him, his selected weapon for the fight. The underling then scampered off to the gate before it closed. Armando's chosen weapon was a massive one, a double-headed battle-axe. The weapon possessed an axe blade at each end of a long shaft, and Armando immediately set it into a deadly and intimidating spin.

"Okay ... let's begin now," he announced. He grasped the double axe, his favorite thing to kill with, and swung and spun it skillfully around him. "Do feel free to try another shot of your blaster on me; I'd welcome the energy gain and the enhanced strength and speed you'd grant me!" Armando teased.

Seeing no significant moves from the four combatants, he shrugged and charged for Gerrard.

Gerrard brought his immense blade forth in defense, and he deflected repeated strikes with impressive speed. He defeated blow after blow from the towering adversary. And he countered when he could manage it. Armando immediately recognized the talent of the older man. As they traded ineffective blows against each other, Armando only got a greater feel for the skill Gerrard possessed. And it wasn't just the raw skill he had; the weapon he wielded was among the grandest he had ever seen. He might even keep it after he laid this old fool low.

Hector jumped into the fighting then, lunging toward Armando with a wicked-looking weapon, perhaps even more impressive.

What an interesting group this is, the tyrant found himself thinking.

And he came to hold that opinion even more strongly a few moments later when he first felt the mental intrusions of Kazahvir attempting to scatter his thoughts and disrupt his focus. He was mostly beyond the insidious thing's ability to affect him, but it still drew a measure of his attention off other elements of the fight. Even so, he easily parried, deflected, and turned aside Hector's aggressive attacks. And Armando sent the admirable, strong warrior reeling back repeatedly from the mighty force behind his battle-axe swings. Hector barely dodged numerous strikes that came at him. At one point, they came in such rapid succession that he could barely distinguish the individual strikes, and any one of them would surely have felled him.

Armando kept his weapon turning and spinning still, maintaining momentum and building it up constantly. And recurringly, that onslaught of individual strikes came on, looking so much like one fluid, harmonic attack.

Then Regina joined the fray, as well, though she came in with a far less unique-looking sword. Armando thought to make quick work of her, and he moved immediately to do so. Regina, though, perceived a weakness in the man's stance, perhaps a slight vulnerability, which she sought to capitalize on. As Armando lunged suddenly away from the two fighters he was engaged with to land a strike on the woman, she actually managed to get her blade dangerously close to a hit against him. She might have been just an inch from penetrating the man's abdomen and spilling out the contents of his stomach—but then a spinning axe-head smashed into her sword and knocked it aside. Or knocked part of it aside; the blow broke her sword into fractured pieces.

And that same axe blade came spinning back moments later for her throat, in a strike that would slice it open, if not sever her head from her body entirely. But Regina managed to get her shield up at the last instant. An ordinary shield would not have stopped the blow; the force behind the spinning axe-head would have splintered and smashed through such a lesser defense. But this was no ordinary shield. It glowed brilliantly in defiance of the powerful strike and successfully repelled it, turning some of that force back against Armando.

And Armando, to his lasting surprise, actually had to fall back a couple steps to regain his footing. He rebalanced quickly, though, and a smile crept onto his face—perhaps as wide a smile as Mercedes had ever seen on the man, at least on the battlefield.

"Don't get overexcited. Don't be overconfident," she heard herself advising him under her breath.

Armando was entering a state of fascination with these newcomers. He had been longing for a fight so worthy of his time for decades—maybe his whole life. They were just seconds in, and the fourth hadn't even engaged him yet! And that one had another unusual looking weapon—a saber, he recognized, with jewels embedded in it. How Armando reveled in his personal excitement that four such powerful fighters would soon be utterly crushed by him! Yes—he was loving every second of this.

Armando continued to fend off the annoyance that was Kazahvir's pitiful attempt at destabilizing his thoughts. He turned his attention to the fourth of the fighters, thinking to give her a little push into joining the fun. He was intensely curious what sort of thrill this one could offer him. He charged for her, battle-axe-heads spinning viciously.

Andromeda sidestepped the first few swings, wondering if she could begin to slow the momentum that exotic weapon seemed to have. She drove her saber in, out, and across with great technique, dancing around the heavier swings of the axe and trying in futility to land a blow.

Gerrard came in at Armando's side, briefly drawing some of his attention. As he did so, Andromeda managed a glancing blow, a slight scratch, on the juggernaut's arm. She couldn't get close enough to get much force behind the slash, though, and she knew all she had managed was a superficial cut. She nearly lost hold of her saber in the process, as a glancing blow from Armando's weapon nearly sent it flying. She instantly fell back to avoid being sent flying herself, by what was a much heavier follow-up strike.

Gerrard continued swinging his claymore, defending against the ferocity of Ezmondia's emperor and his relentless double-headed battle-axe. And Armando continued to feel impressed, continued to feel his battle lust escalate the longer the smaller man defended against his attacks. That magnificent sword of his held up against blow after blow from the usually weapon-shattering axe-heads.

Gerrard suddenly pressed hard for a few quick but more forceful strikes, even as he began to tire. Then he fell back immediately, hoping he had bought himself a few moments' rest with that pulse of ferocity. Armando recognized the tactic, and he thought to pursue him and keep on him to deny him that breath-catching moment. His curiosity overwhelmed him, though, and he let Gerrard break off from the fight.

He smiled wickedly as he regarded Gerrard and his companions, who had regrouped at his side. They all seemed to be tiring already, and he himself hadn't even broken a sweat—though he was shocked that that saber had somehow managed a scratch on him. He looked over them all now, his confidence completely untarnished.

"I can't help but wonder if this is actually the best this world can offer up against me," the titan boasted. "I am all-powerful," he droned on. "I own all of Ezmondia, and soon far more. I have what I want; I take all I desire."

"What you desire," Gerrard shouted back between breaths, "is slavery for all but your power-obsessed self. And death and pain for those who don't deserve it. And a plethora of wealth, and the means to acquire even more, which you surely don't need. And other misguided desiderata destructive to you, Ezmondia, and all Gracyr."

Then the four companions observed something they took as a little unnerving, for some odd reason: they saw the emperor's confident smile vanish.

"You," Armando accused, pointing at Gerrard. "There is something familiar about you. Why do you seem so familiar? Do you remind me of someone?" he asked, though more to himself than anyone else. He was genuinely curious. He needed a little more information from this one before he sent him to his grave.

"What are you trying to accomplish?" Armando went on, still questioning, trying to lead himself to the answer that felt just barely beyond his mind's grasp. "Surely it's not to live as long as possible—not given that you're here in front of me now, on the battlefield." He paused for a few silent moments before his next question came on. "What did you come here looking for?" he asked.

That was it, Gerrard thought. That was the same question he remembered this terrible man asking so many years ago. And even despite all the time that had passed, he felt in that moment how it did so little to shield him from the emotional long-ago event he recalled now as vividly as ever.

It was the question that had been asked of his father, by the monster of a man who had killed him. He saw now that Armando was that monstrous man—shrouded in the darkness of his incomplete memory—who had mercilessly ended his father's life.

Gerrard regarded the gigantic adversary with renewed clarity. He took another breath and steadied his shaking body against the rage welling up within him. He pushed the emotions aside to what extent he could; he knew they threatened to cloud the clarity he had now achieved.

Gerrard came again at the tyrant, with a ferociousness tempered as much as he could manage. This behemoth who had robbed him of his father those many years ago—he had no concept of the accountability or justice he rightly deserved. And Gerrard very much wanted to help him realize it.

Gerrard came close—closer than anyone ever had to sealing Armando's fate. But that door to victory, maybe just momentarily ajar, was quickly identified and immediately slammed shut.

Gerrard's sword came on in a flurry of impossibly fast strikes for so large a weapon, a number of them nearly connecting with various parts of the giant's body. Armando countered with several of what would have been life-ending blows had they connected. Then he caught the smaller man off guard with a sudden head bash, slamming his head into Gerrard's. And then a left-handed punch sent Gerrard tumbling back and to the ground.

Nearly defeated and knowing Armando would quickly close the distance between them and end his life, Gerrard again drew his blaster. He squeezed that trigger to release what Duncan had promised him was the most powerful blast in his new arsenal.

Armando stopped suddenly in his advance and stood there steadfast against the oncoming bullet. He fully expected his magic-absorbing gauntlet would turn the power of Gerrard's own bullet back against him. The bullet was encircled in a spiraling violet-red hue as it torpedoed through the short distance it had to travel to reach the giant man. It struck with a roaring inferno, which ignited a spectacular conflagration and engulfed the entire arena in that rich, vibrant color.

But it damaged only Armando and the gauntlet he called on to try to contain its power. Still, that magic-stealing defense of his managed to ensnare a measure of that power, and Armando immediately turned it back on Gerrard. While the searing flames of the magic burned into Armando's flesh, his gauntlet erupted and shot a blast of energy back at the commoner who had dared to bring this pain upon him.

Armando knew that what was perhaps a fatal fraction of the magic was still at work and tearing at his life force, and he howled as he rushed ahead to more directly seal the lesser man's fate, should his magic blast happen to fail.

Regina summoned the magic of her shield to try to defend Gerrard, but had to alter her plan as she saw Andromeda also throwing herself in the way of the emperor's counterblast. Andromeda smashed into the kneeling Gerrard, forcing him out of the way, but landed in the way of that oncoming blast from Armando. She braced herself, but that blast—which should have ended her—never struck.

She opened her eyes to see a bright white glow encompassing and protecting her—and even felt a comforting warmth as it did so. The strange magic persisted a few more comforting seconds before it finally faded.

Then Regina fell to her knees in front of her, collapsing in a state of exhaustion.

When the final remnants of magic fizzled out, the five combatants considered each other again. The four companions all appeared worn down, not far from defeat—though Hector was at least still standing, still seeming like he had some fight left in him.

Armando's skin was badly scorched in multiple areas, with some of his body even charred black from the magic flames that had assailed him. And his gauntlet was a sparking, malfunctioning, broken mess of a thing, which he regarded briefly before removing it and tossing it to the ground.

"Well, I think we can safely say that would have been the death of you," the burnt behemoth remarked to Gerrard.

Armando prepared himself. He wasn't defeated yet—though he was surely injured, and he had a growing distaste for dragging out this fight that wasn't quite the level of fun he wanted anymore. But there was still something nagging at him, and questions seemed to persistently cross his mind that could perhaps get him a measure closer to whatever it was. He had some final questions occurring to him now, and he voiced them to Gerrard—to all of them.

"What is it you are seeking to accomplish here today?" he asked. Then his eyes landed on Gerrard again. "What is it you desire here? Why do you fight that which you know cannot be defeated? You are, after all, in a fight you know you can't win," he said with cold finality.

Do I know that? Gerrard asked himself then.

He could understand that logical conclusion. They were outmatched, unable to defeat this titan, a practically invincible enemy. He could reason out the insanity of what he and his friends were engaging in well enough without any help at all. And yet he understood more deeply that there was something profoundly wrong with that assessment. His heart rejected that undeniable path of reason and logic.

He defiantly spoke again to the titan. "There is a dissonance between what is in my heart and what is in my mind, and I gladly lay down my life now for a chance to harmonize it."

The larger man considered those words. And he considered, too, that these were remarkable people, of a caliber he had previously thought—in the modern era—to be lost to time.

Then he quite succinctly determined, with even more certainty than before, that they all had to die.

How such rare people had managed to come together in their dark world, and align to come against him now, was a question that astounded him.

In those final moments before the battle resumed, Andromeda felt a magical clarity come over her. She looked down at her saber, and it illuminated with a brilliant bluish hue. She felt a new power in it she hadn't felt before. Indeed, she hadn't even known the weapon to be magic at all before. It was just a family heirloom her father had given to her, so it had a sentimental element to it, she supposed—but a magical one?

In an instant, she knew things about what was unfolding that she could not explain. She felt Kazahvir's ongoing mental attacks on Armando's mind. She felt its power, and for the first time, understood its magical sentience. And she knew what she had to do with unexplainable surety. She understood that her weapon's true power had been tapped into by her act of sacrifice in trying to save Gerrard—her friend she cared deeply for. And her friend who, she realized in that moment, she might actually even love.

She harnessed the newfound magic of her saber, calling on it to amplify Kazahvir's assault on Armando's mind. And the enhanced mental attack cratered the giant man's attention on the physical aspects of the battle.

"Pick up your sword, Regina!" she called to her ally.

"It's bro—" began Regina, before realizing it wasn't broken at all. It was back in one piece, lying at her feet. She felt the magic of her shield being replenished, too, and she felt it beckoning her to call on its power again to defend herself and her friends.

Then Andromeda looked to Gerrard. "Give him one more shot," she bid him.

Gerrard nodded, pulling himself up from the ground, just before he unloaded another round from his blaster.

Armando moved first to try to get to them, but then, seeing he couldn't in time, he opted to try dodging out of the way. He was fast—incredibly so—but he came far short of escaping the magical round. The explosive bullet plunged into his body. He knew he had other tactics to defeat such an attack, even without his gauntlet, but he couldn't think with clarity anymore. Kazahvir's mental attacks had grown to far more than a mere annoyance.

"Summon the scorpion!" Andromeda yelled to Hector.

Not pausing to reflect on how it was that she even knew about that special ability of his weapon, he did as he was instructed. The phantom scorpion appeared and struck with its piercing tail, with its debilitating venom.

Then Andromeda and Regina dove in together after, slashing at the stunned and weakened Armando. He suffered many cuts and vicious gashes, but his magical defenses held and stole away much of the strength and damage of the women's attacks.

Armando roared and began returning their blows with a multitude of his own, any of which should have sufficed to kill either of them. He fought through the searing and burning of those magic flames from the blaster bullet, and Kazahvir's incessant mental intrusions, even as Hector came on with powerful slashing strikes of his own.

And now Armando could see through the mess of blades against him that Gerrard was moving in to join the fray, as well.

The failing tyrant let out a tremendous roar, and with incredible force, drove all the companions back with a rapid succession of strikes, sending them tumbling to the ground. Regina felt her magic shield fade as its energy was depleted again—and all four of them felt similarly. They had drained themselves and their magics, driven themselves to exhaustion.

The ground and the room around them were trembling now. The concentration of magical power and the blaster bullets had weakened the structure and stability of the arena around them. And now Armando's own magic pulsing wave, which one of his magic items had begun emitting when he let out that defiant roar, was further compromising the integrity of the Castle's structure. The ground began to quake and split, and several large pillars supporting the Castle began to crack.

The crowd began to scream and dart for the exits. Large sections of the ceiling fell onto the crowd as one of the pillars collapsed, killing many of Armando's staff and military officers. Casualties were mounting fast, and even Armando reflected in that moment that he had taken his obsessive pursuit of greater challenges and greater power too far this time.

Still, he stood firm and strong, ready to finish the job if his opponents dared to come at him again.

Gerrard was the first of the companions to pull himself back up from the ground, and he stood there, returning Armando's gaze. They both continued to stand there, each gasping for breath, sincerely wondering if the other had already been beaten—and mutually wondering whether the other would simply collapse from the further effort of simply attempting another strike.

The Castle rumbled and shook, the blasts and the combined energies having compromised the structure beyond salvation. And the combatants all understood acutely that the place was collapsing around them.

Andromeda found her footing next, and she moved over, joining Gerrard as she looked around at the devastated arena.

"Gerrard, come on, let's go!" she pleaded with him, tugging his arm. "That broken giant has lost too much of his will and strength to chase after us, and he's wondering the same as us—if he can even just escape with his life," she pressed.

Gerrard looked to his companions, and then back again at Armando, who clenched his jaw in steely determination. But Gerrard understood, without any magic at all, that what Andromeda said was so.

And within the span of a just few racing heartbeats, the companions were on their way, together, out of that broken place.

Epilogue

The companions went on to make their way safely back to Cid's place in Akastair, back in the country of Makeva.

When they returned, they found that Malcolm, Mariana, and Rhoda had made substantial progress with their atomic fusion generator. With the help of the substance, verium, they were containing the extreme temperatures necessary to make the generator possible, and the substance had a stabilizing effect on the plasma of the reaction.

The verium they used was also found to have even further, previously undiscovered uses. Malcolm and Mariana had been using it, in something of a throwback to their earlier days obsessing over hydrogen energy, to make better electrolyzers. And with these improved electrolyzers, they could split molecules of salty seawater, something still in relative abundance, more practically and efficiently into hydrogen that could be used as a fuel source. Their work held compelling potential for making hydrogen fuel dramatically more available, and at significantly lower costs to the train stations across Makeva and beyond.

Old Guard Mining, Gerrard's past employer, also had made some advancements of its own. They had started development of a new operation at the mining site outside Serazema—the very site Gerrard had tipped them off to. And the mining practices they followed, and which they continued to develop and improve there, were far more sustainable and in line with acceptable standards than those of Oranlak's previous operation.

* * *

The Makevan authorities had been efficient at removing the mining operations of the Order of Oranlak from the area, not long after the companions had left. And as Old Guard Mining found after Gerrard tipped them off, the authorities had, in so doing, essentially cleared the way for a company like theirs to seize a grand and lucrative opportunity there.

Regarding their company, but also more broadly regarding mining in general, there were many legislative changes in process. And despite a fair measure of disagreement on many associated topics, some were still widely agreed upon and held great promise.

A helpful factor in the midst of all the proposed changes was that there was a frame of mind being adopted by the Makevans and the Gatekeepers Council that the tactics of this company, Old Guard Mining, were far healthier and more environmentally sound than pursuing the alternative path now before them. That alternative path was the rise and spread of the empire's promethium power plants. And those were showing themselves to be increasingly harmful to Gracyr and its citizens, especially as time passed and as those new power plants became more widespread on the continent.

Plus, Old Guard Mining was conducting much of its mining at the new operation outside Serazema with nascent laser drill technology. The new technology eliminated waste and limited pollution, and allowed for deeper digs, and even still, it had efficiency that rivaled that of past practices.

Out of touch, archaic, and poorly worded—or vaguely interpreted—regulations had long been an obstacle for the industry. But the rise of promethium had led many to turn a fresh eye to some such red tape that now clearly appeared to be doing more harm than good. And so, new perspectives came to hold great potential for Gracyr in mining and in many associated fields that impacted Gracian society.

Regina also resumed her public talks. She often volunteered her time to spread awareness of the needed energy transition away from hydropower. Hydropower was failing now, if not utterly collapsing, due to Gracyr's changing climate. She also sought to speak out against what the empire was doing for energy—turning to the promethium power generators.

Regina continued to advocate for the advancement of geothermal energy.

She described new processes of drilling into magma for energy. She spoke up about and in support of geothermal heat pumps, which moved heat rather than generated it—and which used far less energy to meet the heating and cooling needs of Makevans.

The other companions came into greater contentment with themselves and the world, too, developing as it now was.

Hector found his hunger for battle and persistent wanderlust satiated ... for a time. Kazahvir's urging this way or that went on, but even *it* seemed to appreciate that things could have gone very differently during that fateful fight at the capitol building.

Gerrard was able to come to terms with and put to rest the events of a past that had long weighed on him, at a level he perhaps didn't fully appreciate before the companions' recent ordeal with Armando. He felt at greater peace with the circumstances of his past.

All of the companions came into a fair degree of fame after accomplishing what they had that day—with some reports, arguably embellished, even claiming the four of them had brought down an empire.

With her newfound fame, Andromeda was able to rekindle public concern for the ranches—an important food source in their country. She even worked with the Gatekeepers Council to institute policy changes that protected and supported ranches, their livestock, and associated supply chains across Makeva. Work in the field and in related areas was bolstered, and it grew more sustainable for working families again. She was also pleased with her blossoming relationship with Gerrard, which came along well, as did those of Regina and Blaine and Saoirse and Hector.

Ezmondia fell into a time of troubles after the collapse of that great symbol of the empire's strength, the Castle. Armando had survived, as had Mercedes, but many of the elites and the infrastructure that had secured his power had been lost on that fateful day. Perhaps even more damning had been the mental toll it took on Armando. It had been a stalemate that day, he felt. His mind ran through the circumstances surrounding what happened many times—and often involuntarily, and painfully. However he chose to perceive what had transpired, he still recognized clearly that he had not been victorious. And the fragmentation of his empire that resulted led to many instabilities that Mercedes lamented.

There were many dissenting voices and opinions that consequently ensued, and Armando's grasp over Ezmondia had clearly been fractured deeply. It would have been putting it mildly to say he had many long headaches over his choices that final day in the Castle. His ambitions were set back, if not outright canceled for the foreseeable future. It even occurred to him regularly now that he might never even reach the point of his previous level of glory, let alone build it up beyond that. Still, in time he knew he would rebuild, that he would be stronger tomorrow than he was today—and that the strength he had today was still, by most any standard, formidable.

Perhaps, though, he would not have longed for quite the same things if he had bothered to turn his eyes back to his previous operation at the underwater facility in the Eastern Sea. The structure had been abandoned, deemed not worthy of further unnecessary headaches. Their empire already had plenty of promethium to take them well past the span of the lifetime of anyone currently alive in Gracyr.

But deep under those waves was a brewing darkness, the beginnings of what would come to be a greater army than any Armando would ever command—an army of malicious and hungry alien monsters, creatures of nightmares, horrors descended from the vast recesses of outer space. And they and their gargantuan mother were far from content to remain harmless and hungry in the isolated depths of Gracyr's Eastern Sea.

www.ingramcontent.com/pod-product-compliance
Lightning Source LLC
Chambersburg PA
CBHW060814310726
48980CB00002B/302
* 9 7 9 8 9 9 2 3 2 3 5 2 8 *